About

Scarlet Wilson wrote her first story aged eight and has never stopped. She's ~~worked~~ ~~for~~ ~~the~~ ~~NHS~~ ~~for~~ twenty years, trained ~~as~~ ~~a~~ ~~nurse~~ ~~and~~ ~~a~~ ~~midwife.~~ Scarlet now works in public health and lives on the West Coast of Scotland with her fiancé and their two sons. Writing medical romances and contemporary romances is a dream come true for her.

Andrea Bolter has always been fascinated by matters of the heart. In fact, she's the one her girlfriends turn to for advice with their love lives. A city mouse, she lives in Los Angeles with her husband and daughter. She loves travel, rock n' roll, sitting at cafés, and watching romantic comedies she's already seen a hundred times. Say hi at andreabolter.com

With two beautiful daughters, **Lucy Ryder** has had to curb her adventurous spirit and settle down. But, because she's easily bored by routine, she's turned to writing as a creative outlet, and to romances because—'What else is there other than chocolate?' Characterised by friends and family as a romantic cynic, Lucy can't write serious stuff to save her life. She loves creating characters who are funny, romantic and just a little cynical.

Romantic Escapes

Romantic Escapes:
New York

SCARLET WILSON

ANDREA BOLTER

LUCY RYDER

MILLS & BOON

First Published in Great Britain 2022
by Mills & Boon, an imprint of HarperCollins*Publishers* Ltd,
1 London Bridge Street, London, SE1 9GF

www.harpercollins.co.uk

HarperCollins*Publishers*
1st Floor, Watermarque Building,
Ringsend Road, Dublin 4, Ireland

ROMANTIC ESCAPES: NEW YORK
© 2022 Harlequin Books S.A.

English Girl in New York © 2014 Scarlet Wilson
Her New York Billionaire © 2017 Andrea Bolter
Falling at the Surgeon's Feet © 2015 Bev Riley

ISBN: 978-0-263-30403-9

MIX
Paper from
responsible sources

FSC™ C007454

This book is produced from independently certified FSC™ paper to ensure responsible forest management.

For more information visit: www.harpercollins.co.uk/green

Printed and Bound in Spain using 100% Renewable electricity at CPI Black Print, Barcelona

ENGLISH GIRL IN NEW YORK

SCARLET WILSON

My first Mills & Boon® Romance story has to be dedicated to my own three personal heroes, Kevin, Elliott and Rhys Bain. This story is set in New York, and they helped me celebrate my 40th in New York in style!

Also to my editor Carly Byrne, who is soon to have her own adventure! Thank you for your support, and I hope to collaborate with you on lots more stories. x

CHAPTER ONE

THE SUBWAY RATTLED into the station, the doors opened and Carrie felt herself swept along with the huddled masses on the platform, barely even looking up from her hunched position in her woefully thin coat. It had looked better on the internet. Really. It had.

She resisted the temptation to snuggle into the body in front of her as the carriage packed even tighter than normal. Just about every train in the city had ground to a halt after the quick deluge of snow.

The streets had gone from tired, grey and bustling to a complete white-out with only vaguely recognisable shapes in a matter of hours.

An unprecedented freak snowstorm, they were calling it.

In October.

In the middle of New York.

The news reporters were having a field day—well, only the ones lucky enough to be in the studio. The ones out in the field? Not so much.

And Carrie appreciated why. Her winter coat wasn't due to be delivered for another two weeks. She could die before then. Her fingers had lost all colour and sensation ten minutes ago. Thank goodness she didn't have a dripping nose because at these temperatures it would freeze midway.

'They've stopped some of the buses,' muttered the woman next to her. 'I'm going to have to make about three changes to get home tonight.'

An involuntary shiver stole down her spine. *Please let the train get to the end of the line.* This part of the subway didn't stay underground the whole way; parts of it emerged into the elements and she could already see the thick white flakes of snow landing around them.

A year in New York had sounded great at the time. Magical even.

A chance to get away from her own *annus horribilis.*

A chance to escape everyone she knew, her history and her demons.

The only thing she'd taken with her was her exemplary work record.

In the black fog that had been last year it had been her one consistently bright shining star.

She should have known as soon as her boss had invited her into his office and asked her to sit down, giving her that half sympathetic, half cut-throat look. He'd cleared his throat. 'Carrie, we need someone to go to New York and represent the London office, leading on the project team for the next year. I understand this year has been difficult for you. But you were my first thought for the job. Of course, if it feels like too much—or the timing is wrong...' His voice had tailed off. The implication was clear. There were already two interns snapping at her heels, anxious to trample her on the way past.

She'd bit her lip. 'No. The timing is perfect. A new place will be just what I need. A new challenge. A chance for some time away.'

He'd nodded and extended his hand towards her.

'Congratulations. Don't worry about a thing. The firm has an apartment in Greenwich Village in the borough of Manhattan. It's a nice, safe area—easily commutable. You'll like it there.'

She'd nodded numbly, trying not to run her tongue along her suddenly dry lips. 'How long until I have to go?'

He'd cleared his throat, as if a little tickle had appeared. 'Three weeks.' The words were followed by a hasty smile. 'One of the partners will be leaving for business in Japan. He needs to brief you before he leaves.'

She'd tried hard not to let the horror of the time frame appear on her face as she'd stood up and straightened her skirt. 'Three weeks will be fine. Perfectly manageable.' Her voice had wavered and she'd hoped he didn't notice.

He'd stood up quickly. 'Perfect, Carrie. I'm sure you'll do a wonderful job for us.'

The train pulled into another station and Carrie felt the shuffle of bodies around her as the passengers edged even closer together to let the hordes of people on the platform board. It seemed as if the whole of New York City had been sent home early.

A cold hand brushed against hers and a woman gave her a tired smile. 'They've closed Central Park—one of the trees collapsed under the weight of the snow. I've never heard of that before.' She rolled her eyes. 'I'm just praying the school buses get home. Some of the roads are closed because they don't have enough snow ploughs and the grit wasn't due to be delivered for another two weeks.' Her face was flushed as she continued to talk. 'I've never seen it so bad, have you? I bet we're all snowed in for the next few days.'

Carrie gave a rueful shrug of her shoulders. 'I'm not

from around here. I'm from London. This is my first time in New York.'

The woman gave a little sigh. 'Poor you. Well, welcome to the madhouse.'

Carrie watched as the train pulled out of the station. It didn't seem to pick up speed at all, just crawled along slowly. Was there snow on the tracks, or was it the weight of too many passengers, desperate to get home before the transport system shut down completely? *Please, just two more stops.* Then she would be home.

Home. Was it home?

The apartment in West Village was gorgeous. Not quite a penthouse, but part of a brownstone and well out of her budget. West Village was perfect. It was like some tucked away part of London, full of gorgeous shops, coffee houses and restaurants. But it still wasn't home.

Today, in the midst of this snowstorm, she wanted to go home to the smell of soup bubbling on the stove. She wanted to go home to the sound of a bubble bath being run, with candles lit around the edges. She wanted to go home somewhere with the curtains pulled, a fire flickering and a warm glow.

Anything other than her own footsteps echoing across the wooden floor in the empty apartment, and knowing that the next time she'd talk to another human being it would be with the man who ran the coffee stall across the street on the way to work the next morning.

She wrinkled her nose. It might not even come to that. The sky was darkening quickly. Maybe the woman next to her was right. Maybe they would end up snowed in. She might not speak to another human being for days.

She shifted the bag containing the laptop in her hands. She had enough work to last for days. The boss had been clear. Take enough to keep busy—don't worry about getting into the office. If the snow continued she couldn't count on seeing any of her workmates.

The people in her apartment block nodded on the way past, but there had never been a conversation. Never a friendly greeting. Maybe they were just used to the apartment being used by business people, staying for a few weeks and then leaving again. It would hardly seem worthwhile to reach out and make friends.

A shiver crept down her spine and her mind started to race.

Did she have emergency supplies? Were there any already in the apartment? How would she feel being snowed in in New York, where it felt as if she didn't know a single person?

Sure, she had met people at work over the past two months. She'd even been out for a few after-work drinks. But the office she worked in wasn't a friendly, sociable place. It was a fast-paced, frenetic, meet-the-deadline-before-you-die kind of place. She had colleagues, but she wasn't too sure she had friends.

The train shuddered to a halt at Fourteenth Street and the door opened. 'Everybody out!'

Her head jerked up and the carriage collectively groaned.

'What?'

'No way!'

'What's happening?'

A guard was next to the door. 'This is the last stop, folks. Snow on the tracks. All trains are stopping. Everybody out.'

Carrie glanced at the sign. Fourteenth Street. One subway stop away from the apartment. She glanced down at her red suede ankle boots. She could kiss these babies goodbye. The ground outside was covered in thick, mucky slush. She didn't even want to think about what they'd look like by the time she reached the apartment.

The crowd spilled out onto the platform and up towards the mezzanine level of the station on Fourteenth Street. Carrie could hear panicked voices all around her trying to plan alternative routes home. At least she knew she could walk from here, no matter how bad it was outside.

The sky had darkened rapidly, with thick grey clouds hanging overhead, continuing their deluge of snow.

Snow. It was such a pretty thing. The kind of thing you spent hours cutting out of paper as a kid, trying to make a snowflake. Then sticking on a blue piece of card and putting on the classroom wall or attaching to a piece of string and hanging from the Christmas tree.

It didn't look like this in the storybooks. Thick wads of snow piled at the edges of the street, blanketing the road and stopping all traffic. The whiteness gone, leaving mounds of grey, icy sludge.

There was a creaking noise behind her and across the street, followed by a flood of shouts. 'Move! Quickly!'

In slow motion she watched as a large pile of snow slowly slid from a roof four storeys above the street. The people beneath were hurrying past, blissfully unaware of what was happening above their heads.

It was like a slow-moving action scene from a movie. All the inevitability of knowing what was about to happen without being able to intervene. Her breath caught in her throat. A woman in a red coat. A little boy. An elderly couple walking hand in hand. A few businessmen with their coat collars turned up, talking intently on their phones.

There was a flash of navy blue. The woman in the red coat and little boy were flung rapidly from the sidewalk into the middle of the empty street. The elderly couple pressed up against a glass shop window as some frantic shouts alerted the businessmen.

The snow fell with a thick, deafening thump. A cloud of powdered snow lifting into the air and a deluge of muddy splatters landing on her face.

Then, for a few seconds, there was silence. Complete silence.

It was broken first by the whimpers of a crying child—the little boy who had landed in the road. Seconds later chaos erupted. Onlookers dashed to the aid of the woman and small child, helping them to their feet and ushering them over to a nearby coffee shop. A few moments later someone guided the elderly couple from under the shelter of the shop's awning where they had been protected from the worst of the deluge.

'Where's the cop?'

'What happened to the cop?'

A policeman. Was that who had dived to the rescue? Her eyes caught the flicker of the blue lights of the NYPD car parked on the street. It was such a common sight in New York that she'd stopped registering them.

Some frantic digging and a few choice expletives later and one of New York's finest, along with one of the businessmen, emerged from the snow.

Someone jolted her from behind and her feet started to automatically move along the sludgy sidewalk. There was nothing she could do here.

Her own heart was pounding in her chest. Fat use she would be anyway. She didn't have a single medical skill to offer, and the street was awash with people rushing to help. She could see the cop brushing snow angrily from his uniform. He looked vaguely familiar but she couldn't place him. He was holding his wrist at a funny angle and looking frantically around, trying to account for all the people he had tried to save.

A tissue appeared under her nose. 'Better give your face a wipe,' said another woman, gesturing towards her mud-splattered coat, shoes and face.

Carrie turned towards the nearest shop window and did a double take. She looked like something the cat had dragged in. 'Thanks,' she muttered as she lifted the tissue to her face, smudging the mud further across her cheek. Her bright green coat was a write-off. The dry-clean-only label floated inside her mind. No dry-cleaning in the world could solve this mess.

She stared up at the darkening sky. It was time to go home. Whether it felt like home or not.

Daniel Cooper coughed and spluttered. His New York skyline had just turned into a heavy mix of grey-white snow. Wasn't snow supposed to be light and fluffy? Why did it feel as if someone were bench-pressing on top of him? A pain shot up his arm. He tried his best to ignore it. *Mind over matter. Mind over matter.*

There was noise above him, and shuffling. He spluttered. Snow was getting up his nose. It was strange being under here. Almost surreal.

He didn't feel as if he was suffocating. The snow wasn't tightly packed around his face. He just couldn't move. And Dan didn't like feeling as if things were out of his control.

The scuffling above him continued and then a few pairs of strong arms pulled him upwards from the snow. His head whipped around, instantly looking to see if the mother and child were safe.

There. On the other side of the sidewalk. He could see the flash of her red coat. Throwing them towards the street probably hadn't been the wisest move in the world, but the street was deep in snow, with not a car in sight. People were crowded around them but they were both safe, if a little shocked. The woman lifted her head and caught his eye. One of her hands was wrapped around her son, holding him close to her side, the other hand she placed on her chest. She looked stunned, her gaze registering the huge mound of snow that they would have been caught under, the horror on her face apparent. *Thank you,* she mouthed at him.

He smiled. The air left his lungs in a whoosh of relief. Snow was sticking to the back of his neck, turning into water that was trickling down his spine. As if he weren't wet enough already.

The elderly couple. Where were they? And why was his wrist still aching so badly? He spun back around. The elderly couple were being escorted across the street towards a sidewalk café. Thank goodness. He gave a shiver. He didn't even want to think about the broken bones they could have suffered—or the head injuries.

'Buddy, your wrist, are you hurt?' A man in a thick wool coat was standing in front of him, concern written all over his face.

Dan looked down. The thing he was trying to ignore. The thing he was trying to block from his mind. He glanced at the pile of snow he'd been buried under. There, in amongst the debris, were some slate shingles. Who knew how many had fallen from the roof above. He was just lucky that one had hit his wrist instead of his head.

Darn it. His eyes met those of the concerned citizen in front of him. 'I'll see about it later,' he muttered. 'I'm sure it will be fine. Let me make sure everyone's okay.'

The man wrinkled his brow. 'They've called an ambulance for the other guy.' He nodded towards the sidewalk, where one of the businessmen was sitting, looking pale-faced and decidedly queasy. Truth be told, he felt a little like that himself. Not that he'd ever let anyone know.

He tried to brush some of the snow from his uniform. 'Who knows how long the ambulance will take to get here. We might be better taking them to be checked over at the clinic on Sixteenth Street.' He signalled across the street to another cop who'd appeared and was crossing quickly towards him. 'Can you talk to dispatch and see how long it will take the ambulance to get here?'

The other cop shook his head and threw up his hands. 'The whole city is practically shut down. I wouldn't count on anyone getting here any time soon.' He looked around him. 'I'll check how many people need attention—' he nodded towards Dan '—you included, then we'll get everyone round to the clinic.' He rolled his eyes. 'It's gonna be a long shift.'

Dan grimaced. The city was in crisis right now. People would be stranded with no way of getting home. Flights were cancelled. Most of the public transport was shutting down. How much use would he be with an injured wrist?

A prickle of unease swept over him as he looked at the streets crowded with people. He should be doing his job, helping people, not sloping off to a clinic nearby.

He hated that. He hated the elements that were out of his control. He looked at the crowds spilling out onto the sidewalk from Fourteenth Street station and took a deep breath.

Things could only get worse.

Carrie stared out of the window. The sun had well and truly disappeared and the streets were glistening with snow. Not the horrible sludge she'd trudged through earlier—but freshly fallen, white snow. The kind that looked almost inviting from the confines of a warmly lit apartment.

Her stomach rumbled and she pressed her hand against it. Thank goodness Mr Meltzer lived above his store. Every other store in the area had pulled their shutters and closed. She glanced at the supplies on the counter. Emergency milk, water, bread, bagels, cheese, macaroni and chocolate. Comfort food. If she was going to be snowed in in New York she had every intention of eating whatever she liked. It would probably do her some good. After the stress of last year she still hadn't regained the weight she'd lost. Gaining a few pounds would help fill out her clothes. It was so strange that some women wanted to diet away to almost nothing—whereas all she wanted was to get her curves back again.

Her ears pricked up. There it was again. That strange sound that had brought her to the window in the first place. This apartment was full of odd noises—most of which she'd gotten used to. Rattling pipes with trapped air, squeaking doors and floorboards, sneaky unexplained drafts. But this one was different. Was it coming from outside?

She pressed her nose up against the glass, her breath steaming the space around her. The street appeared deathly quiet. Who would venture out on a night like this? The twenty-four-hour news channels were full of *Stay indoors. Don't make any journeys that aren't absolutely necessary.* Anyone, with any sense, would be safely indoors.

She pushed open the window a little, letting in a blast of cold air. Thank goodness for thermal jammies, bed socks and an embossed dressing gown.

She held her breath and listened. There it was again. It was like a mew. Was it a cat? Downstairs, in the apartment underneath, she could hear the faint thump of music. It must be the cop. He obviously wouldn't be able to hear a thing. She didn't even know his name. Only that he must be a cop because of the uniform he wore. Tall, dark and handsome. But he hadn't looked in her direction once since she'd arrived.

Who had left their cat out on a night like this? Her conscience was pricked. What should she do? Maybe it was just a little cat confused by the snow and couldn't find its way home. Should she go downstairs and investigate? She glanced down at her nightwear. It would only take a few seconds. No one would see her.

She could grab the cat from the doorway and bring it in for the night. Maybe give it a little water and let it curl in front of the fire. A cat. The thought warmed her from the inside out. She'd never had a cat before. It might be nice to borrow someone else's for the night and keep it safe. At least she would have someone to talk to.

She opened her door and glanced out onto the landing. Everyone else was safely ensconced in their apartments. Her feet padded down the flights of stairs, reaching the doorway in less than a minute. She unlocked the heavy door of the brownstone and pulled it open.

No.

It couldn't be.

She blinked and shut the door again. Fast.

Her heart thudded against her chest. One. Two. Three. Four. Five. Her brain was playing horrible tricks on her. Letting her think she was safe and things were safely locked away before springing something out of the blue on her.

Maybe she wasn't even awake. Maybe she'd fallen asleep on the sofa upstairs, in front of the flickering fire, and would wake up in a pool of sweat.

One. Two. Three. Four. Five.

She turned the handle again, oh-so-slowly, and prayed her imagination would get under control. Things like this didn't happen to people like her.

This time her reaction was different. This time the cold night air was sucked into her lungs with a force she didn't think she possessed. Every hair on her body stood instantly on end—and it wasn't from the cold.

It was a baby. Someone had left a baby on her doorstep.

CHAPTER TWO

FOR A SECOND, Carrie couldn't move. Her brain wouldn't compute. Her body wouldn't function.

Her ears were amplifying the sound. The little mew, mew, mew she'd thought she'd heard was actually a whimper. A whimper that was sounding more frightening by the second.

Her immediate instinct was to run—fast. Get away from this whole situation to keep the fortress around her heart firmly in place and to keep herself sheltered from harm. No good could come of this.

But she couldn't fight the natural instinct inside her—no matter how hard she tried. So she did what any mother would do: she picked up the little bundle and held it close to her chest.

Even the blanket was cold. And the shock of picking up the bundle chilled her.

Oh, no. The baby.

She didn't think. She didn't contemplate. She walked straight over to the nearest door—the one with the thudding music—and banged loudly with her fist. 'Help! I need help!'

Nothing happened for a few seconds. Then the music switched off and she heard the sound of bare feet on the wooden floor. The door opened and she held her breath.

There he was. In all his glory. Scruffy dark hair, too-tired eyes and bare-chested, with only a pair of jeans clinging to his hips—and a bright pink plaster cast on his wrist. She blinked. Trying to take in the unexpected sight. His brow wrinkled. 'What the—?'

She pushed past him into the heat of his apartment.

'I need help. I found this baby on our doorstep.'

'A baby?' He looked stunned, then reached over and put a hand around her shoulders, pulling her further inside the apartment and guiding her into a chair next to the fire.

'What do I do? What do I do with a baby? Why would someone do this?' She was babbling and she couldn't help it. She was in a strange half-naked man's apartment in New York, with an abandoned baby and her pyjamas on.

This really couldn't be happening.

Her brain was shouting messages at her. But she wasn't listening. She couldn't listen. *Get out of here.*

She stared down at the little face bundled in the blanket. The baby's eyes were screwed shut and its brow wrinkled. Was it a girl? Or a boy? Something shifted inside her. This was hard. This was so hard.

She shouldn't be here. She absolutely shouldn't be here. She was the last person in the world qualified to look after a baby.

But even though her brain was screaming those thoughts at her, her body wasn't listening. Because she'd lifted her hand, extended one finger and was stroking it down the perfect little cold cheek.

Dan Cooper's day had just gone from unlucky to ridiculous. He recognised her. Of course he recognised her. She was the girl with the sad eyes from upstairs.

But now she didn't look sad. She looked panicked.

He was conscious that her gaze had drifted across his bare abdomen. If she hadn't been banging on the door so insistently he would have pulled on a shirt first. Instead, he tried to keep his back from her line of vision as he grabbed the T-shirt lying across the back of his sofa.

He looked back at her. Now she didn't look panicked. She'd stopped babbling. In fact, she'd stopped talking completely. Now she just sat in front of the fire staring at the baby. She looked mesmerised.

His cop instinct kicked into gear. *Please don't let her be a crazy.* The last thing he needed today was a crazy.

He walked over and touched her hand, kneeling down to look into her eyes. He'd heard some bizarre tales in his time but this one took the biscuit. 'What's your name?'

She gave him only a cursory glance—as if she couldn't bear to tear her eyes away from the baby. 'Carrie. Carrie McKenzie. I live upstairs.'

He nodded. The accent drew his attention. The apartment upstairs was used by a business in the city. They often had staff from their multinational partners staying there. His brain was racing. He'd seen this girl, but had never spoken to her. She always looked so sad—as if she had the weight of the world on her shoulders.

He racked his brain. Had she been pregnant? Would he have noticed? Could she have given birth unaided upstairs?

His eyes swept over her. Pyjamas and a dressing gown. Could camouflage anything.

He took a deep breath. Time was of the essence here. He had to ask. He had to cover all the bases. 'Carrie—is this your baby?'

Her head jerked up. 'What?' She looked horrified. And then there was something—something else. 'Of course not!'

A feeling of relief swept over him. He'd been a cop long enough to know a genuine response when he saw one. Thank goodness. Last thing he needed right now was a crazy neighbour with a baby.

He reached over and pulled the fleecy blanket down from around the baby's face. The baby was breathing, but its cheeks were pale.

The nearest children's hospital was Angel's, all the way up next to Central Park. They wouldn't possibly be able to reach there in this weather. And it was likely that the ambulance service had ground to a halt. He had to prioritise. Even though he wasn't an expert, the baby seemed okay.

He stood up. 'How did you find the baby?'

Her brow wrinkled. 'I heard a noise. I thought it was a cat. I came downstairs to see.'

He couldn't hide the disbelief in his voice. 'You thought a baby was a cat?'

Her blue eyes narrowed as they met his. His tone had obviously annoyed her. 'Well, you know, it was kinda hard to hear with your music blaring.'

He ignored the sarcasm, even though it humoured him. Maybe Miss Sad-Eyes had some spunk after all. 'How long since you first heard it?' This was important. This was really important.

She shook her head. 'I don't know. Five minutes? Maybe a little more?'

His feet moved quickly. He grabbed for the jacket that hung behind the door and shoved his bare feet into his baseball boots.

She stood up. 'Where are you going? Don't leave me alone. I don't know the first thing about babies.'

He turned to her. 'Carrie, someone left this baby on our doorstep.' His eyes went to the window, to the heavy snow falling on the window ledge as he slid his arms into his jacket. 'Outside, there could be someone in trouble. Someone could be hurt. I need to go and check.'

She bit her lip and glanced at the baby before giving a small cursory nod of her head. He stepped outside into the bitter cold, glancing both ways, trying to decide which way to go. There was nothing in the snow. Any tracks that had been left had been covered within minutes; the snow was falling thick and fast.

He walked to the other side of the street and looked over at their building. Why here? Why had someone left their baby here?

There were some lights on in the other apartment buildings on the street. But most of the lights were in the second or third storeys. Theirs was the only building with lights on in the first floor. It made sense. Someone had wanted this baby found quickly.

He walked briskly down the street. Looking for anything—any sign, any clue. He ducked down a few alleyways, checking behind Dumpsters, looking in receded doorways.

Nothing. Nobody.

He turned and started back the other way. Checking the alleys on the other side of the street and in the opposite direction. His feet moving quickly through the sludgy snow.

He should have stopped and pulled some socks on. The thin canvas of his baseball boots was soaked through already. The temperature must have dropped by several degrees since the sun had gone down. He'd only been out here a few minutes and already he was freezing.

He looked up and his heart skipped a beat. Carrie was standing at his window, holding the baby in her arms.

There was a look of pure desperation on her face—as if she were willing him to find the mother of this child.

It was a sight he'd never expected to see. A woman, holding a child, in his apartment. She'd pulled up his blinds fully and the expanse of the apartment he called home was visible behind her. His large, lumpy but comfortable sofa. His grandmother's old high-back chair. His kitchen table. His dresser unit. His kitchen worktop. The picture hanging above the fireplace.

Something niggled at him. His apartment was his space. He'd rarely ever had a relationship that resulted in him 'bringing someone over'. He could count on one hand the number of girlfriends who'd ever made it over his doorway. And even then it seemed to put them on an automatic countdown to disaster.

He didn't really do long-term relationships. Oh, he dated—but after a few months, once they started to get that hopeful look in their eyes, he always found a way to let them down gently. They eventually got the message. It was better that way.

So seeing Carrie standing in his apartment with a baby in her arms took the wind clean out of his sails. The sooner all this was over with, the better.

Still, she was cute. And even better—from London. She'd have no plans to stay around here. Maybe a little flirting to pass the time?

He gave himself a little shake and had another look around. There was no one out here. The streets were completely empty.

It was so funny being on the outside looking in. He loved his home. He cherished it. But he'd never really taken a moment to stand outside and stare in—to see what the world must see on their way past if he hadn't pulled the blinds. His grandmother had left it to him in her will and he knew how lucky he was. There was no way a single guy on a cop's salary could have afforded a place like this.

But it was his. And he didn't even owe anything on it. All he had to do was cover the bills.

A little thought crept into his mind. He hadn't quite pulled the blinds fully tonight. He just hadn't gotten round to it. Was that why someone had left their baby here?

Did they see into his home and think it would be a safe place to leave a baby?

It sent a shudder down his spine. The thought that a few minutes ago someone could have been out here having those kind of thoughts.

The snowfall was getting even heavier—he could barely see ten feet in front of him. This was pointless. He was never going to find any clues in this weather. He had to concentrate on the immediate. He had to concentrate on the baby.

He hurried back into the apartment. Carrie turned to face him. 'Nothing?' The anxiety in her voice was obvious. Was she just a concerned citizen? Or was it something else?

He shook his head and pulled off his jacket, hanging it back up behind the door.

He walked over to where she was standing at the window and had another quick look out into the deserted street, searching for something, anything—a shadow, a movement. But there was nothing. Just the silence of the street outside.

He stood next to her, watching the way she cradled the baby in her arms. She was holding the baby, but he could sense she was uneasy. She'd said she didn't know the first thing about babies—well, neither did he. And in a snow-storm like this, it was unlikely they could get any help.

Most of the people who stayed around here were pro-fessionals. He couldn't think of a single family that stayed on this street. There were a couple of older people who had lived here for years. Mrs Van Dyke upstairs, but her family had long since moved away. There really wasn't anyone they could call on for help.

He watched her. The way her blue eyes were fixed on the face of the baby, still swaddled in its blanket. It was then he noticed the way her arms were trembling. It was slight—ever so slight. Making her chestnut curls waver and the pink flush of her cheeks seem heated.

She was beautiful. Now that he was close enough to take a good look at her, Carrie McKenzie was beautiful. Even if she didn't know it herself. Even with the realm of sadness in her blue eyes. He wondered what they looked like when they were happy. Did they sparkle, like the sun glinting off a turquoise-blue sea?

They were standing too close. He was sure his warm breath must be dancing across her skin. He could smell the orange scent of her bath oils, still present on her skin. He liked it. It was nicer than the cloying scent of some perfumes that women wore. The ones that prick-led your nose from the other side of the room. This was like a warm summer's day. Here, in his living room, in the middle of a snowstorm in New York.

She looked up at him with those sad blue eyes. She didn't pull away from him. She didn't seem to think he had invaded her personal space. It was quite unnerving. He couldn't remember the last time he'd been this close to a beautiful woman in his apartment—and certainly not one in her nightwear.

A smile danced across his face. If he'd ever pictured

a woman in his apartment in her nightwear it certainly hadn't been in fluffy pyjamas and bed socks. She blinked and it snapped him out of his wayward thoughts and back to the current situation.

'I don't even know your name,' she whispered.

Wow. He hadn't even introduced himself. What kind of a New Yorker was he that his neighbour didn't even know his name? His grandma would kill him for his lack of manners and hospitality.

Why hadn't he ever introduced himself? Was it because he was so used to the constant flow of traffic up above him that he hadn't thought it worth his while? The thought shamed him. Because this woman definitely looked as if she could do with a friend. 'Dan. Daniel Cooper.'

'Daniel,' she repeated, as if she were trying to associate his face with the name. Her lips curled upwards. 'It's nice to meet you, Daniel,' she whispered, her gaze steady on his. 'Even if I am barely dressed.' He liked that about her. Even though her arms were trembling and she was clearly out of her depth, she could still look him clear in the eye and make a joke at her own expense.

The baby let out a whimper, reminding them of its presence, and he jerked back to reality. 'Maybe it's time to find out whether we've had a boy or a girl.' He raised his eyebrows at her and held out his hands to take the bundle from her.

It only took a few seconds to relieve her of the weight. There was a noticeable sigh of relief in her shoulders as she handed the baby over.

He walked closer to the fire and unwound the little blanket. His cast made it awkward. There were no baby clothes underneath—no diaper. Just a little wrinkled towel. Carrie let out a gasp, lifting her hand to her mouth at the sight of a piece of string and a barely shriv-elled umbilical cord.

Dan sucked in a deep breath. 'Well, like I said, I'm no expert but I guess this means we have a newborn.' A million thoughts started to flood into his head but he tried to push them aside. 'And I guess I should say con-gratulations, we've got a boy.' He rewrapped the blanket and lifted the little one onto his shoulder, trying to take in the enormity of the situation.

'I have a friend who works at Angel's, the children's hospital. Let me give her a call.'

'Her?'

He lifted his head. It was just the way she said the word *her*. As if it implied something else entirely.

'Yes. She's a paediatrician. Since neither of us know what we're doing and we can't get any immediate help, I guess she's the best bet we've got.'

He walked over to the phone and dialled quickly, put-ting the phone onto speaker as he adjusted the baby on his shoulder, away from his cast. 'Can you page Dr Adams for me? Tell her it's Sergeant Cooper and it's an emer-gency. Thanks.'

It only took a few seconds to connect. 'Dan? What's up?'

The relief he felt was instant. Shana was the best kids' doctor that he knew. She would tell him exactly what to do.

'Hi, Shana. I've got a bit of a problem. I've had a baby dumped on my doorstep and from the looks of it, it's a newborn.'

'What?' He could hear the incredulous tone in her voice. 'In this weather?'

'Exactly.'

Shana didn't mess around. She was straight down to business. 'Is the baby breathing?'

'Yes.'

'How cold? Do you have a thermometer? What's the baby's colour? And how is it responding?'

Carrie burst in. 'We think he was outside for just over five minutes. His skin was cold when I brought him in—and he was pale. But he's started to warm up. He looks pinker now.' Her brow was furrowed. 'Do you have a thermometer, Dan?' She was shaking her head. 'I don't.'

'Who's that?'

Daniel cleared his throat. 'That's Carrie, my neighbour from upstairs. It was she who heard the baby crying. And no, Shana, we don't have a thermometer.'

'No matter. Crying? Now that's a good sign. That's a positive.'

Carrie shook her head. 'Not crying exactly, more like a whimper.'

'Any noise is good noise. You said he's a newborn. Is the cord still attached? Is it tied off?'

'Yes, it's tied with a piece of string. Doesn't look the cleanest. But the baby was only wrapped up in a blanket. No clothes. No diaper.'

'Sounds like no preparation. I wonder if the mother had any prenatal care. Does the baby look full term?'

Daniel shrugged and looked at Carrie, who shook her head and mouthed, *I don't know.*

'To be honest, Shana, neither of us are sure. I guess he looks okay. What does a full-term baby look like?'

'Does he have a sucking reflex? Is he trying to root?'

'What? I have no idea what you're talking about.' He was trying hard not to panic. This was all second nature to Shana. These types of questions were the ones she asked day in, day out. To him it all sounded like double Dutch.

They could hear the sound of muffled laughter at the other end of the phone. 'One of you, scrub your hands thoroughly under the tap then brush your finger around the side of the baby's mouth. I want to know if he turns towards it, as if he's trying to breastfeed or bottlefeed.'

Daniel nodded at Carrie, who walked over to the sink and started scrubbing her hands. 'Give us a second, Shana.'

Carrie dried her hands and then walked back over and lifted her finger hesitantly to the side of the baby's mouth. It took a few gentle brushes to establish that the little guy was reacting to her touch, turning towards it and opening his mouth.

'Yes, Shana. We think he is responding.'

'Good. That's a sign that he's around full term.' She gave an audible sigh. 'Okay, Daniel, you're not going to like this.'

'What?' Did she think something was wrong with the baby?

'There's no way I can send anyone from Angel's to get that baby. Our emergency room is packed and the roads around us are completely impassable. And from the weather report it's going to be like that for a few days.'

'Is that the good news or the bad news?' The mild feeling of panic was starting to rise.

Shana let out a laugh. 'Probably both. It sounds as if your baby is doing okay. Thank goodness. He will need a proper assessment as soon as possible. I'll put the necessary call in to social services, but they are on the other side of the city from you and everyone is in crisis right now. It will be a few days before they get to you. In the meantime the first thing you need to do is feed the little guy. Do you have somewhere local you can get some supplies?'

Blank. His brain had instantly gone blank. He'd never had any reason to look for baby supplies before. Where on earth would he get them?

Carrie touched his arm. 'Mr Meltzer stays above his store. I'm sure he'll have some powdered baby milk and diapers we can buy.'

Instant relief, followed by a sickening feeling in the pit of his stomach. 'Shana, you can't seriously expect us to look after a baby. Me, Shana? Seriously?'

'Daniel Cooper, you're one of the most responsible guys I know. I can't think of a single other person I would trust with a newborn baby right now. You're like any brand-new parent. None of them have experience. They just learn as they go. You'll need to do the same.'

'But they have nine months to get used to the idea. They read dozens of books about what to do—'

'And you have your own personal paediatrician at the other end of a phone. Not that I think you'll need me.'

Daniel could feel his heartbeat quicken in his chest. He wasn't afraid—not really. As a New York cop he'd dealt with most things in life. He'd had a gun pulled on him, a knife—on more than one occasion. He'd stopped a young girl from being abducted once, and managed to resist the temptation of doing what he really wanted to the potential kidnapper. He'd even talked a guy down from the edge of a rooftop before. But this? Looking after a baby? Why did it seem more intimidating than anything else?

'Shana, I don't think I'm the best person for the job.'

'Why not? You're practical. You're resourceful. And right now you're the best that baby's got.' She was beginning to sound exasperated. Angel's must be under an enormous amount of pressure right now, and he really didn't want to add to it. 'You've even got some help from your neighbour.'

He glanced over at Carrie, who was shaking her head frantically. *No,* she was mouthing.

'Suck it up, Daniel—and call me if you have any problems.' There was a click at the other end of the phone.

Carrie's chin was practically bouncing off the floor. 'Suck it up, Daniel? Suck it up? That's what she says to you?' Her voice was getting higher pitched by the second and the baby was starting to squirm in his arms, reacting to the noise.

Reactions? Was that a good sign, too? He really didn't have a clue.

He shrugged. 'She's my best friend's older sister. It isn't the first time Shana's told me to suck it up—and it won't be the last.' He walked over to the sofa and sank down onto the cushions. This little guy weighed more than he thought. Or maybe it was just because he couldn't swap him between his arms.

'I'm going to have to put a call in to the station, to let my captain know about the abandoned baby.'

Carrie sagged down next to him on the sofa. She shook her head and squeezed her eyes shut. 'I know we've just met, Daniel, but I'm sorry. I just can't help you with this. I can't do it. Babies—' she hesitated '—they're just not my thing. I won't be any help anyway. I don't know a thing about babies.'

He stared at her. Hard. 'You've got to be joking, right?'

Her eyes opened and widened. It was clear she was instantly on the defence. 'No. Why?'

He shook his head in disbelief. 'You turn up at my door with a baby, and now you're expecting to dump it on me in the middle of a snowstorm.'

When he said the words out loud they were even worse than the thoughts in his head.

Her face paled. 'But I...'

'I nothing.' A grin appeared on his face. 'Suck it up, Carrie.'

She drew back from him and he could sense her taking some deep breaths. 'It's not quite like that.'

He shook his head. There was no way she was leaving him high and dry. He waved his cast at her. 'What am I supposed to do? How am I supposed to bath a baby with one of these? Sure, I can probably manage to feed a baby and make up some bottles. But be practical, Carrie. I'm hardly the ideal babysitter right now.' He could see her staring at his pink cast and trying to work things out in her head. 'Least you can do is give me some help.'

Her cheeks flushed with colour, as if she'd just realised how mean it looked to walk away.

She pointed at his cast. 'How did you end up with that anyway? And what made you pick a pink cast?'

He snorted. '*Pick* isn't the word I would choose. There was an accident earlier today, a tonne of snow fell off a roof and I got trapped underneath it pushing people out of the way.'

Her eyes widened. 'On Fourteenth Street? That was you?'

He sat up a little straighter. 'How do you know about that?'

'I was there. I saw it happen.' She tilted her head to the side and stared at him again. 'I didn't realise it was you—I mean, I didn't know you.' She reached over and touched his cast. 'I remember. I remember seeing you hold your wrist at a funny angle. I guess it's broken, then?'

He nodded.

'And the pink?'

He smiled. 'It seems that today was the biggest day in the world for fractures at the clinic on Sixteenth Street.' He waved his wrist. 'Pink was the only colour they had left.'

She started to laugh. 'I can just imagine the look on your face when they told you that.'

He started to laugh, too. 'I was less than impressed. The air might have been a little blue.'

'Not pink?'

'Definitely not pink.'

She shook her head. 'That was really scary. I just remember the noise and the shouts. What about that woman in the red coat and her little boy? And that elderly couple?'

She really had been there. And she could remember the details. The lady could be a cop. 'All checked out and okay. One of the businessmen twisted his ankle and the other was being assessed for a head injury. He kept being sick.'

'Wow. Thank goodness you were there.'

Her words struck a chord with him. He hadn't really thought about that. He'd been too angry at breaking his wrist and being out of action for the NYPD. He hadn't really had time to stop to think about what could have happened to that elderly couple, or the woman and her young son.

A vision flashed in his eyes. The woman in the red coat cradling her son with one arm as if he was the most precious thing on earth. Then looking at him, with her hand on her heart, and mouthing, *Thank you*. He hadn't really had time to talk to her properly, but that one action had been more than enough for him. He didn't do this job for the thanks.

The little bundle shifted in his arms and started to

whimper again. There was colour coming into the baby's cheeks and his tongue was starting to play around the edge of his mouth. He sighed. 'I guess our boy is getting hungry. I'll give Mr Meltzer a call and see if he can open the store so we can get some supplies. Know anything about making baby bottles?'

Carrie shook her head quite forcefully. 'I've told you—I can't help. This isn't my thing.'

But Dan was already on his feet, shifting his weight and moving the baby into her arms, whether she was ready or not. 'My computer's right next to you. Do an internet search while I'm gone.' He flicked through the nearby phone directory and punched a number into his phone. 'I'll only be five minutes.'

He grabbed his jacket and headed for the door again. What was her problem? He wasn't so chauvinistic that he expected all women to want to be mothers, but he did expect any responsible adult to help out in an emergency situation.

Maybe it was just the cop in him. Maybe his expectations of the average person were too high. But he'd seen the way she'd looked at the baby. She might not have experience, but she couldn't hide the tenderness in her eyes.

Maybe she was just uncomfortable with the pyjama situation. Maybe he should offer to let her go back upstairs and get changed.

He pressed the send button on his phone as he headed along the white street. Whatever it was, she'd better get over it quick. There was no way he was doing this on his own.

Carrie sat frozen on the sofa.

This wasn't happening. This couldn't be happening.

There was a weight pressed firmly against her chest.

Like a huge dumb-bell just sitting there, taunting her to try and pull some air into her lungs.

He was scowling at her again. The baby. Nearly as much as Daniel Cooper had scowled at her when she'd tried to pull out all the lame excuses under the sun to get out of here.

It must make her seem like a bitch. But right now she didn't care.

She could feel tears starting to flood into her eyes. This was someone's precious baby. Someone's living, breathing, precious bundle. What on earth could happen in this life that would make you leave a baby on someone's doorstep in the middle of a snowstorm?

It wasn't fair. Life wasn't fair.

Last time she'd held a baby it hadn't been moving. Its little chest didn't have the rise and fall that this little boy's had. It didn't have the pink flush to its cheeks.

She blinked back the tears. The tightening in her chest was getting worse.

It.

A terrible term.

But she couldn't use any other right now. She couldn't think about her daughter. She couldn't think about Ruby McKenzie. She couldn't let that name invade her thoughts.

Because then she would spiral downwards. Then she would remember the nursery and pram. Then she would remember the routine check at the midwife's, followed by the urgent scan. Then she would remember the forty-eight-hour labour, with no cry of joy at the end of it.

Then she would remember the disintegration of her five-year relationship, as both of them struggled to cope with their bereavement.

The whimpering was getting worse, turning into full-blown screams.

She'd have given anything to hear the screams of her daughter. She'd have given anything to see her daughter screw up her face and let out a yell like that.

She shifted the baby onto her shoulder. Five minutes. Dan would be back in five minutes.

She put her hand on the keyboard of the computer and did a quick search. If she could keep her mind on something else, she could fight back the feelings. She could stop them from enveloping her. *How to sterilise and prepare bottles*.

She read the screen in front of her, scanning quickly. Her hand automatically moving and patting the baby on the back. She could do this. She could help him make a bottle and then leave.

He couldn't expect any more. She couldn't *give* any more.

She could feel herself pulling in—withdrawing inside herself. Turning into someone else. Stepping outside herself to a place where there was no hurt, no memories. Switching off.

It was the only way she'd coped before. And it was the only way she could cope now.

She glanced at the clock. Ten minutes maximum.

She could keep this face painted in place for ten minutes when he got back. That was how long it would take to sterilise the bottle, make up the powdered milk and leave him positioned on the sofa.

Her eyes registered something on the screen. Darn it! Cooled boiled water. How long did the water have to cool for before it was suitable to give a baby?

Maybe he'd only just boiled the kettle. She juggled the baby in her arms and walked over to the kitchen countertop, putting her hand on the side of the kettle. Stone cold. She picked it up and gave it a shake—and practically empty.

Nightmare.

She ran the tap and filled the kettle, putting it back into position and flicking the switch for it to boil.

Then she felt it—and heard it.

That first little squelchy noise. Followed by a warm feeling where her hand was resting on the baby's bottom.

No nappy. This little boy had no nappy on.

Her heart sank like a stone as she felt the warm feeling spread across her stomach. Could this night really get any worse?

CHAPTER THREE

DAN ENDED THE CALL on his phone. His captain had let out the loudest, heartiest laugh he'd ever heard when he'd told him about the baby. It hadn't helped.

He could hear pandemonium in the background at the station. He should be there helping. Instead of doing a late-night recce for baby supplies.

Mr Meltzer, on the other hand, had been full of concern. Loading up supplies on the counter and waving his hand at Dan's offer of payment.

'If I help the little guy get a better start in life that's all I need.'

The words tormented him. Ground into him in a way they shouldn't. If only everyone felt like Mr Meltzer.

He pushed open the door to the apartment building and kicked the snow off his favourite baseball boots. They were really beyond repair.

Carrie was waiting and she pulled open the inside door. 'Did you get some milk?'

He nodded and dumped the bags on the counter.

'Wow, how much stuff did you get?'

He pulled his arms out of his jacket. 'Who knew a baby needed so much? Mr Meltzer just kept pulling things off his shelves and saying, "You better take some of that".'

Carrie tipped one of the bags upside down. 'Please tell me you got some nappies and dummies. We need both—now.'

'What? What are you talking about?'

She waved her hand in the air. 'Oh, you Americans. Nappies—diapers. And dummies—what do you call them? Pacifiers? He's starting to get restless and it will take a little time to sterilise the bottles.' She rummaged through the bags. 'You did get bottles, didn't you?'

'What's that smell?' He wrinkled his nose and caught sight of the expression on her face. 'Oh, no. You're joking. He can't have. He hasn't eaten yet.' He pulled out a pack of baby wipes. 'I take it we'll need these?'

She nodded. 'Do you have a towel we can lay him on? I'd say getting a nappy on the little guy is a priority.'

Dan walked over to the laundry cupboard and started throwing things about. 'I know I've got a brand-new set of towels in here somewhere. My friend Dave just got married. He was drowning in the things. Ah, here we are!' He pulled out some navy blue towels and laid one down on the rug, a little away from the fireplace. He glanced at his cast. It was more inconvenient than he first thought—to say nothing about the constant ache that was coming from his wrist. 'Can you do this?'

He could see her taking a deep breath. 'Fine,' she muttered through gritted teeth. She grabbed the bag of diapers from the counter, along with the wipes and some diaper sacks. 'Did you get some cream?'

'Cream? What for?'

'For putting on the baby's bum, of course. Everyone knows you put cream on a baby to stop them from getting nappy rash.'

He shrugged his shoulders. 'Mr Meltzer didn't seem to know—and he knew everything else.' He pulled something from a second plastic bag. 'Look—ready-made for-mula in a carton. We've got the powdered stuff, too, but he said this was ready to use.'

She scowled at him as she laid the baby down on the fresh towel and peeled back the blanket.

'Eww!'

'Yuck!'

The smell was awful and filled the apartment in-stantly. The baby, on the other hand, seemed to quite like the freedom the open blanket gave and started to kick his legs.

'How can all that stuff come from one tiny little thing?' He really wanted to pinch his nose shut.

Carrie was shaking her head, too, as she made a dive for the baby wipes. 'I have no idea, but the next one is yours.'

He looked at her in horror. 'No way.' He waved his pink cast again. 'Can you imagine getting a bit of that caught on here? It would stink forever. I would smell like this for the next six weeks.' He shook his head. 'At least you can wash your hands.'

Carrie was deep in concentration, wiping and thrust-ing the dirty wipes into the supposedly scented diaper sack. She pulled out one of the diapers and held it up. 'Well, at least you seemed to have got the right size.'

Dan bit his lip. 'Actually, there was a whole shelf of the things. Mr Meltzer picked them out.'

She raised her eyebrow. 'Can you ask him to come babysit, too, please? He seems to be the only person around here who knows anything about babies.'

'I tried. He wasn't buying it.'

Carrie positioned the diaper under the clean little bot-tom and snapped the tapes into place. 'There, that's bet-ter. Pity the smell hasn't disappeared.' She picked up the blanket by the corner. 'This will need washing. Where's your machine?'

'In the basement.'

She let out a sigh. 'I don't get that about New York. Why does everyone have their washing machine in the basement?' She waved her hands around. 'You've plenty of room in here. Why isn't your washing machine in the kitchen? Everyone in London has their washing machine in their flat. You don't have to walk down miles of stairs to do the laundry.'

'Worried about leaving your underwear unguarded?'

There it was again. That cheeky element coming out. He couldn't help it. She seemed so uptight at times.

Just as he suspected, a pink colour flooded her cheeks. He could almost hear the ticking of her brain trying to find a way to change the subject quickly.

She nodded over to the counter. 'We need to sterilise the bottles.'

'I think he gave me some tablets for that.' Dan started to root around in one of the bags.

'He probably did, but according to the internet the bottles would need to be in the sterilising solution for thirty minutes. It only takes ten minutes if we boil them. That way you can use the ready-made formula and get it into him quicker.'

'What about one of these? Can we give him a pacifier in the meantime?'

Carrie shook her head. 'I think we need to sterilise them, too. And we need to use only cooled boiled water with the powdered milk. But I've no idea how long water takes to cool once you've boiled it. And I don't know whether we should put the milk in the fridge or keep it at room temperature—everyone seems to have a differ-ent opinion on the internet.' She was getting more harassed by the second, the words rattling out of her mouth and her face becoming more flushed. 'I told you—I'm not an expert in all this. I have no idea what I'm doing!'

Something clenched in his stomach. He could sense the feelings overwhelming her, and he had a whole host of some himself.

Deep down, having a woman in his apartment—without an expiry date—was freaking him out. But these weren't normal circumstances. He *needed* Carrie McKenzie's help. He couldn't do this on his own and right now he could sense she wanted to cut and run.

He was feeling a bit flustered himself. Flustered that some gorgeous Brit was in his space. But this wasn't about him. This wasn't about Daniel Cooper and the fact he liked his own space. This wasn't about the fact his relationships only lasted a few months because he didn't want anyone getting comfortable in his home—comfortable enough to start asking questions. This was about a baby. A baby who needed help from two people.

So, he did what his grandma had always taught him. Her voice echoed in his head. *You get the best out of people when you compliment them—when you thank them for what they do.*

He reached over and touched Carrie's hand. She was getting flustered again, starting to get upset. 'Carrie McKenzie?' He kept his voice low.

'What?' she snapped at him.

Yep, he was right. Her eyes had a waterlogged sheen. She was just about to start crying.

He gave her hand a little squeeze. 'I think you're doing a great job.'

The world had just stopped because she wasn't really in it.

This was one of those crazy dreams. The kind that

had your worst type of nightmare and a knight in shining armour thrown in, too. The kind that made no sense whatsoever.

She wasn't here. She wasn't awake.

Her earlier thought had been true. She was actually fast asleep on the sofa upstairs. She would wake up in a few minutes and this would all be over. This would all be something she could shrug off and forget about.

Except those dark brown eyes were still looking at her.

Still looking as if he understood a whole lot more than he was letting on. As if he'd noticed the fact she was seconds away from cracking and bursting into floods of tears.

But he couldn't, could he? Because he didn't really know her at all.

Daniel Cooper was an all-action New York cop. The kind of guy from a romance movie who stole the heroine's heart and rode off into the sunset with her. A good guy.

The kind of guy who looked after an abandoned baby.

She was trying to swallow. Her mouth was drier than a desert, and it felt as if a giant turtle had started nesting at the back of her throat.

She looked down to where his hand covered hers. It was nice. It *felt* nice.

And that was the thing that scared her most.

When was the last time someone had touched her like that? At the funeral? There had been a lot of hand squeezing then. Comfort. Reassurance. Pity.

Not the same as this.

He smiled at her. A crooked kind of smile, revealing straight white teeth.

A sexy kind of smile. The kind that could take her mind off the nightmare she was currently in.

There was a yelp from the towel. Dan moved his hand

and looked down. 'I guess baby's getting hungry. I'll stick the bottles in the pot.'

Carrie left the baby on the towel and started to look through the bags on the counter. Five prepacked cartons of formula, two different kinds of powder, more dummies and a whole mountain's worth of baby wipes.

She folded her arms across her chest as she watched Dan dangle the bottles and teats from his fingertips into the boiling water. 'Clothes, Dan. What are we going to put on him?'

His brow wrinkled and he shook his head. 'Darn it, I knew I'd forgotten something. There weren't any baby clothes in the general store, and there's no place else around here that sells any. Can't we just leave him in the diaper?'

Carrie shook her head. 'Want me to do a search on that?' She started to pace. 'Don't you know anyone around here with kids who might still have some baby clothes? How long have you stayed here?'

He blinked and his lips thinned. As if he was trying to decide how to answer the question. He averted his eyes and started busying himself with the coffee maker. 'I've lived here on and off my whole life. This was my grandma's place.'

'Was it?' She was surprised but it made perfect sense. After all, how did a young guy on a cop's salary afford a gorgeous brownstone West Village apartment? She looked around, starting to take in the decor of the place. There were a few older items that didn't look quite 'him'. A rocker pushed in the corner near the window, a small antique-style table just at the front door, currently collecting mail and keys, a dresser in the more modern-style kitchen. It was kind of nice, to see the old mixed in with the new. 'It's a lovely place. Big, too. You're a lucky guy.'

He made a noise. More like a snort. 'Yeah, I guess. Just born lucky, me.'

Carrie froze, not really knowing how to respond. What did that mean?

But he must have realised his faux pas because he changed the subject quickly. 'The ten minutes will be up soon. Once we've fed the little guy I'll go on up to Mrs Van Dyke's place. Her family used to stay here. She might have some things in storage we could use.'

'Mrs Van Dyke? Which one is she? Is she the one on the second floor who looks as if she came over on the Mayflower and is about six hundred years old?'

He raised his eyebrows. 'Watch it. According to her, her family were amongst the original Dutch settlers. And I don't think she's quite six hundred years old. She's as sharp as a stick, and she hasn't aged in the past twenty-five years.' He gave her a wink as he switched off the burner. 'Maybe you should ask her what cream she uses.'

Carrie picked up an unopened packet of pacifiers and tossed them at his head. They bounced off the wall behind him.

'Careful, careful, we've got a baby in the apartment. We don't want anything to hit him.' He glanced at his watch. 'On second thought, it's getting kind of late. Maybe it's too late to go knocking on Mrs Van Dyke's door.' His gaze was still fixed on the baby, lying on the floor, grizzling impatiently for his milk.

Carrie folded her arms as she stood next to him. 'You've got to be kidding. Mrs Van Dyke is up watching TV until four a.m. most nights. And I take it she's getting a little deaf, because I can't get to sleep in my apartment because of the *Diagnosis Murder* or *Murder, She Wrote* reruns that I hear booming across the hall. Seriously, the woman needs a hearing aid.'

'And seriously? She'll be far too proud to get one.'

There was something nice about that. The fact that he knew his elderly neighbour so well that he could tell exactly why she didn't have a hearing aid. 'So what was wrong with me, then?' She couldn't help it. The words just spilled out.

'What do you mean?'

'You obviously know your other neighbours well, but it was too much trouble to even say hello to me in the foyer.'

The colour flooded into his cheeks. Unflappable Dan was finally flapping. He could deal with a tonne of snow falling from a roof, he could deal with a baby dumped on his doorstep, but this? This was making him avert his eyes and struggle to find some words.

'Yeah, I'm sorry about that. I just assumed you were staying for only a few days. Most of the others seemed like ships that pass in the night.'

'I've been here two months, Dan. Eight long weeks—' she let out a little sigh '—and to be honest, this isn't the friendliest place I've ever stayed.'

He cringed. 'I can hear my grandmother shouting in my ear right now. Shaming me on my bad manners. I did see you—but you always looked like you had a hundred and one things on your mind. You never really looked in the mood to talk.'

This time Carrie felt like cringing. There was a reason Dan was a cop. He was good at reading people. Good at getting to the heart of the matter. And she had only herself to blame for this, because it was she who'd called him on his behaviour.

She gave a little shrug, trying to brush it off. 'Maybe a cheery good morning would have been enough.'

She walked over and lifted the pot, tipping the boiling water into the sink.

He appeared at her back, his chin practically resting on her shoulder, as he lifted the plastic bottles and teats out onto the worktop with a clean dish towel. 'You're right, Carrie. You're absolutely right. I should have said hello. I should have said good morning.'

She turned her head slightly. He wasn't quite touching her, but she could feel the heat emanating from his body. She wanted to step away, to jerk backwards, but her body wasn't letting her.

Her lips were curving into a smile—even though she was telling them not to—as she stared into those brown eyes again. It was nice. Being up close to someone again. His lips were only inches from hers. She wondered if he was having the same kind of thoughts she was. The kind of thoughts that made her forget there was a baby in the room…until he let out an angry wail from the floor.

They jumped back, both at the same time. She reached for one of the cartons. 'Do you have a pair of scissors?'

He opened a drawer, pulled out the scissors, snipped the edge of the carton and upended the contents into one of the cooled bottles. Carrie picked up one of the teats by the edge of its rim and placed it on the bottle, screwing it in place with the retaining ring.

The bottle sat on the middle of the counter and they stared at each other for a few seconds.

'Don't we need to heat the milk up now?'

She shook her head. 'According to the internet, room temperature is fine.'

'Oh, okay.'

Silence. And some deep breathing, followed by a whole host of screams from the floor. It was like a Mexican stand-off.

'So, who is going to do this?'

'You. Definitely you.'

'But what if I do it wrong?'

'What if I do it wrong? Don't you dare suggest that I can do it better because I'm a girl.'

He raised his eyebrows. 'Oh, I'd never refer to you as a girl.'

'Stop it. He's mad. Just feed him.' She opened one of the kitchen drawers and handed him a dish towel. 'Here, put this over you.'

'What do I need that for?'

'In case he pukes on you.'

'Ewww…'

Dan picked up the bottle, holding it between his hands as if it were a medical specimen. He squinted at the markings on the side of the bottle. 'How much do I give him?'

'I don't know.'

'Well, look it up on the internet while I start.'

Relief. Instant relief. She wasn't going to be left to feed the baby. She could sit on the other side of the room and do a search on the computer.

Dan picked up the baby from the floor and settled him on his lap, resting him in the crook of his arm that had his cast in place. He held the bottle with his other hand and brushed the teat against the baby's cheek.

There were some angry noises, and some whimpering, before finally the baby managed to latch on to the teat and suck—furiously.

Carrie was holding her breath on the other side of the room, watching with a fist clenched around her heart. A baby's first feed.

One of those little moments. The little moments that a parent should share with a child.

Daniel seemed equally transfixed. He glanced over at her. 'Wow. Just wow. Look at him go. He's starving.'

And he was. His little cheeks showed he was sucking furiously. But it was Dan who had her attention. The rapt look on his face, and the way the little body seemed to fit so easily, so snugly against his frame.

Her mouth was dry and the hairs were standing up on the back of her neck. Worse than that, she could feel the tears pooling around her eyes again.

What was wrong with her? This had nothing to do with her. Nothing to do with her situation. She shouldn't be feeling like this. She shouldn't be feeling as if she couldn't breathe and the walls were closing in around her.

But Dan looked so natural, even though he kept shifting in the chair. He looked as if he was born to do this. Born to be a father. Born to be a parent.

The thing that she'd been denied.

She glanced at the screen and stood up quickly.

She had to leave now, while he was trapped in his chair and before the tears started to fall. She needed some breathing space.

'You should stop after every ounce of milk, Dan. Take the bottle out and wind the baby. I'm sorry. I have to go.'

'What? Carrie? Wait a minute, what does *wind* mean? How do I know how much an ounce is?'

But she couldn't stop. She couldn't listen.

'Carrie? Come back.'

But her feet were already on the stairs, pounding their way back up to the sanctuary of her solitude.

CHAPTER FOUR

DAN STARED AT the wall. What had just happened?

One minute she seemed fine, next minute a bundle of nerves, ready to jump out of her skin at the slightest noise.

She'd caught him unawares. She'd caught him while he was in no position to run after her. Probably planned it all along.

Still, it wasn't as if she could go anywhere. The city was at a standstill and if this little guy started screaming she was right upstairs. Whether she liked it or not.

He shifted on the sofa. The little guy was feeding fast and furious. Was this normal?

He heard some rumbling, the noises of the milk hitting the baby's stomach. How much was an ounce anyway? And how on earth could he tell if the baby had drunk that much when the bottle was tipped up sideways? At this rate he was going to need Shana on speed dial. He glanced at the clock and let out a sigh.

This was going to be a long, long night.

Carrie slammed the apartment door behind her and slid down behind it. Her mind was on a spin cycle. She couldn't think a single rational thought right now.

What Dan must think of her.

She tried to take some slow, deep breaths. Anything

to stop her heart clamouring in her chest. Anything to stop the cold prickle across her shoulder blades.

She sagged her head into her hands. *Calm down. Calm down.*

This was ridiculous. Avoiding babies for the past year was one thing. Body-swerving pregnant friends and brand-new mothers was almost understandable.

But this wasn't. She had to stop with the self-pity. She had to get some perspective here.

What would she have done if Dan hadn't been in the building?

There was no way she would have left that baby on the doorstep. No matter how hard the task of looking after him.

And if she'd phoned the police department and they couldn't send anyone out? What would she have done then?

She lifted her head from her hands. She would have had a five-minute panic. A five-minute feeling of *this can't be happening to me.*

Then what?

There was a creeping realisation in her brain. She pushed herself back up the door. Her breathing easing, her heartbeat steadying.

Then she would have sucked it up. She would have sucked it up and got on with it.

Because that was what any responsible adult would do.

She strode over to the bedroom, shedding her dressing gown and bed socks and pulling her pyjama top over her head. She found the bra she'd discarded earlier and fastened it back in place, pulling on some skinny jeans and a pink T-shirt.

Her pink baseball boots were in the bottom of her cupboard and she pushed her feet into them.

There. She was ready.

But her stomach started to flutter again.

The light in the bathroom flickered. Was the light bulb going to blow again? Which it seemed to do with an annoying regularity. She walked inside and ran the tap, splashing some cold water over her face.

She stared into the mirror, watching the drops of water drip off her face. Dan would have labelled her a nutjob by now. He probably wouldn't want her help any more.

But the expression on his face was imprinted on her brain. He'd looked stunned. As if he couldn't understand—but he wanted to.

She picked up the white towel next to the sink and dried off her face. Her make-up was right next to her. Should she put some on? Like some camouflage? Would it help her face him again?

Her fingers hesitated over the make-up bag. It was late at night. She'd been barefaced and in her pyjamas. He wouldn't expect anything else.

But it might give her the courage she needed. It might make her feel as if she had some armour to face the world.

She pulled out some mascara and a little cream blusher, rubbing some on to her cheeks and then a touch on her lips. There. She was ready.

She crossed the room in long strides before any doubts could creep into place. There was no point in locking her apartment door. She would only be down two flights of stairs.

She placed her hand on the balustrade, ready to go down, and then halted. The television was booming from the apartment across the hall. Mrs Van Dyke.

The neighbour she'd only glimpsed in passing and never spoken to. The neighbour who might have some baby supplies they could use.

She hesitated and then knocked loudly on the door. 'Mrs Van Dyke? It's Carrie from across the hall. Daniel Cooper sent me up.'

She waited a few minutes, imagining it might take the little old lady some time to get out of her chair and over to the door—praying she'd actually heard her above the theme tune from *Murder, She Wrote*.

She could hear the creaking of the floorboards and then the door opened and the old wizened face stared out at her. Oh, boy. She really could be six hundred years old.

'And what do you want, young lady?'

Carrie jerked back a little. She had such a strong, authoritative voice, it almost reminded her of her old headmistress back in London.

She took a deep breath. 'I'm sorry to disturb you, Mrs Van Dyke, but we found a baby on the doorstep and Dan said you might be able to help.'

As the words tumbled out of her mouth she knew she could have phrased it better. If this old dear keeled over in shock it would be all her fault.

But Mrs Van Dyke was obviously made of sterner stuff.

'Oh, dear. What a terrible thing to happen. What does Dan need?'

Just like that. No beating about the bush. No preamble. Just straight to the point. Wonderful.

'We got some things from Mr Meltzer's store. He opened it specially to help out. We've got nappies—I mean, diapers—and pacifiers and bottles and milk.'

There was a gleam of amusement in the old lady's eyes. 'Just as well. I doubt I would have had any of those.'

Carrie shook her head. 'Of course. I mean—what we don't have is any baby clothes. Or any clean blankets. Do you have anything like that? Dan wondered if you might have some things packed away.'

Mrs Van Dyke nodded slowly and opened the door a little wider. 'I might have a few things that you can use, but most of them will be at the back of my cupboards. Come in, and I'll see what I can do.'

Carrie stepped into the apartment and stifled her surprise. 'Wow. What a nice place you have here.'

Clutter. Everywhere.

The floor was clear, but that was pretty much it.

There was no getting away from it—Mrs Van Dyke was clearly a hoarder.

She gave a smile and stepped further, keeping her elbows tight in against her sides for fear of tipping something off one of the tables or shelves next to her.

On second thoughts, Mrs Van Dyke wasn't your typical hoarder. Not the kind you saw on TV with twelve skips outside their house so it could be emptied by environmental health.

There were no piles of papers, magazines or mail. In fact, the only newspaper she could see was clearly deposited in the trash. And all the surfaces in the apartment sparkled. There was no dust anywhere. Just…clutter. Things. Ornaments. Pictures. Photo frames. Wooden carvings. Tiny dolls. Ceramics. The place was full of them.

No wonder Dan had thought she might have something they could use.

'They're mementos. They're not junk. Everything holds a memory that's special to me, or my family.'

Carrie jumped. Mrs Van Dyke seemed to move up silently behind her. Had she been so obvious with her staring?

'Of course not,' she said quickly.

Mrs Van Dyke picked up the nearest ornament. 'My husband used to carve things. This one he gave me on our first anniversary. A perfect rose.'

Carrie bent down and looked closely. It really was a thing of beauty. She couldn't even see the marks where the wood had been whittled away—it was perfectly smooth.

'It's beautiful.'

Mrs Van Dyke nodded. 'Yes, it is.' She walked slowly through the apartment, pointing as she went. 'This was the globe he bought me at Coney Island. This was a china plate of my grandmother's—all the way from Holland. This—' she held up another carving, this time of a pair of hands interlinked, one an adult's and one a child's '—is what he carved for me after our son Peter died when he was seven.'

Carrie's hand flew to her mouth. 'Oh, I'm so sorry.'

Mrs Van Dyke ran her finger gently over the carving as she sat it back down. 'It shows that we'd always be linked together, forever.'

She reached a door and gestured to Carrie. 'This is my box room. This is where I keep most of my things.'

Carrie was still taken aback by her comment about her son, so she pushed the door open without really thinking. She let out a gasp of laughter. 'You're not joking—it *is* a box room.' And it was. Filled with boxes from floor to ceiling. But there was no randomness about the room. Every box was clearly labelled and facing the door, and there was a thin path between the boxes. Room enough for someone of slim build to slip through.

'The boxes you're looking for are near the back.' She touched Carrie's shoulder. 'Your baby—is it a boy or a girl?'

Just the way she said it—*your baby*—temporarily

threw her for a second. It took her a moment to collect her thoughts. 'It's a boy. It's definitely a boy.'

Mrs Van Dyke nodded. 'Straight to the back, on the left-hand side somewhere, near the bottom, you'll find a box with David's name on it. And behind it, you might find something else that's useful.'

Carrie breathed in and squeezed through the gap. The labelling was meticulous, every item neatly catalogued. Did this really make Mrs Van Dyke a hoarder? Weren't those people usually quite disorganised and chaotic? Because Mrs Van Dyke was none of those things.

The box with David's baby things was almost at the bottom of a pile. Carrie knelt down and started to gingerly edge it out, keeping her eyes on the teetering boxes near the top. The whole room had the potential to collapse like dominoes—probably at the expense of Mrs Van Dyke, who was standing in the doorway.

She pushed her shoulder against the pile, trying to support some of the weight wobbling above her as she gave a final tug to get the box out.

In that tiny millisecond between the boxes above landing safely in place, still in their tower, she saw what was behind the stack and it made her catch her breath.

A beautifully carved wooden cradle.

She should have guessed. With all the other carefully carved items of wood in the apartment, it made sense that Mr Van Dyke would have made a cradle for his children. She weaved her way back through the piles, careful not to knock any with her box, before sitting it at the door next to Mrs Van Dyke. 'Do you want to have a look through this to see what you think might be appropriate?'

She chose her words carefully. Mrs Van Dyke had already revealed she'd lost one child; there might be items in this box that would hold special memories for her.

Items she might not want to give away. 'I'll go and try and get the cradle.'

It took ten minutes of carefully inching past boxes, tilting the cradle one way then another, before she finally managed to get out of the room.

She sat the cradle on the floor. Mrs Van Dyke was sitting in a chair with the open box on her lap, setting things in neat piles next to her.

Now that she had the cradle in the light of the room she was able to appreciate how fine the carving was. The cradle actually rocked. Something Carrie hadn't seen in years. The wooden spindles were beautifully turned, with a variety of ducks and bunnies carved at either end on the outside of the crib. Something like this would cost a small fortune these days.

She ran her fingers over the dark woodwork. 'This is absolutely beautiful. It looks like the kind of thing you would see in a stately home. Did your husband really make this himself?'

Mrs Van Dyke's eyes lit up at the mention of her husband. She smiled proudly. 'Yes, he did. It took him nearly four months.' She leaned forward and touched the cradle, letting it rock gently. 'This held all five of my children. Just for the first few months—they quickly outgrew it.'

'Are you sure we can borrow it? It looks like a precious family heirloom.'

Mrs Van Dyke nodded. 'A cradle is only really a cradle when it holds a baby. That's its job. You'll bring it back, mind?'

Carrie nodded. 'Social services have been called—' she held out her hands '—but with the snowstorm it might be a few days before they can collect the baby.'

Mrs Van Dyke handed her a small pile of clothes. 'I'm

sorry. I didn't keep too much. There's some vests, socks and some hand-knitted cardigans. Oh, and a blanket.'

'These will be great. Thank you so much. I'll launder them and bring them back to you in a few days.' She fingered the edge of the intricately crocheted blanket. 'This is beautiful and it looks brand new. Are you sure we can use this?'

Mrs Van Dyke smiled and shook her head. 'It's not new. I made a new blanket for every child. This was the final one. You're welcome to use it.'

Carrie smiled gratefully. 'Thank you, it's gorgeous and I'm sure it will be perfect.' She sat the clothes inside the cradle and picked it up. 'I'm sure Dan will be really grateful to you, too. If there's anything you need in the next few days be sure to let us know. We can ask Mr Meltzer to open his store again.'

Mrs Van Dyke shook her head. 'I'll be fine. My pantry is well stocked.'

Carrie walked over to the door. 'Thanks, Mrs Van Dyke.' She opened the door and gave a little smile. 'You have a beautiful home here.'

Mrs Van Dyke smiled. 'And you're welcome in it any time.'

Carrie juggled the cradle in her hands and closed the door behind her quietly.

Wow. Not what she'd expected at all.

Mrs Van Dyke was lovely, a real pleasure to be around. And she could imagine that Mrs Van Dyke could regale Carrie with hundreds of stories about her life and her family.

She thought of the little carving of a mother's and child's hands interlinked. It was heartbreaking—and it was beautiful. It hadn't felt right to ask any questions about her son Peter. She'd only just met Mrs Van Dyke and that would be intrusive.

But she'd felt the *connection*. The connection that only another mother who had lost a child could feel.

Obviously she hadn't said anything to Mrs Van Dyke. The woman hardly knew her. But that little feeling in the pit of her stomach had told her that this woman would be able to understand exactly how she felt.

Their circumstances were obviously different. Mrs Van Dyke had spent seven years loving and cherishing her son, getting to know his thoughts and quirks, growing together as mother, child and part of a family. Carrie had missed out on all that.

She'd spent seven months with her hands on her growing stomach, with a whole host of hopes and expectations for her child. In her head she'd been making plans for the future. Plans that involved a child.

None of those plans had been for a future without her daughter.

Her hands were starting to shake a little. Was it from the weight in her hands—or was it from the thoughts in her head?

A cradle is only really a cradle when it holds a baby.
How true.

She'd loved the white cot she'd bought for her daughter. But it hadn't been nearly as beautiful as this one. It had been dismantled and packed off to the nearest charity shop, along with the pram, because she couldn't bear to look at them.

Hopefully some other baby had benefitted from them.

Carrie walked down the stairs carefully, making sure she didn't bang the cradle on the way. Who knew what Dan would say to her? She wouldn't be surprised if he let rip with some choice words.

Her ears pricked up. Crying—no, wailing. The baby was screaming at the top of his lungs. Her steps quickened and she pushed open Dan's door with her shoulder.

'Dan, what on earth is going on?'

Dan's ears were throbbing. Weren't there environmental laws about noise? No one seemed to have told this little guy.

He changed him over to the other shoulder. This had been going on for the past fifteen minutes. What on earth had gone wrong?

He screwed up his face. Why was he even thinking that? He knew exactly what had gone wrong. The little guy had nearly finished the entire bottle without burping once. And according to what he'd read on the internet—that wasn't good.

He tried to switch off from the screaming. Tried to focus his mind elsewhere. Who would leave a baby outside in the cold?

The thought had been preying on his mind since the second Carrie had found the baby. Sure, he'd done the cop thing and made a half-hearted attempt to look for the mother—to see if someone was in trouble out there.

But truth be told—he wasn't that sure he wanted to find her.

Some people just weren't fit to be parents. Fact.

He was living proof and had the scars to back up his theory.

Even twenty-five years ago social services had tried to support his mother to keep him, when the truth of the matter was they should have got him the hell out of there.

Thank goodness his grandmother had realised what the scars on his back were. The guys in the station thought they were chicken-pox scars, and he wasn't about to tell them any different. But cigarettes left a nasty permanent burn.

The expression on Carrie's face had said it all. She'd felt compassion; she'd felt pity for the person who'd left this baby behind. He felt differently. Maybe this little guy was going to get the start in life he deserved.

There was a light tap at the door, then it was shouldered open. Carrie—with a wooden crib in her hands.

She wrinkled her nose at the noise. 'What did you do?' She crossed the room and sat the crib at his feet. Had she been with Mrs Van Dyke all this time? It was the only place she could have got the crib.

He shrugged his shoulders. 'Fed him.'

She shook her head. 'He shouldn't be squealing like that. Give him here.' She held out her arms and he hesitated. What was going on? This woman had hightailed it out of here as if there were a fire licking at her heels. Now she was back as if nothing had happened?

He placed his hand protectively on the little guy's back. 'What happened, Carrie?' He didn't care how blunt it sounded. He didn't care how much help he really wanted right now. He needed her to be straight with him.

She looked him straight in the eye. But he could see it—the waver. The hesitation in her blue eyes. 'I needed a little space for five minutes. And now—I've had it. I spent a little time with Mrs Van Dyke. She's great. I wish I'd had the opportunity to speak to her before today.' She walked over to the sink and lifted one of the pacifiers out of the sterilising solution. 'Has this been in there thirty minutes?'

He glanced at the clock and nodded, watching as she put the pacifier in the baby's mouth and lifted him from his shoulder. 'Let's try something else, then.' She sat down on the sofa and laid the baby across her lap, face down, gently rubbing his back.

Dan looked at the crib and shook his head. 'I hadn't even thought about where he was going to sleep.'

Carrie smiled. The kind of smile that changed the whole expression on her face. There it was. That little glimpse again of who she could be if she let herself.

'Neither did I. I asked Mrs Van Dyke if she had any clothes and it was she who suggested the crib.' She peered over at him as she continued to rub the baby's back. 'We don't have a mattress, though. Do you have something we could put inside?'

Dan tried to rack his brain. 'What about those new towels? We used one earlier, but I have plenty left. I could fold some of them to make a mattress for the crib.'

'That sounds perfect. I don't have a lot of clothes. A few cardigans, some embroidered vests and some socks. She also gave me a beautiful crocheted blanket. It looks brand new.'

The baby had stopped crying. Dan turned his head just in time to see a little pull up of the legs and to hear the loudest burp known to man.

'There we go. Is that better, little guy?' Carrie had turned him over and lifted him up again, staring him in the face. She put him back on her shoulder and kept gently rubbing his back. Her tongue ran along her lips. 'I remember somebody mentioning that trapped wind makes a baby cranky.'

Dan let out a snort. 'Cranky? You call that cranky? You only had to listen to five minutes of it.'

She bit her lip. 'Yes, I know. Sorry.' He could see her take a deep breath. 'I find this difficult, Dan. And I'm not sure I'll be much help.' She stood up and walked over to the window with the baby on her shoulder. 'I can't help feeling really sorry for whoever is out there. Why didn't they think they could take care of their baby? I wish I could help them.'

There it was again. The sympathy vote. The thing he just couldn't understand.

'Maybe they don't want our help. Maybe they just weren't designed to be a parent. There's a good chance they didn't have any prenatal care for the baby. Why on earth would they leave a baby on a doorstep? They didn't even ring the doorbell! This little guy could have frozen out there—he wasn't properly dressed or even fed. No diaper. He could have died during delivery. This isn't a person who wants a baby, Carrie. This is a person who has no sense of duty or responsibility.'

She spun around. 'You don't know that, Dan. You don't know anything. This could be an underage girl's baby. She might have been terrified to tell anyone she was pregnant—afraid of the repercussions. What if she was abused? What if she lives with her abuser? Have you thought of that?'

He was trying not to get mad. He was trying not to shout. He took a long, slow breath, his eyes lifting to meet hers. 'It could also be the baby of someone who wasn't interested in prenatal care. Someone who wasn't interested in making sure their baby was delivered safely. Someone who doesn't really care what happens to their baby.'

There was a tremble in her voice. 'You don't know that, Dan.' She looked down at the baby. 'You don't know anything. I just can't imagine what would make someone dump their baby on a doorstep. But I've got to believe they were desperate and wanted their baby to get help.' Her hand stroked the baby's head. 'A baby is a precious gift. I don't know any mother who would give their baby up willingly.'

'Then I guess our experiences of life are different.' The words were out before he knew it. No hesitation. No regrets.

Her eyes met his. It was as if she was trying to take stock of what he'd just said. As if she was trying to see inside his head.

He gave himself a shake and walked over next to her. 'I agree with you, Carrie. I think babies are precious and they should be treated with respect. So I think we should do something.' He lifted his finger and touched the baby's cheek.

'What?'

'I think we should give our baby a name.'

CHAPTER FIVE

SHE LOOKED STUNNED.

As if he'd just suggested packing up the car and heading off into the sunset with a baby in tow.

'What? We can't keep calling him "the little guy". You know what happens with abandoned babies. At some point somebody, somewhere gives them a name.'

'But we don't have any right. This isn't our baby.' She gave a little shake as if the thought was too alarming.

'Actually, right now, he is our baby. And might continue to be so for the next few days. We have to call him something in the meantime. Calling him "baby", "him" or "it", it's just not right. You know it isn't.'

She'd started pacing now. Walking about the apartment. Her eyes refusing to meet with his. 'Well, what's your suggestion, genius? Do you want to call him Dan?'

She was mocking him. For some reason, she was uncomfortable with this.

'I don't want to call him Dan. That will just get confusing. I'm trying to make this *less* confusing, not more.' He looked at her again; her pacing was slowing. 'What kind of names do you like?'

'I'm not naming him.' The words snapped out of her mouth.

'Why not?'

'Because he's not my baby.'

He shook his head. 'We know this. That's not the point. Let's find something we can agree on. Do you like crazy names like Moonwind or Shooting Star? Do you like modern names, celebrity names or something more traditional?'

Her chin was on the floor. 'Moonwind? Shooting Star? You've got to be kidding?'

He shook his head and rolled his eyes. 'You forget. I'm a cop in New York. I've heard everything.'

'Wow.' She sat back down on the sofa and picked up the bottle of milk. 'I'm going to try and give him a little more of this.' She watched as his mouth closed around the teat and he started to suck. 'I guess I like more traditional names,' she finally said.

'Plain? Like John or Joe or Bob?'

'No. They are too plain. Something proud. Something that makes you sit up and take notice.'

'I thought you'd ruled out Moonwind?'

There was a sparkle in her eyes as she turned to him. 'How about really traditional? How about something biblical?'

'Now you're really testing me. I'll need to think back to my Sunday school days.'

'Then you do that. How about Joseph? Or Isaac, or Jeremiah?'

He grabbed the first names that sprang into his mind. 'Noah, or David, or Goliath?' he countered. He wanted to make her smile again. And it worked. She was sitting up a little straighter. Trying to beat him at this game.

He could see her start to rack her brains. 'Peter, Paul or Matthew?'

'Adam, Moses or Joshua?'

There was silence for a few seconds as they both concentrated hard.

'Abraham.'

'Abraham.'

Their voices intermingled. And a smile appeared across both their faces.

Carrie stared down at the baby. 'Abraham,' she whispered. 'Now there's a proud name. What do you think of that one?'

He sat down next to her. 'Abraham, I like it. Also the name of one of our finest presidents. It's perfect.'

'It does seem perfect.' She was staring down at the little face as he sucked at the bottle. She nodded. 'You're right. We do need to give him a name—even if it's temporary. What a pity his mum didn't leave a note with what she'd called him.' There was a wistfulness in her voice. The sympathy vote that grated on him.

'Might have been better if she'd actually left some clothes. Or some diapers. Or anything at all to show us she cared about her son.'

Carrie gave the tiniest shake of her head as she eased the bottle out of Abraham's mouth, then sat him upright, putting her hand under his chin to support his head while she rubbed his back. 'Let's see if we can get a burp out of you this time.'

She turned to face him. 'You're really hard on people, Dan. And I find it really strange. You didn't hesitate to try and help this baby. You weren't even too upset when Shana told you that you'd need to keep him a while. We have no idea what's happened here. Can you at least try to give his mother the benefit of the doubt?'

'No.'

Just like that. Blunt and to the point.

Abraham arched his back and let out a big burp.

'Good boy.' His head started to sag. 'He's tired. Maybe we should put him down to sleep.'

Dan nodded and started folding up the towels he'd pulled from his cupboard, forming a makeshift kind of mattress in the crib. 'What do you think?'

'Perfect.' She had to put him down. She had to put him down now. She was starting to feel a little overwhelmed again. A baby cuddling into the nape of her neck and giving little sighs of comfort was making a whole host of emotions wash over her. None that she wanted to share.

She adjusted Abraham and laid him down in the crib, covering him with the hand-knitted shawl, and held her breath, waiting to see if he would stir.

It took her a few seconds to realise Dan was holding his breath right next to her.

But Abraham was out cold. His first feed had been a success.

'Darn it. Do you think we should have changed his nappy again?'

Dan raised his eyebrows. 'I think if you touch Abraham right now and wake him up I will kill you.'

She gave a little laugh. 'It's kind of strange, isn't it? Standing here waiting to see if he'll wake up again?'

Dan straightened his back. 'What time is it?' He looked over at the kitchen clock. 'Ten-thirty? Wow. No wonder I'm starved. I haven't eaten dinner. What about you? Are you hungry, Carrie?'

She shook her head. 'Maybe I should go.'

'You are joking, right?'

She shook her head firmly. All of a sudden there wasn't a baby as a barrier between the two of them.

All of sudden there wasn't a whole lot of space between them. And it was as if a little switch had been flicked.

Everything about Dan was making her feel self-conscious. How was her hair? Was her make-up still in place?

She'd spent the past few months going around in a fog. It had never once crossed her mind how she looked to the opposite sex.

But there was something about Dan. Something about being in close proximity to him that was making her feel uncomfortable. She didn't want to have to think about all those kinds of feelings resurrecting themselves. Not when she knew where they could eventually lead.

Now, she was fixating on his straight white teeth, the little lines of fatigue around his eyes and the sincerity in his face.

Then he snapped her out of it by giving her a cheeky wink and folding his arms across his chest. 'If I have to arrest you, I will.'

She jolted out of her daze. 'Arrest me?'

He smiled. 'To keep you here. To force you to help me look after Abraham overnight. What do I know about a newborn baby?'

'And what do I know?' She felt the rage surge inside her along with something else she couldn't quite work out. 'Because I'm a woman you think I should know about babies?'

'No.' His words were firm and strangely calming. They must have taught him that in cop school. How to calm a raging bull. 'I think you're another human being and two heads are better than one.'

It sounded logical. It sounded sensible. And it made all the chauvinistic arguments that had leaped into her head feel pathetic.

She didn't want to spend the night with a new baby. How on earth would she cope? It could end up bringing back a whole host of memories she didn't know how to deal with.

Then there was Dan. With his short dark hair and big brown eyes that made her skin itch. No, that made her skin *tingle*.

Every now and then he flirted with her, as if it was his natural demeanour. Flirting with women was obviously second nature to a guy like him. But it wasn't second nature for her. And she just didn't have the defences for it yet. She didn't want to be drawn in by his twinkling eyes and cheeky grins. She would look like some hapless teenager around him. This was feeling more awkward by the minute.

Carrie walked back over to the window, sneaking a look at Abraham on the way past.

'How long do you think he'll sleep?'

She shook her head. 'Yet another thing I'll need to look up. Isn't it usually around four hours for new babies?'

Dan glanced at the clock. 'So we've got until two-thirty.' He smiled. 'Do you want the night shift or shall I?'

Carrie hesitated. 'I'm not sure about this, Dan. I told you I've got no experience with babies. How am I supposed to know if something is wrong or not? I can't read everything you're supposed to know about babies in a few hours. What if we do something we shouldn't?'

He lifted his hands. 'We can only do our best. And anyway, look at you earlier—you were a natural.'

The words sent a chill down her spine. She knew he didn't mean for that to happen—he probably meant the words as a compliment. But her mind and body just couldn't react that way.

She was trying to partition this whole experience in her head. Put it inside a little box that could be safely stowed away somewhere.

Somewhere safe.

This was hard. And the reality was, it was only going to get harder. She'd felt herself waver a few moments before when Abraham had snuggled into her neck and she'd caught that distinctive baby scent in her nostrils.

She knew it was time to back off. To give herself a little space. And if she could keep doing that she might actually survive this experience.

And let's face it. Dan was hardly a strain on the eyes.

Why hadn't they ever spoken before? Had she really seemed so unapproachable? So caught up in her own world?

She watched as he looked in his cupboards, trying to find something to eat. Eventually he pulled some glasses and a bottle of soda from the cupboard. She could see the taut muscles across his back through his thin T-shirt. She tried not to stare at the outline of his behind in the well-worn jeans.

Her eyes automatically went downwards. Would he look at her the same way? Maybe she should have given some more thought to what she was wearing.

'I see you've finally got some clothes on.'

She gave a little smile as she walked over and sat down at the table. 'I didn't really have time to think earlier. I don't often roam around strange men's apartments in my nightclothes.'

'You don't?' He had a gleam in his eyes. He was trying to lighten the mood. Ease the stress they were both under. 'Is your apartment cold upstairs? You were bundled up like you live in an igloo.'

She took a sip of the soda he'd just poured for her. 'No. It was comfort clothes. I was freezing when I got in—I ruined my suede boots walking in that mucky slush. My raincoat was covered in muddy splatters and all I could think about was getting inside, heating up and eating myself silly.'

He tilted his head as he sat down. In this dim light in the kitchen he had really dark brown eyes. Comforting kind of eyes. The kind you could lose yourself in.

'And what does eating yourself silly involve?'

She shrugged. 'Chocolate. In all varieties. Macaroni cheese. Grilled bagels with melted cheese. Porridge. Pancakes.' She pointed towards the ceiling. 'I bought some stuff at Mr Meltzer's before I came home. I was worried I'd be stuck inside for a few days with no comfort foods.' She gave him a grin and shook her head. 'Believe me, that would *not* be pretty.'

He eyed her closely, the smell of pizza starting to fill the apartment. 'And would you be willing to share some of your stash?'

Her smile widened. The atmosphere was changing between them. They were going from frantic neighbours to something else entirely. Were they flirting here? Was that what was happening? It had been so long for Carrie she wasn't sure she remembered how.

She rested her elbows on the table, sitting her head in her hands. 'Oh, I don't know about sharing. I might be willing to trade.'

'Aha, a wolf in sheep's clothing.'

'What does that mean?'

The gleam wasn't disappearing; in fact, if it was possible, it was getting naughtier. 'You come down here with your innocent smiles, woolly socks and grandma pyjamas—not forgetting an abandoned baby—with your tales of a huge pirate haul of comfort foods upstairs, and now you're trying to hold me to ransom.' He leaned back in his chair and tapped the surface of the table. 'You're not really a grandma-pyjamas girl, are you? That was all just a ruse—you're really a sexy negligee kind of girl.' He lifted his hand and tapped his chin. 'The question is, what colour?'

She could feel her cheeks start to pink up. She hadn't been imagining it. He was flirting with her. And the thing that amazed her—or terrified her—was she wanted to flirt right back. Could she trade her bagels for a kiss?

Wow. That thought made the blood rush into her cheeks. 'What's wrong with grandma pyjamas? They hide a multitude of sins.'

He didn't hesitate. 'You don't have any sins to hide.'

She felt her breath stall. She couldn't breathe in. She definitely couldn't breathe out. She was stuck in that no man's land. He'd said it so quickly. He didn't even have to think about it twice.

What did that mean?

She made a vague attempt to laugh it off—feeling like a nervous teenager instead of a capable twenty-seven-year-old woman. 'You're a man. You really have no knowledge of water-filled bras or hold-your-gut-in underwear.'

He leaned across the table towards her. A cheeky smile across his face. 'And you have no need for either.'

He stayed there. Inches away from her face. Letting her see the tiny, fine laughter lines around his eyes and the smattering of freckles across his cheeks.

Up close and personal Daniel Cooper looked good enough to eat.

And then there was the smell. His cologne. It was affecting her senses. Everything seemed heightened.

Her skin prickled, her hairs standing upright. Her mouth felt dry, her tongue running across her lips.

She couldn't take her eyes off his mouth. Or maybe it was his brown eyes. The kind you could melt into. Both were distracting her. Both were making entirely inappropriate thoughts about a man she hardly knew invade her brain and send a warm feeling to her stomach.

A feeling she hadn't felt since…

It was like a bucket of cold water being tipped over her head. That, and the awareness of the little contented noises from the crib off to the side.

That was why she was here.

Not for any other reason. Dan wasn't interested in her. Not really. He just didn't want to be stuck with some strange baby on his own. He'd made that perfectly clear.

The rest?

She hardly knew the guy, and with handsome looks and a job like his? He probably had women eating out of the palm of his hand.

The thought made her pull back in her chair, her sudden movement causing him to blink and a wrinkle to appear on his brow.

She fixed her eyes on the table. They were safe there.

'Don't you have a friend you can call to help you with Abraham overnight? I'm sure you must have plenty of female friends who'd be willing to give you a hand.'

'What does that mean?'

She shrugged, trying to look complacent. Trying to pretend she hadn't just almost asked him out loud if he had a girlfriend. 'It means there must be someone other than me who can give you a hand.'

He shook his head. 'All the female cops I know are currently run off their feet on duty. My friends who are married all stay too far away to get here and help.' He rolled his eyes. 'And the past few female companions I've had—I wouldn't let within fifty feet of this little guy.'

She almost choked on her soda. 'Then maybe you should be more selective with your female friends.' It was meant to sound playful, but it came out like a chastisement. All because her insides were wound up so tightly.

He shrugged his shoulders. 'Maybe I should.'

It was left hanging in the air between them.

She had no idea what to make of that. She shifted uncomfortably in the chair. 'You mean there's absolutely no one you can ask to help you out?'

'Just you.'

'Dan...' She looked out at the falling snow. If it were even possible, it seemed to be falling even heavier.

She looked around the apartment and threw her hands in the air. 'I don't like this, Dan. I don't know you and you don't know me. It doesn't matter that you're a cop and one of the "good guys".' She put her fingers in the air and made the sign. 'Baby or no baby, I can't stay in an apartment with some strange guy. I'm just not comfortable.'

He leaned back in his chair, watching her with those intense brown eyes.

'What if I promise not to come near you at night? You can sleep in my room and I'll sleep on the sofa. We can move the crib during the night. That way—you'll still have some privacy but we'll both know the other is there if we need a hand.'

Her. In a room by herself with Abraham in a crib. She was going to throw up right there and then.

And then Dan did something. He reached across the table and took her hand. 'I need help, Carrie. I need you. Don't say you can't do it.'

A lump a mile wide appeared in her throat.

He was leaning towards her in the dim light. Her eyes fixated on his lips. What was wrong with her? And what was wrong with her emotions?

Everything about her wanted to run right now.

But her ethics and her goodwill were making her

stay. She couldn't abandon Abraham right now. His own mother had already done that.

She had been the one to find him. She should be the one responsible for him.

'I feel really awkward about all this, Dan.' She sighed.

'Then let's see if we can make you feel unawkward.'

'Is that even a word?'

'It is now.' He put his head in his hands. 'So, Carrie McKenzie, what's your favourite movie?'

'What?' It was so not what she was expecting. She was expecting him to pry. To ask why she'd reacted like that. To ask what had been wrong with her this whole evening.

The question was totally random and took her by surprise. It took a few seconds for her brain to think of an appropriate response. 'If it's adults' it's *Dirty Dancing.* If it's kids' then definitely *Toy Story.* What kind of a question is that anyway?'

'A getting-to-know-you question,' he said as he took a sip of his soda. Just like that. So matter-of-fact. Boy, this guy didn't mess around. He raised his eyebrows at her. 'What? You've never been on a date and done the getting-to-know-you questions before?'

She opened her mouth to react, to ask what he meant, then stopped herself dead. He was being casual. He was being cool. And anything she would say right now would be distinctly *uncool*.

One moment she'd been staring into his eyes wondering what it would be like to kiss him—next they were having a first-date kind of conversation.

She took a deep breath. 'It's been a while,' she said quietly. 'I guess I'm out of practice.'

'How long?'

His question was fired back straight away. She could tell a lie here and try and pretend to be blasé. But it just didn't suit her. 'About seven years.' She lifted her head and looked him straight in the eye. She'd had to think about that. Had it really been that long? She'd dated Mark for five years before she was pregnant with Ruby, and it had been more than a year since then. To Dan's credit he didn't even blink, no smart remarks, no more questions. It was as if he just filed the information away for use at a later date.

She shouldn't have said anything. It was time to move things back to the original question. Get off this subject completely. 'You do realise I had to leave out the musicals—for obvious reasons.'

The eyebrows lifted even further. 'What obvious reasons?'

She shrugged. 'I couldn't possibly count them. I'll have you know I know the words to every song of every musical ever made.' She gave him a cheeky wink. 'And some of the dance moves.'

He leaned across the table towards her. 'The thing that scares me about that is—I believe you.' He kept his eyes fixed on hers. 'I might ask to see some of those dance moves.'

She gulped. Colour was rushing to her cheeks. She'd been premature with that wink. Trying to appear sassier and way cooler than she actually was. Maybe not her best idea. Especially when she could almost feel the heat radiating from him. It was time to get this back to safer territory. 'What about you?' That was easy. That kept everything on an even keel.

'Definitely *The Great Escape,* with Steve McQueen on the motorbike. Nothing can beat that.'

She nodded. She'd watched the movie a hundred times— knew some of the lines by heart. 'And a kids' movie?'

He had the good grace to look a little bashful. 'You

might be surprised. But I love *Finding Nemo*. I love Marlin and Dory. It's one of those movies that you turn the TV on, walk past and find yourself sucked in for two hours. Just like that.' He snapped his fingers.

She couldn't help the smile that was plastered on her face. 'I wouldn't have taken you for a *Finding Nemo* kind of guy.'

He took another sip of soda. 'See? There's lots you don't know about me. And vice versa. Are you feeling a little less awkward now.'

She let out a little laugh. 'Just because I know what films you like doesn't mean I feel comfortable about staying in your apartment overnight.'

He nodded slowly. 'So, what brought you to New York, then, Carrie? I know your business owns the apartment upstairs, but why you? Why now?'

There it was. The killer question—sneaked on in there when her defences were down. She should have seen this coming.

How could she answer that? How could she answer any of that without giving herself away?

She picked up her glass and walked over to the sink. 'I'll do the dishes.' She started running the hot water and putting some washing-up liquid into the basin. 'Seems only fair.'

'But what if we're not finished yet?'

He knew. He knew exactly what she was doing. Distraction. Avoidance.

She jumped. His voice was just at her shoulder. His warm breath next to her ear. 'What do you mean?' Darn it. Her voice was wavering. He would have heard it. He would know the effect he was having on her.

So much for acting cool.

He slid his glass in next to hers, his arms on either side of her body, capturing her between them.

She could feel him up against her. One part of her wanted to relax. To let herself relax against him as if this was the most natural thing in the world.

But her frantically beating heart wouldn't let her. And her oxygen-deprived brain wasn't playing ball, either.

She watched the bubbles form in the warm water. Letting them come halfway up her arms.

And what did he mean anyhow?

His hands slid into the basin next to hers. His head coming forward and almost resting on her shoulder. 'I mean, what if we're not finished with this conversation? What if I think you just avoided my question and I want to know why?' His hands were over hers now and her breath hitched in her chest. 'What if I want to get to know you a little better, Carrie McKenzie? Despite our unusual meeting—and despite our chaperone.'

He lifted up a finger and held it in the air. It was covered in bubbles, with the light reflecting off them revealing a rainbow of colours. She couldn't speak. She didn't know what to say—how to respond. Plus she was mesmerised by the bubbles popping one by one. He gave a little laugh, moved his finger and smudged the bubbles on her nose.

She breathed in quickly in surprise, inhaling half the bubbles, leading to a coughing fit. All she could hear was Dan's hearty laughter as she half choked to death, doubled over, then she felt his hand on her back, sharply at first, giving a few knocks to ease her choking, then soothing, rubbing her back while she caught her breath again.

She finally stood upright, his hand still positioned on her back, damp from being in the sink. His other hand fell naturally to her hip.

She turned her head to look at him. 'What was that for?'

'Fun.' He was grinning at her. Showing off his perfect teeth and American good-boy looks.

It was like temptation all in one package.

She bit her lip. 'You've got me all wet.' She squirmed as she pulled her T-shirt from her back. Then cringed at her words. No! She hadn't really said that out loud, had she? She could feel the blood rush to her cheeks. *Please don't let him take anything from that.*

But he just gave her that sexy smile again. 'We can't have that. Do you want something else to wear?' He walked towards one of the doors in the apartment—most likely his bedroom. 'I'm sure I've something in here for you.'

It was blatant. It was obvious. He was full of it.

She folded her arms across her chest. She should be insulted, but the truth was she wasn't really. She was a tiny bit flattered.

She shook her head. 'You were the college playboy, weren't you?'

He leaned against the doorjamb. 'What if I was?'

'Then you should be used to women thinking you're too big for your boots.'

The tension in the air was killing her. If this were a movie she would just walk over, wink and lead him into the bedroom.

He sighed and looked skyward. 'I love it when you talk dirty to me. It's the accent. It's killing me. Every time you talk I just—'

There was a little grunt from the corner of the room and they both leaped about a foot in the air.

Every other thought was pushed out of the window.

In the blink of an eye they were both at the side of the crib, leaning overtop the still-sleeping baby.

'Did that mean something?' asked Dan.

'How am I supposed to know?' she whispered back.

She watched Abraham's little chest rise and fall, rise and fall. It was soothing. It was calming.

'Did we decide on who was doing the night shift?'

She wanted to say no. She wanted to say she couldn't do it and retreat back upstairs to the safety of her silent apartment.

She wanted to put the random flirtations out of her head.

But there was so much churning around in her mind. This baby. Abraham.

He didn't have a mother to comfort him right now. Being around him was hard. Being around him was torture.

But what if this was something she had to do? What if this was something she had to get past?

Sure, she'd grieved for her daughter. She'd wept a bucketload of tears and spent weeks thinking 'what if?' She'd watched her relationship slowly but surely disintegrate around her and Mark. They'd both known it was inevitable, but that hadn't made the parting any easier.

So she'd been bereft. She'd been empty.

But had she allowed herself to heal?

And Dan wasn't anything like Mark. Mark hadn't walked from their relationship—he'd practically run.

And here was Dan stepping in, and taking responsibility—albeit temporarily—for an unknown baby on their doorstep. Maybe for five minutes she should stop judging all men by Mark's standard. Maybe she should take a little time to get to know someone like Dan. Someone who might restore her faith in humanity again.

And did she even know how to do that?

She straightened up, pushing her hands into her back and cricking her spine. Dan was at her back again. 'Carrie, are you okay? Is there something you want to tell me?'

This was it. This was her opportunity to tell him why she was acting so strangely around him and this baby. This was a chance for her to be honest.

This was a chance to clear the air between them.

But she was torn. There was a buzz between them.

They were both feeling it. She liked the flirtation. It made her feel good. It made her feel normal again. Even though there was nothing about this situation that was normal.

She barely knew Dan, but just being in his company made her feel safe. The way he'd reacted to the abandoned baby. The way he'd immediately gone out into the snowstorm to look for the mother, even if he really didn't want to. The way he wasn't afraid to roll up his sleeves and help take care of a baby, even with no experience.

But what would happen right now if she told him?

She could almost get out a huge crystal ball and predict it. The moment she said the words, *'I had a stillbirth last year. My daughter died,'* it would kill anything between them stone dead. It would destroy this buzz in the air.

It would destroy the first feel-good feelings she'd felt in over a year.

So, no matter how hard this was, and for what were totally selfish reasons, she wanted to stay. She might feel a sense of duty, a sense of responsibility towards Abraham, but that wasn't all she was feeling.

And right now she wanted to do something for herself. For Carrie.

Was that really so selfish?

She took a deep breath and turned around to face him.

It would be so easy. It would be so easy to lean forward just a little and see what might happen.

To see if this buzz in the air could amount to anything.

To hold her breath and see if he was sensing what she was feeling—or to see that it had been *so* long that her reactions were completely off. Completely wrong.

He reached up and touched her cheek. 'Carrie?'

She swallowed, biting back the words she really wanted to say and containing the actions she really wanted to take.

She didn't want anything to destroy that tiny little buzz that was currently in her stomach. It felt precious to her. As if it was finally the start of something new.

'How about I take the first shift? I'll sleep on the sofa next to the crib and do the first feed and change at night. You can take over after that.'

She kept her voice steady and her words firm.

She could see something flicker behind his eyes. The questions that he really wanted to ask. He nodded and gave her a little smile.

'Welcome to your first night shift, Carrie McKenzie.'

She watched his retreating back as she sat down on the sofa.

Was she wrong about all this?

Only time, and a whole heap of snow, would tell.

CHAPTER SIX

CARRIE STRETCHED ON the sofa and groaned. The early morning sun was trying to creep through the blinds. It was brighter than normal, which probably meant it was reflecting off the newly laid white snow. All thoughts of everything returning to normal today vanished in the drop of a snowflake.

There was no getting away from it—Baby Abraham was hard work.

She hadn't had time last night to feel sorry for herself and neither had Dan—because Abraham had screamed for three hours solid. She certainly hadn't had time for any romantic dreams. It seemed neither of them had the knack for feeding and burping a new baby.

'Carrie?' Dan came stumbling through the doorway, bleary-eyed, his hair all rumpled and his low-slung jeans skimming his hips.

She screwed up her eyes. Bare-chested. He was bare-chested again. Did the guy always walk about like this? Her brain couldn't cope with a cute naked guy this early in the morning, especially when she was sleep-deprived.

She pointed her finger at him. 'If you wake him, I swear, Dan Cooper, I'll come over there and—'

'Cook me pancakes?'

She sighed and sagged back down onto the sofa, landing on another uncomfortable lump. 'You have the worst sofa known to man.' She twisted on her side and thumped at the lump. 'Oh, it's deceptive. It looks comfortable. When you sit down, you sink into it and think, *Wow!* But sleeping on it?' She blew her hair off her forehead. 'Not a chance!'

'Wanna take the bed tomorrow night?'

With or without you?

She pushed the wayward thought out of her head. How did parents ever go on to have more than one child? Hanky-panky must be the last thing on their minds.

She stood up and stretched. Abraham had finally quietened down around an hour ago. He was now looking all angelic, breathing steadily as if sleeping came easily to him.

'The offer of pancakes sounds good. Do you think you can cook them without waking His Lordship? Because at this rate, ancient or not, Mrs Van Dyke's going to have to take her turn babysitting.'

Dan nodded. 'Right there with you, Carrie. For some reason I thought this would be a breeze. You've no idea how many times I nearly picked up the phone to call Shana last night and beg her to come and pick him up.'

Carrie leaned against the door, giving him her sternest stare. 'Well, maybe you need to think about that a little more.'

'What do you mean?'

'You've been pretty down on Abraham's mum. We're presuming he was just born. But what if he's actually a few days old? Maybe she was struggling to cope. Maybe she's young—or old—and didn't have any help. Maybe she's sick.'

The dark cloud quickly descended over Dan's face again. 'Stop it, Carrie. Stop trying to make excuses for her. And if Abraham's not newly born, then where were his diapers? Where were his clothes? And no matter how hard she was finding it to cope—is that really a good enough reason to dump a baby on a freezing doorstep?'

She shrugged her shoulders. 'I'm just throwing it out there, Dan. I'm not trying to make excuses for anyone. What I am going to do is take a shower and change my clothes.' She headed over to the door. 'I'll be back in ten minutes and I expect my breakfast to be waiting.' She gave him a wink.

He lifted his eyebrows. 'Hmm, getting all feisty now, are we? I think I preferred you when you were all *please help me with this baby.*'

She picked up the nearest cushion and tossed it at his head. 'No, you didn't,' she said as she headed out the door.

'No. I didn't,' he breathed as he watched her head upstairs.

Carrie took a few moments to pull open her blinds and look outside.

A complete white-out with no signs of life. Not a single footprint on the sidewalk. Every car was covered in snow, with not a single chance of moving anywhere soon. It seemed that New York City would remain at a standstill for another day.

For a moment she wished she were in the middle of Central Park. Maybe standing at Belvedere Castle and looking out over the Great Lawn, or standing on Bow Bridge watching the frozen lake. It would be gorgeous there right now.

She didn't care that it was closed because of the snowfall. She didn't care about the potential for falling trees.

All she could think about was how peaceful it would be right now—and how beautiful.

But with daydreams like this, was she just looking for another opportunity to hide away?

She tried to push the thoughts from her head. There was too much going on in there. What with virtually bare baby and bare-chested Dan, her head was spinning.

She switched on the shower and walked through to her bedroom, stripping off her clothes and pulling her dressing gown on while she waited for the water to heat.

The contents of her wardrobe seemed to mock her. A sparkly sequin T-shirt. Trying too hard. A red cardigan. Impersonating Mrs Van Dyke. A plain jumper. Frumpy.

She pulled out another set of jeans and a bright blue cap-sleeved sweater. It would have to do.

Her eyes caught sight of the silver box beneath her bed and her heart flipped over.

It was calling her. It was willing her to open it.

She couldn't help it. It was automatic. She knelt down and touched it, pulling it out from under the bed and sitting it on top of the bed in front of her.

Her precious memories, all stored in a little box. But how could she look at them now after she'd just been holding another baby?

It almost seemed like a betrayal.

She ran the palm of her hand over the lid of the box. Just doing it made her heartbeat quicken. She could feel the threat of tears at the backs of her eyes.

She couldn't think about this now. She just couldn't.

Steam was starting to emerge from the bathroom. The shower was beckoning. She couldn't open the box. Not now. Not while she was in the middle of all this.

For the contents of that box she needed space. She needed time.

She needed the ability to cry where no one could hear. No one could interrupt.

She sucked air into her lungs. Not now. She had to be strong. She had to be focused. Her hand moved again—one last final touch of the silver box of memories—before she tore herself away and headed inside, closing the door firmly behind her.

There was a whimper in the corner. Dan's pancakes were sizzling; was the noise going to wake the baby? He sure hoped not. He didn't know if he could take another cry-fest.

The television newscaster looked tired. He'd probably been stuck inside the New York studio all night. The yellow information strip ran along the bottom of the news constantly. Telling them how much snow had fallen, how the city was stranded, all businesses were closed, food supplies couldn't get in. Nothing about how to look after a newborn baby.

It was time to do an internet search again. They must have done something wrong last night. There was no way a baby would cry like that for nothing. At least he hoped not.

He tossed the pancakes and his stomach growled loudly. He was starving and they smelled great.

A jar of raspberry jam landed on the counter next to him. She was back. And she smelled like wild flowers—even better than pancakes.

'What's that for?'

'The pancakes.'

'Jelly?' He shook his head. 'Pancakes need bacon and maple syrup. That's what a real pancake wants.'

She opened his fridge. 'Pancakes need butter and raspberry jam. It's the only way to eat them.'

He wrinkled his nose, watching as she flicked on the kettle.

'And tea. Pancakes need tea.'

He grimaced. 'You might be out of luck, then. I've only got extra-strong coffee.'

She waved a bag at him. 'Just as well I brought my own, then.'

Dan served the pancakes onto two plates and carried them over to the table, pulling some syrup from his empty cupboards and lifting the brewing coffee pot. 'I can't tempt you, then?'

Something flickered in her eyes. Something else. Something different. She gave him a hesitant smile. 'I'm an English girl. It's tea and butter and jam all the way.'

They both knew that the flirtation was continuing.

And right now he wanted to tempt her. The cop in him wanted to forget about the mountain of paperwork he'd need to complete about this baby. The cop in him wanted to forget about the investigation that would have to be carried out.

The guy in him wanted to concentrate on the woman in the lovely blue sweater sitting at his table with her jar of raspberry jam. He wanted to reach over to touch the curls that were coiling around her face, springing free from the clip that was trying to hold them back. He wanted to see if he could say something to make her cheeks flush even pinker than they currently were. He wanted a chance to stare into those cornflower-blue eyes and ask her what she was hiding from him. What she was guarding herself from.

He lifted the maple syrup and squirted it onto his pancakes. She was concentrating on spreading butter on her pancakes smoothly and evenly with one hand while stirring her tea with the other hand.

He'd opened the blinds partly to let a little natural light into the apartment. And seeing Carrie McKenzie in the cold light of day was more than just a little shock to his system.

The girl was beautiful. From the little sprinkle of freckles over her nose to the way she wrinkled her brow when she was concentrating.

He'd felt a pull towards her last night, when he'd seen her in the dim lights of his apartment. But now he had a chance to look at her—to really look at her—and all he could think about was why on earth he hadn't noticed her before.

How on earth could he have stayed in an apartment building with someone so incredibly pretty and not have noticed? He could just imagine the cops at the station if they ever got wind of that.

Carrie put a teaspoon into the jam jar and spread some jam onto her pancakes. 'Are you going to watch me eat them, too?' she asked, a smile spreading across her face.

He jerked backwards in his seat. 'Sorry. I was just thinking.'

'About Abraham?'

Wow. No, Abraham was the last thing he'd been thinking about, and as if in indignation there was a squawk from the crib. Dan set down his cutlery, gave a sigh and waved his hand at her as she went to stand up. 'Stay where you are—you're still eating. I'm finished. Maybe he's hungry again. I sterilised the bottles so we should be fine.'

It was amazing how quickly you could learn to make a baby bottle. A few minutes later he lifted Abraham from the crib and settled him onto his shoulder for a bit.

'Carrie? Does he look okay to you? What do you think about his colour?'

She set down her mug of tea and walked over. 'It's kind of hard to tell.' She shrugged her shoulders. 'We don't really know anything about the ethnicity of his parents, so I'm not entirely sure what normal will look like for him.'

She walked over to the window and pulled the blinds up completely. 'Bring him over here so I can get a better look at him.'

Dan carried him over and they stood for a few seconds looking at him in the daylight. 'He looks a tiny bit yellow, don't you think?'

She nodded. 'Jaundice. Isn't it supposed to be quite common in newborns?'

He gave her that smile again. The why-are-you-asking-me-something-I-couldn't-possibly-know smile.

They both glanced at the computer. Carrie took a few seconds to punch in the words and then—nothing.

She turned towards him. 'Looks like your internet has just died.'

'Really? It's usually really reliable. Must be the weather.'

She stared out the window. 'It must be something to do with the snow. I hope the power supply doesn't get hokey. That sometimes happens in storms back home.'

He looked at her with an amused expression on his face. 'Hokey?'

She raised her eyebrows. 'What? It's a word.'

'Really? Where?'

She gave him a sarcastic smile. 'I'd look it up for you online but your internet is down.'

'Ha-ha. Seriously—what are we going to do about Abraham? Do you think it's dangerous? I mean, he's drinking okay and—' he wrinkled his nose '—he certainly knows how to poo.'

She raised her eyebrows at him. 'Really? Again? Then maybe you should phone a friend. It's a bit like the blind leading the blind here. I guess you'll need to phone Shana. There really isn't anyone else we can ask.'

He gave her a smile as he walked over to put Abraham on the dark towel to change him. He could only imagine the chaos going on at Angel's Children's Hospital right now. Last thing he wanted to do was add to Shana's headache. But he wanted to make sure that Abraham was safe in his care. Screamer or not, he wanted to do the best he could for this baby.

'Do you think this is how all new parents feel? As if they don't know anything at all?'

Carrie turned her back and walked over to the countertop, picking up her mug of tea. Trying to find the words that would counteract the tight feeling in her chest. She was trying so hard. So hard not to let these things creep up on her. Then—out of the blue—some random comment would just cut her in two.

She set her mouth in a straight line. 'Most new parents would have a whole host of textbooks or family to ask—we don't.'

He pulled his mobile from his pocket. 'I guess I'll phone Shana, then.' He dialled the number and waited for Shana to be paged, pressing the button to put her on speakerphone as he wrestled with Abraham's nappy.

'What?'

Not good. She sounded snarky. 'Shana, it's Dan.'

'Is the baby okay?' Straight to the point as usual. Did she ever stop—just for a second?

He took a deep breath. 'We're not sure. Abraham looks kinda yellow. Carrie thinks he might be jaundiced.'

'Who is Abraham?'

'The baby. Who did you think I was asking about?'

'Oh, so you've given him a name. Abraham—I like it.'

'I'm glad I've got your approval. What about his colour?'

'More common in breastfed babies—but not unusual. It could be jaundice.' It was clear she was thinking out loud. 'Could be serious if it's appeared within twenty-four hours of birth—but then we don't know that, do we?'

'So what do we do now?'

'Ideally, I'd like to check him over and draw some blood.'

'Well, that's not gonna happen any time soon. What should we do in the meantime?'

'Monitor him—I mean, watch him. Make sure he feeds regularly and he's not too sleepy. Don't be afraid to wake him up to feed him. Let him get some natural light onto his skin. Put his crib next to the window and keep a close eye on his colour. If you think it's getting worse—or he has any other symptoms—phone me, straight away. Check the whites of his eyes. If they start to turn yellow you need to call me.'

Dan couldn't help it. He lifted a sleepy eyelid immediately, much to the disgust of Abraham, who squealed loudly at being disturbed.

Shana let out a laugh at the other end of the phone. 'If he's that annoyed, he's doing okay. But let me know if you're concerned.' She ended the call abruptly—probably a thousand other things to do.

Dan stared at the receiver in his hand. 'She never even told me if she contacted social services,' he murmured.

'Probably too busy.' He jumped at the quiet voice in his ear. He should have realised she'd stepped closer to him. The wave of wild flowers seemed like her trademark scent.

He held his breath. Did she realise she was standing so

close? Was there something, somewhere that kept pulling them closer together? Because it sure felt like it.

Her gaze dropped to the floor and he was sorry, because he liked when she was so close he could see the other little flecks of colour in her cornflower-blue eyes. Tiny little fragments of green that you could only see up close. She tugged at the bottom of her sweater, obviously feeling a little self-conscious.

'I heard a little of that,' she said. 'Shall I move his crib over to the window?'

He nodded and she moved swiftly, pulling all the blinds up completely and drowning the room in the reflected brilliant white light from outside. He flinched, his hand on Abraham's back. 'Wow. Well, if that can't beat a bit of jaundice I don't know what will.'

She turned around and shot him a killer smile.

His reactions were automatic. Abraham was put down in the brightly lit crib and Dan found himself standing right at her side.

He was obviously going stir-crazy. Being trapped in his apartment with a beautiful lady was playing havoc with his senses. He was going to have to try and find some other way to distract himself.

All his usual self-control was flying out the window around Carrie McKenzie and he had no idea why.

She was hiding something from him. And who could blame her? They hardly knew each other. He couldn't expect her to tell him her every dark secret.

But Dan's instincts were good. Probably due to his experiences as a child. Experiences that had affected his ability to form real, trusting relationships with women.

So why was it that the first time he ever really wanted to get to know someone, he picked the one woman who was clearly hiding something? Was he crazy?

He had to do something—anything—to distract himself from all this. 'Any plans today, Carrie?'

She folded her arms across her chest. 'Apart from strapping on my jet pack to fly across New York, get to work, put in a ten-hour day, find some groceries and clothes for a stranded baby, no, nothing at all.' She was shaking her head, staring out at the five-foot-deep snow. She was obviously as stir-crazy as he was.

He waved his pink cast at her. 'Well, I'm going to go swimming. Then I'm going to strap on my skis—can't waste good snow like this—and finally I'm going to ship Shana over here to check out Abraham and make sure he's okay.' He gave her a little smile. 'And if she could bring some beers, sodas and a fresh pizza, that would be great.'

Carrie leaned against the window and sighed. 'What are we going to do all day?'

'If we can't play our imaginary games?'

Carrie counted off on her fingers. 'We could have a soapathon. You know, watch all the soaps that you haven't for years. Watch them all day.' Her brow wrinkled. 'I don't really know the names of any of the soaps in America. Are they any good?'

He shook his head. 'Next idea.'

She looked around. 'We could reorganise. Everyone needs a spring clean. It could be the perfect time.'

'Get your hands off my stuff, McKenzie,' he growled at her. 'Anyway, haven't you already realised there's nothing in my cupboards to reorganise?'

She laughed. 'Okay. I didn't think you'd go for that one.

'Do you have games? Board games? I could challenge you.' She could obviously see him racking his brain. 'Chess?' She was getting desperate.

'I might have some board games. But they will be years old. Some are probably originals.'

He walked over to a cupboard and went down on his hands and knees, crawling right inside. She heard some groans as some sports-kit bags, rackets and balls shot past her ankles. 'Need some help in there?'

There was a little cloud of dust followed by a coughing fit and Dan crawled out with a pile of games in his hands. He held them out towards her. 'How about these?'

She carried them over to the table. 'Wow. You were right—some of these are originals.' And even better than being originals, they all showed visible signs of wear and tear. It was obvious that these games had been used and loved at some point in their history. 'I think these would be perfect.'

He appeared at her side, a big smudge across his cheek. 'What does the winner get?'

She couldn't help it. Her fingers reached up to wipe the smudge from his cheek. He froze, then caught her hand in his before she could pull it away. 'What does the winner of this games tournament get?'

His words were quiet this time, the jokey aspect removed, and she could sense the feeling hanging in the air between them.

A whole variety of answers sprang to mind; some of them would make her hair curl and save her hours at the hairdressers.

Then a safe option shot into her mind. 'Can you bake?'

'What?' He looked stunned. He'd obviously had something else in mind.

'I said can you bake?'

'I suppose so. My grandmother baked all the time. But it's been years since I've tried anything like that.

Anyhow, you've seen my cupboards. Old Mother Hubbard had nothing on me. I don't have any ingredients.'

'But I do. There—it's settled. The loser has to make the winner a cake. Just what we need on a day like this.'

'You'd trust me to make you a cake?'

'I love cake. I'd trust anyone to make me a cake.' She held out her hand. 'Do we have a deal?'

He hesitated for just a second, before his competitive edge took over. 'I'm a chocolate cake kind of guy. You better get your apron out.'

The waft of baking filled the whole apartment. It had been years since the place had smelled like this. It only made him miss his grandmother more.

Apple pie. That had been the thing she'd baked most frequently. And it was the smell he most associated with his grandmother. Freshly baked juicy apples bubbling under the surface of the golden pie, topped with a sprinkling of sugar. Bliss.

Now the smell was a little different. The timer on the oven buzzed. He hadn't even known that his oven had a timer, let alone how to use it. But Carrie had insisted it was essential to bake the perfect cake.

Or cakes as it had turned out.

The game marathon had resulted in a dead heat.

And now his kitchen was filled with the smells of chocolate cake and carrot cake. He pulled the door open as a waft of heat flooded out from the oven. The chocolate cake that Carrie had baked for him looked spectacular. His carrot cake? Not so much. A little charred on top. But nothing that the mound of frosting she'd made him prepare couldn't hide.

He lifted both out and watched as she tipped them onto a wire rack to cool—yet another thing she'd brought down from her apartment upstairs. Along with the mixing bowls, spatulas, ingredients and cake tins. She probably had more of her possessions currently in his apartment than her own.

Baking was definitely her thing. She seemed relaxed, she seemed happy and she liked it. Even Abraham seemed to be more chilled out. Two feeds, lots of wind and no crying fits. Finally things were starting to settle.

'We need to let the cakes cool before we ice them. So let's give them a minute.' She pulled out some plates from the cupboard, then shook her head and went back to look for more.

'What's wrong with my plates'?

'Nothing.' Her voice was muffled as she crouched in one of his kitchen cupboards. 'But cake-eating is an art form. You have to have better plates than those. Aha.' She pulled herself back out of the cupboard with something in her hand. 'These are much better.'

She stood up and put the fine bone china plates on the countertop. White with tiny red flowers painted on them. Another remnant of his grandmother. She'd used them for eating cake, too—probably why they were now hidden in the depths of his cupboards.

The lights flickered around them.

'Uh-oh,' murmured Carrie. 'That's the third time that's happened now.'

Dan walked over next to her. 'This could be a problem.'

She turned to face him. 'Why?'

'Because I don't have any candles.'

She looked at him in mock horror and held up her hands. 'You don't? What kind of emergency guy are you? Aren't you cops supposed to be prepared for anything?'

He didn't move, just kept his eyes fixed on her face.

'Not everything.' His voice was quiet, barely a whisper. There was no mistaking the alternative meaning.

She looked up at him. He was only inches from her face, inches from her lips. The lights flickered again, so he moved a little closer, his hand resting on her hip.

She didn't move. Not an inch. Her tongue came out slowly and ran along her lips, as if, without even realising it, she was preparing them for kissing.

She could feel the pull. She could feel the same draw that he felt. He wasn't wrong about this—he could tell.

It had been there all day and they had been dancing around the edges of it. But now it wasn't hiding any more. It was right there in front of them.

His fingers pressed into her hip, pulling her pelvis a little closer to his, giving her every opportunity to object—to resist.

But she didn't.

He leaned forward. 'Carrie McKenzie, I'm going to kiss you now.' His voice was low, trying to entice her to edge forward to hear it.

But she didn't do that.

She did something totally unexpected. She lifted her hands and wrapped them around his neck. 'It's about time,' she whispered as she rose up on her toes to meet his lips.

Honey. She tasted of honey. Was there honey in the chocolate cake she'd just baked? At least that was what it felt like. The kiss started out shy—tentative. He didn't want her to feel forced. He didn't want her to feel as if she couldn't say no. He just prayed she wouldn't.

Her fingers wound up across his shorn hairline as the kiss deepened. As her tongue teased with his. Then she let out a little sigh that almost undid him completely.

He should pull back. He should let her out of his arms

to give her time to think about this. There was still so much about Carrie McKenzie he didn't know.

But right now he didn't want to. Letting her go was the last thing he wanted to do right now. Not when she seemed to be matching him move for move.

And in an instant everything was black.

They jumped apart, then instantly moved back together again, bashing noses.

'Oops.' Carrie started to giggle as she rubbed her nose. 'I guess that will be the power cut, then.'

'I guess it is. Do you have any candles?'

'Yeah, I have some upstairs in my apartment. Not the emergency kind. More the bathroom kind.'

'What's a bathroom kind of candle?'

'The scented kind. The kind you light around your bath.'

He shook his head. 'I guess I'll take your word for it. We'll need something.'

'I'll go up and get them.'

He slipped his hand into hers. 'Let me come with you.'

'What about the baby?' She glanced over in the direction of the silent crib.

'Leave the door open. We'll only be a few minutes. He's sleeping. Nothing's going to happen.'

He liked holding her hand. It felt right inside his. It fitted.

They stumbled towards the door, leaving it wide open, and stepped out into the hallway. There was no light in the hall at all. No street lights shining in. No gentle glow underneath the opposite door. It was weird. He couldn't remember the last time there had been a power cut—probably why he didn't have any candles. He reached out for the banister and started up the stairs, giving her a gentle tug behind him.

They reached her door and she glanced in the direction of Mrs Van Dyke's apartment. 'Do you think we should check on her?'

'Maybe. Do you have any extra candles she could have?'

She let out a little laugh. 'Oh, I have a whole year's supply in here.' She pushed open the door to her apartment and walked over to the bathroom, bending down and pulling things from one of the cupboards.

Dan looked around as best he could. It took a few seconds for his eyes to adjust to the dark. The only available light was the moonlight outside, streaming in through one of the windows.

Neat. Tidy. Everything in its place.

There was nothing strange about that. Lots of women he knew were tidy. But there was something else. Something he couldn't quite put his finger on.

He moved across the room, putting his hand on the back of the leather sofa.

This wasn't Carrie's place, so she wouldn't have chosen any of the furnishings. But she'd been here for a few months now.

The darkness wasn't helping. Nor was the sight of Carrie's behind in her jeans as she bent over the cupboards and pulled out an array of candles.

She walked back over, fumbled through a drawer for a box of matches and lit the candle she was holding in a glass jar. The warm light spread up around her face, illuminating her like some TV movie star.

Candlelight suited her. Her pale skin glowed, her brown curly hair shiny and her eyes bright. She smiled as she held it out towards him and the aroma from the melting wax started to emerge.

He wrinkled his nose. 'What is that? Washing powder?'

She waved her hand in the air to waft the smell a little further. 'Close. Cotton fresh. I've also got lavender, orange, cinnamon, raspberry, spring dew and rain shower.'

'Sheesh. Who names these candles?'

She lit another one and moved over next to him again. 'I think it would be a great job. Right up there with naming paint shades.'

'You'd have a field day doing that.'

'You can bet on it. Imagine the fun. Shades of yellow—sunshine rays or daffodil petals. Shades of purple—sugared violet, lavender dreams or amethyst infusion.' Even in this dim light he could see the twinkle in her eyes and the enthusiasm in her voice were completely natural.

'Wow. You weren't joking, were you?' He took a little step closer.

She shook her head slowly. 'I don't know how the careers advisor missed it from my career matches.'

He could see her automatic reaction. She was drawn towards him.

A thought jumped into his head, tearing him away from the impure thoughts starting to filter through his brain. He groaned. 'What about the power? How can we sterilise the bottles and make the milk for Abraham?'

She touched his arm and an electric current shot straight up towards his shoulder, sending his brain straight back to his original thoughts. There was hesitation. She'd noticed it, too. 'We should be fine,' she said quietly, lifting her eyes slowly to meet his. 'I had just boiled the kettle and resterilised the bottles. We can make up one when we go back downstairs.' She was staring at him. Even in the dark light he could see the way her pupils had widened, taking over most of her eyes. Natural in the dark, but it didn't feel like that kind of response. It felt like another entirely.

He set his candle down on a nearby side table, letting the glow shine upwards, emphasising the curve of her breasts and hips. He couldn't pretend any more. He couldn't hide his reactions. He didn't want to.

He put his hand on her hip, pulling her closer, leaving her with a candle jar clutched to her chest. 'So, not only am I marooned here—' he waved his other hand around '—in a snowstorm, with the power out, with a lady who found a baby on the doorstep and knows all the words to every musical known to man—' his hand came back to rest on her other hip, pulling her even closer with only the burning candle between them '—I find out she's also slightly crazy. With career ambitions even the career-matching machine couldn't have predicted.'

There was hesitancy there. A little apprehension—even though they had been lip-locked a few minutes ago. But Carrie was gradually relaxing. He could feel the tension leaving her arms and her body easing into his. She moved the flickering candle from between them, pressing her warm breasts against his chest. If she moved any more, things could start to get out of hand.

But she was smiling. A happy, relaxed smile. A warm smile. The kind he'd only glimpsed on a few rare occasions over the past two days. The kind that showed she'd let her guard down. The metal portcullis that was kept firmly in place was starting to ease up—ever so gently.

It revealed the real Carrie McKenzie. The kind of person she could be—if she was brave enough. The kind of person he'd like to know more about—be it vertical or horizontal.

Stop it! He tried to push those thoughts from his crowded head. Carrie just wasn't that kind of girl. And instead of lessening the attraction it only heightened it.

He reached up and pulled one of her long chestnut curls from behind her ear. 'I like your hair down. It's beautiful. Really flattering.' He hesitated a second as his finger brushed the side of her face. He didn't want to push this. He didn't want to scare her off.

Even though his male urges were giving him a whole other vibe his brain kept jumping in to keep him in check. 'Sexy,' he murmured, holding his breath to see the effect of his words.

He could almost predict she would tense and pull away. It was the biggest part of Carrie that he'd seen over the past couple of days.

But something had changed. The dim lights, the candles or just her new relaxed state meant that instead of pulling away she brushed closer against him and rested her hands on his shoulders. 'Sexy—I like that.' Her breath was dancing against his skin. He had to let her be the one to make the move. He had to be sure about this.

Those few seconds seemed like forever.

But she did move. Her body pressed against his a little more firmly and he felt her rise up on her tiptoes. Her lips brushed gently against his, then with a little more confidence her kisses became surer. His hands moved to her ribs; he could feel her deep breaths against the palms of his hands. He couldn't stop them. He wanted to do more.

She had one hand on his back, the other at the side of his face as she deepened their kiss, teasing him with her tongue.

It was driving him crazy. *She* was driving him crazy.

He wanted to release the emotions and passions that were currently stifled in his chest doing their best impression of a smouldering volcano. But Carrie had to feel in control. He could sense how important that was.

He had to concentrate. He couldn't lose himself in this. It was far too tempting. Far too tempting by half.

All he had to do was edge his hands a little higher and then he would feel her warm skin, be able to cup the warm mounds of her breasts and...

He stepped back. Slowly, pulling his lips apart from hers. Careful to let her know he hadn't suddenly changed his mind about this.

His voice was hoarse. Too much pent-up expectation. 'I hate to remind you, Carrie McKenzie, but we have a sleeping baby downstairs. We've only been gone a few minutes but if you distract me for another second...' He let his voice drift off, leaving her in no doubt as to his meaning.

He wasn't pulling away from her because he didn't want to kiss her.

He was pulling away because right now he *should*.

She bit her lip.

A tiny movement. And one that could be the complete undoing of him. He wanted to slam her apartment door shut and drag her through to the bedroom. And forget about everything else and everyone.

But on the floor underneath them lay a little boy. He'd already been abandoned by one adult. He certainly didn't need to be abandoned by two others.

Daniel's sense of duty ground down on his chest.

He tugged at his jeans, trying to adjust them. Some human reactions were as natural as breathing.

Others he would have to control.

She nodded. 'Let me grab a few things that I might need.' She picked up one of the candles and walked over to her bedroom, opening a cupboard and pulling a few items of clothing out.

In the flickering candlelight he could make out the outline of her bed and possessions scattered around the room. A smile danced across his lips. Carrie McKenzie's bedroom. Would he ever get an invite into there?

It wasn't entirely what he'd expected. No flowers. No pink.

A bright green duvet, a mountain of pillows and a matching fleece comforter across the bottom of the bed. An electronic tablet and a few books were scattered on the bedside table, along with a few other obligatory candles. He wondered what scent they were. What scent she liked to fall asleep to.

A silver box lay on top of the bedclothes.

Her eyes flickered over to it and there was something—was it panic?—before she moved quickly, picked up the box and tucked it under the bed. She tucked the assorted clothes under her arm and appeared under his nose. 'Ready.'

It was just a little too bright. A little too forced. As if she was trying to distract him.

He'd just been kissing this woman but there were still parts of her she wanted to keep hidden. A tiny flare of anger lit in his stomach, only for him to extinguish it almost as quickly. He should know better than most. Everyone had secrets they wanted to hide. Parts of their life they wanted to remain hidden. Why should Carrie be any different?

'Let's go. We need to check on Abraham, and Mrs Van Dyke.'

He turned to follow her out of the door. And then it hit him.

That was what was wrong with this place.

There was nothing really of *Carrie*.

Oh, she might have her candles and a few books.

But there were no photos. Not a single one.

It sent a strange sensation down his spine. Every woman he'd ever known had pictures of their friends and family dotted around. Even he had some family pictures in various places around his apartment.

Carrie didn't have one. Not a single one.

What did that mean? She'd been here two months, surely enough time to get some family snaps out. Wasn't there anyone to miss back home?

'Dan, what's wrong? Let's go.' Carrie stuck her head back around the door, her impatience clear. Or was it her hurry to get him out of her apartment?

With one last look around he followed her out and pulled the door shut behind him.

There was more to Carrie McKenzie than met the eye.

And he was determined to get to the bottom of it.

CHAPTER SEVEN

WHEN CARRIE OPENED her eyes that morning it was to a totally different sight.

Blue walls and white bed linen.

The disorientation was over in an instant. She drew in a deep breath. It was strange waking up in someone else's bed.

She'd felt like that the first few nights in the apartment upstairs. Then, after a week, she hadn't even noticed. It just proved to her how much *home* in London hadn't really felt like *home* any more.

Dan's place was much more lived-in than hers. But then, he'd spent most of his life here. In amongst the state-of-the-art television and digital sound system, there were tiny ornaments, old picture frames and the odd piece of antique furniture. The little dark wood side table next to the door was her favourite. He hadn't really said much about how he'd ended up living with his grandmother and she didn't want to pry.

Just as she didn't want him to pry too much, either.

An unconscious smile crept across her face. He'd kissed her.

And she'd kissed him back.

Her first kiss since...

And it felt nice. It felt good.

Actually it felt a lot more than all that. Nice and good made it sound like a safe kiss. A kiss that was taking her on the road to recovery.

But Dan's kiss had ignited a whole lot more than that in her. She almost couldn't sleep last night when they'd parted. It was amazing how long you could lie staring up at the ceiling while your brain was on a spin cycle.

She looked around the room. A pair of his boots were on the floor, along with a pair of jeans slung across a chair. She could almost still see the shape of his body in those jeans. And it sent another lot of little pulses skittering across her skin.

Dan had decided to do the night shift last night. She was almost sure another two slices of her chocolate cake had been the appropriate bribe for him to spend the night on his lumpy sofa.

Abraham. He appeared in her thoughts like a flash and she sat upright in bed.

She hadn't heard him. She hadn't heard him at all.

A chill spread across her body instantly, reaching straight down into the pit of her stomach. Sending its icy tendrils around her heart.

No. Surely not.

She was up and out of the bedroom before her feet even felt as if they'd touched the wooden floor. Her steps across the floor the quickest she'd ever moved. Her breath caught in her throat and she leaned over the crib.

Empty. It was empty.

She spun around. 'Dan—' And stopped dead.

Dan was upright on the sofa, fast asleep with Abraham tucked against his shoulder. She'd obviously missed quite a bit last night. Why hadn't he woken her up? More importantly, why hadn't she heard?

In her haste across the room she hadn't even looked

over at his slumped frame. She'd been so focused on Abraham. So focused on the baby.

Dan's eyes flickered open and he lifted his hand covered in the cast to rub his sleep-ridden eyes. 'Wake my baby and I'll kill you,' he growled, echoing her words from the day before.

'I'm sorry,' she gasped. 'I just woke up and realised I hadn't heard him all night. I thought something was wrong. Then he wasn't in the crib and I—' She stopped to draw breath, conscious of the look on Dan's face. 'What? What is it?'

The coldness of the wooden floor was starting to seep through her toes and up her legs, making goosebumps erupt on her skin—her woefully exposed skin.

'Oh!' She lifted her arms across her breasts. Some body reactions weren't for public view.

Dan had been right about her other nightwear. Her tiny satin nightie covered her bum and not much more. Last night she'd been wearing her dressing gown—her eternal protection—and hadn't removed it until she'd climbed into bed. The power had come back on and the temperature in the apartment was warmer than usual, both having agreed that due to the lack of appropriate clothing for Abraham they needed to raise the temperature slightly. So she couldn't have bundled up in her usual fleece pyjamas—not without melting completely—and Dan would never see her in her nightie anyway, would he? Until now.

The cold floor had the ultimate effect on her body. Her nipples were firmly pressed into the sides of her arms across her chest. They had obviously been the feature that had caught his attention.

'Give me a second,' she blurted as she made a run for the bedroom and the sanctity of her dressing gown.

Too late she realised how much her slight nightie must have flapped around her behind, leaving little to the imagination.

She emerged a few minutes later, trying not to look completely flustered.

'I'll make breakfast this morning,' she said brightly. 'It was American yesterday—you made pancakes. So I think it will be tea, toast and marmalade this morning.'

Dan couldn't wipe the smile off his face, even though she was trying desperately to change the earlier subject. He shook his head. 'I sense distraction techniques, Carrie McKenzie. But since I'm a gentleman with an empty stomach I'll let it go. As for toast and marmalade? No, you don't. You sabotaged the pancakes with your butter and jam. And don't even think about making me tea after the night I've had. I need coffee. With at least three shots.'

Guilt surged through her and she sat down next to him. She was safe now; she was completely covered. 'Was Abraham really bad last night? I'm so sorry. I never heard a thing.'

'I noticed.' He shook his head and gave her a weary smile. 'If I'd needed you, Carrie, I would have woken you up. But it was fine.' He paused. 'Well, actually, it wasn't fine, but I closed the door so you wouldn't hear. I figured this was hard enough for you and a night with no sleep wouldn't help.'

She was stunned.

It was no secret she hadn't managed to hide things from Dan. He'd already asked her on more than one occasion what was wrong and she hadn't responded. Because she didn't feel ready to.

It had only been a few days. And she didn't know him that well—not really. But Dan had taken actions last night to make sure she had some respite. He was reading her better than she could have ever thought. Was it the cop instincts? Did he just know when to push and when to back off?

Did they even teach things like that in cop school? Or was he just good at reading her? At sensing when things were tough and she needed to step back. She wasn't ready to share. Or was she?

Her friends back home all knew about the stillbirth. And they either tiptoed around her or tried to make her talk. Neither way worked for her.

She needed to talk when *she* was ready. Not when they were ready.

Maybe it would be easier to share with someone from outside her circle of friends. Someone who could be impartial and not try to hit her with a whole host of advice about what to do and how she should feel.

Dan was the first guy to cause her stomach to flutter in a whole year. She'd thought that part of her had died. And nothing would cause it to wake up again. But the close proximity was definitely a factor. How much of a risk would it be to tell him, to trust him?

Looking at the snow outside, they could be here for at least another whole day. The flickering TV in the corner of the room still had the yellow strip running across the news report, telling about more snowfall and more people cut off from their family and friends. 'I see there's going to be more snow.' She nodded at the TV.

He sighed. 'Yeah.' He shrugged his shoulders as his eyes met hers. 'Seems like we're not going anywhere fast.'

'At least the electric shower will be working. And the kettle and hob. I'll be able to sterilise things and make some more bottles for Abraham.' The practical things. The things that always came into her brain first.

But there was something else there. Something else drumming away inside her head.

They were stuck here. For at least another day.

Another day with delectable Dan.

Another day with a baby. Could she cope? Could she do this again?

It was as if something happened inside. A little flare sparked inside her brain. This was it. This was her chance.

If only she had the courage.

She held out her hands towards Abraham. Would Dan notice they were trembling? 'May I?'

He nodded and handed over the half-sleeping babe to her. Abraham didn't seem to mind who was holding him. He snuggled instantly into her shoulder, obviously preferring the upright position.

There was a loud splurging noise, closely followed by a smell creeping around the apartment. Carrie wrinkled her nose. 'Oh, Abraham. How could you?'

Her hand felt along his back and came into contact with a little splurge at the side of the nappy and half-way up his back. She let out a sigh and set him down in the crib.

'I guess it's going to be a bath for you, little sir.'

'How are we going to manage that? We don't have a baby bath.'

Carrie walked over to the deep kitchen sink. 'We'll improvise. This is the best we've got. Don't you remember ever getting bathed in the kitchen sink as a child?'

He shook his head. 'Can't say that I do. Is it an English tradition?'

Carrie had started to scrub the sink within an inch of her life. 'I guess it must be, then. My gran's got some pictures of me sitting bare naked in her kitchen sink. I thought everyone did that.'

She filled the sink with some tepid water and baby bubble bath before testing the temperature. She stripped Abraham's clothes and put them in a bucket of cold water to soak. Dan wrinkled his nose. 'I'm going to wash these? Really? Wouldn't it be better just putting them in the garbage?'

Carrie shook her head. 'We don't have that luxury, Dan. We only have a few things that fit him. They'll just need to be soaked and then boil washed.'

Dan lifted the bucket and headed down to the laundry. 'Be back in five,' he said.

Carrie lifted Abraham from the towel he was squirming on. 'Let's see if we can get this all off you,' she said as she gently lowered him into the warm water.

The expression on his face was priceless. First he squirmed. Then he let out a little yelp of dismay. It only lasted for a few seconds before the shock of being cold disappeared and his little body picked up the surrounding warm water. He gave a little shudder. Then started to kick his legs.

She smiled. His first baby bath.

Her first baby bath. And it was just the two of them.

There was something about it that was so nice. She knew this should be a moment that he shared with his mother. But it was almost as if this were meant to be. She watched as his little legs stretched out and kicked in the water in the sink. She lapped the water over his stomach and chest. He let out a range of little noises. If she didn't know better she could imagine he was almost smiling.

Some babies screamed when they hit the bathwater, hating being stripped of their warm cocoonlike clothes. But not Abraham. He seemed to relish it, enjoying kicking his legs in the water.

She lifted some cotton wool balls, being careful to

make sure he was entirely clean. Turning his position slightly, so she could make sure there was nothing left on his back.

That was when it happened.

That was when he gave a little judder.

She knew instinctively something was wrong. She turned him over, her hands struggling to hold his slippery body as she panicked. He was pale. Deathly pale. Almost as if he was holding his breath.

No. No!

She let out a scream. She couldn't help it. The whole world had just started to close in all around her. She grabbed him beneath the arms and thrust the dripping baby into Dan's arms as he strode back through the door.

'Carrie, what's wrong?'

She couldn't stop. She couldn't breathe. Her feet carried her outside the apartment door and out onto the steps. The cold snow-covered steps where she'd found him. As soon as she reached the cold air it was as if her legs gave way and she collapsed down onto the steps, struggling to catch her breath.

There were tiny little black spots around her vision. She put her head between her legs and told herself to breathe slowly. But nothing could stop the clamouring in her chest.

That sight. That pale little body. That still little chest. It had been too much for her. That momentary second of panic had made her head spin. No one should have to go through that twice in their life.

No one was meant to experience that again.

Breathe. In through her nose, out through her mouth. And again. Breathe. In through her nose and out through her mouth.

She tried to get control. Her senses were picking up

something else. A noise. A background noise. A baby crying.

Then she started to sob. Uncontrollably sob. Abraham was fine. She knew that. She'd panicked. If she'd stopped to think—even for a moment—she would have realised he'd only been holding his breath for a second. But she couldn't. She didn't possess those rational kinds of thoughts any more. And she doubted she ever would.

Then she felt it, a hand creeping around her shoulders and a body sitting on the step next to her. The heat of another body touching hers. The comfort of an arm around her shoulders and the feeling of somewhere she could lay her head.

But he didn't speak. Dan just held her. She didn't know how long passed. She didn't know how long she sobbed. All she knew was his arms were around her and he was holding her—as if he would never let go.

His hand was stroking her hair. It was bitter cold out here, but neither of them seemed to notice. 'Tell me, Carrie,' he whispered. 'Tell me how to help you.'

'You can't, Dan.' It was a relief to say the words out loud. 'I panicked. I thought Abraham had stopped breathing.'

'He's fine, Carrie. Abraham is absolutely fine.' His voice washed over her, like a calm, soothing tonic. He lifted her chin towards his face. 'But you're not.' His finger traced the track of tears down her cheek. 'You're not fine, Carrie. Tell me why not.'

It was time. It was time to tell the truth. 'Why do you struggle with babies?'

The million-dollar question.

'Because I had one.'

She heard his intake of breath, but to his credit he never reacted the way she expected. There was a few moments' silence while he obviously contemplated her news. 'When did you have one?' His voice was low, comforting. The question wasn't intrusive. He made it feel like an everyday conversation.

'Last year.'

'Oh.'

'Yes, oh.' A shiver danced along her spine. Was it a reaction to the cold? Or was it a reaction to saying those words out loud?

Dan stood up and pulled her along with him. 'Let's do this inside. Let's do this inside with Abraham.'

Even now he didn't want to leave the baby on his own. Dan was being a good parent. It made this seem so much easier.

Abraham was wrapped in a towel, his bare toes kicking at the air above. As Dan closed the door behind them, shutting out the cold winter air, she knew what she had to do. She knew what would help her through this.

She picked up the kicking bundle and held him close to her chest, taking some deep breaths in and out.

She couldn't think of a single reason why this made her feel better. The thought of holding another baby in her arms had terrified her for so long. But the past few days had been cathartic.

Never, in a million years, would she have thought that holding another baby in her arms while she talked about the one she had lost would feel okay. Would actually feel quite right. If she'd ever planned to share, it would never have been like this.

'It wasn't too long ago.' Her words were firmer than she expected. She'd always thought that she'd never be able to get them out.

Maybe it was because she was with Dan. Maybe it was because he was literally a captive audience with no place to go. Maybe it was because she knew he couldn't run out on her if he didn't like what he heard. Maybe it was because she was beginning to feel as if she could tell this guy anything.

'Fifteenth of May last year, I had a little girl. Ruby. She was stillborn.'

There was silence.

It seemed important. Even though she hated the word *stillborn* it seemed important to her to tell him what had happened to her baby. She didn't want him to think she'd given her baby up for adoption, or done the same as Abraham's mother and abandoned her.

What was he thinking? And then a warm hand crept up and covered hers, squeezing gently. 'I'm sorry you lost your daughter, Carrie. That must have been a terrible time for you.'

The quiet acknowledgement made tears spring to her eyes. 'Thank you, Dan,' she whispered.

For Ruby. He was expressing his sorrow for the loss of her daughter. For Ruby. Some people didn't like to acknowledge a baby who had been lost. Some people didn't even want to say their names. It was easier to pretend they'd never existed. After all, babies who had never drawn breath in this world, they practically hadn't been here.

Except Ruby had been here.

She'd kicked under her mother's expanding stomach for seven months. She'd twisted and turned in the middle of the night, constantly having dancing competitions that kept her mother awake into the small hours. Sometimes a little foot or hand had been clearly visible as Carrie had lain watching her belly.

Ruby McKenzie had definitely existed. And it was so

nice to finally talk about her. Talk about her in a normal way instead of in hushed, quiet tones.

'Is that what's in the silver box upstairs?'

Now he had surprised her. 'How do you know about the box?'

'I saw it sitting on your bed when we were in your apartment. I saw the way you looked at it.' He gave her a little smile. 'It's pretty. And it seemed important.' His finger traced along the knuckles of her hand, small circular motions. 'Your place. You didn't have pictures up. For a woman, that struck me as strange. I figured you had a good reason and didn't want to ask.'

A tear slid down her cheek. 'I'm trying to get away from memories. That's why I'm in New York. It seemed like a good time to get away. Everything and everyone back home just reminded me of last year. It made sense. Coming here, getting away from it all.'

Dan traced his finger from her hand to her breastbone. His voice was intense. 'You can't get away from what's in here, Carrie. It stays with you all the time—no matter where you go.'

Wow. Her breath caught in her throat.

It was the way he said the words. The understanding. How could Dan be so in tune with things? There was an intensity she hadn't seen before. A darkening of his brown eyes from caramel tones to deep chocolate colours.

He knew. He understood her straight away, and she didn't know why.

'I know that. But sometimes what's in here feels easier if you've got room to deal with it yourself.' Easier than everyone clamouring around you, suffocating you with *their* grief.

'And has it been? Has it been easier, Carrie?'

'I thought it was. I thought I was coming to terms

with things.' Her eyes went down to Abraham. 'Until now. Until him.' She could hear the waver in her voice, feel the tremble in her throat. She desperately wanted to keep it together. She wanted to put her thoughts, feelings and frustrations into words—in a way she'd never managed before.

But Dan's reaction was flooring her. She couldn't have asked for more.

Dan shook his head. 'No wonder you didn't want to help out. No wonder you tried to make excuses.' His eyes were still heavy with weariness and she could see the lines on his face. He was fighting fatigue with every bone in his body.

He turned around on the sofa so he was facing her entirely. 'I'm sorry, Carrie. I had no idea how hard this was for you. But I really needed your help. I couldn't do this on my own. I don't know the first thing about babies.'

The gentle tears were still flowing. 'And neither do I, Dan. I never got the chance to find out. And I'm so worried I'll do something wrong. What if I caused Ruby to be stillborn? What if it was something I did? Something I ate? I'm not sure I should be around babies. I'm terrified that I'll do something wrong. What if he's sick and I don't know it? What if the jaundice gets worse instead of better?' She shook her head. 'I've already held one dead baby in my arms. I couldn't live with myself if anything happened to Abraham.'

Panic was welling up inside her and threatening to take over.

Some things were still too much for her. Still too raw.

Dan put his hands on her shoulders. 'Don't, Carrie. Don't do this to yourself. We've spoken to Shana. You heard what she said. As soon as possible, she'll arrange to examine Abraham and make sure everything is fine.

Nothing happened today when you bathed him. Abraham must have just held his breath. As soon as you handed him to me, it was almost as if he let out a little squawk. It was nothing you did, Carrie. Nothing at all. As for doing something wrong—I'm more likely to do that than you. You're a natural. Everything you do is right. No matter how hard you're finding this, you still make a much better parent than I do. I couldn't even get a diaper on straight!' He pressed his fingers into the tops of her arms. 'I don't know what happened to Ruby, but I don't believe for a second it was your fault. Did they ever tell you? What did the medical examiner say?'

Carrie took a deep breath. 'Nothing. They found nothing. Although she was early Ruby was the right size and weight. There was nothing wrong with my placenta. There was nothing wrong with the umbilical cord. I hadn't been in an accident. I didn't have any infections. My blood pressure was fine. They couldn't give me a single reason why Ruby stopped moving that day. She was perfect. She was perfect in every way.'

Her voice was cracking now. Her head was filling with pictures of that room. The expression on the radiographer's face as she swept Carrie's abdomen, trying to find a heartbeat with no success. The quiet way she had spoken, mentioning she needed to look for a colleague before disappearing out of the door.

And Carrie, sitting in the semi-dark room, knowing, just *knowing,* that life was about to change in an unimaginable way. Placing her hands on her stomach, ignoring the gel, and just talking to her baby. Telling her that Mummy loved her. Forever and ever.

Ruby's name had been picked weeks before. The hand-painted letters already adorned the door of the room in their flat that had been dedicated as the nursery. The nursery that Ruby would never see—never live in.

She could see the empathy on Dan's face. He understood. He understood the pure frustration of having no reason, no answer to the worst thing that could happen to her.

He lifted his heavy eyelids with caution. 'What about Ruby's dad?'

'What about Ruby's dad?' She shook her head. A small bit of guilt still weighed on her soul. 'Mark was a good guy. But neither of us could cope with what happened. Things just fell apart. He got another job and moved away. He's met someone now. And I'm happy for him. We just couldn't stay together—it was far too hard. Like having a permanent reminder etched on your brain.'

'Seems to me that Ruby will be permanently etched on your brain anyhow. Whether you're with Mark or not.'

She stared at him. That was blunt and to the point. And for the first time Dan had a deep crease across his forehead. A crease she wanted to reach up and smooth away with her fingers.

She was feeling it. This connection to Dan. Just as he was feeling it, too.

Mark was a chapter of her life that was over. And although she thought about Ruby frequently, she barely ever thought about Mark.

Dan's last remark seemed almost protective, and a tiny bit territorial. And the strangest thing was she didn't mind. Why had she been so scared to talk about this?

It wasn't comfortable. It wasn't comfortable at all. But Dan seemed to understand more than she would have expected him to.

And Dan was everything Mark wasn't. Mark couldn't bear to be around her once she'd lost Ruby. It was too hard. Too hard for them both. But Dan was nothing like that. She couldn't imagine Mark in this situation. Looking after an abandoned baby. Mark would have wanted nothing to do with that at all. But Dan had taken it all in his stride. A totally different kind of man.

And timing was everything. If New York hadn't been hit by this freak snowstorm she and Dan might never have talked. Might never have got to know each other and started to show these little glimmers of trust.

She sagged back on the sofa as Abraham let out a little sigh, his warm breath against her neck. 'I don't ever want to forget my daughter, Daniel. I couldn't, and I wouldn't ever want to. I have things in the box, her first scan, her scan at twenty weeks. A few little things that I'd bought for her that she never got to wear.' She stared off into the distance. 'I had to buy something new. Something for very premature babies to put on her. And some photos. I have some photos. But—'

She broke off, unable to finish. The photographs were just too painful.

His hand was wrapped back around hers again. 'So, how do you feel about helping me with Abraham? I know it's hard for you, Carrie. But I really need your help.' His words were said with caution, as if he didn't want to cause her any more pain.

She took a few moments before she answered, trying to sort it all out in her brain. 'It's strange. It's not quite what I'd expected. I've avoided babies for months. Any of my friends who were pregnant and delivered, I just made excuses not to see them and sent a present. I think they all understood. Most of them felt awkward around me anyway. I thought Abraham would be my worst nightmare.'

'And?'

'And—' she looked down at the little face, snuggled

against her shoulder '—I won't pretend it's not hard. I won't pretend that I don't sometimes just need a minute. Just need a little space. But it's not as bad as I expected.'

The heat from Abraham's little body was penetrating through her dressing gown, like an additional hot-water bottle. But it felt good. It felt natural. It didn't make her want to run screaming from the room. Not in the way she would have expected.

'Then can you do this, Carrie? Can you keep helping me for the next day or so?' He pointed to the TV. 'It doesn't look like New York is opening back up for business any time soon.' He touched her arm, and she could sense the frustration he was trying to hide from her. 'I'll understand, Carrie. I'll understand if you say no and want to go back up to your apartment and stay there.'

She thought about it. There was no hiding the fact that for a few moments she actually considered it. But just at that point Abraham moved and snuggled even closer to her neck.

What was up there for her? An empty apartment with no one to talk to. There was only so much news she could watch on TV saying the same things over and over again.

There were only so many times she could rearrange her wardrobe and shoes. There were only so many times she could reread her favourite books.

She sucked in a deep breath. He was watching her. *He* was holding *his* breath, waiting for her response. 'You understand now, but you didn't understand a couple of nights ago.' She could remember the stunned expression on his face when she'd bolted for the door.

He nodded in defeat. 'You're right. I thought you were distinctly weird. But I was crazy and desperate enough not to care.' He pointed to his chest. 'But I know, Carrie, I know in here if someone is a good person. And don't think it's anything about being a cop. I've been like this since I was a kid. I always knew who had a good heart—no matter what their appearance or surroundings. And I always knew who to steer clear of, no matter what they told me.'

There were shadows in his eyes. He was revealing a tiny part of himself here. Maybe without even knowing it. And that was the second time this had happened. First with the comment about things always staying inside you, and now about knowing people—who to stay away from. How had he learned that lesson? It was painful to even think about it.

She reached up and touched the side of his face with her free hand. Bristles. Dan hadn't managed to shave yet and they felt good beneath her smooth skin. She even liked the sound.

'And do you want to steer clear of me, Dan?' He was staring at her with those dark brown eyes. Pulling her in. Thank goodness she was sitting or her legs would currently be like jelly.

There was comfort here. Because she knew what he was about to say. Didn't doubt it for a second. This connection was the truest thing she'd felt in a long time.

He gave her that sexy smile. The one that made her stomach flip over. 'Not for a second,' he whispered, and leaned forward and brushed his lips against hers.

It was beautiful. The gentlest of kisses.

Just as well. She still had Abraham in her arms. Under any other circumstances she might feel the urge to throw her dressing gown to the wind and jump up onto his lap.

He was concentrating solely on her mouth. His hand still only brushing the side of her face as their kiss deepened and his tongue edged its way into her mouth.

She could feel the heat rush through her, warming

her chilled legs and feet and spreading to a whole host of other places.

She could concentrate solely on this. She could concentrate solely on Dan. Once he started kissing her nothing else mattered. Her brain didn't have room for a single thought.

But as if sensing where this could go, Dan pulled back.

And for a second she felt lost. Until she opened her eyes again and realised he was smiling at her.

'What do you think, Carrie McKenzie? Will you be my partner in crime? Can Abraham and I count on you?'

She narrowed her eyes at him. Boy, he was good. With his fancy words and his kisses. His help-the-baby plea. This man could charm the birds out of the trees.

Just as well she was the only bird around.

She lifted her eyebrows. 'Are you doing this for the chocolate cake?'

He smiled. 'I'm definitely doing it for the chocolate cake.'

'Well, that makes us even, 'cause I'm doing this for the carrot cake—and the pancakes.' She liked this. She liked that they could fall back into flirting so easily, even after her monumental revelation.

'Just what I like—a woman with her priorities in order.' He pushed himself up from the sofa and held out his hands for Abraham.

'Don't you want me to take a turn for a while?'

'Oh, no.' He shook his head firmly as he gathered Abraham into his arms and took a long look at her bare legs and painted toenails. 'What I want is for you to put some clothes on. You're *way* too distracting without them.'

She stood up, deliberately letting her dressing gown open, just to annoy him. 'Well, we wouldn't want any distractions, would we?' she teased as she headed to the door.

There was some colour in his cheeks. A guy like Dan couldn't be embarrassed. Not when he looked like that. He must have women throwing themselves at him all the time—particularly when he was in uniform.

She saw him shifting uncomfortably, adjusting himself. No! She'd caused an age-old reaction with a few cheeky words and a flash of skin. Her cheeks started to blush, too.

And then she started to smile.

It was starting to feel as if she had some control back. As if everything in life wouldn't just slip through her fingers like grains of sand on the beach.

She turned the handle on the door.

'Carrie?'

She spun around.

Dan was standing with Abraham in his arms. Looking every inch the gorgeous family man. Looking every inch like the man she pictured in her dreams about the life she wanted to have.

'Hurry back.'

She tried to think of something witty or clever to say. But she had nothing.

'Absolutely,' she muttered as she sped up the stairs as fast as her legs would carry her.

Her brain had just flipped into a spin cycle again.

It was certifiable. Daniel Cooper was driving her crazy.

CHAPTER EIGHT

By now Dan should have been a crumpled heap on the floor. He'd spent most of last night walking the floor with a sometimes whimpering, sometimes screaming baby. At one point he'd put Abraham back in the crib and gone to stand in the kitchen for a few minutes to catch his breath.

But from the moment Carrie had appeared, all bright-eyed and bushy-tailed after a good night's sleep, he'd felt instantly invigorated.

There was something about her brown curls, blue eyes and flash of skin that was slowly but surely driving him crazy.

And now he knew.

Now he understood.

Well, not entirely. God willing he'd never really understand what it felt like to lose a child. But at least now he had an explanation for the shadows beneath her eyes. The moments of panic that he'd seen and recognised. Her abruptness. Her lack of confidence in herself.

What he couldn't understand was why Carrie couldn't see what he could see. A remarkably caring and competent woman who seemed to have a real empathy with this little baby.

For some reason Carrie's news reassured him a little. He'd known there was something wrong but hadn't quite been able to put his finger on it. His instincts told him she was a good person and not a crazed baby-snatcher or madly unstable.

Carrie McKenzie was probably the bravest woman he'd ever met. And that included his grandmother.

She'd put the needs of this little baby—a child she didn't know—before her own needs, even though it was apparent at times her heart was clearly breaking. How many other people did he know who could have done this?

A smile danced across his lips as he remembered her reaction to Shana's 'suck it up' comment. No wonder she'd been so horrified.

This was truly her worst nightmare and she'd just lived through thirty-odd hours of it, with only a few minor hiccups along the way.

He'd been right to let her sleep. It seemed to have given her new strength and the confidence to share. And he was glad she'd shared.

He'd just resisted the temptation to gather her into his arms and try to take her pain away. Because something told him this was all new for her. Sharing about this was all new for her, and he had to let her go at her own pace.

And while it seemed the most unlikely solution, holding Abraham had seemed to give her comfort at that moment. Which was why he'd resorted to the smallest movement—the hand squeeze—to show his support.

What did this mean now for them?

Now that she'd shared he'd given her the opportunity to walk away. To stop making things so hard on herself. But she was determined to stay and help. And his sense of relief was overwhelming. If left to himself, he was sure he could muddle through. But having someone else there—even a little reluctantly—was more help than she could imagine.

As for the kiss?

How much was Carrie ready to move on?

Because being in a confined space with her was going to drive him crazy—in a good way. Now that he'd tasted her sweet lips and felt the warmth of her body next to his it just made him crave her all the more.

Carrie wasn't like any other woman that he'd met.

Girls in New York weren't shy. *Reserved* was an extinct term around here.

He was used to women throwing themselves at him, in pursuit of either a relationship or something far hotter.

It was just the way of the world these days.

But truth be told, it wasn't really Dan's world. It wasn't really the family values his grandmother had brought him up with. They, in themselves, were almost laughable. His mother certainly hadn't had any family values—no matter what her family had taught her. And that had reflected badly on Dan.

His grandmother had patched him up, fought fiercely for him and his mother's name was never mentioned in the house again.

And that was fine with him. For years she haunted his dreams most nights anyway.

But Carrie McKenzie, with her too-blue eyes and quiet nature, was slowly but surely getting under his skin in a way no other woman had.

It was clear there were some aspects of life they disagreed on. But did that mean it would be pointless to pursue anything else? Dan wasn't sure. He still had his own demons to deal with. And the situation with Abraham was only heightening a whole host of emotions he'd buried for so long.

His stomach grumbled loudly just as Carrie burst back through the door, wearing a pink shirt and jeans, her hair tied up in a loose knot. She laughed at the sound of his stomach. 'You called?'

He nodded at her hands that were clutched to her chest holding a jar of lemon marmalade. 'It's getting to the stage I won't even fight you about the toast and marmalade. You've starved me so long I'm ready to concede.' He walked over to the crib and laid Abraham back down.

She strode over to the toaster and slid the last of the bread into place. 'I'll concede on one thing. I'll make you coffee instead of tea—but only since you had such a bad night. I might make some scones this afternoon and make you drink tea, then.'

He felt his ears literally prick up. The cupboards' supplies were getting low—even though it had only been a few days. The cakes yesterday had been a real boost. Scones today? Even better.

'I've never really had the scone things. What do you have them with?'

She shrugged. 'It should be jam and cream, but jam and butter will do. Do you want fruit scones or plain?'

He rolled his eyes upwards. 'I take it bacon's not an option?' He smiled at the horrified expression on her face. 'You've got a secret stash of dried fruit up there, too?'

She put her hand on her hip and gave him a sassy look. 'I've got a whole host of things you know nothing about up there.'

He let out a stream of air through his lips. 'Woman, you're going to drive me crazy.'

The toast popped behind her and she started spreading butter and marmalade, pulled out two plates and mugs and finished making breakfast in record time.

It was almost as if Abraham had an inbuilt antenna.

As soon as Carrie's backside hovered above the chair he started to grizzle in his crib. She glanced at the clock. 'When did he have his last feed?'

Dan looked at his watch. 'I think it was around four. This little guy is like clockwork. He couldn't possibly let it go any more than four hours.'

'It must be my turn to feed him. Let me make up a bottle.' She picked out the bottle and teat from the sterilising solution and measured out the formula. 'I wish we could get some more of the ready-made formula. It's so much easier.' She peered into the contents of the formula tub. 'How many bottles does this make? I know it's only a small can but it seems to be going down mighty quickly.' She turned back to face him.

Dan wasn't listening. He was staring at the toast and lemon marmalade as if it had sprouted legs and run across the floor.

'Dan? Dan? What's wrong.'

He took another bite of the toast. 'This is much nicer than I remember. Or maybe it's just that I'm so hungry that I would eat anything.' He stared at the toast. 'I always thought marmalade was—you know—yeuch.' He let a shiver go down his spine. 'I don't remember it tasting like this.'

She gave him a smile. 'It's one of my secrets. You probably had orange marmalade as a child. I don't like it, either. This is much nicer, made with lemons. I brought it with me from London.'

He narrowed his eyes. 'Where do you keep the jar?'

She tapped the side of her nose. 'Aha, that's a secret. You'll never make me tell.'

'Never?' He stood up, his chair skidding across the floor and his hands on her hips in an instant. She could hardly even remember him crossing the space.

Oh, no. Those come-to-bed eyes again. The kind that gave her ideas she really shouldn't be having at this time of day.

He didn't wait. He didn't ask. He just claimed her lips as his own. His hand coming up and cupping her cheek. There was an element of ownership in his actions.

But the strange thing was, instead of being annoying, it sent little sparks of heat all the way down to the tips of her toes.

The past year had been lonely. The past year had been more than lonely. The past year had been dark and bleak and, at times, scary.

Sometimes she felt as if the black cloud around her would never lift, no matter how hard she tried.

For the first time she was feeling something other than despair. Other than hopelessness.

Maybe her senses were overreacting. Maybe it had just been too long since she'd been in a position like this, where her hormones couldn't keep themselves in check.

All she knew was she wanted Daniel Cooper's lips on hers. She wanted Daniel Cooper pressed up against her. She wanted to feel his arms around her body, touching her skin, stroking her cheek...

She wound her arms around his neck as his hands found their way to the bare skin at the small of her back. Would his fingers creep any lower? Or any higher? She wasn't quite sure which way she wanted them to go.

There was a howl from the corner of the room and they jerked apart instantly.

Baby. There was a baby in the room. She made to move towards the crib. 'Don't. I'll do it,' he said, his hands still pressed firmly against her hips.

'But you did all of last night.' She touched his shoulder. 'You're exhausted, Dan. You really should get some sleep.'

He nodded. 'And I will, as soon as you've eaten. You haven't had a chance yet. Finish breakfast, then come and take over from me.'

She eyed her toast with oodles of butter and marmalade and her steaming-hot cup of tea. How long would it take her? Five minutes? Then she could take over from Dan for a good part of the day.

From the shadows under his eyes it was clear that he needed a few hours' sleep. Could she cope with Abraham on her own for a few hours?

No matter how hard she was trying here, the thought still struck fear in her heart. What if something happened? What if she did something wrong?

The truth was she felt safer when Dan was around. Even though he told her she was doing a great job she wasn't sure she wanted to do it alone.

One of the little cardigans was hanging on the side of the crib and the solution was with her in an instant. Of course! That was what she would do. She would take Abraham upstairs to visit Mrs Van Dyke—at least then she wouldn't be on her own. And even though Mrs Van Dyke was elderly she had lots of experience with babies. She might even be able to give Carrie some tips.

She looked over to the sofa. Dan was already taking the bottle out of Abraham's mouth. He was feeding really quickly. A thought crossed her mind. 'Is your internet working yet?'

Dan shrugged his shoulders. He was deep in concentration. 'Haven't checked yet. Why?'

'Do you think there's any way we could weigh Abraham? Maybe we aren't giving him enough milk. He always seems to gulp really quickly then gets lots of wind.'

The news anchor was telling the same story over and over again. Wasn't she wearing that same suit jacket a few days ago? Pictures filled the screen of stranded cars, a collapsed tree in Central Park, aerial shots of all the roads completely covered in snow. More pictures of people being rescued by police and, in some cases, helicopters. It looked as if there had been barely any improvements in the past two days. Her voice was starting to annoy Carrie.

'Snow ploughs cleared most of New York State Thruway the I-87 this morning, only for the hard work to be destroyed less than three hours later after another record deluge of snow. Some people had been waiting two days to get their cars out of the snowdrifts, only to get snowed back in a few miles down the thruway. Emergency services can't give an estimate on how much longer it will take to clear the thruway again. They are stressing that people in the area should only travel in emergency cases. Every resource possible is currently being used to try and restore the fluctuating power supplies to the city. Some areas of the city have been without power for more than twenty-four hours. Authorities assure us that all power supplies should be connected in the next twelve hours.'

Dan pointed at the screen. 'That's the bad news. Now wait for it—here comes the good news story.'

Carrie turned back to the screen. She definitely had seen that jacket before. Wardrobe at the news station must be as closed down as the rest of New York.

'And finally, community kitchens are springing up all over New York City. The latest is in Manhattan's Lower East Side at Sara D. Roosevelt Park and the locals have been enjoying the opportunity to gather somewhere with some hot food and heating.' The camera shot to children building a giant snowman in the park and several residents holding cups with something steaming hot inside.

'Wow, that snowman is enormous. There's no way a kid made that. They couldn't reach that high.'

'Do I sense a little snowman envy?' Dan had an amused expression on his face.

Carrie shrugged. 'Maybe. Can't even tell you the last time I made a snowman. I must have been around ten. Back home in London I don't even have a garden.'

Dan headed over to the back window, juggling Abraham in his arms. It was time for winding again. 'Most of the apartments around here don't have gardens. But there are gardens. Have you managed to get to Washington Square Park yet?'

She joined him at the window, looking out over the snow-covered back alley. 'If I even thought we'd have a chance of making it there I'd ask you to take me.' She reached over and touched Abraham's little hand. 'But we pretty much can't take this little guy anywhere with no proper clothes, jacket or snowsuit. I guess that means we're stranded.'

It was the wrong thing to say. Almost as soon as she said the words she wanted to pull them back. She could instantly see Dan's back and shoulders stiffen, the atmosphere changing around them in a second.

'I guess the actions of others impact on us all.'

She was still touching Abraham's hand, letting his little fingers connect with hers. 'We don't know, Dan. We don't know anything.'

He spun around to face her. 'Of course we do. Look at him. Look at this defenceless little baby. Left out in the cold with hardly any clothes. He could have died out there, Carrie. He could have died.'

'Don't. Don't say that. I don't even want to think about that. I can't think about that.'

She stared him down. He had to know how much his

words impacted on her. How she couldn't even bear to think the thoughts he was putting in her head.

'Why are you so critical, Dan? You must see a whole host of things in your line of work. I thought that would make you more sympathetic to people out there. Not sit as judge and master.'

'I don't judge.' His words were snapped and Abraham flinched at the rise in his voice.

'Well, I think you do. I think that's what you've done since the second I found Abraham and brought him to you.'

He opened his mouth, obviously ready to hit her with a torrent of abuse. But good sense waylaid him. She could almost see him biting his tongue and it annoyed her. She didn't want Dan to hide things from her. He should tell her how he really felt. It didn't matter that they would disagree.

'Spit it out, Dan.'

'I don't think that's wise.' His words were growled through clenched teeth.

She walked right up to him, her face directly under his chin. He was angry. She could tell he was angry. But she wasn't intimidated at all. Dan would never direct his anger at her.

'So, you can kiss me to death, but you can't tell me how you feel?'

Dan walked over to the crib, placed Abraham down and raked his hand through his short hair, his hand coming around and scraping at the bristles on his chin. 'Just leave it, Carrie.'

'Why? Isn't it normal to disagree about things? I just can't understand why the guy who was prepared to risk his life for a bunch of strangers can't take a minute to show a little compassion to a woman who is clearly desperate.' She pointed over at the crib. 'No woman in her right mind would abandon her baby. Not without good reason. I bet she's lying crying and terrified right now. I bet the past two nights she hasn't slept a wink with worry over how her son is doing.'

He shook his head. 'You're wrong, Carrie. You're more than wrong. Good people don't do things like this. Good people don't abandon their babies or make them suffer. Everyone who has the responsibility for children should put their needs first—before their own.'

She wrinkled her brow. 'What are you getting at, Dan? What need do you think Abraham's mother was putting first?'

He couldn't meet her eyes. He couldn't look at her. His eyes were fixed either on the floor or the ceiling. He walked towards the window, staring out at the snow-covered street, his hands on his hips. 'Drugs, Carrie. I think his mother was looking for her next fix.'

Carrie's hand flew up to her mouth. It hadn't even occurred to her. It hadn't even crossed her mind.

Maybe she was too innocent. Maybe she'd lived a sheltered life.

'No.' She crossed quickly to the crib and looked down at Abraham. His eyelids were fluttering, as if he was trying to focus on the changing shapes around him. He looked so innocent. So peaceful. The thought of his mother being a drug user horrified Carrie.

She hadn't lived her life in a plastic bubble. There had been women who clearly had drug problems in the maternity unit next to her's. But they were in the unit, being monitored for the sake of their babies. Although they had other issues in their lives, their babies' health was still important to them.

She reached out and stroked Abraham's skin. It still

had the slightest touch of yellow, but these things wouldn't disappear overnight. Could his mother really have been taking drugs? It was just unimaginable to Carrie.

She felt a little surge of adrenalin rise inside her. 'No, Dan. No way. It can't be that. It just can't be. We would know. Abraham would be showing signs. Drug addicts' babies show signs of withdrawal, don't they? If Abraham's mother was an addict he would be scream-ing by now.'

'Hasn't he screamed the past two nights?'

She shook her head firmly. It didn't matter that she was no expert. She'd heard enough to know a little of the background. 'He would be sick, Dan. He would be *really* sick. And Abraham's not. Look at him.' She walked around to the other side of the crib to give Dan a clear view. 'He's not sick like that. Sure, he gets hungry and has wind. He pulls his little knees up to his chest. That's colic. Nothing else. And there are pages and pages on the internet about that.' She folded her arms across her chest. 'If we had a baby in withdrawal right now, we'd need Shana to airlift him to the hospital. There's no two ways about it.'

It was clear from the tight expression on Dan's face that he wasn't ready to concede. He wasn't ready to con-sider he was wrong.

She could feel her hackles rising. She could feel they were on the precipice of a major argument and she just didn't want to go there. All her protective vibes were coming out, standing over Abraham like some lioness guarding her cub. But why would she have to guard him against Dan? The man who'd opened his door and wel-comed them both in?

She took a deep breath. 'Dan, you're tired and you're cranky. I know what that feels like. Let's leave this. Go and sleep for a few hours. I'm going to take Abraham upstairs to see Mrs Van Dyke. She'll be happy to see him and, who knows, she might even give me some tips.'

She could see he still wanted to argue with her but fatigue was eating away at every movement he made. His shoulders were slumped, his muscular frame sagging.

'Fine. I'll go to sleep.' He stalked off towards the bedroom—the bed she'd recently vacated—before he halted and turned around. 'Mrs Van Dyke, ask her if she needs anything. Anything at all. I can phone Mr Meltzer and go back along to the shop in a few hours and get us some more supplies. We'll need things for Abraham anyhow.'

There it was. Even in his inner turmoil, the real Dan Cooper could still shine through. He was still thinking about others, still concerned about his elderly neighbour.

She picked up Abraham from the crib, tapping her finger on his button nose and smiling at him.

Just when she thought Dan had gone he appeared at her elbow, bending over and dropping a gentle kiss on Abraham's forehead.

'I'm not going to let anything happen to this little guy, Carrie. Nothing at all.' His words were whispered, but firm, and he turned and walked off to the bedroom, closing the door behind him.

CHAPTER NINE

CARRIE WALKED UP the stairs slowly, Abraham cradled in her arms.

The way that Dan had come over and kissed him had almost undone her. She was ready to fight with him, to argue with him over his unforgiving point of view.

But Daniel Cooper was a good guy—his most recent action only proved that. There was so much more to this than she could see. Maybe she'd been so wrapped up in her own grief and struggling with her own ability to cope with the situation that she'd totally missed something with Dan.

It just didn't figure for a warm-hearted Everyman hero to have such black-and-white views. To be so blinkered. Maybe it was time for her to crawl out of the sandbox and get back in the playground—to start to consider those around her.

She reached Mrs Van Dyke's door and gave a little knock. 'Mrs Van Dyke? It's Carrie from across the hall. May I come in?'

She heard the faint shout from the other side of the door, once again almost drowned out by the theme tune of *Diagnosis Murder*. She turned the handle and walked in, crossing the room and kneeling next to Mrs Van Dyke's brown leather armchair.

She adjusted Abraham from her shoulder, laying him between her hands so Mrs Van Dyke could have a clear look at him. 'Guess who I brought to visit,' she said quietly.

Mrs Van Dyke reached out for the remote control and silenced the television. 'Well, who do we have here?' she asked, one frail finger reaching out and tracing down the side of Abraham's cheek.

'We call him Abraham. It's been three days now and there's still no sign of his mother.'

'May I?' Mrs Van Dyke held out her thin arms. For a second Carrie hesitated, instant protective waves flooding through her, wondering about the steadiness of Mrs Van Dyke's hands. But she pushed the thoughts from her mind. This woman had held more babies, more little lives in her hands than Carrie probably would in this lifetime. She had a wealth of experience to which Carrie really needed even the tiniest exposure.

She placed Abraham in her shaky hands and watched as Mrs Van Dyke repositioned him on her lap, with her hand gently supporting his head as she leaned over and spoke to him quietly, all the while stroking one cheek with her bent finger.

It was magical. Even though Mrs Van Dyke was obviously feeling the effects of age, from her misshapen joints to her thin frame, a new life and sparkle seemed to come into her eyes when talking to Abraham. It was as if he released a little spark of life into her.

Carrie couldn't hear what she was saying. It was as if she were having an entirely private conversation with him. His little blue eyes had opened and were watching her intensely. Could he even focus yet? Carrie wasn't sure. But the conversation brought a smile to her face.

Abraham was wearing one of the beautiful hand-knitted blue cardigans that Mrs Van Dyke had given her, along with the white crocheted shawl. The recognition made Mrs Van Dyke smile all the more as she fingered the delicate wool. They still had hardly any clothes for him and without Mrs Van Dyke's contribution Abraham would have spent most of the time wrapped in a towel.

Carrie settled onto the antique-style leather sofa. 'Dan asked me to check if you needed anything. He's hoping to give Mr Meltzer a ring and go along to the shop later. Can you give me a list of what you're running short of?'

A smile danced across Mrs Van Dyke's lips. 'He's such a good boy, my Daniel.'

She almost made it sound as if he were one of her own. 'I'm surprised he didn't come up himself.'

Carrie felt her cheeks flush. She wasn't quite sure what to say. 'He's really tired. Abraham kept him awake most of the night. I told him to get some sleep and I would come up and see you.' It almost made them sound like some old married couple. She was hoping that would pass Mrs Van Dyke by.

But the old lady was far too wily for that. The smile remained on her lips and as she regarded Carrie carefully with her pale grey eyes it was almost as if she were sizing up her suitability. 'I could do with some things,' she said slowly.

'No problem. What do you need?'

'Some powdered milk—there won't be any fresh milk left. And some chocolate biscuits and some tins of soup.'

'What kind of soup do you like?'

Mrs Van Dyke smiled as she played with Abraham on her lap. 'Oh, don't worry about that. Daniel knows exactly what to get me.' She eyed Carrie again. 'Sometimes I wonder what I'd do without him.'

The words seemed to drip with loyalty and devotion to Daniel. These two had known each other for most of Daniel's life. How much had they shared?

Carrie pushed the queries out of her head. She was fascinated by how content Abraham looked, how placid he was on Mrs Van Dyke's lap, with her wholehearted attention. 'You're much better at this than me. Maybe you can give me some tips.'

Mrs Van Dyke raised her head. 'Tips? Why would you need tips?'

'Because I'm not very good at this. I think he's feeding too quickly. He gets lots of wind and screams half the night.' She pointed over at his little frame. 'I've no idea what he weighs. So I don't know if we're giving him enough milk or not. This baby stuff is all so confusing.'

Mrs Van Dyke gave her a gentle smile as Abraham wrapped his tiny fingers around her gnarled one. 'I'm sure you're much better at this than you think you are. He's around six pounds,' she said.

'How do you know that?' Carrie asked in wonder.

Mrs Van Dyke smiled. 'I just do. Years of experience. I think he might have been a few weeks early.' She touched his face again. 'But his jaundice will settle in a few days. Have you been putting him next to the window, letting the daylight get to him?'

Carrie nodded. 'Dan has a friend who is a paediatrician at Angel's Hospital. She told us what to do. I just wish we could actually get him there so he could be checked over.'

'He doesn't need to be checked. He's fine. As for the wind—he's a new baby. It will settle.' She slid her hands under his arms and sat him upright. 'It's a big adjustment being out in the big bad world. A few days ago he was in a dark cocoon, being fed and looked after. Now he's got to learn to do it for himself.'

Carrie felt a prickle of unease. 'I wish Dan felt like that.'

Mrs Van Dyke's eyes were on her in a flash. 'Felt like what?' There was the tiniest sharp edge to her voice. A protective element. Just like the way Carrie felt towards Abraham. It heightened Carrie's awareness. Mrs Van Dyke had known Daniel since he was a child. What else did she know?

Carrie gave a sigh. 'Dan doesn't think that Abraham's mother cared about him at all. He doesn't think she looked after him. He thinks she might have been a drug user.'

She could see Mrs Van Dyke's shoulders stiffen and straighten slightly. Maybe she was wrong to use the drug word around someone so elderly.

But Mrs Van Dyke just shook her head. 'No.' Her eyes were focused entirely on Abraham. 'His mother wasn't a drug user.'

Carrie leaned back against the leather sofa. Even though it looked ancient, it was firm and comfortable. Much more comfortable than Dan's modern one. How many people had rested on this sofa over the years, laid their hands on the slightly worn armrests and heard the pearls of wisdom from Mrs Van Dyke?

'Then what happened?' She gave a sigh. 'I just can't get my head around it. I keep thinking of all the reasons in the world that would make you give up your baby, and none of them are good enough. None of them come even close. I keep thinking of alternatives—all reasons a mum could keep her baby. None of them lead to this.'

'Not every woman will have the life that you've had, Carrie.' The words were quiet, almost whispered and spoken with years of experience. The intensity of them brought an unexpected flood of tears to Carrie's eyes.

Her voice wavered. 'You say that as if I've lived a charmed life.'

'Haven't you?'

She shook her head firmly. 'I don't think so. Last year I lost my daughter. I had a stillbirth.' She looked over at Abraham, her voice still wavering. 'I came to New York to get away from babies—to get away from the memories.'

Mrs Van Dyke was silent for a few moments. Maybe Carrie had stunned her with her news, but, in truth, Mrs Van Dyke didn't look as if anyone would have the capability of stunning her.

Her answer was measured. 'It seems as if we've shared the heartache of the loss of a child. At least with Peter, I had a chance to get to know him a little. To get to share a little part of his life. I'm sorry you didn't get that opportunity, Carrie.'

The sincerity in her words was clear. She meant every single one of them. And even though Carrie didn't know her well, it gave her more comfort than she'd had in a long time. Maybe this was all on her. She'd kept so much bottled up inside for so long. She didn't want to share. And now, in New York, the only two people she'd shared with had shown her sincerity and compassion—even though they were virtual strangers.

'You had five children, didn't you?'

Mrs Van Dyke nodded. 'Peter was my youngest. David, Ronald, Anne and Lisbeth all have families of their own now.'

'Are any of them still in New York?'

There was a sadness in Mrs Van Dyke's eyes. 'Sadly, no. David's in Boston. Ronald's in Washington. Lisbeth married a lovely Dutch man and is back in Holland. Anne found herself a cowboy and lives on a ranch in Texas. She spends most of her time trying to persuade me to go and live with her and her family.' Mrs Van Dyke showed some pride in her eyes. 'She has a beautiful home—a beautiful family. But I find Texas far too hot. I visit. Daniel takes me to the airport and I go and stay with Anne for part of the winter. But New York is home to me now. It always will be.' She hesitated for a moment, before looking at Carrie with her pale grey eyes. 'And Peter's here, of course. I would never leave my son.'

It was as if a million tiny caterpillars decided to run over her skin. Tiny light pinpricks all over.

Ruby. Her tiny white remembrance plaque in a cemetery in London. She'd visited it the day she left and wondered if anyone would put flowers there while she was gone. The chances were unlikely. Most people had moved on.

Part of her felt sympathy for Mrs Van Dyke not wanting to leave her beloved son. Should she feel guilty for coming to New York? All she felt was sad. Ruby wasn't there any more. Her talismans were in the box upstairs and in her heart—not on the little white plaque next to hundreds of others.

She was trying to put things into perspective. Her past situation and the current one. Trying to find a reason for Abraham's mother's behaviour.

Mrs Van Dyke's voice cut through her thoughts. 'You have to remember, Carrie. Our children belong to God. We're only given them on loan from heaven. Sometimes God calls them home sooner than we expected.'

The words of the wise. A woman who'd had years to get over the death of her young son, but it was clearly still as raw today as it had been at the time. But here she was, with the help of her faith, rationalising the world around her. Getting some comfort from it.

Carrie moved from the sofa and knelt on the ground next to Mrs Van Dyke's armchair. 'Then why would we waste any of that precious time? Why would we want to miss out on the first feed, the first smile? It's all far too precious, far too fleeting to give it up so easily. I can't believe that Abraham's mother doesn't care. I can't believe she abandoned him without a second thought.'

'It's a sad world, Carrie. But sometimes we have to realise that not everyone has the same moral standing and beliefs that you and I have. Not everyone values babies and children the way that they should.'

It was a complete turnaround. The absolute opposite of what she'd expected Mrs Van Dyke to say. But as she watched the elderly face, she realised Mrs Van Dyke was lost—stuck in a memory someplace. She wasn't talking about the here and now; she was remembering something from long ago.

It sent a horrible, uncomfortable feeling down her spine. She'd seen the awful newscasts about abused and battered children. She'd seen the adverts for foster carers for children whose parents didn't want them any more. The last thing she wanted was for Abraham to end up in any of those categories. It was just unthinkable.

She was staring at him again. Transfixed by his beautiful skin and blinking blue eyes. 'I just can't think of him like that. I just have the oddest feeling—' she put her hand on her heart '—right here, that I'm right about him. I can't explain it, but I just think that Abraham's mother didn't abandon him because she didn't love him. I think it's just the opposite. She abandoned him because she *did* love him.'

Mrs Van Dyke sat back in her chair, cradling Abraham

in her arms. Carrie was almost envious of her years of experience. The strength she had to draw on. It radiated from her. Being around Mrs Van Dyke was like being enveloped in some warm, knowledgeable blanket. She could only hope that one day she would be like that, too.

After a few moments she eventually spoke. 'It seems to me like it's time to ask some hard questions, Carrie.'

The words made her a little uncomfortable. Could Mrs Van Dyke read her thoughts? See all the things that were floating around her brain about Daniel? That would really make her cheeks flush, because some of those thoughts were X-rated.

But surely Mrs Van Dyke had no inkling that anything had happened between them. She hadn't even seen them together. She couldn't possibly know.

'What kind of questions?' she finally asked.

'The kind of questions you're skirting around about. Why exactly would a mother leave a baby on our doorstep? What reasons could she possibly have? And why this doorstep? Why not another?'

Carrie sat back in her chair. All the things that had been circling in her brain for the past few days. Even though they were in the background, she hadn't really focused on them, or given them the attention they deserved. Looking after Abraham, and trying to decipher her emotions towards Daniel, had taken up all her time and energy.

It was time to sit back and take a deep breath. To look at things from a new angle, a new perspective.

'I guess I need to take some time to think about this,' she said quietly.

'I guess you do.'

It was like being in the presence of an all-knowing

seer. A person who knew what was happening but left you to find it out for yourself.

She stood up and walked over to pick up Abraham again. Just holding him close seemed to give her comfort. It was amazing how quickly she was becoming attached to this tiny person.

'I'll get Dan to bring your shopping up later.'

'That's perfect, Carrie.' She gave a little nod of her head. 'You've taken on a big job, and I commend you for it. But Abraham is someone else's baby. It's so easy to love them, and it's so hard to let them go. You need to protect yourself. You need to look after your own heart.'

Carrie placed her hand across Abraham's back. 'I know that. I know that this won't last. As soon as the snow clears, Abraham will go to Angel's to be assessed. Social services already know about him. I'm sure they will already have somewhere for him to go.'

She nodded towards the television. The title for a new episode of *Diagnosis Murder* was just beginning to roll. 'I'll let you get back to your television.' Had she really been up here for an hour? 'Thank you for letting us visit, Mrs Van Dyke.'

'No, thank *you,* Carrie. I hope I'll be seeing you again soon.'

'I hope so, too.'

She headed towards the door. Even before she opened it Abraham twitched in her arms as Mrs Van Dyke reached for the remote control and the sound boomed around the apartment again.

Carrie smiled as she closed the door behind her.

She lifted her head. It was as if her own doorway was beckoning from across the hall. She'd barely been in there for the past few days. Just twice for a shower, a change of clothes or to pick up some baking ingredients.

Last time she'd been in there Dan had kissed her.

After this morning that almost seemed like a lifetime ago.

She propped Abraham up on her shoulder. She knew exactly what she was going to do now. She wanted to leave Dan to sleep a little longer. Hopefully then he would be in the mood to talk.

In the meantime she and Abraham would have some quiet time together. It didn't feel like a betrayal to have him in her arms any more. It just felt right. As if he belonged there.

But most importantly she had someone she wanted him to meet. Someone she wanted to talk to him about.

To let him know that there was room in her heart for everyone.

CHAPTER TEN

THREE HOURS LATER she was back downstairs. Abraham had slept for a few hours while she sat quietly and looked through the things in Ruby's box.

It was the first time she'd ever managed to do it without breaking her heart. She was still sad, a few tears had still slid down her cheeks. But this time it hadn't been so hard to put the things back in the box. It hadn't felt as if her life was over. It hadn't felt as if there was nothing to fight for any more.

And that wasn't just because Abraham was in her arms. It was because she was beginning to feel different.

Daniel appeared in the doorway, his hair rumpled and sticking up in every direction but the right one. 'Hey, how long did I sleep?'

She glanced at her watch. 'We've been gone for four hours. We had to come back down because Abraham needed another bottle.' She hesitated for a second. 'We need some more supplies, and Mrs Van Dyke needs some things. How would you feel about leaving Abraham with her for a little while?'

He nodded and rubbed the sleep out of his eyes. 'I think that sounds like a plan.'

'Are we almost out of nappies already?'

Dan looked over and nodded, staring into the bottom

of the powdered-milk can. 'We're almost out of everything. I definitely need to buy some more coffee. It's the only thing that keeps me awake. I'm usually never this tired.'

Carrie walked over to him, leaving Abraham to kick his legs freely on the towel for a few minutes. 'You're usually never looking after a baby. How do you do on night shifts?'

He gave her a rueful look. 'The busy nights are fine. The quiet nights? I drink about six cups.'

'Will Mr Meltzer have anything left?'

Dan shook his head. 'No. We'll need to go further afield. Do you have rain boots?'

'Wellies? Sure I do.'

'Then get them. Go and get changed and I'll make a few calls to see where we can get some supplies. Are you okay walking a few blocks?'

'Of course. Do you want me to take Abraham up to Mrs Van Dyke?'

He shook his head. 'No, I'll do it. You go and get changed.'

She should have known. Dan wanted to check on Mrs Van Dyke himself. He really was a good guy. So why was he so down on Abraham's mother? It just didn't fit with the rest of his demeanour.

Ten minutes later she was ready. Her pink wool coat, purple scarf and purple woolly hat pulled down over her ears. Her wellies firmly in place with her jeans tucked inside.

The nip of frost was still in the air as they stepped outside. Dan pushed a piece of paper into his pocket and held out his gloved hand towards her.

Carrie hesitated for just a second. There was nothing in this. He was being mannerly and making sure she didn't fall over in the snow. This wasn't about the kiss that they'd shared—not at all.

She put her hand in his. 'How far do we need to go?'

The snow was deeper than she'd expected. Not quite deep enough to reach the tops of her wellies, but not too far off it. 'A few blocks,' he murmured.

It only took a few minutes for her to realise that trudging through the snow was harder work than she first thought. She could feel her cheeks flush and her breathing get harder. This was the most exercise she'd had in days. But there was something almost magical about being the first set of footprints in the clean, bright snow.

They walked for ten minutes before they came across their first snowman. He was built in the middle of the sidewalk at a peculiar angle. The hat had slipped and one of the stones that had been an eye had fallen out.

Dan smiled as she stopped to admire him. 'Oh, no. Here she goes. Snowman envy again.'

'What do you mean?'

'I saw your face when you watched the news report. The shops we're visiting are right next to Washington Square Park. If you really want we could stop and build one.'

She shook her head. 'But I didn't bring a carrot. Every good snowman needs a carrot for a nose.' She smiled. 'Actually, I'd much prefer to do a snow angel. Less work, more fun.'

They walked around the edge of the park towards the shops. There were a number of independent stores with lights on inside. Dan pushed open one of the doors quickly and shouted through to the back. 'Aidan, are you there?'

'Hi, Dan.' The guy appeared quickly from the back of the shop. 'Sorry, the phone keeps going ever since I got

here. Seems the whole world needs supplies right now.'
He nodded to the bags on the counter. 'I think I've got
everything you requested—including the baby supplies.
Anything you want to tell me, buddy?'

He looked from Dan to Carrie, and back again. 'It's
not what you think. We found a baby on our doorstep a
few days ago. Social services can't get through to pick
him up and we need some supplies to take care of him.'

Dan's face was a bit flushed. As if he knew exactly
what Aidan had been thinking. Was he embarrassed?
Was he embarrassed that people might think they were
actually a couple?

'This is my neighbour Carrie. She's giving me a hand
with the baby.'

It seemed so.

Aidan nodded at Carrie and rang up the purchases on
the register. 'Hopefully this will last only another day or
so. Then you'll both be able to stop playing babysitter.'

The phone started ringing again and he headed back
through to the back of the store. Dan had picked up the
bags from the counter but seemed frozen. A bit like Carrie.

Another day or so. Abraham would be gone in a matter of days—maybe hours. What would happen to him
then? Would he just get lost in the New York care system and be handed out to a foster family? The thought
made Carrie feel sick. Before she'd been worried about
Dan being embarrassed by her. Now, she realised she had
much more to worry about.

She was going to have to say goodbye to another baby.

They walked out into the clear day. The snow was
still thick everywhere, but the sky was clear and bright.
Maybe this was the beginning of the end of the bad
weather. Maybe it was time to move forward.

Dan seemed as lost in his thoughts as Carrie. Was he thinking about Abraham, too, or was he thinking about her?

They reached the edge of the park, near the Washington Arch. There were a few figures dotted around the park and a whole host of snowmen. 'Look.' Carrie pointed. 'It's like a whole little family.' She stood next to the father snowman and looked down at the carefully erected snow family. 'Dad, mum, a son and a daughter. How cute.' Her voice had a wistful tone that she couldn't help. Even the snow people had happy families.

Dan lifted his eyebrows at her. 'Snow angels?' he asked.

She wanted him to say so much more. She wanted to know how he was feeling. But Dan just wouldn't reveal that side of himself to her. In a way he was even more closed off to her than Mark had been.

She gave a little nod. 'Snow angels.' This could be the last thing they would do together. She might as well have a little fun.

They found a bit of untouched ground. 'It's perfect,' said Carrie. 'Are you ready?'

She walked as gingerly as she could in her wellies and turned around holding her hands open wide. Dan left the bags on the ground and stood next to her, hands wide, their fingers almost touching. 'You do realise you're about to get soaked, right, Brit girl?'

'It's a question of whether I care or not,' she responded as she leaned backwards, arms wide, letting herself disappear in a puff of powdery snow. She waved her hands through the snow as fast as she could, laughing, as Dan tried to keep up with her. Snow was soaking through her coat quickly, edging in around her neck and up her coat sleeves.

Then she felt it, her fingers brushing his, and she stopped.

She turned her head to face his. All of a sudden it seemed as if they were the only two people in New York. The only two people in this park, in this universe.

Dan moved. His breathing just as quick as hers. The warm air spilling into the cold around him, and then he was on her. His legs on either side of her, his warm breath colliding with her own.

'What are you doing to me, Carrie McKenzie?' His brown eyes were full of confusion and it made her heart squeeze. There it was. For the first time. Daniel Cooper stripped bare.

'What are you doing to me, Daniel Cooper? I thought I was doing fine till I met you.'

She pushed her neck up, catching his cold lips with hers. Wrapping her hands around his neck and pulling him even closer. She didn't mind the cold snow seeping through her coat around her shoulders and hips. She pushed aside the fact that a few minutes ago she'd felt a little hurt when he'd introduced her as his neighbour. She was as confused about all this as he was.

She'd told him everything. She'd told him about Ruby. She'd told him about Mark. But how much did she know about Daniel Cooper? And why did she feel as if she'd only scraped the surface?

In a few days the snow would be cleared, Abraham would be gone and their lives would return to normal. But what was normal any more? What would happen to her and Dan? An occasional hello on the stairs? She couldn't bear that.

He pulled away and stood up, holding out his hands to pull her up from the snow. 'Let's go, Carrie. You'll catch your death out here.'

The moment was past. It was over. Just as they would soon be.

She swallowed the lump in her throat. Now the wet patches were starting to feel uncomfortable. Starting to make her notice the cold air around them.

'I guess it's time to get back,' she said quietly.

'I guess it is.' He picked up the bags and started towards the exit, leaving her feeling as if she'd just imagined their kiss.

Two hours later, dried off and with clean clothes, Carrie finished making coffee for Dan and tea for herself, before adding the fruit scones that she'd made upstairs to a plate. Baby Abraham was in a good mood and feeding happily after being picked up from Mrs Van Dyke's.

Dan grinned at her. 'I wondered what the smell was. Do you know it drifted down the stairs and woke me up earlier? Not that I'm complaining.'

'Butter and raspberry jam. I hope you like them.'

'I'm sure I will.' He held her gaze for a minute and it made her wonder what he was thinking about. Was he regretting having her help with Abraham? Because she wasn't regretting it for a second.

'What did you do when I was sleeping—apart from baking?'

'I went upstairs and visited with Mrs Van Dyke. She's lovely—really lovely. Abraham seemed to like her, too.'

'Everybody likes her. She's just one of those people.'

'Was she good friends with your grandmother?'

Dan nodded. 'They lived in the same apartment block for sixty years and spoke to each other every day. Things were a bit different in those days—they used to borrow from each other all the time. There was hardly a day that went by where my grandmother didn't send me up the stairs to borrow or return something.'

'Did you meet her family?'

Dan adjusted himself in the seat as he fed Abraham. He looked slightly uncomfortable. 'They were all a good bit older than me.'

'The same age as your mother?' She couldn't help it. Both of them were tiptoeing around the issue. She didn't want to ask him about his mother, and he hadn't volunteered any information.

'Yeah, around about the same age.'

Nothing else. It was his prime opportunity to tell her a little more and he hadn't taken it. Should she give up? Maybe some things were best left secret. But it just felt so strange.

She took a deep breath.

'How come you ended up staying with your grandmother? Was your mum sick?'

Dan let out a laugh, causing Abraham to startle in his arms. But it wasn't a happy laugh. It was one filled with anger and resentment. 'Oh, yeah, she was sick all right.'

'What does that mean?'

'It means that some people shouldn't be mothers, Carrie.'

He didn't hesitate with his words and it made the breath catch in her throat.

What did that mean? Was that just aimed at his mother? Or was it aimed at her, too?

Was this why he was so screwed up about Abraham? He thought Abraham's mother wasn't fit to have a child?

'Is your mother still alive, Dan?' It seemed the natural question.

'No.' His words were curt and sharp. 'She died ten years ago. Drug overdose.'

The words were a shock and not what she was expecting to hear. Lots of people she knew had lost their mum or dad to various illnesses, cancer or some tragic accident. But no one had ever had a parent die from a drug overdose. One boy that Carrie had gone to school with had died a few years ago from drugs, but that was the only person she knew.

Chills were flooding over her body. Dan's reactions were acidic, obviously affected by years of bitter experience. What kind of a relationship had he had with his mother? It couldn't have been good.

'I'm sorry, Dan. I'm sorry that your mother died of a drug overdose. That must have been awful for you.'

He stood up as Abraham finished his bottle and propped him up onto his shoulder. 'It wasn't awful at all. I hadn't seen her in years. Nor did I want to.'

Carrie was at a loss. Should she ask more questions or just stay quiet? There was that horrible choice between seeming nosey or seeming uninterested. The last thing she wanted to do was upset Dan—he'd been so good to her. But she also wanted to support him as much as he'd supported her. Surely there was something she could do.

And then she remembered. His touch, and how much it had meant to her.

She walked over and laid her hand on his arm. His eyes went to her hand, just for a second, then lifted to meet her eyes.

She could see the hesitation, the wariness in them. He'd revealed a little part of himself, but there was so much more. She'd shared the most important part of her. It had hurt. It had felt as if she were exposing herself to the world. Taking her heart right out of her body and leaving it for the world to spear.

And what hurt most here was that Dan didn't feel

ready or able to share with her. Had she totally mis-
read the situation? She'd thought they had connected.
She thought that there might even have been a chance of
something more. But if Dan couldn't share with her now,
how on earth could they go any further?

The television flashed in the background. Pictures
of snow being cleared in some areas, with aerial shots
of previously deserted streets now with a few people on
them, or a single car slowly edging its way along. The
snow was finally going to stop. New York was going to
return to a sense of normality.

Maybe it was for the best. Abraham would be able to
go to Angel's Hospital and be checked over by Shana.
That was good, except it made her want to run over and
snatch him out of Dan's arms.

How much longer would she be able to cuddle him?
Would this be their last night together? And what hurt
more, the thought of being separated from Abraham, or
the thought of not having a reason to spend time with
Dan any more?

It was almost as if Abraham sensed her discomfort.
He chose that precise moment to pull his little legs up, let
out a squeal and projectile vomit all over Dan's shoulder.

Her reactions were instant. She held out her arms to
take Abraham from him.

'Yeuch!' Dan pulled his T-shirt over his head, trying
to stop the icky baby sick from soaking through. It was
an almost unconscious act and she tried not to be distracted by his flat abdomen and obvious pecs. If only her
stomach looked like that.

But it didn't—ever. No matter what the TV ads said,
women's abdomens just weren't designed to look like
that, even *before* they'd had a baby.

Stifling a sigh, she pretended to fuss over Abraham

as Daniel walked past on his way to the laundry basket. What about his shoulders? And his back? Was the view from behind just as good?

She tried to take a surreptitious glance and her breath caught in her throat. While Daniel's torso was something a model would be envious of—his back was entirely different.

Scars. Chicken-pox scars all across his back. She winced inwardly, remembering how itchy she'd been as a child when she was covered with the spots. She'd only had a few on her back and they'd driven her insane because she couldn't—probably thankfully—get to them to scratch them.

'This is my favourite T-shirt,' he moaned as he flung it into the laundry basket. 'I bet no matter what I use, I'll never get rid of that smell.'

He looked up and caught sight of her face. She felt her cheeks flush and looked down at Abraham again.

But it was too late. He'd seen the expression that she'd tried to hide. He'd seen the shock. And maybe a little bit of horror.

She wanted to take back the past few seconds. She wanted to stand here with a smile fixed on her face. But it was too late.

Dan made to walk past, heading to his bedroom to get another T-shirt and cover up, the shadows apparent in his eyes. But something made her act. She put Abraham down in the crib and grabbed Dan's arm on the way past.

'What?' he snapped.

'Stop, Dan. Just stop for a second.'

She had no medical background. She had no training whatsoever. But something had registered in her brain. Something inside was screaming at her.

She nervously reached her fingers up and touched his

back. He flinched, obviously annoyed at her touch. His voice was lower. 'What are you doing, Carrie?'

Her fingers were trembling. She was almost scared to touch his flesh. But something was wrong. Something was very wrong.

The scars weren't what she'd expected. She had chicken-pox scars herself. And she and her fellow friends had spent many teenage years debating over how to hide their various scars.

Chicken-pox scars were pitted and uneven. No two looked the same.

But that wasn't the case on Dan's back. All his scars looked the same. Uniformly pitted circles across his back with not a single one on his chest, arms or face. Nothing about this was right.

Her pinkie fitted inside the little uniform scars. They were all the same diameter, all perfect scars, but of differing depth. Almost as if…

'Oh, Dan.' Her hand flew to her mouth and tears sprang to her eyes. She'd seen scars like these before. But only single ones, caused by accident by foolish friends.

These hadn't been caused by accident. These had been inflicted on a little boy. One at a time. Cigarette burns. She couldn't even begin to imagine what kind of a person could do this to a child. What kind of a person could willingly and knowingly inflict this kind of pain on another human being. It was beyond unthinkable.

Everything fell into place. Dan's reactions. His feelings towards his mother. The fact he'd ended up staying with his grandmother.

She reached her hands up around his neck and pulled him towards her. 'Oh, Dan, I'm so sorry. Your mother did this to you, didn't she?'

He was frozen. Frozen to the spot at his secret being exposed.

Even as her hands had wrapped around his neck her fingers had brushed against some of the scars. It was so unfair. So cruel. It made her feel sick to her stomach.

Finally, he answered. 'Yes. Yes, she did.' She could feel the rigid tension disperse from his muscles.

He walked back over and sagged down on the sofa, Carrie at his side. She didn't want to leave him—not for a second. Carrie couldn't stop the tears that were flowing now. Tears for a damaged child. Tears for a ruined childhood.

She shook her head. 'Why? Why would she do something like that? Why would *anyone* behave like that towards a child?'

The words he spoke were detached. 'Not everyone is like you, Carrie. Not everyone is like Mrs Van Dyke or my grandmother.' The words were catching in his throat, raw with emotion. 'My mother should never have had children. I was a mistake. She never wanted me. I ruined her drug habit. As soon as her doctor knew she was pregnant my mother was put on a reducing programme—even all those years ago. She couldn't wait to get her next fix. When she didn't use, she was indifferent to me, when she did use, she was just downright nasty. My grandmother tried time and time again to get her to give me up. Most of the time my mother kept moving around the city, trying to stay out of the way of my grandmother, social services and the drug dealers she owed money to.' He ran his fingers through his hair. 'Drugs aren't a new problem in New York. They're an old one. One that affected me since before I was even born.'

His other hand was sitting on his lap and she intertwined her fingers with his.

Touch. The one thing she knew to do that felt right.

So many things were making sense to her now. So many of the words that he'd spoken, or, more importantly, not spoken. So many of his underlying beliefs and tensions became crystal clear, including his prejudices towards Abraham's mother.

She would probably feel the same herself if she'd been in his shoes. But something still didn't sit right in her stomach about this whole situation.

She squeezed his hand. 'So how did you end up with your grandmother, then?'

'The cops phoned her. Our latest set of neighbours heard the screams once too often.' Carrie flinched. She didn't like any of the pictures her mind was currently conjuring up. 'They were concerned—but didn't want to get involved. Fortunately for me, one of their friends was a cop.'

'And he just picked you up and took you out of there?'

Dan shook his head. It was apparent he didn't like the details. 'It was more complicated than that. Social services were involved, as well as the police—it took a little time to sort out. But from the second I set eyes on the cop in my mother's house I knew I would be safe. There was just something about the guy. He wasn't leaving without me—no matter what happened.'

She gave him a smile. 'I guess he paved your way to the police academy.'

'I guess he did. He even gave me a reference eighteen years later when I needed it.'

'And what did your grandmother say?'

He shook his head. 'Nothing. Nothing at all. My mother's

name was never mentioned again. As far as I know she never had any more contact with my mother. Neither of us did. I can only ever remember a woman from social services coming to the door once. That was it. Nothing else.'

There was silence for a few seconds, as if both of them were lost in their thoughts. 'Thank you,' Carrie whispered.

'For what?' He looked confused.

'For sharing with me.'

'But I didn't. Not exactly.'

'It doesn't matter. Now I understand why you're so concerned about Abraham.'

They both turned towards the crib. 'I can't allow him to have a life like that, Carrie. If his mother didn't want him, then maybe this is the best thing for him. To go to loving parents who do want him. There are thousands of people out there who can't have kids of their own, just waiting for a baby like Abraham.'

Carrie hesitated. She didn't want to upset him. What he said made sense, but it still just didn't ring true with her.

'I get that, Daniel. I do. But I still think there's something else—something that we're both missing here.'

'Like what?'

She stood up and walked over to the window. The newscaster had been right. She could see the difference in the snow outside. It wasn't quite so deep. It wasn't quite so white. No freshly lain snow was replacing its supplies and what was there was beginning to disintegrate, to turn to the grey slush that had been on the streets before.

This time tomorrow Abraham would be gone. Gone forever. And the thought made her heart break.

She turned to face him again, her arms folded across

her chest. 'Why here, Dan? Why this house? There are plenty of nice houses on this street. What made Abraham's mother leave him *here?*' She pointed downwards, emphasising her words.

Daniel lifted his hands. 'What do you mean, Carrie? We've been through this. The lights were on. This place was a safe bet. Even if the mother didn't ring the bell.'

'That's it.' She was across the room in a flash, a little light going on in her brain. 'A safe bet. Don't you get it?' She grabbed hold of his arms.

'Get what?'

Her frustration was mounting. 'Dan, I knew you were a cop—even though you'd never spoken to me. I saw you every day in your uniform. Walking along this street and into our apartment building.'

'So?' A wrinkle appeared on his brow.

'So!' Her face was inches from his. The compassion in her eyes more prominent than anything he'd ever seen. 'What's a safer bet than a cop? If you had to leave a baby at anyone's door, who would you choose, Dan? Who would you choose?'

A horrible feeling of realisation started to wash over his skin. A horrible feeling that he'd missed something really important.

'You think the baby was left here because someone knew I was a cop?'

'I *know* he was. Think about it, Dan. It makes perfect sense. If I wanted to keep my baby safe—and couldn't tell anyone about it—where safer than at a cop's door.'

'But who? Who would do something like that?'

Their eyes met. It was as if a mutual thought had just appeared in their heads. One that left a sinking feeling in his stomach. But Carrie wasn't about to stand back and leave things unsaid. Leave possibilities unchallenged.

She looked at Abraham again and tried to keep the tremble from her voice. 'Dan, is there any chance—any possibility at all—that Abraham could be your baby?'

'What? No! Of course not.' There was pain in her eyes. Hurt there for him to see. It didn't matter to her how painful the suggestion was, Abraham came first. She was thinking only of him.

It was there, in that split second, that he knew. Carrie McKenzie was the girl for him. He loved her, with his whole heart. The past few days had let deep emotions build, heartbreaking secrets revealed by both of them.

But as he looked at her flushed face, her blue eyes trying to mask the pain she didn't want him to see, her teeth biting her plump bottom lip as she tried to digest his answer, he absolutely knew. This was a woman who was prepared to push her feelings aside for a child she had no responsibility for, no connection with. If he pulled her to the side right now and told her there was a strong likelihood that Abraham was his—even though that wasn't a possibility—he knew she would just nod quietly and say nothing. All for the sake of the child.

The one thing he'd never been able to do—connect with a woman—he'd found here, in his own home and right on his doorstep. His fractured relationship with his mother had made him erect barriers even he couldn't see. But here, and now, with Carrie McKenzie, they were gone. She wasn't shying away from him because he'd been an abused child. She was only trying to understand him better.

'Are you sure?' She was struggling with the words,

trying to be steady and rational even though he knew inside she wasn't.

It only took a step to reach her and touch her cheek—no, cradle her cheek in his hand. 'I promise you, Carrie. There's no chance that Abraham is mine. That's not why he's been left here.'

There were tears brimming in her eyes. Tears of relief? She let the air out of her lungs with a little whoosh. Her bottom lip was trembling and he ached to kiss her. But it wasn't the time. They were on the precipice of something here. The precipice of something for them and something for Abraham. And they both had too much duty and responsibility to know what came first.

He didn't ever want to do that to her again. He didn't ever want to do anything to cause Carrie McKenzie even a second of hurt, a second of pain. Once was enough. She was far too precious to him for that.

She looked at him with her big blue eyes, words hovering on her lips, before she broke eye contact and looked down at the floor. Anything they had to say to each other would have to wait, if just for a few hours. She lifted her head again. 'Then it must be someone else, Dan. Someone that knows you're a cop and trusts you.'

He tried to rack his brain. 'I just can't think, Carrie. Most of my friends don't stay around here. And none of them are pregnant.' He glanced towards the window again. 'And the snow might be beginning to clear now, but it was thick on Monday night. It could only have been someone around here, someone local....' His voice tailed off and he pressed his hand against the window.

'What if it isn't a friend, Dan? What if it's a neighbour? Or someone you've come into contact with because of your job? Is there anyone around here you've been called out to see?'

'I usually work in the middle of the city. I've only ever covered a few shifts down here. It doesn't do any good covering your own patch.'

'Who did you get called out to see when you visited? Anyone that sticks in your mind?'

He felt the blood rush from his head right down to his toes. He could be sick, right now, all over the floor.

He made a mad dash for the phone, pressing the numbers furiously. 'It's Daniel Cooper. I need to speak to the captain. Now!'

'Dan, what is it? What have you remembered?'

He shook his head. He didn't have time for small talk. All he could do was pray that some of the roads had cleared and help would be available if needed.'

'Captain, it's Dan. This baby? Yes, he's fine. But I think I know who put him here. Look up Mary and Frank Shankland.... Yes, that's them. A list of domestics as long as your arm. Last time I was there, she was pregnant, he was mad and he'd beat her so badly she lost the baby. Told her if she ever got pregnant again, he'd do the same.'

Carrie's hand flew to her mouth. 'Oh, no! That's awful.'

Dan lifted his hand to silence her as he listened to the other end of the phone. 'That's why she was unprepared. She couldn't buy anything for this baby or else he might notice. She must have hidden her pregnancy from him. How are the roads? Can you send a unit? I'm going there. Now.'

He slammed down the phone and headed straight for the door. 'Wait, Dan, you can't go there alone. Look at your hand—you're already injured. How will you be able to protect her with a broken wrist?'

He spun around, his eyes furious. 'I can't, no, I *won't* wait another second, Carrie. Why didn't I think of this? After what he did to Mary the last time, we'll be lucky if she's still alive.' He pointed over to the crib. 'Take care of Abraham. Take care of Abraham for his mother. And just pray I get there in time.'

And in an instant he was gone.

CHAPTER ELEVEN

IT WAS THE longest two hours of Carrie's life. Every time she heard a siren her heart was in her mouth. Every time she heard the start-up of a car engine she would run to the window to peer outside.

Abraham was perfect. He fed and winded like a little dream. It was as if he knew how stressed and on edge she was. The noise of the snow plough coming down the street nearly tipped her over the edge. Most of the snow was starting to melt and it merely ploughed the dirty slush ahead of it.

Finally, there was a flashing blue light and the sound of a door slamming. She ran and opened Dan's apartment door.

There was a scuff mark on his cheek, as if he'd hit a wall. And his clothes, although still intact, were definitely rumpled. As if someone had clutched them in a tight grip.

Behind him, a uniformed officer was lurking, obviously waiting to hear their interaction. She couldn't stop herself. With Abraham in one arm, her other was wrapped around Dan's neck in an instant. 'Are you okay? Are you hurt? What about Abraham's mother? Please tell me that she's okay?'

Dan turned and nodded to the other cop. 'Give me five minutes, Ben. I'll be right out.' It was then Carrie noticed the baby car seat in Ben's hands. He nodded at Dan, and left it sitting next to the door.

Dan closed the door and leaned against it for a few seconds, catching his breath, before finally leaning over and dropping a kiss first on Abraham's head and then on Carrie's.

He walked over to the sofa and put his head in his hands.

Her heart was breaking for him. It was obvious he was blaming himself for this. Even though it had been entirely out of his control.

She sat next to him, the length of her thigh in contact with his. Even the slightest touch gave her a little comfort. But she couldn't find the patience to wait. Two hours had been long enough. She had to know. She had to know Abraham still had a mother.

'What happened, Dan? Does Abraham belong to Mary Shankland?'

He nodded and lifted his head from his hands. His eyes were heavy with fatigue and strain. 'It was just as I suspected. She hid the pregnancy and gave birth in secret. She knew she would have to hide him from Frank, and thought she would have made it to a women's shelter or a hospital. But everything conspired against her.' He held up his hands. 'The weather. The snow. Then Abraham came four weeks early. She was desperate. She didn't know what to do. Frank was at the pub and was due home any minute. She didn't have time to pack up the kids and leave, and they didn't have anywhere to go.' He shook his head in frustration. 'She couldn't even get through to emergency services.'

'So she left the baby here, with you?' Carrie wrinkled her nose. 'Why didn't she ring the bell? Why didn't she ask for your help?'

He thumped his hand on the table. 'She did, Carrie! She did ring the bell. My darn music was on too loud. I never heard it. Frank was due back any minute and she'd left the children by themselves. She had to get back home before he knew anything was wrong.' He turned to face her, his eyes full of sorrow. 'If you hadn't been upstairs and heard Abraham...' He was shaking his head, obviously imagining the worst.

She clutched at his hand. 'But I did, Dan. And Abraham's safe.' She took a little moment to look at the sleeping baby on her lap. Perfect. Perfect in every way. And more importantly, safe. Something squeezed at her heart. Every baby like Abraham and every child like Dan had the right to be safe. Had the right to be cared for and loved. Had the right to be treated with respect. If only everyone in this world felt the same.

'How are Mary and the other kids?'

Dan nodded slowly, letting a long stream of air out through his pursed lips. 'She's safe now. We arrived just as Frank was kicking off. It looks as if his temper has got worse and worse over the past few days with the family being snowed in together. Mary was crouched in a corner sheltering her youngest son.' The words sent a horrible shiver down her spine.

'Oh, those poor children.'

He nodded. 'Frank's been arrested. Mary is being checked over at Grace Jordan Hospital.' He reached over and touched Abraham's tiny fingers. 'I almost couldn't persuade her to go. She wanted to come straight here and check on Abraham. It was awful, Carrie. The tears of pure relief when she saw me and knew that I was there to help. It was a look I recognised.' He shook his head again. 'I should have got there sooner. I should have known.'

'But you didn't know, Dan. *We* didn't know.'

'But you didn't let your past history cloud your judgement—stop you from looking at other possibilities.'

'Of course I did, Dan! How many times did I tell you I couldn't do this? I couldn't look after Abraham? I couldn't help you?'

But Dan was still fixated on his own failings. 'I shouldn't even be doing this job. How can I be a good cop when I can't even think straight?'

'Stop it. Stop it right now. You're the finest cop I've ever met, Dan Cooper. You have the biggest, kindest heart in the world. You can't help what happened to you in the past. And even though you had a crummy mother with a terrible addiction, even though you experienced things a child should never experience, it's shaped you, Dan. It's made you become the fine man that you are.' She reached over and touched his cheek. 'You feel passionately about things. You have a clear sense of right and wrong. You have the courage of your convictions. You looked at the example of the cop who looked out for you and used him as your role model. Him, Dan—not your mother. He would be proud of you. I know he would. Just like your grandmother would be.' She could feel her eyes pooling with tears. 'I couldn't have got through the past few days without you.' She looked at Abraham in her lap. 'No, *we* couldn't have got through the past few days without you.'

The tension seemed to dispel from his muscles, the frustration to abate from his eyes. He reached over and cupped her cheek, brushing her curls behind her ears. 'Carrie, you know what I need to do now, don't you? I need to take Abraham to Angel's. Shana is waiting to see him. And I need to reunite him with his mother.'

Carrie could feel the pooled tears start to spill down her cheeks. Of course. This was what she'd always wanted to happen. For Abraham to be safe, to be returned to his mother. So why did it feel as if her heart were breaking?

These past few days had been hard. But they'd also been wonderful. She finally felt healed. She finally felt as if she could start to live again.

And she'd found someone she wanted to do that with.

But their cosy little bubble was about to burst. The snow was melting. Things would get back to normal. New York would get back to normal.

Dan would get back to normal. There would be no reason for them to be stuck in his apartment together. There would no reason for her to be in his life at all.

She tried to concentrate. She tried to focus. Last thing she wanted to do was appear like a blubbing wreck.

Abraham's eyes flickered open and she leaned over him. 'Well, Abraham, it's time to say goodbye. Or maybe I should call you Baby Shankland now?' She raised her eyebrows at Dan and he shook his head and gave her a sad little smile.

'Mary loved the name. He's definitely going to stay an Abraham.'

A tiny bit of the pressure in her chest felt relieved. He wouldn't have another name. He'd have the name that they'd given him—together. At least that little part of their time together would live on, even if nothing else did.

She ran her finger lightly over his face, touching his forehead, his eyelids, his nose, his cheeks and his mouth. Trying to savour every second, trying to imprint on her brain everything about him. Something caught her eye. His little soft fontanelle, it was pulsing. She could see the proof of his heartbeat right before her eyes. She hadn't noticed it before and it gave her even more comfort than she could have imagined.

She tried not to let her voice shake. 'I'm going to wish

you a long, happy and healthy life, Abraham. I'm going to tell you that you're blessed. You're blessed to have a mother who did her best to protect you. And every time I see snow I'm going to think of you and remember you here—' she pressed her hand to her chest '—in my heart. Now and always.'

She wrapped him a little tighter in Mrs Van Dyke's crocheted shawl. She was sure Mrs Van Dyke wouldn't mind it going to a good home. She couldn't even lift her head to look at Dan right now. She already knew he was holding out his hands, waiting for Abraham, to take him away.

She must have paused. She must have waited just a little too long. Because his hand touched her arm. 'Carrie.' It wasn't a question. It was a prompt, in the quietest, subtlest way.

She put one final kiss on Abraham's forehead and held him out with shaky hands. It took all her self-control not to snatch him back from Dan's grasp.

She felt his hand on her shoulder. A tight squeeze. Followed by his voice murmuring in her ear. 'I don't know how long I'll be, Carrie. I could be all night. I need to stay with Abraham at the hospital, then fill out a mountain of paperwork downtown.'

She was nodding automatically at his words. Not really taking any of them in.

Her heart was thudding in her chest. Was this it? Was this it for them, too?

Dan hadn't said anything. She had no idea what would happen next.

All she knew was she wanted him to stay. She wanted him to stay with her. She wanted him to wrap his arms around her and tell her that everything would be okay. She wanted him to reach out and tuck her hair behind her ears. She wanted him to look at her the way he had the night before, right before he'd kissed her. She wanted to feel her heartbeat quicken and flutter in her chest as it did when they were together.

Anything other than this horrible leaden feeling that was there right now.

He released his fingers on her shoulder and she heard his footsteps heading for the door.

No words. He hadn't said anything to her. He hadn't told her to stay. He hadn't told her to go.

She heard the final hesitant steps and then the click of the door behind her.

It sounded so final. It sounded like the end of everything.

And it probably was.

And then the sobs that had been stifled in her chest finally erupted.

CHAPTER TWELVE

DAN'S WHOLE BODY wanted to go into shutdown mode. But his brain was buzzing. It had been twenty-four hours since he'd slept.

The check-over at the hospital for Mary Shankland had taken much longer than expected. She had three broken ribs and a minor head injury. It had taken hours before she was cleared for transfer and Dan didn't want anyone else to have the job of reuniting her with her son.

He wouldn't have missed it for the world.

Abraham was fine and healthy. He'd even managed to squirt a little pee all over Shana, much to Dan's amusement, as she'd examined him.

But the real heart-stopping moment had been when Mary finally got to hold her baby in her arms. She sobbed and sobbed, telling him how much she loved him and how she just wanted to protect him. The hospital social worker had been standing by to help find the family alternative accommodation and to assess them. And even though Frank had been taken to jail, a temporary restraining order had been put into place to protect the family in the meantime. All of which added to the mountain of paperwork toppling over on his desk.

His captain had been as understanding as could be. But there were still professional requirements that Dan had to fulfil. Pages and pages of paperwork that had to be completed before he could leave the station and get back home to Carrie.

Back home to where he wanted to be.

Back home to the one he wanted to be with.

Things had been too hard. Taking Abraham away from Carrie had been hard, and he'd tried his best not to make it any more difficult than it already was.

There was so much to say. So much to do. He didn't have a single doubt in his head about Carrie McKenzie. But would she have any doubts about him? There was only one way to find out.

He'd made three pit stops on his way home, his stomach churning the whole way. Thankfully the New York florist he'd visited hadn't even flinched when he'd asked her for 'rose-coloured' roses. There might have been a slight glimmer of a smile while she'd walked to her back storeroom and reappeared with beautiful, rich pink-coloured roses with the tiniest hint of red, and tied them with a matching satin ribbon.

Perfect. Just like the roses his grandmother used to fill the apartment with. It was time to do that all over again.

He walked up the stairs to his apartment building with trepidation in his heart. As he pushed open the door to his apartment he already knew she wasn't there. He could feel it. Just her presence in a room made it light up.

His feet were on the stairs in an instant, thudding upstairs and knocking on the door of her apartment. The snow had started to clear, but most people hadn't returned to work yet; the subway still wasn't completely open.

Please don't be at work. Please don't be at work.

'Carrie? Are you there? It's Dan. I need to speak to you.' He waited a few seconds, then dropped to his knees and tried to peer through the keyhole.

The door behind him creaked open. Mrs Van Dyke's thin frame and loose cardigans filled the doorway. 'I think the person you're looking for is in here,' she whispered.

'She is? What's she doing?'

Mrs Van Dyke shrugged. 'It appears I need some help with tidying up. She's in my spare room.'

He hurried inside, knowing exactly where to go. That was just like Carrie. Now that she knew about Mrs Van Dyke's hoarding she would be doing her best to try and help. He walked over to the room, hearing the muffled noises of falling cardboard boxes inside.

'Yikes!'

His heartbeat accelerated as he elbowed his way into the room, past the teetering piles and fallen boxes, finally reaching Carrie in a heap on the floor. He grasped her hand and pulled her upwards, straight into his arms.

'Dan!' She looked dazed, and it took him a few moments to steady her. Then the arms that had rested on his shoulders fell back to her sides.

'What do you want, Dan?' She sounded sad, tired even.

'I wanted to see you.'

'Why? Why did you want to see me, Dan?'

He reached up and touched her cheek. 'I wanted to speak to you. I wanted to make sure you were okay.'

Her hand reached up and covered his. 'I'm fine, Daniel. I'm just glad that Abraham is back with his mother.'

His gut was twisting. She was still hurting, still in pain because of the whole situation he'd allowed her to become involved in.

'Abraham is fine. Mary Shankland is fine—well, not really, but she will be. But what I'm most interested in is you, Carrie. Are you fine?'

Her eyelids widened, as if she was surprised at his words.

He pulled her a little closer. 'I've been thinking about you all night and all day. I couldn't get away—I had a mountain of paperwork to fill out. I'm so sorry I had to leave you, Carrie. I know how hard it was. But I had to take Abraham back to his mother. I had to make sure they were both okay. Even though the person I wanted to be with was you.'

'It was?' Her lips were trembling. Her whole body was trembling.

'Of course it was, Carrie.'

'But you didn't say anything. You didn't ask me to stay.' She was shaking her head as if she was trying to make sense of things.

'I couldn't, Carrie. I didn't want to start a conversation with you that I couldn't finish. Not when I had things to sort out. I wanted us to have time. Time to talk. Time to see what you wanted.' He brushed her hair behind her ear and whispered, 'What do you want, Carrie? What do you want to happen now?'

She was hesitating. As if she was scared to say the words out loud. He was praying inside it was because she was nervous and not because she wanted to let him down gently.

He lifted up the hand-tied bouquet and handed it to her. 'My grandmother's favourite roses. I bought you some, to say thank you for helping me these past few days.'

'Oh.' The little spark that had lit up her eyes disappeared. He wasn't doing this right. He wasn't saying the right things. None of this was working out how he'd planned.

'They're beautiful. Thank you.' She was disappointed. She'd been hoping for something more. And so had he.

He moved forward, pulling her close, and whispered in her ear, 'Look closely, Carrie.'

She held up the bouquet to her nose and took a deep breath, savouring the smell of the roses. 'Where did you get them in the middle of this snow, Dan? They must have cost a fortune.' She still hadn't noticed. She still hadn't seen what he'd done.

He held up the bag he had in his other hand and pulled out a bundle—also tied with pink ribbon. She looked surprised and took the bundle from his hands. It was DVDs. *The Great Escape, Dirty Dancing, Finding Nemo, Toy Story* and a whole host of musicals. A little smile appeared on her face. 'What did you get these for, Dan?'

He gulped. He was going to have to spell it out. 'I figured if we were staying in a lot, we might need to expand our DVD collection. I thought we'd start with some favourites for us both.'

Her eyes finally caught sight of it. The key hanging from the pink ribbon on the bouquet. 'What's this for?'

'It's for you.'

'For me?' Her smile was starting to broaden and the sparkle to appear in her eyes again.

He caught a whiff of her scent. Freesias. More subtle than the roses. Sweeter. Something he could happily smell for the rest of his life. Who needed candles?

He pressed his hands firmly on her hips, pulling her closer to him. 'What's the point of having two apartments when we could easily have one?'

She wound her hands around his neck. 'One?'

He nodded and smiled. 'One.'

'What about the getting-to-know-you dates?'

'What about them?'

'Aren't we missing some stuff out here?'

'Honey, if you want to do some getting-to-know-you, then I'm your man.'

He bent to kiss her.

'You know, Dan, I think you could be right.'

'Carrie McKenzie, you're killing me. Will you look inside the roses, please?'

She wrinkled her nose and caught the glint of a diamond nestled inside one of the roses.

He sighed. 'Finally!'

He got down on one knee. 'Carrie McKenzie, I've never connected with anyone the way I've connected with you. I don't care where we stay, whether it's here or in London. All I know is I want us to be together. Carrie McKenzie, will you be my wife?'

He slid the ring onto her finger. She smiled. 'Aren't you supposed to wait for an answer?' She held up the ring, watching the perfect diamond glint in the sun.

He whispered in her ear, 'I'm not going to risk it. I'm hoping it's a yes.'

'Oh, it's definitely a yes,' she whispered as she wrapped her hands around his neck and started kissing him.

* * * * *

HER NEW YORK
BILLIONAIRE

ANDREA BOLTER

For Alex

CHAPTER ONE

"WHY IS YOUR face blue?"

Holly froze in shock. She had just opened the door to the apartment she'd expected to find empty. But instead of flicking on the lights in a vacant living room she'd walked in on lamps already blazing. And a shirtless man sitting in the center of the sofa. Reading a newspaper. A gorgeous brown-haired shirtless man was reading a newspaper.

"Why is your face blue?" he repeated. Broad shoulders peeked out over the newspaper he was holding.

Why is your face blue? Holly heard the individual words but couldn't put them together to understand them as a question. She could hardly get over the fact that there was a man in the apartment, let alone make sense of the sounds coming from his mouth.

She checked the keys in her hand. Perhaps she was somehow in the wrong place.

And then she saw.

Her hands were blue. Cobalt Blue Two Eleven, to be exact. She'd know that color anywhere. It was one of her favorites.

It suddenly made sense. Just a few minutes ago she'd ducked out of the rain and under the front awning of the building to rifle through her duffel bag for the piece of paper that confirmed the address. The duffel held paint tubes and brushes, paperwork, clothes and heaven knew what else. The cap must have come off her Cobalt Two Eleven.

And she must have touched her face with paint-covered hands.

"What are you doing here?" Holly asked the shirtless man.

"This apartment belongs to my company."

He lowered his newspaper, folded it matter-of-factly and laid it beside him. Giving Holly a full view of his long, lean torso that led down to the plaid pajama bottoms covering the lower half of his body.

"What is it that *you* are doing here?"

The lump that had balled in Holly's throat delayed her response. She hadn't seen a half-naked man in a very long time. And she hadn't seen a man who looked like he did while he was busy being half-naked in...well, possibly ever.

"I'm staying here," she answered.

It had been a grueling journey, and the last thing she'd expected was to have to reckon with someone once she got here.

She blinked her eyes hard to pull herself together and tried not to panic. "I was told I could use this apartment."

"That must have been a mistake."

Mistake? What was this man talking about?

"I've just arrived from Florida. My brother, Vince, works in the Miami office of Benton Worldwide Properties. This is one of the apartments they keep for visitors to New York."

"That is correct."

"Vince arranged for me to stay here. He confirmed it last week. And he called again yesterday to Benton Boston headquarters."

"I am Ethan Benton, Vice President of Benton Worldwide. As you can see from my…" he gestured down his chest "…state of undress, *I* am staying here at the moment."

"Okay, well, I'm Holly Motta and I was counting on using this apartment. See?" She shook the blue-painted keys. "The Boston office left the keys in my name with the doorman downstairs."

"I apologize for the mistake. I have just arrived tonight myself. In the morning I will look into who is responsible for this egregious error and have their head lopped off."

The left corner of his mouth hitched up a bit.

Ethan Benton and his bare chest sat on a black leather sofa. Matching armchairs faced opposite, separated by a modern glass coffee table. The furnishings were spare. Two large framed photos were the only adornments on the wall. Both black and white, one was of a potted orchid and the other a maple tree.

Bland as a plain piece of toast. A typical corporate apartment, Holly guessed, having never been in one before. Elegant, yet all business. With no personal touches.

It was hardly the type of place where a beautiful shirtless man should be reading a newspaper. Not at all the kind of place where one brown curl of hair would fall in front of that man's forehead as if it were no big deal. As if that wasn't the most charming thing that a wet and exhausted young woman from Fort Pierce, Florida could imagine.

"Again, so sorry for the miscommunication," said the man that curl belonged to, "but you are going to have to leave. I will have the doorman hail you a taxi."

"Not so fast."

Holly snapped out of her fascination with his hair. She stomped over to one of the chairs opposite the sofa. Keeping her blue hands in the air, so as not to get paint anywhere, she lowered herself down.

"If your corporate office didn't have you scheduled to stay here, maybe it's *you* who should leave."

The corner of his mouth ticked up again—which was either cute or annoying. Holly wasn't sure yet.

"Obviously I am not going to leave my company's apartment."

Holly couldn't believe this was happening. This morning she had taken a bus from Fort Pierce to West Palm Beach airport. Then her flight to Newark, New Jersey had been delayed. When it had finally landed she'd taken another bus to the Port Authority terminal in Manhattan. It had been raining and dark by then, and there had hardly been a taxi to be had. She'd got drenched flagging one down. The cab brought her to this address on the Upper East Side.

And now—same as always, just when she was trying to do something for herself—someone else's need was somehow one-upping hers.

"What am I supposed to do?"

"I would suggest you go to a hotel."

Hotels in New York were expensive. Holly had been saving money for months to make a go of it when she got here. She couldn't use up any of her funds on a hotel stay.

"I can't afford it."

Ethan fixed a strangely searching stare on her.

While he assessed her Holly's eyes followed his long fingers as they casually traced the taut muscles of his chest down and then back up again. Down. And up. Down. And up.

After seemingly giving it some thought, he reasoned, "You must know people in New York that you can stay with?"

"No. I don't know anyone here. I came here to…"

Holly stopped herself. This man was a total stranger. She shouldn't be telling him anything about her life. He didn't need to know about her ex-husband, Ricky the Rat, her crazy mom, or any of it.

Maybe all that chaos was behind her now. Maybe the whole world was at her feet. Or maybe there were more hard times ahead.

Holly didn't know. But she was going to find out.

Hard rain continued to pelt against the window.

An unwelcome tear dropped its way out of her eye. When she instinctively reached up to brush it away before Ethan noticed she found Cobalt Two Eleven was smeared on the back of her hand as well.

"Are you *crying*?" Ethan asked, as if he were observing a revolutionary scientific function.

"I'm not crying," Holly denied. "It's been a long day."

"Perhaps you would like use the bathroom to wash up," Ethan offered. He pointed behind him. "It is the door on the right."

"Thank you." Holly hoisted herself up without touching anything, and made her way past Ethan and his curl of hair. "By the way—I'm not leaving."

Behind the sofa was a small dining table made of glass and steel like the coffee table. Four orange leather dining chairs provided a much-needed pop of color. Beyond that was a teeny kitchen.

Her brother had told her it was a very compact one-bedroom apartment. It would do quite fine. This was to be a temporary stepping stone for Holly. Either she was in New York to stay or it was merely a transition to somewhere else. Only time would tell.

She found her way into the marble-appointed bathroom and tapped the door closed with her boot. Made a mental commitment to also slam the door shut on her intense immediate attraction to Ethan Benton…astoundingly handsome, half-naked. Although it took her a stubborn minute to stop wondering what it might be like to lay her cheek against the firmness of one of those brawny shoulders.

Oh, no! She caught her reflection in the mirror above

the sink. It was so much worse than she could have envisioned. She had Cobalt Two Eleven streaked across her face in horizontal stripes. Like a tribal warrior. Her black bangs were plastered to her forehead in sweaty points. She was a scary mess. What must this man think of her?

Not wanting to get anything dirty, she used her elbow to start the faucet. With both hands under the running water, she saw color begin swirling down the drain. She rubbed her hands together until enough paint was removed that she could adjust the tap to make the water hotter and pick up the pristine bar of white soap.

Eventually her hands were scoured clean—save for a little residual blue around the cuticles and under the nails. As usual. She reached for the fluffy towel hanging on the rack.

Next, Holly wanted to get her jacket off before she tackled washing her face. She unzipped the sleek and stylish black leather jacket she had bought at the shopping mall in Fort Pierce yesterday. With Florida's mild climate, there hadn't been a lot of selection, but she'd needed something warm for New York. When she'd seen it, she'd known it was the one for her.

Ricky the Rat would have hated it. He'd have said it was highfalutin'. Yeah, well, falute *this*! Decisions were going to be made *by* her, *for* her from now on. Not based on what other people wanted or thought.

After her face was scrubbed she towel-dried her bangs and peeled off her ponytail band. Fluffed out the dark hair that had grown far past her shoulders. With the longer hair, she realized she already had a new look. New hair. New jacket. New city. She was ready for a new life.

Giving a yank on her tee shirt and a tug on her jeans, she was more than a little concerned about how she'd look to Ethan when she went back into the living room. Which was, of course, completely ridiculous because she didn't even know him.

* * *

My, my, but Holly Motta cleaned up well. Distracted by the blue paint on her face, Ethan hadn't noticed the other blue. The crystal color of her eyes. How they played against her lush jet-black hair.

As soon as she returned from the bathroom a rush of energy swept through the living room. He didn't know what kind of magic she held, but it wasn't like anything he had been in the same space with before.

All he could mutter was, "Better?"

It wasn't really a question.

He was glad he had nabbed a tee shirt from the bedroom, although he was still barefoot.

"Yes, thanks." She slid past him to her luggage, still at the front door.

He reached for his computer tablet and tapped the screen. Best to get Holly out of the apartment right now. For starters, he had no idea who she was. Ethan knew firsthand that there were all sorts of liars and scammers in this world, no matter how innocent they might look. He had his family's company to protect. The company that he was to run.

As soon as he could get his aunt Louise to retire.

As if a heart attack hadn't been enough, his beloved aunt was now losing her balance and mobility due to a rare neurological disorder that caused lack of feeling in her feet. Benton Worldwide's annual shareholders' gala was this Saturday. Ethan hoped Aunt Louise didn't have any bruises on her face from the fall he'd heard she'd taken last week.

Ethan owed everything to Aunt Louise and to Uncle Melvin, who had passed away five years ago. Without them he would just have been an abandoned child with no one to guide him toward a future.

His aunt had only one final request before she retired from the company that she, Uncle Mel and Ethan's late father had spent fifty years growing into an empire. She wanted to be sure that Ethan was settled in all areas of his life. Then she'd feel that everything was in its right place before she stepped down and let him take over. One last component to the family plan.

Ethan had lied to his aunt by claiming that he'd found what she wanted him to have. But he hadn't. So he had a lot to take care of in the next few days.

His temples pulsed as he thought about it all. Commotion was not an option. This exhilarating woman who had blown into the apartment needed to leave immediately. Not to mention the fact that there was something far too alluring about her that he had to get away from. Fast.

On top of it all he had a conference call in a few minutes that he still had to prepare for.

But with a few swipes across the tablet's screen he confirmed that all the Benton properties in New York were occupied.

Holly slung her jacket on the coat rack by the door and sat down on the floor. After pulling off one, then the other, she tossed her boots to the side. Ethan was mesmerized by her arms as they rummaged through her bag. She seemed to be made up only of elongated loose limbs that bent freely in every direction. Lanky. Gangly, even.

Downright adorable.

Nothing about Holly was at all like the rigid, hoity-toity blondes he usually kept company with. Women who were all wrong for him. Since he wasn't looking for someone right, that didn't matter. It kept his aunt happy to see him dating. But, of course, now he had told Aunt Louise that was all coming to an end. And he had a plan as to how to cover that lie.

Under her boots, Holly was wearing one red sock and one striped. She rolled those off and wiggled her toes. "That feels good..." She sighed, as if to herself.

Ethan's mouth quirked. "Miss Motta, please do not make yourself at home."

"I have nowhere else to go."

Holly death-stared him right in the face, putting on her best tough guy act. In reality she looked terrified that he was going to throw her out. She'd already been in tears before she washed up.

"Can't *you* be the one to leave?"

His stern expression melted a bit. What was he going to do? Toss her out into the cold rain?

She said she didn't know anyone in New York that she could stay with. Funny, but he didn't either. There were dozens—hundreds—of colleagues and workers in the city, connected with various Benton projects. Yet no one he'd call late on a rainy night to see if they had a sofa or guest room he could use.

Ridiculous. He'd sooner go back to the airport and sleep on his private jet.

He could pay for Holly's hotel room. Or he supposed he himself could go to a hotel. But—good heavens. He'd been in flight all day, had already unpacked and undressed here. Why on earth should he leave his own property?

"I do not suppose it will do for either of us to try to find other accommodation at this late hour."

"What's your plan, then?"

Ethan always had a plan. His life was structured around plans. He was about to embark on his biggest yet—moving Aunt Louise into retirement and taking the CEO seat.

"We will both spend the night here."

"Oh, no, I couldn't. I'm sure you're a very nice per—"

"I assure you, Miss Motta, I have no motive other than getting a peaceful night's rest. You will sleep in the bedroom and I will make do out here." He gestured toward the sofa.

"I need to think about that. That doesn't seem right.

Maybe I should call my brother. Let me just get my things straightened out." Holly returned to her task of sorting out her duffel bag, quarantining paint-stained items in a plastic bag.

She didn't look up at him until she lifted out a pair of white socks. They were splattered with the same blue that had been disguising her lovely face. "Occupational hazard."

"You are a painter, I take it?"

"Yup."

"And you have come to New York to pursue fame and fortune?"

"Ha! That would be nice. Who wouldn't want their work to hang in a museum or a gallery here…?"

"I sense there is a *but* at the end of that."

"I've been making money doing large pieces and collections for corporate properties."

"Office art, lobby art, art for furnished apartments?"

Ethan was well aware of that kind of work. He'd spent many hours with interior designers making decisions about the art at Benton developments all over the world.

"Indeed, the right pieces are vitally important to a unified decor. They announce a mood."

"A point of view," Holly chimed in.

"It sets the tone." He pointed at the two black and white nature photos on the wall. "Those, for example."

"Dull."

"Safe."

"Yawn."

They both laughed in agreement. A sizzle passed between them. It was so real Ethan was sure he saw smoke.

How alive Holly was. The type of person who said exactly what she thought. A bit like Aunt Louise. And nothing at all like most of the women he knew.

He flashed on a possibility.

Then quickly thought better of it.

"My aunt's new husband selected this apartment. He frequently comes down from Boston."

Ethan rolled his eyes. Fernando Layne was no favorite of his. Definitely no substitute for Uncle Mel. Fernando was a plaything for Aunt Louise. Ethan tolerated him.

"I will remodel this property while I am in New York. Perhaps you can advise me?"

What a stupid thing to say. He was never going see Holly again past this awkward evening interlude. An unfamiliar sense of disappointment came over him.

He generally steered clear of his feelings. When they did arrive they were usually of the painful variety and proved too confusing.

"Do you want to look at my website?" Holly gestured to the tablet he still had in his hand.

"I am sorry to be rude but I have a phone meeting in five minutes. I need to prepare."

"At this time of night?"

"I am expecting a call from Tokyo, if you must know." He also wasn't used to explaining himself to anyone. "I will take it in the bedroom," he declared.

Then he picked up a roll of architectural blueprints from the desk and marched down the hall, perturbed in twenty different ways.

Ten o'clock on a rainy New York night.

Holly had left Fort Pierce at eight that morning.

Hungry and tired, she absentmindedly ran her hand along the sofa where Ethan had been sitting when she came in. The leather still held his warmth.

She probably should have been afraid when she'd opened the door to find a total stranger in the apartment. Yet she hadn't felt the slightest inkling of fear. She'd felt ticked off, maybe. Or something else entirely.

It might have something to do with the fact that Ethan Benton looked less like a serial killer than he did the lord of a countryside manor. With his imposing height and lean muscles and that stunning wavy brown hair that had a touch of red flecked in it.

His tone was bossy, but she supposed it must have been quite a shock for him that a woman with a blue face, a tattered duffel bag and a squeaky-wheeled suitcase had just barged into the apartment he'd thought he had to himself.

Now she was trapped here with him unless she was willing to face the stormy night. The man—who may or may not have a British accent—definitely had the most soulful eyes she had ever seen. The man who was now in the next room, conducting business halfway around the world.

New York was getting off to a rollicking start.

Would he be angry with her if she checked to see if there was anything to eat? Should she care, given that this apartment was supposed to be *hers*?

A rumbling stomach propelled her to the kitchen. She'd picked at snacks all day, but had not had a proper meal. On the counter lay one basket of fruit, and another of breads and bagels. The refrigerator held beer, milk, eggs and cheese.

Had this food been purchased for her arrival as a hospitality custom? Or was it Ethan's? Or did it belong to his aunt's husband, who Ethan had said used this apartment frequently?

The sight of the food rendered Holly too hungry to care. Being hungry was a unique ache that she had experience with. Surely Ethan wouldn't mind if she took one shiny red apple.

She hoisted herself up to sit on the countertop. Let her legs and bare feet dangle. Smiled remembering the apple's symbolism here in New York. Like so many others, she was here to take her bite. With one satisfying chomp after the next, her mind wandered about what might be.

"Miss Motta!" Ethan looked startled to find her sitting on the kitchen counter after he finished his call. "Must you always make yourself so…so *comfortable*?"

Holly shrugged her shoulders and slid off the countertop. *Whatever.* If her sitting on the counter was a big deal to him, she wouldn't do it.

She jutted out her chin. "I bet you haven't eaten."

"Not since early this afternoon on the flight," he confessed. "Is there food?"

"Looks like there's eggs and some things for breakfast."

"We will have something delivered."

"Sounds good to me."

"What would you like?"

"You know what? I haven't been to New York in years. Want to get some famous New York pizza?"

"Pizza it is." He swiped on his tablet. "Yes, Giuseppe's. I ordered from there quite a bit when I was last in New York, working on a project. What type of pizza do you like?"

It was nice of him to let her choose. This man was a bundle of contradictions. Scolding one minute, courteous in the next.

"Everything," she answered, without having to think twice.

"Everything?"

"You know—pepperoni, sausage, salami, mushrooms, onions, peppers, olives. The whole shebang."

"Everything…" he repeated. "Why not?"

"I'll pay for my half."

His mouth twitched.

"Twenty minutes," he read out the online confirmation. She eyed the kitchen clock.

"I guess I'm staying tonight." She crunched on her big apple.

A bolt of lightning struck, flashing bright light through the window.

CHAPTER TWO

ETHAN HAD A peculiar urge. The minute he'd said he'd sleep on the sofa tonight he'd wanted to lie down on the bed with Holly. Not to get under the covers. Just to lie on the bed with her. He wanted to relax. To hold her body against his. Caress her hair. Find out if those ebony locks were as silky as they looked.

Huh. A woman he had never met before, who had charged into his apartment and refused to leave. He had no idea who she really was or what she was doing here.

Yet he wanted to hold her.

The thought had interrupted his phone call several times.

He wasn't going mad. He'd just been working too hard. That was it. It had already been a long evening.

From the moment his flight had landed it had been one thing or another. He'd managed to sort out some of the details for the shareholders' gala. Many more remained. He'd heard there were construction delays on the low-income housing development in the Bronx that was so dear to his heart. He'd talked to a few people at the Boston headquarters to see how Aunt Louise was doing after the fall she'd taken. The news was not good. Then he'd worked on trying to resolve problems with a building permit in Detroit.

It had only been about an hour ago that Ethan had

changed into pajama bottoms and quieted down to read the newspaper. Before Holly had arrived, with the sparkling blue eyes and the creamy skin he now couldn't take his gaze off.

"While we're waiting for the pizza would it be okay if I took a shower?" she asked.

It would be okay if I took it with you.

Ethan surprised himself with the thought he didn't voice. He settled for, "Go right ahead."

Ethan did not like the way warmth resonated from Holly's body when she passed by him en route to the shower. Did not like it a bit because it stirred sensations low within him. Fierce sensations. *Urgent.*

The bathroom door shut with the quick smack that only happened when you closed it with a foot. Did she *always* shut doors with her feet?

His tongue flicked at his upper lip when he heard the sound of the shower. He couldn't help but imagine which article of clothing Holly was removing first. What each long limb might look like uncovered. Her torso was straight, rather than especially curvy, and he envisioned the smooth plain of her back. When he started to imagine what her... Well, he begged his brain to move to a different topic. No easy task.

Normally Ethan maintained a controlled world, without surprises. A world that allowed him to keep the upper hand. Maneuver as he saw fit. Because he was usually right.

Mushroom pizza, for heaven's sake.

A thirty-four-year-old man knew his own ways. Protected his orbit. Holly seemed to tip the universe off-kilter. Made the earth spin off its axis.

He preferred his pizza with only mushrooms on it!

She had to be stopped.

Yet he hadn't the heart to force her out on the street—

especially given the time of night. He didn't doubt that she was capable of fending for herself. But he didn't want her to.

That insane idea glimmered again. He needed to get it out of his head.

Ethan had too much to think about already. He was in a bind. Aunt Louise needed to retire. She'd had a distinguished career, and Ethan wanted her to go out on top. Concern was growing that she would sustain a fall in public. That word would spread. That people might remember her as a woman who had stayed on past her prime. That she was doddering, weak, bruised… All things that Louise Benton was most certainly not.

His aunt and his Uncle Melvin—his father's brother— had taken Ethan in as their own when he was nine years old. Now the time had come for the roles to be reversed. Ethan needed to make sure his decisions were in his aunt's best interests. His father would have told him to. Uncle Mel would have counted on him. It was the very least he could do.

But Aunt Louise had that one condition before she stepped down and moved from frigid Boston to the sunny compound in Barbados they'd had built for just that purpose. She wanted to know that Ethan would run their global business with a stable home life as a foundation.

Even though she and Uncle Mel hadn't been able to have children of their own, they'd experienced the joys and the heartaches of parenting through Ethan. In turn, his aunt wanted *him* to know the profound love of a parent for a child. And the united love and partnership that only came with decades of a shared life.

Aunt Louise would retire once Ethan was engaged to be married.

And because he'd become so alarmed about his aunt's

escalating health problems, and his responsibility to guard her reputation, Ethan had lied to her.

"You always say that deep down in your gut you know when something is right," Ethan had said, twisting his aunt's advice when he'd given her the news that he had met the soul mate he would wed.

Trouble was, Ethan had no such fiancée. Nor would he ever.

That was why he'd come to back to the States a few days ahead of the shareholders' gala. Tomorrow he was having lunch with the woman he planned to marry. In name only, of course.

He'd found a beautiful actress who'd be a suitable bride-to-be. This was New York, after all. There was hardly a better place to find a performer capable of pulling off this charade. He clicked on his tablet to the talent agency website where he'd located Penelope Perkins, an educated and sophisticated blonde with a stately neck.

It was a simple matter, really, in Ethan's mind. He'd chosen the actress and scheduled a meeting with her under the guise of hiring her for a promotional campaign for his company. If he found her to be acceptable and unencumbered he'd have her thoroughly investigated by Benton Worldwide's Head of Security, Chip Foley.

While Chip was completing a background check and every other kind of probe there was, Ethan and his stand-in fiancée would get to know each other and create a history for their relationship. Their engagement would be announced at the gala.

Penelope would also sign numerous non-disclosure and confidentiality agreements. She'd understand that if she were ever to reveal the arrangement she would be sued. Benton lawyers played hardball. They never lost their cases.

For her services, this performer would be paid generously.

It was a solid plan.

"Clean at last." Holly emerged from the bathroom while towel-drying her hair. A fresh tee shirt and sweatpants made her feel cozy after the day's journey. "Traveling makes you so grimy, you know?"

"Yes. I showered on the plane before arrival," Ethan agreed.

"You showered on the plane? How does someone shower on a plane?"

"I have a corporate jet. It does have a number of creature comforts."

Holly whistled. Highfalutin'. "I haven't flown that many times in my life. I'm still excited to get free soda and peanuts."

"Yes, well…perhaps you would enjoy all the amenities on private planes."

She tilted her head to one side and squeezed a little more moisture from the tips of her hair onto the plush towel. Sure, she'd like to be on a private plane, with a shower and enough room for her legs not to feel cramped into a ninety-degree position the entire flight. But that wasn't something that was ever going to happen, so she didn't see any point in discussing it.

"You have a little bit of an accent. And a kind of formal way of talking." Holly had a sometimes bad habit of blurting aloud everything that came into her mind. She called 'em as she saw 'em. "Are you American, or what?"

That left side of his mouth quivered up again in the start of a smile. "Boston-born. Oxford-educated. I would be the complete cliché of an entitled rich boy save for the fact that my father died when I was nine and I was raised by my aunt and uncle."

"What about your mother?"

The landline phone on the desk rang. Ethan turned to answer it. "Thank you. Please send him up." He headed toward the door. "Our pizza is here."

With his back to her, Holly was able to take in the full height of his slim, hard build. Probably about six foot three. Much taller than she was, and she always felt like a giant rag doll.

Ethan moved with effortless authority and confidence. Of course this was a man who showered on planes. This was a man who had been born to shower on planes.

Speaking of showers…it had been weird to shower in the apartment with him there. She knew there was no way he was an axe murderer who was going to hack her to bits. But she couldn't be a hundred percent sure that he was a gentleman who wasn't going to come into the bathroom while she was undressed.

A devilish thrill shot through her at the thought that he might have.

Attraction to a man during her first evening in New York was not on her itinerary. Especially not a man who had put all her plans in jeopardy.

She'd just have to make it through the night. In the morning her brother would help straighten things out about the apartment.

Staying here for a few weeks was meant to be the leg-up that she desperately needed. It would buy her time to find work and decide whether New York was where she should be. It had been two years since she'd kicked out Ricky the Rat. Two years was enough time to move on and move forward.

It was her brother, Vince, who had finally convinced her to take a chance. To take a risk. To take something for her own.

Maybe someday a man would fit into the picture. Not any time soon. She needed to concentrate on herself.

"Join me." Ethan gestured for her to come sit on the sofa after the delivery. He laid the pizza down on the coffee table, then dashed into the kitchen, returning with two plates, a stack of napkins and two bottles. "Will you have a beer?"

She took one from him and popped the cap with a satisfying twist.

As they sat down beside each other Holly winced involuntarily and moved away a bit. Being close to him felt scary. Strange. Strangely great…

He noticed her sudden stiffness. "I do not bite."

Pity. She held back a laugh. It wasn't fear that he'd bite that was bothering her. It might have been fear that he wouldn't.

Ethan flipped open the box and a meaty, cheesy, tomatoey aroma wafted up to their noses.

"I do not believe I have ever seen a pizza with this many ingredients on it."

As if performing a delicate procedure, he used two hands to lift one hefty slice onto a plate and handed it to Holly. Then he served himself.

"Ah…"

They groaned in unison as the first bites slid down their tongues. Unable even to speak, they each quickly devoured their slices.

Holly was the first to reach for a second. Then she sat back on the sofa and put her bare feet up on the coffee table.

"'Everything' is now officially my favorite pizza topping," Ethan confirmed, after taking another slice.

Observing Holly stretched out and seemingly comfortable, he did the same. His leaned back against the sofa.

Tentatively he extended one leg and then the other onto the coffee table, and crossed them just as Holly had hers.

And there they sat, both barefoot, eating pizza, as if they had known each other for eons rather than minutes.

She thought of something to ask. "Where did you fly in from?"

"Dubai. Before that I was in Stockholm. I have been out of the country for a month."

"Where do you live?"

"I keep a small apartment in Boston, near our head-quarters. Although I travel most of the time."

"Your company has properties all over the world?"

He nodded and washed down his pizza with a sip of beer. "Yes. Some we build. Some we buy and refurbish. In the last couple of years I have been spending a lot of my time on affordable housing for low-income buyers."

"Vince told me about the development you built in Overtown. He said he was so proud to have been part of a project helping people in one of Miami's neediest areas."

That left side of Ethan's mouth rose up again, but this time it continued until the right side lifted to join it in one full-on heart-melting smile.

Holly almost choked on her pizza. She thought a person might enjoy looking at that smile for the rest of her life.

"After my aunt retires I plan to turn most of Benton's focus toward housing for homeless or low-income fami-lies."

"When will she retire?"

Ethan sized Holly up in a gaze that went from the tip of her head down to her toes. As if he were taking her all in. Measuring her for something.

When she couldn't stand the moment any longer she reached for another piece of pizza and pressed, "Does your aunt *want* to retire?"

Holly watched his concentration return to the conversation at hand.

"I think she must, whether she wants to or not. She has peripheral neuropathy. It is a rare inherited condition. She's starting to lose some of her faculties."

"I'm sorry."

"I am, too. She is a wonderful woman."

"She's lucky to have you looking out for her wellbeing." Holly didn't think anyone would ever care about *her* that much.

"I would like to see her relaxing in Barbados. Swimming in warm waters and enjoying her silly trophy husband."

"But she doesn't see it that way?"

"She has a stipulation that she is insistent on before she retires, the details of which have not been worked out yet." Ethan reached for his beer. "So, tell me, Miss Holly Motta, you have come to New York completely on your own?"

What did his aunt want? Was there a family secret?

Holly was dying to know. In fact she wanted to know about all of Ethan's joys and triumphs and struggles and defeats. Wanted to tell him all of hers. Though she couldn't fathom why.

Even if she had been open to meeting the right man—a man with whom she would share the deepest, darkest nooks and crannies of her life—it wouldn't be a man who showered on airplanes.

A man like Ethan Benton had no business with a girl who had grown up in a trailer park in Fort Pierce. *Never going to happen.* And she wasn't looking for someone, anyway. This was *her* time.

She chewed her pizza, suddenly agitated by the way Ethan continued to examine her, as if she was an object he was considering purchasing.

"I have to say I cannot remember the last time I was with a woman who ate half a pizza in one sitting."

"Of course not. You probably only keep company with women who eat one green bean and then tell you how full they are."

That crooked grin broke into a hearty belly laugh. "You are absolutely right. If they eat anything at all. You are definitely not like the women I tend to meet."

"Should I consider that a compliment?"

"Please tell me why you have come to New York alone."

"Who would I have come with if not alone? I haven't seen my mother in years. My brother, Vince, is doing well in Miami. I have no other ties."

She'd grown up strategizing and compensating for her unreliable mother. Looking out for Vince. Then working around Ricky's bad behavior. Juggling two or three jobs. Keeping the house clean. Making sure people were fed. Paying bills. Always being the responsible one. Day after day. Year after year.

"I'm through with being cautious." She couldn't believe she was blathering this out to a man she'd only just met. "Yes, I came to New York alone. No job. No permanent place to live. I don't even know if here's where I belong. That's why I was going to stay in this apartment for a while—to figure it out. I'm sure it all sounds insane to you."

"How it sounds is brave."

Ethan furrowed his brow. A minute ago Holly had confided that she wasn't in contact with her mother. No mention of a father. He sensed there was plenty more that she hadn't said. That she'd been through more than her share of trouble and strife. Although it might be a made-up story meant to evoke sympathy from him to let her stay in the apartment.

Every previous experience he'd had with women other than Aunt Louise had led him to believe that they were never what they seemed.

Starting with his own mother.

Do not trust *trust*. It was a lesson he'd learned decades ago.

That was why he'd devised this scheme to set up a fake relationship, so that Aunt Louise would think she had gotten her wish. She would retire with her mind at ease and her attention on her health.

An imitation fiancée would suit him perfectly. The women he'd known before had always wanted something from him. With this arrangement he'd dreamt up everyone would get what they were after. Clean and upfront, with clear expectations and no disappointment.

After he and Holly had finished eating she retrieved a pad and pencils from her luggage and sat herself in the window, with its second-floor view out onto the street. She turned sideways, somehow wedging her long legs into the windowsill, and propped her sketchpad on her knees.

"You are welcome to pull a chair over," Ethan tossed out, not in the habit of contorting himself to fit into small spaces.

"I'm fine, thanks."

Unsure what to do with himself, he picked up his tablet to check emails. If he'd been there alone, as planned, he would have gone to bed. It was going to be a busy week.

He could ask Holly to take her things into the bedroom. Then he could turn off the lights, try to get comfortable on the sofa and hope to fall asleep.

Yet it was so unusual for him to be in an apartment with someone he craved her company and wanted to prolong it. He wasn't ready for her to retreat to separate quarters.

How crazy was the idea that kept popping into his mind?

As Holly drew, he began telling her more about Aunt

Louise. About the cruel medical condition that was taking away pieces of her.

"How did your family's company get started?" she asked, while working on her drawing.

"With nothing. When my father and Uncle Mel were in their twenties they saved their money from doing carpentry work until they had enough to buy the South Boston apartment they grew up in. Then they bought the whole building. And then the one next to it."

"That takes focus and determination. Hmm…" She shook her head.

"Hmm—what?"

She kept her eyes on her pad. "It's just that nobody I've ever known has done anything like that."

"After my uncle married Louise, she helped them grow the business. My father died twenty-five years ago. Then Aunt Louise took over as CEO when Uncle Mel died five years ago."

Ethan had only vague memories of his father. But he so missed the uncle who had become a second father to him. Melvin Benton had been a smart leader. A just and fair man.

"Uncle Mel would have agreed that it is time for Aunt Louise to step down. Before industry gossip sullies her reputation as the competent successor to his legacy that she was."

"What is it that your aunt wants you to do before she'll agree to retire?"

Oh, so Holly had been paying close attention earlier, when he'd started to tell her about Aunt Louise's request and then stopped himself.

"She wants to see me established in my personal life. For me to have what she and Uncle Mel had. She is waiting for me to be engaged to be married."

"And now you are?"

"So to speak…"

"There's no 'so to speak.' You're either engaged or you're not."

"Not necessarily."

Why had he started this? He'd revealed more than he should have.

"Tell me," she persisted, without looking up.

"I would rather talk about you. You have come to New York with no work here at all? This city can be a very tough place."

"I know. But I do have some people to contact. You're probably thinking my coming to New York was a really reckless bet. But if I didn't do it now I never would have."

When Ethan glanced down to the inbox on his tablet his eyes opened wide at the latest email. It was the talent agency, apologizing for contacting him so late in the evening and asking for the duration of his booking for Penelope Perkins, his soon-to-be "fiancée." Because, the representative explained, Mrs. Perkins had just informed them of her pregnancy. She expected to be available for a few months but, after that her altered appearance might be an issue for any long-term acting assignment.

Good heavens. *Yes*, Mrs. Perkins's blossoming pregnancy was going to be an issue! That would be too much to disguise from Aunt Louise. First an engagement and then a pregnancy right away? Not to mention the fact that Penelope was apparently *Mrs.* Perkins. And a certain *Mr.* Perkins was be unlikely to be agreeable to such an arrangement.

The veins in Ethan's neck pulsed with frustration. As if he didn't have enough to do! Now the engagement plan he'd worked so hard to devise was in jeopardy. Could he choose someone else and get an appointment with her in time? He quickly tabbed through the photos of the other actresses on the website. They were all of a suitable age. Any one of them might do.

Then he glanced up to lovely Holly, sketching in the windowsill.

What if…?

He'd been exchanging pleasant conversation with Holly all evening. Why *not* her? It might work out quite nicely. Perhaps they could have an easy, friendly business partnership based on mutual need. He had a lot he could offer her.

Of course the fact that he found her so interesting was probably *not* a plus. It might add complication. But who was to say that he wouldn't have been attracted to Penelope Perkins, or some other actress he'd chosen?

A sense of chemistry would be palpable to Aunt Louise and anyone else they would encounter. It would make them believable as a couple. And he certainly wouldn't be acting on any impulses. It wasn't as if he was open to a genuine relationship.

A fake fiancée was all he was looking for. Holly was as good a bet as any.

He gazed at her unnoticed for a moment. She turned to a new page on her sketchpad. Then, when she asked him again about whether or not he was engaged, he finally told her the truth.

He picked up the beer he had been drinking with the pizza. Carefully peeling off the label that circled the neck of the bottle, he rolled it into a ring. And then stepped over to Holly in front of the window. Where anyone in New York could be walking by and might look up to see them.

"I was intending to hire an actress," he explained. "But I think Aunt Louise would like you. You remind me of her. There is something very…real about you."

He got down on one knee. Held up the beer label ring in the palm of his hand.

She gasped.

"Holly, I do not suppose you would… If you might consider… Would you, please? Can you pretend to marry me?"

CHAPTER THREE

"HEAR ME OUT," Ethan said, still on one knee.

Holly had been so stunned by his proposal that moments stood still in time. It was as if she watched the scene from outside her body.

In an Upper East Side apartment in New York an elegant man with wavy brown hair waited on bended knee after proposing to his dark-haired intended. Would she say yes?

Holly couldn't remember if she had dreamt of a moment like this when she was a little girl. A dashing prince, the romantic gesture of kneeling, white horse at the ready. She'd probably had those fantasies at some point but she couldn't recall them. They were buried under everything else.

Most of Holly's memories were of hard times.

Growing up, it had been her alarm clock that had snapped her out of any dreams she might have had. The clock had made her spring her up quickly to check if her mother had woken up and was getting dressed for work. Or if she wasn't going to get out of bed. Or hadn't made it home at all during the night. Leaving Holly to scrounge together breakfast and a sack lunch for her and Vince.

No, Holly hadn't had much time for fairy-tale dreams. She'd been proposed to before. After all, she'd been married. But Ricky's offer had been about as heartfelt as their marriage had been. It had been on a sweaty, humid day in his beat-up old truck and it had gone something like, "I guess you want to get married…"

At the time, she'd thought that was about as good as it was going to get.

"It would be strictly business, of course." Ethan continued with his proposition. "An engagement in name only."

So Holly's second marriage proposal was to be just as unromantic as her first.

A twinge of despair pinged through her.

Ethan was suggesting a fake engagement to appease his aunt and get her to retire before poor health tarnished her standing. She understood why he was asking, but she didn't see what would be in it for her.

He anticipated her immediate trepidation and added, "We can negotiate a contract that is mutually beneficial."

"That certainly sounds cut and dried, Mr. Benton."

Even having this discussion was making her uncomfortable. Because it brought up notions like a little girl's dreams and happily-ever-afters. Thoughts she couldn't afford to linger on. Not then and not now.

She squinted at him. "Could you please get up?"

"I can."

He rose, yet still held out the beer bottle label. Looking down at it he assured her, "We would purchase a proper engagement ring."

"Let's put the paper ring down for a minute, okay?"

He laid it gently onto the coffee table as if it was a thing of great value. "I have a scenario…" He gestured toward the sofa.

She followed him, but this time didn't sit next to him as she had when they were eating pizza. She chose one of the black chairs opposite him. Best to keep her distance.

"May I be frank?"

"Oh…okay," Holly answered with apprehension.

"You are new to New York. You mentioned that you do

not yet have work. You mentioned that you could not afford to stay in a hotel. I am offering you very easy temporary employment. Pose as my fiancée. What I would pay you will help you establish yourself here. Shall we bring it to the bargaining table? Name your price."

"Name my *price*!" Such a ruthless businessman! Everything was a deal to him. "Are you used to getting everything you want simply by demanding it?"

"Oh, I always get what I want." His stare drilled into her.

Wow, what a predator. And why did that excite her rather than repel her?

Just for entertainment's sake, she took a minute to fantasize what being his pretend fiancée might be like. She'd probably be physically near him quite a bit. He'd have his arm around her shoulder. Sometimes around her waist. They'd hold hands. He'd probably even place a kiss on her cheek in front of other people, just to put on a convincing show.

Holly snuck a glance at his mouth. Ripe lips that looked to be endlessly kissable. No way would a plan that involved her standing close to his lips ever, *ever* be a good idea.

But it didn't matter, because she was just playing along hypothetically. "I'm not for hire by the hour!" She feigned indignation.

"There need not be anything sordid about it, Miss Motta." Ethan eyed the paper ring on the table. "I assure you I am only proposing a trade agreement."

She didn't doubt that. This was a man who'd already said he kept company with stunning, glamorous women who ate one green bean. He'd never be interested in her romantically. She'd have nothing to worry about there.

But she couldn't resist throwing in for fun, "My brother, Vince, is up for a promotion in your Miami office. Let's say this deal included helping him along in his career…"

"Done," Ethan answered quickly. "I would have to look at his human resources file and speak with the people who work with him. But if he is deserving, I would certainly look to promote my future brother-in-law."

He leaned forward. Even though there was the coffee table between them, she could feel him zeroing in on her. Coming in for the kill. Determined to make the sale.

"What else, Miss Motta?"

He was so maddeningly sure of himself. Holly hadn't met many people who were like that.

She sat dumbfounded, way out of her league.

Ethan raised a finger in the air with a thought. "Shall we consider it another way? You need somewhere to live. How about if I give you this apartment? I will put it in your name."

Holly tried to keep her eyes from bugging out. *How about if I give you this apartment?* Who even *said* that?

"As you can imagine, real estate is something I have as a bartering tool. Regardless of what happens, you will have a home in New York."

A home in New York. He really did know how to persuade a deal.

"What is it that might happen?" She had no intention of taking him up on his offer, but she was curious. "How is it that you see this working?"

He'd obviously thought this through well. Today was Monday. His aunt Louise and her boy-toy husband, Fernando, would be coming down from Boston this week in preparation for their Saturday shareholders' gala. He'd present Holly to them on Wednesday night.

"Dinner. Le Cirque. Or one of the new Asian-Spanish fusion restaurants in Tribeca. Something flashy that shows us as a hip New York couple on top of the trends."

"How about instead I throw a pot roast in the slow cooker?" Holly countered, batting him the idea.

His mouth tipped. "A home-cooked meal? Like she and Uncle Mel used to make on Sundays? Brilliant!"

Holly was no gourmet cook, but she knew how to work with the basics. She'd had to learn if she and her brother were ever going to eat. When they were kids she'd search through the pockets of pants left on the floor. Between the couch cushions. Under the seats in the car. Somehow she'd find enough money to buy a few groceries and put a meal together for her and Vince. Restaurant visits had been few and far between.

"Mashed potatoes. Roasted carrots. Apple pie…" She completed the menu.

"Perfect. I will try to be of assistance."

"Continue," she requested.

It was amusing to hear Ethan's outline for the masquerade that she wasn't actually going to be any part of.

Their next appearance would be at the shareholders' gala on Saturday, where Holly would be formally introduced as Ethan's fiancée.

"So I'd look amazing that night? Dress? Jewels? Hair and makeup? The whole nine yards?"

He sat silent for a minute, as if lost in his own memories. But then he snapped back with, "Of course. A couture gown would be chosen for you. My tuxedo tie will match your attire."

"It'd be a crime if it didn't."

Then there would be an engagement party in Boston. A month or so later would come the announcement that Aunt Louise was stepping down. A grand retirement luncheon would send her off in style.

"In between those dates," Ethan explained, "I would travel, so that you and I should not have to attend many events together. I will devise reasons that I have to spend prolonged periods in Florence or Sydney or the like."

Ethan went on. After those appearances Aunt Louise

and Fernando would move to Barbados as planned. Ethan and Holly—the happy couple—would fly to the island for long weekends three or four times during the first year. In between those visits Holly would be free to live the life she chose, as long as there was nothing criminal or anything that attracted attention.

Then they'd evaluate. They could continue to visit Aunt Louise and make excuses as to why they hadn't yet married. Or they could tell fibs about a lavish wedding that would take an entire year to plan.

"Or," he continued, "especially if you were to meet someone else and need to be free, we could call off the engagement. Aunt Louise would be settled into her island life of leisure. By that point there would not be any danger of her wanting to return to frigid Boston and the working grind."

"And what if *you* were the one to meet someone?" she clipped, pretending to advocate a deal for herself.

"Impossible!" he spat immediately. "I will never marry."

His harshness hit her like a slap in the face.

Or perhaps it was a warning.

"I see," she assured him, and knew she'd understood his underlying message.

"Therefore, when we split up, you will own this apartment outright—which you can either keep, lease or sell. And the engagement ring. And whatever clothing and jewels have been purchased. Your brother's position will be secure. We can also agree on a monetary settlement. In exchange for very little labor on your part, I can provide you with a lifetime of comfort and luxury."

Game over.

Enough was enough.

Even if it could be as simple as he made it sound she had come to New York to get her own life straightened out. Not to get tangled up in someone else's.

"Ethan, I appreciate the offer. And I think it's great that you've done so much planning on this. It shows how much you care about your aunt. But this is not for me."

He swallowed hard. His Adam's apple bobbed in his throat. His jaw tightened.

Was he upset?

Of course. This was a man who was used to getting everything he wanted. It wasn't personal. She was a mere obstacle for him to overcome in order to reach his goal.

Ethan tapped his tablet. "Holly Motta dot com—is that it?"

She nodded, yes. What was he up to?

He typed.

"Huh…" His thumb slid through what she assumed to be her website's gallery. "Huh…"

What was he thinking? She took great pride in her work. Suddenly it mattered to her what he thought of it. Which was silly, because his opinion was of no concern to her at all. Yet she sat on the edge of the chair, spine held stiff as she waited for a comment.

His thumb continued to swipe the tablet.

"Hmm…" His next sound was at a higher pitch than the one before. It sounded like approval.

"Why are you looking at my website?"

Ethan ignored the question and continued. His finger slid less frequently. He was spending more time on each piece of work.

Holly imagined what it might feel like to have that thumb slide across her cheek instead of the tablet screen. Or slowly down the center of her chest. That thumb and its nine partners on those two big hands looked as if they'd always know exactly what to do.

More fantasy. She hadn't been touched in a long, long time.

Finally Ethan looked from the screen to her. "These are extraordinary."

"Thank you," she breathed with gratification—and relief.

He raised a finger in the air again. "Perhaps we can negotiate a merger that would be satisfying to both of us."

She squished her eyebrows.

"In exchange for you posing as my fiancée, as I have outlined, you will be financially compensated and you will become legal owner of this apartment and any items such as clothes and jewels that have been purchased for this position. Your brother's career will not be impacted negatively should our work together come to an end. *And...*" He paused for emphasis.

Holly leaned forward in her chair, her back still board-straight.

"I have a five-building development under construction in Chelsea. There will be furnished apartments, office lofts and common space lobbies—all in need of artwork. I will commission you for the project."

Holly's lungs emptied. A commission for a big corporate project. That was exactly what she'd hoped she'd find in New York. A chance to have her work seen by thousands of people. The kind of exposure that could lead from one job to the next and to a sustained and successful career.

This was all too much. Fantastic, frightening, impossible... Obviously getting involved in any way with Ethan Benton was a terrible idea. She'd be beholden to him. Serving another person's agenda again. Just what she'd come to New York to get away from.

But this could be a once-in-a-lifetime opportunity. An apartment. A job. It sounded as if he was open to most any demand she could come up with. She really did owe it to herself to contemplate this opportunity.

Her brain was no longer operating normally. The clock on Ethan's desk reminded her that it was after midnight. She'd left Fort Pierce early that morning.

"That really is an incredible offer…" She exhaled. "But I'm too tired to think straight. I'm going to need to sleep on it."

"As you wish."

Holly moved to collect the luggage she'd arrived with. Ethan beat her to it and hoisted the duffel bag over his shoulder. He wrenched the handle of the suitcase. Its wheels tottered as fast as her mind whirled as she followed him to the bedroom.

"Good night, then." He placed the bags just inside the doorway and couldn't get out of the room fast enough.

Before closing the door she poked her head out and called, "Ethan Benton, you don't play fair."

Over his shoulder, he turned his face back toward her. "I told you. I always get what I want."

Holly shut the door with her bare foot and leaned back against it. She pursed her lips together to keep from screaming. Her heart thumped so loud she was sure Ethan would hear it in the other room. *Goodness gracious.*

Ethan Benton and his proposition were quite simply the most exciting things that had ever happened to her!

A rush went through her as she recalled that devilish grin creeping slowly up his mouth. Those deep brown eyes that had stayed glued on her, assuring her he was listening to her when she spoke.

Holly hadn't talked and listened as much as she had tonight in a long time. She hadn't dated anyone since leaving Ricky the Rat two years ago. With her in Fort Pierce and Vince a two-hour drive away in Miami, she usually saw her brother twice a month. There was a girls' night here and there with friends. That was about it.

She hadn't really thought about it, but now when she did she realized she led a fairly solitary existence. Hopefully New York would jostle that, along with everything else.

But the change *wasn't* going to come by stepping into Ethan Benton's life. Although it might be the most fun she'd ever have. A jet-set world she'd only read about in magazines… Who wouldn't want to dash off to Barbados for long weekends? To walk on pink sand with her toes in sparkling blue water. Attend glitzy parties…throw some of her own. Buy clothes without looking at the price tag. Never worry about where the rent or her next meal was coming from. Have the best of everything.

It would be amazing—even if it was only for a short time—to be completely taken care of. After all those years of putting other people ahead of her.

Which reminded her of how this deal could benefit her brother. Becoming part of the Benton family, even in name only, might help him further his career in a way he'd never have the chance to otherwise. He'd get to spend more time with Ethan and Louise. They'd see up close how capable and special he was.

No. This wasn't about Vince. He'd be fine on his own. He was a grown man and his career was underway.

It was time for *her* future to begin. Period. In the morning she would tell Ethan no.

Besides, once he heard that she had already been married and divorced he wouldn't think she was an appropriate choice for his game.

Right now, she needed to get some sleep.

She stopped short at the sight of the room's king-size bed. This was where Ethan Benton had been planning to lay that tall, sturdy frame of his tonight. A wiggle shot up her spine at the mental image of him stretched out on this bed. Perhaps only wearing the plaid pajama bottoms as when she'd first seen him on the sofa.

On the bed she counted one, two…eight plush pillows, overlapped in a tidy row against the brown leather headboard. She imagined Ethan's head against those pillows, with that curl of hair tousled on his forehead.

The luxury pillowcases alternated in color, tan then black. Which coordinated with the tightly fitted tan sheets. She ran a finger along the black duvet, tracing it down the right side of the bed. Then across the bottom. Then up the left. It was all too matchy-matchy for her tastes, but clearly made of expensive fabrics.

She eyed the wall-to-wall closet. If she took Ethan up on his proposal it would become filled with designer gowns for glamorous black tie dinners. Trendy separates for groundbreaking ceremonies. Classic sportswear for sailing jaunts and tennis tournaments. The finest shoes and purses and jewels.

None of that was her. She couldn't picture it. Not even for make-believe.

Back on earth, Holly didn't know whether she should unpack her suitcase full of jeans, comfortable skirts and tee shirts. She slid the blond wood closet door open to see if anything was inside.

Four men's suits hung neatly on wooden hangers, with breathing room in between each. Dark gray, light gray, navy pinstripe and a beautiful maroon. They looked to be Ethan's size. He'd probably look especially handsome in that maroon. It would go well with his brown eyes and that brown hair with its speckles of red.

There were freshly laundered shirts. Complementary ties. Polished shoes. A tuxedo and its accessories. Two pairs of pressed jeans. A pair of casual boots. She resisted the temptation to open any drawers. She had seen an overcoat and a leather jacket on the coat rack by the front door.

It wasn't a large wardrobe. Ethan had said he traveled a lot, but hadn't mentioned how long he was staying in New York.

She fingered the lapel of the maroon suit jacket. Ricky

the Rat had only owned one wrinkly black suit. She could count on one hand the times he'd worn it. He was the jeans and workboots type. There were times she'd thought he was sexy.

One of the times he hadn't been sexy was when she'd come home from work early one day and the workboots were all he'd had on. While he was in bed with their neighbor Kiki.

The rain was heavier outside now. Holly watched the bedroom window being pounded with sheets of the downpour. A rumble of thunder emphasized the storm's strength. *Good.* Let it wash away her past.

Deciding to leave her suitcase on the floor for the night, she pulled back the duvet on the bed and climbed into the king-size reminder of the man who was already making her feel as if she were spiraling away from her old life. Even though her encounter with him would come to an end in the morning, her transition to something new had begun.

The bed was divine. The mattress firm. The sheets crisp. She pulled the thick cover over her. Beyond comfortable, she nestled in the oasis, away from cares and plans. It was a peaceful heaven on earth after such a long day. Time to rest her body and mind. She was going to sleep like a log...

Two hours later Holly tossed and turned with exasperation. She hadn't kept her eyes shut for more than a minute before her brain had assaulted her with more and more opinions.

What Ethan was proposing could be her lucky break. A commission to do the artwork for his big development in Chelsea... A chance to really get started in New York...

She'd come to the city armed with work references, but the life of an artist could be tricky. Maybe nothing would pan out from the names and phone numbers she'd collected. Or she'd get small jobs here and there but they might not lead to anything else.

Ethan's proposition was a multi-phase project that would probably be six months of work at least. In that time she could really put down roots here.

She was determined to make her entire living as an artist. Not to have to work anymore as a maid or a nanny during the lean times. Her goals were clear. New York was the place where dreams were made or broken. If it didn't work out here, so be it—but she was certainly going to take her shot.

Imagine how much easier it would be without any astronomical rent to pay. New York apartment prices were notoriously high. Holly knew that she would probably have to live with a roommate. Maybe several of them. Some might have come to New York for the twenty-four-hour-a-day lifestyle, for the party that never ended. The household might be full of noise and people and activity at all hours of the day and night. It might prevent Holly from getting her work done or resting when she needed to.

Or she might end up with people who were slobs. Not able to tolerate a dirty mess, she would end up cleaning up after them. Cleaning up after people—how much of her life had she already spent doing that? She'd never minded taking care of her brother, but her ex-husband hadn't ever seemed even to know where the trash can or the washing machine were. Nor had her mother.

Maybe these roommate slobs wouldn't pay their share of their rent and she'd get evicted. She might end up having to move from place to place through no fault of her own. That would be maddening.

Ethan was offering work and a place to live. This tasteful apartment all to herself. It was one thing to be allowed to stay here while she looked for a place. It was quite another to have it *belong* to her. She could paint here. Reposition the furniture in the living room to make the most of the natural light.

Wait a minute.

Part of Ethan's bargain was that he would pay her. She would be able to afford to rent studio space. A New York artist with her own studio… If *that* wasn't a dream come true!

But on the other hand…

And she needed to consider…

She couldn't really…

And then what…?

When Holly opened her eyes, a drizzly morning sky crept in through the window. At some point she had finally dozed off, her mind twirling about the past and what the future could hold. Now, with morning's dawn in Ethan Benton's bedroom, certainty hit her like a ton of bricks.

If something seemed too good to be true, it was.

Not cut out to be anyone's pretend anything, Holly was only who she was. Ethan was kidding himself. It could only end in disaster. She would do him a favor by acknowledging the impossibility of his proposal, even though he wasn't able to see it for himself.

His judgment was clouded by his deep love for his aunt Louise. How touching was his concern for her welfare, for her reputation and her happiness. Blood ran thick. A good man took his family responsibilities seriously…

She had to call her brother. She wouldn't tell him about Ethan's offer. But she *did* need his help sorting out this confusion about her staying in the apartment. It would be good to hear his voice. In the end, he was the only one she really had in her corner.

He'd be working out in the garage of the little house he rented in Miami. Lifting weights. Bench pressing and hoisting dumbbells before showering and getting to work at Benton.

"Vinz." She pictured him, no doubt in a muscle shirt drenched in sweat. His close-cropped blond hair so unlike her black. The round blue eyes marking him as her kin.

"Holz! How's the Big Apple so far?"

She explained the mix-up with the apartment.

Vince promised to make some calls as soon as he got into the office. "I'll get it fixed," he assured her.

"I don't know if you can."

"Listen to me, big sis. We're going to sniff out opportunities for you and you're going take them. You'll grab everything that's thrown your way."

"Yeah."

"Remember—straight up or fall down!" He chanted their lifelong rally call—the desperate bravado of two kids with no one but each other to root for them.

After hanging up, Holly held the phone in her hand and stared absently out the window for a while. Thick clouds in the sky moved horizontally across her vision.

There had always been rainy days. No one knew how many more were ahead. It would be such a gift to have an umbrella.

Finally she tossed the phone onto the bed and opened the door.

Ethan was in the kitchen. She watched him start a pot of coffee before he noticed she was there. When he did, she leaned against the doorway. Her hair was probably a mess. Surely she had bags under her eyes from her fitful night. She lifted her hand and looked at her fingers with their perpetual paint around the cuticles and under the nails. She was who she was.

"Okay, Ethan. I'll marry you."

CHAPTER FOUR

SHE SAID YES! Ethan wanted to shout it from the rooftops. *She said yes!*

His blood coursed. His muscles tingled.

She said yes!

And then he caught himself. *Good heavens.* There was no cause for fireworks to be launched from his heart. There was no reason to announce his undying devotion in front of the citizens of Manhattan. He was not a giddy groom filled with bliss and anticipation.

A woman he'd met yesterday had agreed to a jointly beneficial contract. He signed deals every day. This was just another one.

With a flick on the switch of the coffeepot he shook his head, trying to dislodge the obvious cobwebs in his skull.

He'd gotten a bit carried away.

Truthfully, he hadn't been alone with a woman in a long time—and certainly not in the close quarters of a small apartment. Perhaps that had stirred up a primal reaction in him. While the mating ritual wasn't part of his daily life, it *was* a natural phenomenon.

Although Ethan employed thousands of women in all aspects of his business, he shunned intimate social situations with them as much as possible. Keeping a clear and level head was what he did best. Women were distracting. Distractions were to be avoided. Problem—solution.

This was the first lesson he needed in order to carry off his plan. He was going to be spending a lot of time with an attractive woman. He'd need to guard and defend himself against her feminine charms. It wasn't personal. It didn't matter whether it was Holly, pregnant Penelope Perkins or another actress he'd picked from a photograph.

In three measured breaths, with his face toward the coffeepot, he set his focus. *Guard and defend.*

Then he turned to Holly, still standing in the doorway. Dark cascades of hair fell around her pretty face, which had a just-woken flush in her cheeks. Her tee shirt was definitely not concealing a bra.

Involuntarily, his body began to lean toward hers. A kiss pushed forward from his lips.

Guard and defend!

In the nick of time, he pulled himself back. Her allure was something he'd need to get accustomed to. His body's involuntary response to her worried him…told him that might be difficult.

But he would be triumphant. For the sake of Aunt Louise he could conquer anything.

Ethan directed himself to talk, since he couldn't kiss. "How did you sleep?"

"Great," she lied.

Her eyes looked tired. He hadn't got much sleep, either. He was far too tall to stretch out comfortably on that sofa. Plus, his mind had taunted him with replays of the evening.

"That coffee smells good," she said as she massaged the back of her neck.

"It does. How do you take it?"

"Lots of milk or cream. No sugar."

Ethan opened one of the cabinets to look for cups. It held only drinking glasses. He hadn't spent enough time in this apartment to know where everything was kept. His second try yielded large white mugs. Setting them on the black granite countertop, he poured the steaming coffee.

The kitchen was Manhattan Minimal. Pint-size efficiency. Cabinets, sink and dishwasher on one side. Stove and refrigerator on the other. A one-person kitchen. Too cramped for two people to work in.

Which was why when Holly stepped in to open the fridge he felt her hips brush past him. In turn, his hips reacted of their own volition—which, fortunately, she didn't notice.

"What are we eating for breakfast?' she asked as she peered into the refrigerator.

"What do we have?" He'd only had bottles of water when he'd got in yesterday, and beer last night with the pizza.

"Eggs, butter and cheese. And the bread and fruit." She pointed to the baskets on the counter. "We can work with this."

The way she said *we* made Ethan's ears prick up. He wasn't used to *we*. He'd worked very hard at avoiding *we*. This was no time to start. Although for the first time he was curious about *we*. He reasoned that this fake engagement was a perfect way of safely pretending to experience *we*, with both parties knowing fully well that the truth was *me* and *me* achieving individual goals.

Right. However, now it felt somewhat confusing.

Holly pulled the carton of milk out of the fridge and handed it to him. Ethan was keenly aware of their fingertips touching during the exchange.

She laid ingredients on the counter. "How does cheese omelets, toasted bagels and sliced fruit sound?"

"What do you generally eat for breakfast?"

Holly giggled. A bit of blush rose in her cheeks. *How adorable*. "Was that a get-to-know-each-other question?"

"It was. If we are going to be convincing as an engaged couple, we have to know those sorts of things about each other."

He handed her a mug. She took a slow sip and exhaled her satisfaction.

"You put the perfect amount of milk in my cup, so we must be off to a good start."

Ethan felt ridiculously proud that she liked her coffee.

"How do you take yours?" she went up.

"Also without sugar. But not as much milk."

"I'll eat anything…" She went back to his question. "If we hadn't polished off that pizza, that's great cold in the morning."

"Cold pizza? Noted."

"Do you know how to cook?"

"I could probably manage to broil a steak without ruining it."

"Eggs?"

"Not really," he confessed.

"Today you learn, then."

"Is that so?"

"I'll put on a show for your aunt Louise, but surely you don't think I'm going to be cooking and cleaning for you." Her face stilled in a moment of earnest uncertainty. "*Do* you?"

"Of course not, phony fiancée."

"It's just that I've done plenty of taking care of people in my life. I just want to take care of myself."

Holly had been through a lot. He'd been able to tell that about her from the start—had seen it right through her spunky attitude. She was no fresh-faced hopeful, arriving in New York full of delusions and fantasies. There was a past. A past that he suspected included hardship and pain.

Another one of those innate urges told him to wrap his arms around her and promise that he'd make up for all her hurts. That now she would be the one taken care of. That he'd quite like to make it his life's mission to take care of her in every possible way.

Once again he had to chastise himself sternly. He had merely hired her to perform a service. For which she would be paid very well. With that opportunity she would be able to find whatever she'd come to New York to get. She didn't need him.

The agony of that shocked him. A reminder to guard and defend.

Holly handed him the carton of eggs. She gave him a bowl. "Four."

Finding a cutting board and a knife, Holly sliced cheese while Ethan cracked eggs. They stood side by side at their tasks, each dependent on the other in order to get the job done. Ethan appreciated teamwork. That was what made Benton Worldwide, and every other successful venture work. It must be the same in a marriage.

Two bagels were halved and popped into the toaster.

"Frying pan?" she mused to herself, and quickly moved to his other side to find one.

His mind flipped back to the past. To Aunt Louise and Uncle Melvin. It had been almost ten years since they'd done the normal things that married couples did. Mel had died over five years ago. Before that recurrences of his cancer had often had him bedridden. But they'd had moments like these. Hundreds, even thousands of cozy day-to-day moments like preparing breakfast.

Those moments strung together added up to a life shared between two people.

In reality, with their success and privilege it was not as if Aunt Louise and Uncle Mel had often been in the kitchen frying up eggs. But they had always cooked Sunday supper together whenever they could. It had been one of their signatures.

Ethan had potent memories of the two of them together as a couple. The way they'd been with each other. Even if it they had just been at the front door on the way out, helping each other layer on coats, scarves and hats to brave the Boston winter. How they'd maneuvered around each other. With effortless choreography. Totally at ease with each other, aware of each other's moves, each other's needs, each other's comforts.

He understood why Aunt Louise so wanted that same security for him. Why she was concerned with the way he jetted around the globe, working all the time, never stopping, never settling. The wisdom of age had shown her what might happen to a man who didn't balance power and labor with the other things that made life worth living. Family. Love.

But his aunt should accept that after all Ethan had been through love wasn't an option for him. He would never open his heart. Her destiny wasn't his. Yet he couldn't blame her for wishing things were different. That his past hadn't defined his future.

In reflection, Aunt Louise had valued her relationship with Uncle Mel above everything else in her life. She'd had a love so true it had never let her down.

Unlike him.

This ruse was the best solution. If the knowledge that Ethan was engaged to be married made Aunt Louise happy, and put her mind at ease, then he'd have taken good care of her. Ethan was in charge of all decisions now, and he wanted them to be in his aunt's best interests.

He and Holly sat down at the table with their breakfast. Just as she had with the pizza last night, she dug in like a hungry animal. She took big bites and didn't try to disguise her obvious pleasure.

Ethan asked if maybe she had gone hungry as a child.

"My mother was...unpredictable."

Something he himself knew more than a little about. Anger burned his throat.

A bittersweet smile crossed her mouth as she cut circular slices of an orange and handed one to him. "Vince and I used to call these rings of sunshine. There were always oranges in Florida."

He wanted to know how she'd been wronged. But he wasn't going to walk on that common ground.

"Aunt Louise and Fernando are coming for dinner on Wednesday." He cut to the matter at hand. "We need to prepare. Our first order of business is making this apartment look like we truly live here. We will start with…"

"The artwork!" they chimed in unison.

"We will visit my favorite galleries in Soho. You can make the final selection."

Outside, stormy skies had given way to more hard rain.

"Dress accordingly."

He plucked his phone from his pocket and began tapping.

Half an hour later, a stocky man in a suit and chauffeur's cap held a car door open for Holly.

"This is my driver, Leonard," Ethan introduced.

"Ma'am."

Holly darted into the black car without getting too wet from the downpour. Sliding across the tan leather backseat, she made room for Ethan beside her. Leonard shut the passenger door and hurried around to the driver's seat.

As they pulled away from the apartment building, Ethan activated the privacy glass that separated the front seat from the back.

Holly didn't know what she'd gotten herself into. Fear and excitement rattled her at the same time.

Soho galleries and shareholders' galas… She didn't really know how she was going to fake her way through a life so different from hers. Being ferried around New York in a town car with a privacy glass.

Ethan had clearly noticed her discomfort at his shielding his driver from any conversation they were going to have. "Obviously we need complete discretion to pull off our little enterprise, do we not?"

"Yup."

"Off we go, then. Yes?"

As crazy as it was, she'd already said yes to this wild ride with him. "Yes."

She watched New York though the car window. The city was gorgeous in the rain. Buildings seemed even taller and grander beneath the turbulent skies. People in dark clothes with umbrellas hurried along the sidewalks. To her eyes, they looked as if they were from a bygone era. Her mind snapped mental pictures. She wanted to paint all of it.

While Ethan checked messages on his phone Holly was aware of every breath he took. Her lungs couldn't help synchronizing each of his inhales and exhales with her own. They were so near each other on the seat her leg rested along his. She detected a faint smell of his woodsy shampoo.

You'll get used to him, she told herself. *Soon enough, he won't be so enchanting.*

Ethan touched his phone and brought the device to his ear.

"Nathan. Did you receive my text? Have you made all of the appointments for today?"

He nodded once as he listened.

"Diane—got it. Jeremy—got it. Thank you. Set me up for meetings next week with Con East and the Jersey City contractors."

He looked toward Holly and licked his top lip, although she was sure he didn't realize he had.

"I will be in New York for a while this time. As a matter of fact I have quite the announcement to make at the shareholders' gala."

A squiggle shot up Holly's back. No one had ever looked at her the way he did.

Ethan sent a sincere laugh into the phone. "All right, Nathan. I suppose I can spare you your beheading. *This* time."

He clicked off the call. "That explains the mystery about the apartment. Nathan had me booked in for the same dates but next month. You were right—it was meant to be yours. But now, to everyone concerned, the apartment is *ours*."

Holly pulled up the collar on her leather jacket as Leonard shuttled them downtown.

Curbside at the first gallery, Leonard helped them out of the car. And then back in as they made their way to the second. And then to the third.

Naturally the staff at each were overjoyed to see Ethan. They reminisced about art openings and museum dedications. Holly felt completely out of place, with nothing to add to the conversations. But she held her own, making intelligent comments about the art on display.

Ethan didn't mention anything about their upcoming nuptials. That announcement was for the gala. Instead he introduced Holly as a friend and painter from Florida whom he had been lucky enough to enlist for an upcoming commission.

Back in the town car again, they munched on the fancy sandwiches Ethan had had Leonard pick up from a gourmet shop. They discussed the paintings they had seen. Holly wanted two, and explained why she'd chosen them.

"If we had more time I'd have my brother send up some canvases that he's storing for me," she said. "If it was really our apartment I'd like to have my own work on the walls."

"I would like that, too," Ethan agreed, with such unexpected warmth it stretched at her heart.

He was masterful at throwing her off-kilter. When

they'd been making breakfast that morning she'd had the feeling several times that he was going to kiss her. At one moment she had desperately hoped he would, while in the next she'd known she must turn away.

Ethan Benton was a bundle of inconsistencies.

Such a precise way he used a paper napkin to brush away imagined crumbs from the corners of his mouth. He was so definite about everything he did. Hobnobbing with gallery people or eating take-out lunch in the car—he did everything with finesse.

It wasn't as if any crumb would dare stick to those glorious lips. Men who showered on planes didn't get food on their faces.

Yet Holly knew there was something damaged underneath all Ethan's confidence and class…

"Can I paint you?"

He contemplated the question as he slowly popped the seal on his bottle of artisan soda.

"You know those drab black and whites of the tree and the flower on the wall?" she went on.

Last night when they'd been critiquing those photographs, flickers had flown between them.

"Flat, corporate…"

"Impersonal," she finished. "That's where I'd hang a painting of you. It would bring personality to the whole room and really make it ours."

"Yes…" he concurred with reluctance. "I suppose it would."

In a flash, Holly understood his hesitation. People were often uncomfortable at the prospect of her painting them. It involved trust. They had to be reassured that she wasn't going to accentuate their pointy nose or, worse still, the loneliness in their eyes.

A good portrait exposed someone's secrets. What was it that Ethan was worried she would reveal to the world?

"Can I?"

"I doubt we could get a painting done in two days' time."

"Let me show you."

Once people had seen Holly's work, she was able to put them at ease. She pulled out her phone and thumbed to her website. "I don't know if you saw these when you were on my site last night. But look. I don't do a typical portrait."

She showed him the screen. "I call them painted sketches. See how they're a bit abstract? And not all that detailed? I would just catch the essence of you."

He whipped his head sideways to face her. "What makes you think you know the essence of me?" he challenged.

Holly's throat jammed at the confrontation. He was right. She *didn't* know him. They'd met yesterday.

But she knew she could get something. Those big and expressive eyes. And, yes, there was some kind of longing behind them.

She might not know him, but she wanted to. This morning at breakfast he had been visibly shaken when she'd hinted at the hardships she'd endured. She had sensed some kind of connection there—a fierce similarity.

She hadn't explicitly told him about the mother who had never consistently provided food for her children. She hadn't mentioned the father who'd come around every couple of years with promises he'd never kept. How Holly had often had to fend for her younger brother and herself.

Yet the damage that dwelled behind Ethan's eyes had made her want to lay her pain bare to him. And for him to lay all his beside hers. As if in that rawness their wounds could be healed.

But none of that was ever to be. They were business partners. Nothing more. Besides, she wasn't going to make herself vulnerable to anyone ever again.

"Never mind." She called his bluff. "I guess we won't

ever find out how much of the real you I could get on a canvas."

One side of his mouth hiked. "I did not say no."

"So you'll let me paint you?"

"I will have you know right now that I have very little patience for sitting still."

"You probably had to sit for family portraits with Aunt Louise and Uncle Mel, right? Dressed up in uncomfortable Christmas clothes by the fireplace? The dutiful family dog by your side? It was torture. You had to sit without moving for what seemed like an eternity."

"I absolutely hated having to hold one position while a greasy bald man who smelled like pipe tobacco painted us."

Flirty words tumbled out of her mouth before she could sensor them. "I promise I'll smell a lot better than the bald man did."

"No doubt."

"And it won't take long."

"I think it might."

Were they still talking about painting?

He lowered the glass separating them from the driver. "Leonard, we are going to change our next stop to Wooster and Broome."

Leonard let them out in front of a painting supplies store the likes of which Holly had never been in before.

She ordered a lot of her materials online, because there were no shops in Fort Pierce that carried fine products like these. When she was low on money she'd make do with what was available at the local brand-name craft store, that also sold knitting yarn and foam balls for school projects.

She cowered at another memory of her ex-husband. As usual, Ricky hadn't wanted to go shopping with her because he thought painting was silly and that she should spend more time going to motorcycle races with him.

Yelling at her to hurry up while she picked out some tubes of paint, Ricky had lost his patience. With a flick of his hand he'd knocked down a display of Valentine's Day supplies. Heart-shaped cardboard boxes, Cupid cutouts and red and pink pompoms had crashed to the floor as Ricky stormed out of the store.

Humiliated, Holly had been left to make apologies and pay for his outburst.

It had been a few months later that she'd caught Ricky in bed with their neighbor. But she'd known that day in the craft store that she couldn't stay married to him.

Now here she was, a million miles away in Soho, the mecca of the American art world, with another man who would never be right for her. Although in completely opposite ways.

Life had a sense of humor.

She chose an easel, stretched canvases in several sizes, new paint and brushes, and palettes and sketchpads, pastels and charcoals. All top-notch. This was the Holly equivalent of a kid in a candy shop.

At the checkout, Ethan opened up an account for her. "That way you can pick up whatever tools and materials you need for Benton projects."

"My goodness…" Her eyes bugged out. "Thank you."

"Of course, my dearest." He winked. "And the next item on the agenda is buying my pretty fiancée some proper clothes."

CHAPTER FIVE

"What's wrong with my clothes?" Holly demanded as Leonard helped them out of the car in front of a Fifth Avenue shopping mecca.

"Not a thing. You do the artist with paint on her hands bit quite well. All you need is a French cigarette in your mouth and a beret on your head," Ethan answered.

"Very funny."

He laid his hand on the center of her back to guide her through the store's revolving entrance door. Holly's shoulders perked up at his touch.

"However," he continued as they bustled through the busy sales floor, "there is the shareholders' gala, and then there'll be charity dinners and social occasions we will be attending. As we discussed, this arrangement necessitates an appropriate wardrobe."

When they reached the Personal Styling department, an older blonde woman in a sleeveless black dress and pearls was awaiting their arrival.

"Are you Diane?" Ethan extended his right hand. "My assistant, Nathan, spoke with you earlier."

"It's a pleasure to meet you, Mr. Benton." Diane took his outstretched hand with both of hers.

"This is my friend Holly Motta."

"Oh…" Diane gave her a limp handshake, taking notice of the paint under Holly's fingernails.

"Hi!" Holly chirped.

She was going to have to get used to the surprise in people's voices when they met her. Everyone probably knew Ethan as a wealthy playboy who dated fashion models and princesses of small countries. He'd have no reason to be with a mere mortal like her.

Ethan raised his eyebrows at Holly, which made her giggle and feel more at ease.

He peered straight into Holly's eyes while he spoke to the other woman. "Diane, my friend will be accompanying me to numerous events. She is an artist, with little need for formal clothes. Can you help us outfit her in a way that stays true to her creative and unique self?"

Holly's mouth dropped open. Could anyone have said anything more perfect? He wanted to buy her clothes but he didn't want to change her.

Diane was stunned as well. "Cer…certainly," she stuttered. "Can I offer you a glass of champagne?"

And thus began her trip to Fantasyland. While Ethan sipped bubbly on a purple velvet settee, Diane showed Holly into a private dressing room that was larger than all the fitting rooms in the discount shops she usually went to put together.

Six full-length mirrors were positioned to allow for a three-hundred-and-sixty-degree view. The carpet was cream-colored, as was the furniture—no doubt chosen so as not to compete with the clothes. A vanity table with padded chair was ready for any primping needs. Hats, gloves, scarves and purses had been pre-selected and lay waiting in a glass display case. A collection of shoes stood neatly on a shoe rack. Jackets and coats hung from pegs.

Diane ducked away behind one of the mirrors.

Holly whistled out loud as she took it all in. And then

laughed at her predicament. She'd overheard Ethan talking on the phone in the car about a Diane. And a Jeremy. He had prearranged the gallery visits and now this, too. And Holly had thought *herself* to be the taking-care-of-business type! She could take a lesson from him.

"We'll start with daywear," Diane announced as she wheeled in a rack of clothes.

Besides the fact that there hadn't been any money when she was growing up, Holly had never been especially interested in clothes. She dressed functionally and comfortably, and ended up staining most everything with paint anyway. But if she had ever dreamt of wearing stylish garments made of luxurious materials these would be them.

The first ensemble Holly tried on was a white pantsuit. The slim line of the trousers made her legs look eight feet long. And the coordinating blazer with its thin satin lapels was both distinguished and chic. Worn with a navy silk shirt unbuttoned one notch past prim, the outfit delivered "sexy" as well.

Diane moved in quickly to pin the jacket's waist for a trimmer fit.

She suggested Holly try a brown slingback shoe, then plucked the proper size from a stack of boxes waiting at the ready. Diane might be a bit snobby, but she sure as heck knew what she was doing.

"Perhaps you'd like to add a touch of lipstick?" Diane inquired—a polite way of reminding Holly that she'd need to attend to her makeup and hair.

Diane opened a drawer in the vanity table that contained a palette of options. Holly dabbed on some lip gloss, undid her ponytail and brushed her hair. Surveying herself in the mirror, she knew this was without question the best she had ever looked.

"Shall we show Mr. Benton?" Diane suggested.

When Holly stepped into the waiting lounge that

seemed destined for wealthy boyfriends and mothers of brides, Ethan was busy typing into his phone.

He leaned comfortably back on the settee with one leg crossed over the other knee. Effortless elegance. Although the wavy reddish-brown hair that always had a bit of a tousle to it made sure hints of his untamed side came through.

Ethan glanced up. His eyes went through her and then right back down to his phone.

Holly was delighted as recognition gradually took hold. His jaw slackened. Eyebrows bunched. Nostrils flared.

Only then did his eyes rise up again for the double-take.

And take her in he did, indeed. Ever so slowly. From the tip of her head to the pointy toes of her designer shoes. His gaze was wicked. As if she was standing in front of him naked rather than dressed in this finery. The feeling thrilled and aroused her down to her core.

That smile made its way millimeter by millimeter across Ethan's face. "My, my…"

"So you approve?" she flirted.

"To say the least."

"Do you want to see more?"

Focused on the opening of her shirt, where perhaps that questionable button should have been closed but wasn't, he sighed. "I would most *definitely* like to see more."

She pivoted, and when her face was out of view from him let a satisfied grin explode. This was so much fun. She was long overdue for some harmless fun. *Harmless*, right?

Diane helped her into the next outfit and pinned it for alterations. Another silk blouse—this one black, with a square neckline and a gold zipper down the back—tucked into a tan pencil skirt. The look was dressy, but edgy.

Ethan's reaction was all she could have hoped for as he lingered over the snug fit of the skirt across her hips.

Next, dark wash jeans tucked into boots and a flowing

white blouse were complemented by Holly's own black leather jacket.

"More," Ethan demanded.

A crisp red dress with a pleated skirt, short sleeves and matching belt provided a timeless silhouette.

A silver satin cocktail dress draped her curves without being tight. At the sight of her in that one, Ethan shifted in his seat.

As a kid, Holly had sprouted up early and had always been the tallest girl in her class. She remembered feeling big and awkward. It had taken her years to train herself out of slouching her shoulders forward. Slim, but with hips wider than was proportionate to her small bustline, she'd never thought she wore clothes well.

Until today.

With Diane's wizardry to pinch here and fold there, these clothes looked as if they'd been custom-made to flatter her perfectly.

In all, ten outfits were put together, ranging from casual to semi-formal. Extra pieces would be added to mix and match.

Ethan had promised that no matter what happened with their phony engagement the clothes would be hers to keep. That had meant nothing to Holly when he'd said it, but now she understood how important an offer that was.

In these outfits she was *distinctive*. They made a statement. The woman who wore them was someone to take seriously. These were clothes that were the epitome of good taste, that she could—and would—care for and wear for years to come.

But the *pièce de resistance* came when Diane brought out an evening gown for the black-tie shareholders' gala. Tears unexpectedly sprang in Holly's eyes at the artistry of it. She couldn't fathom *ever* needing a dress so fancy.

It was a pearly sky-blue completely covered in hand-sewn crystals. Holly was surprised at how much the gown weighed. Sleeveless with a deep-scooped neck, it skimmed the floor until Diane had her step into coordinating high-heeled sandals.

Whether the dress complemented Holly's icy blue eyes or her eyes enhanced the dress, it didn't matter. There couldn't be a more perfect gown.

She hoped Ethan liked it.

As she stepped into the lounge to model it for him, she wanted to be sure that she was wearing the gown rather than the gown wearing *her*. Standing up straight, with her shoulders back, Holly reminded herself of what she had learned from the posture correction videos that had helped her rid herself of her slump. Stand tall. Ribs over hips. Hips over heels.

She smiled demurely at Ethan as she approached.

He hiccupped as he almost choked on his sip of champagne.

Holly giggled. She high-fived herself in her mind. *Mission accomplished.*

She cooed, high on a unique rush of power she'd never known she had, "Do you still want to marry me?"

Ethan set his champagne flute down on the side table and cleared his throat. "You have no idea…"

"One more stop and then we will go to dinner," Ethan said as he ushered Holly back into the car.

Leonard shut the passenger door, then went around to slide into his place behind the wheel. He deftly maneuvered them away from the curb to join the Fifth Avenue traffic.

Ethan was thinking ahead. "What else do you need for the gala? I assume you would like to have your hair and makeup done?"

"Please."

"I will have Nathan book that."

Holly held her hands up in front of her. There was often a rainbow of colors staining her fingers and nails, but today it was just the Cobalt Two Eleven leftover from last night's spill. "And I think I need a manicure, don't you agree?"

"The way you look in that gown, I doubt anyone would notice."

No fair for him to say things like that. Things that made her want to lean over and cover his luscious lips with an hour-long kiss. Not fair at all for him to speak words that made her contemplate what it would be like to be with someone who made her feel good about herself. Who was on her side.

Not just for business purposes.

Gridlocked traffic was only allowing them to inch forward. The rain had ceased for the moment but the sky was a thick grey. Throngs of pedestrians rushed to and fro. Some darted across the streets, jaywalking quickly in between cars. Horns honked. Drivers yelled at each other. Music blared from taxicab radios. A siren screamed.

Together, it sounded like a riotous symphony. New York was alive and kicking.

One minute she had been crammed into an economy seat on a packed airplane, headed for the Big Apple and who knew what. And then a minute later she was modeling a jewel-encrusted evening gown for a young billionaire.

A smokin' hot young billionaire who had ogled her as if he not only wanted to see those clothes on her, but also wanted to see them in a heap on the floor beside his bed.

By the end of her fashion show Holly had been imagining it as well. How it might feel to have Ethan's big and no doubt able hands unzipping the zippers and unbuttoning the buttons of those finely crafted garments.

How far would it be safe to go with this charade they had embarked on? Surely not as far as clothes being strewn at the bedside.

Holly was going to have to learn to regally accept a peck on the cheek in front of other people without melting into a puddle of desire. She might have to place a reciprocal smooch on Ethan's face at some point. If push came to shove she might even have to receive a kiss on the lips at, say, the shareholders' gala when their engagement was announced.

She had no idea how she'd handle that, but she would cross that bridge when she came to it. However, under no circumstances would her make-believe fiancé's tuxedo—or anything else of his—end up crumpled at the foot of her bed.

No one would ever see them behind closed doors. And she'd do well to remember that to a man like Ethan Benton this was all just a deal. A game. A con. He'd only go as far as was absolutely necessary to do what he deemed right for his aunt Louise's future.

Holly would keep her eye on the prize. A great place to live, steady work, a leg-up for Vince. That was more than she could have ever hoped for. Let alone on her first day here. That was enough. That was astounding.

"Out." Ethan opened the car door in the middle of the street. "This traffic is unbearable. We will go on foot."

"What?"

He firmly grasped Holly's hand and slid them out of the backseat. "Leonard, meet us in front," he instructed, before thumping the door shut. He tugged Holly. "Come on."

"Where are we going?" she asked as he ushered her to the sidewalk.

"I told you. One more stop."

They joined the masses of legs charging north on Fifth Avenue. New Yorkers during rush hour. Always in a hurry. Always somewhere to go. The air was cold. The pace was exhilarating.

Maybe this would become home. Maybe this enthralling city itself would fill up the emptiness she'd always had inside.

Two blocks later she stopped dead in her tracks. They had arrived at their destination. She looked up to take in the majesty of the Art Deco architecture. The bronze sculpture of Atlas holding up the building's clock. The elaborate window displays.

People were moving in and out of the store's entry doors. Many of those leaving held the light blue shopping bags that were known the world over.

"I do not suppose it would do for my fiancée to wear an engagement ring made from a beer bottle wrapper," he said, and winked.

So he hadn't brought her to a jewelry store to get a ring. He'd brought her to *THE* jewelry store.

Ricky had never given her an engagement ring. They'd waited for a sale at the jewelry store in their local mall and bought the two cheapest gold bands there. It had only been last month that she'd gotten around to selling hers for bulk weight to help pay for her plane ticket to New York.

Now she was standing in front of the most well-known jewelry store in the world! Little blue bags!

Inside, Ethan gave his name and they were immediately escorted to the private salon. A man in a pinstriped suit introduced himself as Jeremy Markham.

Again Holly remembered hearing Ethan on the phone that morning with his assistant, Nathan, mentioning a Diane and a Jeremy. Diane was clothes…obviously Jeremy was jewels. Ethan had everything figured out.

"Jeremy, we will need some help with a wardrobe of jewelry in the weeks to come, but today we would like to choose a diamond ring."

"Of course, sir. May I present a selection?"

Ethan nodded.

A private appointment to pick out an engagement ring? Ho-hum, just an ordinary day.

"Please, sit down." Jeremy, chin up high, held a chair out for Holly after giving her a once-over. Like Diane with the clothes, had this salesman who clearly only dealt with VIPs already figured out that Holly was just one big fake? Another opportunist going after a rich man's money.

Using a key extracted from his jacket pocket, Jeremy let himself into a back room.

Ethan pulled a chair next to Holly's.

"Check these out!" she exclaimed at the glass case to the left of them.

A heritage collection of gemstone jewelry was on display. Elaborate necklaces and bracelets made from pounds of gold and carat upon carat of colorful stones. The pieces were too ornate for her taste, but she was attracted to the hues.

What had really caught her eye was a simple ring of blue topaz. The stone was a large oval cut, bordered on each side by two small diamonds.

"Look at how stunning that ring is. That blue is so brilliant it's blinding. Light is bouncing off it in twenty different directions."

Holly's eyes were light blue, like the stone. It had always been her favorite color from as far back as she could remember. Maybe that was why she'd instantly fallen in love with the sky-blue evening gown Ethan had bought for her.

While it had always been pink for girls and blue for boys Holly, as usual, had swum against the stream. It wasn't as if the trailer she'd lived in with her mom and brother had had any décor to it. The walls had been covered in flowery peeling wallpaper. Sheets and blankets had always been chosen by what was on clearance sale, which had usually translated to scratchy fabrics with dark prints. But Holly could remember a few occasions when her father had been in town for a day or so with some money and bought her new clothes. She'd always chosen items in shades of blue.

"It's just dazzling," she continued, pointing to the ring. "I've never seen anything like it."

Ethan glanced over to it and shrugged his shoulders, indifferent.

Jeremy returned with two velvet trays that held a wide variety of ring styles, all with humongous diamonds.

Ethan whispered to Holly, "We ought to be able to find something perfect amongst these."

She shot one final glance at the astounding blue topaz. "Whatever you say. You're the boss…"

"Feng, we will start with hot and sour soup. Follow that with the chef's special duck, beef with broccoli, shrimp chow mein. And oolong tea."

"Thank you, Mr. Ethan." The waiter bowed and hurried away.

After the jewelry store, Ethan had instructed Leonard to drive them to Chinatown. Now he and Holly were comfortably ensconced in a booth at a casual restaurant his family often frequented when they were in New York.

"I am famished," Ethan proclaimed. "Shopping is exhausting."

With a suitably enormous diamond engagement ring now on Holly's finger, the day's checklist was complete. They had been downtown, midtown, and now back downtown, but he was craving familiar food.

"Do you do a lot of shopping?" Holly questioned.

"I suppose I do my fair share, but it is not an activity I have a feeling for one way or another," he lied.

Watching Holly model one comely outfit after another would rank pretty darn high on his list of pleasurable pastimes. Although a lot of his other work had been accomplished today as well, thanks to the convenience of technology. Securing a fiancée had been at the top of his to-do list.

"Do you…" Holly twirled a lock of her raven hair "…shop for women on a regular basis?"

Hmm…fishing, was she?

"Women have dragged me to find gold in China, the finest silks in India, the best leather in Buenos Aires, if that is what you are asking."

She brushed her bangs out of her eyes and sat up straight. "Oh."

The previous women in his life were a sore point with him. In fact Ethan and women had never been a good combination, period. Going all the way back to his mother. Other than Aunt Louise, every woman Ethan had encountered seemed to him to be one hundred percent selfish. Only out for what they could get. Gifts, money, travel, status—you name it.

Which was why he was resolute that he'd never fall in love. To love you had to trust. And that was something he was never going to be tricked into again.

So it was a logical step for him to dream up this scheme that would allow Aunt Louise to think Ethan had found lifelong love as she had with Uncle Mel. Ethan would never have to marry a woman whose motivation he'd question. Intention, compensation and expectation were all upfront with this plan. It might be the brainiest partnership deal he'd ever conceived.

"Hot and sour soup." Feng placed the steaming bowl on the table. While he ladled out two servings he questioned, "May I ask if Mrs. Louise is feeling better?"

His aunt Louise had been in New York several times in the past few months. Feng had probably seen her more recently than Ethan had.

"Was she unwell when she was last here?"

The waiter pursed his lips and bowed his head, which said more than any words could.

Ethan's heart sank. This validated the fact that he was on the right track. Doing whatever it took to get Aunt Louise to retire and relax in Barbados before worse things than stumbles and bruises stole her dignity.

It was all going to work out.

As long as Ethan continued to stare past but not into Holly Motta's face. Because when he did steal a glance she didn't look like a business proposition. Or a gold-digger out to get what she deemed hers. With that slouch she kept correcting, and that milky skin, and the hint of ache in her eyes...

No, she was a living, breathing, kindred spirit who could shred his master plan into a million slices if he wasn't careful.

"Why are you looking at me like that?" she asked with her spoon in the air.

"Like what?" Ethan threw back his head with an exaggerated nonchalance.

She gave him a mock frown.

"Eat your soup," he told her.

One very ungenteel slurp later... *"Yummo!"*

"We should learn more about each other if we are to be convincing as a couple. You clearly like food."

He mocked her slurp until they were both laughing.

"My turn," she said. "You're an only child."

"You have one brother."

"You studied at Oxford."

"What is your favorite movie?"

Holly dismissed him with a wave of her hand. "Are you kidding me? If we're going to get to know each other we have to get real. What is the one thing that has hurt you the most in your life?"

His mother. Of course it was his mother. Nothing could

devastate a nine-year-old boy more than being left behind by his mother. It was horrible enough that his father had died instantly when a drunk driver had plowed into his car at racing speed, killing him instantly. But then shortly after that to lose his mother in the way he had… It was unthinkable.

"Beef with snow peas. Shrimp chow mein. Chef's special duck," Feng announced as he and another waiter positioned the platters in the center of the table. "Please enjoy."

Saved by the duck.

Ethan wasn't going to expose his darkness and despair to someone he'd met only yesterday. As a matter of fact he wasn't in the habit of talking about his feelings with *anyone*. It was better that way.

He scooped a portion of each dish onto his and Holly's plates.

But wasn't it rather amazing that this woman was so genuine she didn't want to discuss trivial matters?

As she lifted her chopsticks to grab at her chow mein he admired the diamond ring he had put on her finger. It was staggering in its size and clarity, and he knew any woman would be filled with pride to wear something so timeless and flawless.

Yet he could kick himself because he hadn't bought her the blue topaz ring she had admired at the store!

Quick thinking had told him to buy the type of ring that was expected of him. Anything other than a traditional diamond engagement ring would invite inquiry. Such as where and why and what sentiments had inspired him to buy such an unusual ring. Those were extra questions they didn't need. It would just add to the risk of them flubbing up as a believable couple.

But now he thought blue ring, purple ring, green ring— what would it matter if that was what she wanted?

Pulsing and vibrant, Holly Motta had careened into his apartment with blue paint on her face and, he feared, had changed his life forever. Forcing him to think about women differently than he ever had. Making him for the first time vaguely envision a role in which he cared if someone was happy. Edging him into speculation about what it would be like if someone cared about his happiness, too.

And now she was making it hard to concentrate on anything other than leaping across the table and planting a kiss on that sweet mouth that was busy with noodles.

After a bite of food to steady himself, Ethan resumed their interview. "Tell me something about yourself that I would not have guessed."

"I used to be—" she blurted, and then abruptly stopped herself. She put her chopsticks down and took a slow sip of her tea. Trying to recover, she finished with, "A pretty good softball player."

Aha, so it wasn't as easy for her to be as open and candid as she wanted him to believe it was. What had she been about to say that had proved too difficult to reveal? And what had she avoided telling him at breakfast that morning about the mother she'd characterized as *unpredictable*?

He'd gone along with her easy sincerity, but Ethan really didn't know the first thing about her. He'd garnered that she'd had a difficult childhood, but it wasn't like him to take anyone at face value. Not after what he'd seen of life.

Guard and defend.

He had his family's empire to protect.

"Excuse me," he said as he put his chopsticks down and pulled out his phone. "I have just remembered one more bit of business for the day."

He texted Chip Foley, Benton Worldwide's Head of Security. Just as he'd intended to do if he'd hired an actress for the fiancée job.

Chip, please run everything you can on a Holly Motta from Fort Pierce, Florida. Claims her occupation is artist. I would place her age at about thirty. Tall, slim, blue eyes, black hair. She says her brother Vince works for us in Miami. I do not know if it is the same last name. Do an across-the-board check on her for me.

After hitting the "send" button, his eyes returned to Holly.

She pointed her chopsticks at him and taunted, "Hey, you never told me what it was in your life that hurt you the most."

CHAPTER SIX

It was the dead of night, but Holly could still hear New York outside the bedroom window. Cars drove by. A dog barked. People laughed boisterously on the street.

The city that never slept.

Lying in Ethan's bed, with her head sinking into his soft pillows, she could hardly make sense of the day. Visiting Soho galleries, buying all those art supplies, a new wardrobe, a diamond ring... Then that dinner in Chinatown.

She'd lived a lifetime in the last twenty-four hours.

Ethan was just beyond the door in the living room. Was he sleeping? Was he working? Or was he lying awake thinking about her as she was of him?

Of course not, Holly reminded herself. Ethan Benton had more important things on his mind then his wife for hire. She'd better remember that.

But when they'd watched each other's faces at the restaurant it had seemed as if maybe she would, in fact, linger in his thoughts and keep him up at night. He'd looked at her as if there was nowhere else he'd rather be. The restaurant might have been crowded and clamoring, but he'd never taken his eyes off her.

Through most of the evening they would have convinced anyone they were an engaged couple. Finishing each other's sentences... Digging their chopsticks into each other's plates...

And then there had been those awkward moments when they'd asked each other questions neither was ready to answer.

Holly hadn't been able to bring herself to tell Ethan that she had been married. She feared he would think of her as a used product and not want to go through with their agreement. He didn't need to know about her mistake in marrying someone who hadn't loved her for who she was. Who hadn't supported the person she wanted to become. Ricky Dowd wasn't a name that *ever* needed to come up in conversation.

They would go through with their pretend engagement so that Ethan could protect his aunt as her health declined. And, as he'd said, either they would continue to meet for official occasions or eventually call off their deal. Whatever happened, Ethan would never have to know about Holly's wasted time on wrong decisions that tonight seemed like a million years ago.

Just as she might not find out what he was hiding because he didn't want to tell her what had caused him the most hurt in his life. It had to be something terrible, because both times when he'd avoided the topic his eyes had turned to coal.

But the rest of the evening was a dream she never wanted to wake from. When they had got to unimportant questions, like favorite movies and television shows, they'd laughed themselves dizzy remembering jokes from silly comedies. Laughed some more about bad childhood haircuts and mean teachers they'd hated in school.

They had stayed long after the restaurant had emptied, until the staff had been ready to leave. Feng had walked them out to the street and waved them goodbye as they'd tucked themselves into the car so Leonard could deposit them home.

Holly drifted off to sleep, replaying over and over again how Ethan had gently kissed the back of her hand and thanked her for an unforgettable day before he closed the bedroom door.

In the morning, Ethan scrutinized his unshaven face in the bathroom mirror. He hadn't laughed as much as he had last night in a long time. Truth be told, he couldn't remember ever laughing that much. Everything was full power with Holly. Near her, he felt alive with a liquid fire.

That might burn down his life as he knew it.

After showering and dressing, he charted a direct route into the kitchen toward the coffeepot.

"Morning," she greeted him.

"Yes."

He was careful not to touch her as he crossed behind her in the tiny kitchen to pour a cup. It took stupendous will not to reach for her, to put his arms around her waist and find out what her hair might smell like if his face was buried in it.

Instead, more guarding and defending.

He gained distance by busying himself with checking the morning's urgencies on his tablet. His approval was needed on important architectural specifications for the Jersey City project. An email chain between several of the interested parties provided updates. Thank heavens for work. He needed the interruption from his growing and wholly off-track desires for more than what he'd signed up for with Holly.

Despite his efforts, his eyes of their own volition kept darting upward from the screen as he watched her lay out a light breakfast of toast and juice.

"Right, then, we have an important day," he directed

as soon as they'd sat down with their food. "Aunt Louise and Fernando will arrive at six o'clock. She does not like to stay out late in the evening. We should have dinner on the table by seven."

"I made a shopping list," Holly reported. "I'll go to the store, then get the pot roast into the slow cooker."

"I have several meetings today. Can you manage the shopping on your own?"

She snickered. "I've been doing the grocery shopping since I was seven years old. I think I can handle a New York City supermarket."

"I am the one who would have trouble."

"But after that I'll need you for the painting. I have the canvas size I want. And I'll use acrylic so it will dry quickly. We'll hang it later this afternoon, and no one will be any the wiser that I only painted it today."

With a busy day ahead, he'd selectively forgotten that he had agreed to her doing a painting of him. He had no time for posing. Although a painting by her would be a very eye-catching and convincing symbol that they were really a couple.

Plus, it would put him in proximity with her from midday. Which he had to admit he'd be looking forward to.

He mentally reprimanded himself for that thought.

In front of the building, Ethan watched Holly walk down the block while Leonard held the car door open for him. Her glossy hair swung to and fro. It was another gloomy day, but dry at the moment. Her jeans and that black leather jacket she seemed to favor would be sufficient for her shopping trip. Why he was concerned with how she was dressed for the weather was baffling. And disturbing.

But what would a Florida girl know about winter? She might catch cold…

Leonard ferried him from one appointment to the next. The low-income housing project in the Bronx was behind schedule and over budget. He pored over blueprints with the architect until they found a way to enlarge the kitchens for the exterior-facing units. The architect was feuding with the contractor over the selection of materials, but that always seemed to be the case. Ethan was able to smooth some ruffled feathers.

He stopped at the hotel where the shareholders' gala would be held on Saturday. Gave his authorization for the layout of the ballroom. Visualizing the room full of formally dressed people, he could picture them raising their champagne glasses as Aunt Louise offered a toast to him and Holly. His bride-to-be would charm the crowd with her engaging smile and shimmering gown...

In the silence of the empty ballroom, Ethan's heart pleaded for something he couldn't fully grasp. A dull ache thudded in the center of his chest.

Swiftly shoving those confusing feelings aside, he hurried out through the hotel doors to Leonard's car and his next meeting.

The multi-use development in Chelsea had come a long way since he'd last seen it. As he strode through he offered dozens of hellos to the many workers laboring on the project's five buildings. It was for this large venture that he'd offered Holly the commission to do the artwork. The opportunity that had sealed the negotiations for her to agree to pose as his fiancée.

Ethan's interior designer had been intrigued to hear about the up-and-coming artist from Florida he had brought onto the job. He had provided Stella with Holly's website address.

Midday, he returned to the apartment. Holly must not have had any trouble with the slow cooker, because the aroma of cooking meat practically had him salivating.

"My, my..." he said as he removed his coat and hung it on the rack.

The open area by the living room window had been turned into a temporary artist's studio.

"I've been working."

"I can see."

The easel they had bought yesterday was unpacked and in use. A side table with a tarp thrown over it for protection had become a paint station. Another tarp covered the area's floor.

"What have you done with my apartment?"

"Hey, I thought it was *my* apartment."

"Tonight it will be *our* apartment."

"Don't worry. I'll clean it all up after I do the painting of you."

"What do we have here?"

Three pastel drawings on paper lay on the floor. Moving vehicles was their theme. One was a bright yellow taxi done in abstracted horizontal lines that made it look as if it was in motion. Ditto for a blue city bus motoring along. And likewise for a silver train car that appeared to be whizzing by.

"I was working out some ideas. Will there be a valet and transportation station at the Chelsea development?"

Of course. He nodded with immediate understanding. Paintings like this would be stylish and hip, and convey the movement of the city. They'd be perfect. Even if their marriage arrangement proved to be the wrong move, Ethan was at least sure he'd hired an artist who would produce what he needed for the multi-million-dollar project.

"Excellent."

"We'd better not waste any time. When can you be ready to sit for me?"

A grin tried to crack at his mouth. "Let me just wash up. Dinner smells delicious."

Minutes later, he stepped onto the tarp of her studio area.

"I am ready for you," he said bravely, with arms out-stretched.

In reality, he didn't know what to expect. Was not at all comfortable with how Holly might portray him. He reminded himself that this was ultimately for the good of Aunt Louise. He could put up with a little uneasiness for the sake of her wellbeing.

"I'll have you sitting on the stool." Holly, all business, gestured for him to take his place.

She studied him intently. Backed away to get one perspective. Inched to the side for another. Then came in close. So close he could feel the heat of her body, which made him want to do anything *but* sit still.

"What are you deciding on?"

"The perspective. I think I'll do it at an angle that's a partial profile."

"Will it be only my face?"

She ran a finger across his upper chest from shoulder to shoulder to illustrate the cut-off point. Blood pumped double-time to every inch of him she touched. He instinctively leaned away.

"Don't worry. I won't bite."

His voice came out a jagged growl. "It was not you I was worried about."

She smiled quizzically for several beats. His chest muscles continued to vibrate from her touch.

It occurred to him that for all the questions they'd asked each other about favorite things and childhood memories, they hadn't talked about past relationships.

Had a man broken her heart? Had she broken someone's? Was she looking for love?

Did she wonder about him?

Love wasn't on the bargaining table in their business deal. He'd never loved. Didn't love. Wouldn't love. That was a contract signed a long time ago.

Holly programmed some upbeat music into her phone and began. She wanted to do a preliminary pencil drawing on paper, and when she was satisfied with that move on to paint and canvas.

With a last adjustment to his angle, she requested, "Try not to move."

"Do I need to be silent?"

"I'll let you know when I'm sketching your mouth. Just keep your head still when you talk."

With his face turned toward the window, it was odd to feel her eyes on him when he couldn't see her face. Odd, but spine-tingling. And erotic. He wished he could rip off his clothes and have her paint him in the nude.

Holly made him want to let go of the well-bred and well-mannered businessman he was. With her, he wanted to howl naked under the moonlight. And to ravage her with the savage passion he kept tightly caged inside him.

"Can you soften your facial expression?" she asked, making him realize that he was not masking his arousal.

He neutralized his jaw.

"Tell me about your morning," she coaxed.

He appreciated her trying to help him relax. "There are ongoing issues with my housing development in the Bronx. I want to build the maximum number of comfortable units on the property to give as many families as possible a home of their own."

"What are the problems?"

"Materials are costly. I have shareholders to answer to. And Aunt Louise. I promised this as a break-even project—not one on which the company would lose a lot of money. I may have to move it into the category of charitable endeavor. I will have to present it accordingly. Tricky."

"Here, take a look." Holly unclipped from the easel the large piece of paper she'd been using for her sketch and held it up in front of her for him to see.

After preparing himself to hate it, he saw that it wasn't bad at all. She'd used those same short lines she had on the transportation drawings. Together, the strokes formed the likeness of a pensive man looking into the distance.

Holly's face was flushed. She was nervously waiting for his reaction.

With a voice tight and caught, she squeaked, "What do you think?"

"Is this how I look?"

"Well, obviously you're handsome. I hoped I could convey your seriousness, too."

She'd said "handsome" as matter-of-factly as it would have been to say he was wearing a white shirt. He liked it that she thought he was handsome.

"I suppose I am serious."

"That feels like your core. You're formal. You're measured."

"Whereas *you* just say or do anything that comes into your mind."

"And you don't seem like someone who ever loses control."

Oh, if she only knew the thoughts he was having about grabbing her and showing her exactly how out of control he could be.

She was uncovering wild ideas in him. Holly, with her mesmerizing black hair and sinewy limbs. He'd stripped open more of his true self to her in the last two days than he had with anyone in his life. Not all his secrets, but he'd revealed a lot.

And he must rein that in right now. She only needed to know what was relevant to their phony engagement. Nothing more.

He stood up from his stool to stretch and take a break. Checked messages on his phone. Fired off a couple of texts.

Using a sketchpad, Holly quickly drew more versions

of his mouth until she was satisfied. Then showed him the one that she liked.

"Interesting… It looks as if it is easy enough for you to make a small correction here and there and come out with a quite different result."

She shrugged her shoulders. "I guess so. Trial and error."

"I would not have a clue how to do that."

"I'll show you sometime."

"I would like that."

How absurd this was—letting someone sketch his mouth. In the middle of a workday. When he had a thousand other things on his mind.

But he didn't care. Inexplicably, he wanted to be near Holly. She'd definitely cast a spell on him.

She lifted a large canvas onto her easel and adjusted the height. Then picked out her first brush.

"I'm ready to paint. Let's begin."

"Holly Motta, this is my aunt, Louise Benton." Ethan made the introduction as soon as he'd ushered in the visitors.

With a welcoming smile Holly shook the older lady's hand. "I'm happy to finally meet you. I've heard so much about you."

"And I so little about you…" Louise assessed her. "How pretty you are, dear."

"I'd say the same about you. Let Ethan take your coat."

Holly reminded herself to stay focused in spite of her nerves. At this moment her end of the contract had come due. Louise had to be convinced beyond a shadow of a doubt that not only was she Ethan's true love, but that he had made the right choice in her.

As Ethan helped his aunt to remove her coat Louise almost lost her balance. A telltale sign of her medical condition. How difficult living with a chronic problem like that must be. Still, Louise had style despite her petite and frail frame. A sheet of thin white hair curled under at her shoulders...her simple dark green dress was the picture of good taste.

She was the type of accomplished woman Holly looked up to. Holly was glad she had chosen to wear the black trousers and gray blouse from the new clothes Ethan had bought her. Even though it was dinner at home, these were not people who dined in jeans.

"Such an unusual silver necklace..." Holly initiated conversation.

Louise looked to Ethan. "Yes, my dear nephew brought it back from...remind me where it was from?"

"Turkey."

"Yes, Istanbul. Ethan always brings me unique trinkets from his travels."

With Louise's head turned toward Ethan, Holly noticed the large bruise across her cheekbone. That must have been from the fall Ethan had said she'd taken last week. Holly understood his wish to shield his aunt from the public eye, with her decline so visible.

"Huh...low...oh..." Louise's husband, Fernando, finally insisted on being acknowledged. Ethan hadn't yet taken his coat, and nor had an introduction been made.

"Yes, Fernando Layne—meet my fiancée, Holly Motta."

"Charmed," Fernando replied, without extending his hand.

"Nice to meet you." Holly rocked back on her heels, unsure how to move on if they weren't going to shake hands.

"Are we having cocktails?" Fernando flung his coat to Ethan.

"Let me mix you something," Ethan offered.

"I know where the drinks are." Fernando rebuffed him and headed to the liquor cabinet.

Ethan had told Holly it was Fernando who had bought

this apartment. On behalf of Benton Worldwide and with the company's money, of course. And that he made frequent shopping trips to New York.

Forty-five years old trying to look twenty-five, judging from his slicked-back hair and skinny pants. No doubt Fernando preferred chic New York to less flashy Boston, although Holly couldn't say for sure having never been there. But in an instant she knew that she wouldn't trust Fernando if her life depended on it.

"Louise." Fernando presented his wife with a glass of brown liquor.

She refused. "You know I'm not drinking with the new medications," she said.

"A sparkling water, then." He took the glass and drank it in one tip, then scurried back to the bar to pour Louise some water. Not asking if Holly and Ethan wanted anything.

Fernando's eye caught the painting of Ethan, now on the wall where those impersonal black and white photos had been. "You two have certainly settled in."

Holly bit her lip. *If he only knew.* About her barging in on Ethan just two days ago... That this apartment Fernando thought was his had become part of Ethan and Holly's agreement... How no one in this room knew that her feelings for Ethan were becoming closer to real rather than the masquerade they were meant to be...

"Did you do this, my dear?" Louise moved toward the painting to take a closer look.

It had turned out well, especially for only an afternoon's work. It was all done in blue—a tribute to the paint color she'd had on her face and hands when she had first rushed into this apartment, expecting it to be empty.

She'd probably had more fun than she should have painting Ethan. What an impressive subject he was. With his upright posture. Finely chiseled jaw. The deep, deep eyes with just a hint of crinkle at the outer corners. And his mouth! That mouth! No wonder it had taken her a few sketches until she got it right. Lips not so full as to be feminine. Lips she longed to explore with her own, not with her paintbrush...

"The first of many to come, I hope." Holly slipped her arm through Ethan's in a way she thought a fiancée in love might. His muscles jumped, but at least he didn't bristle and pull away. "Ethan's not keen on sitting for me."

"He never was," Louise agreed. "Didn't we have to bribe you with sweets in order to get you to stay still for those Christmas portraits every year?"

"I told Holly about that crotchety old painter who smelled of pipe tobacco. She is lucky I was not scarred for life."

Conversational banter. *Check*. This couldn't be going better.

"I see you captured that distinctive curl of hair over Ethan's forehead," Louise noted.

That curl had captured Holly—not the other way around. The magnificent way his wavy hair spilled over in front. Just a little bit. Just enough...

It was the one thing that wasn't completely tamed and restrained about Ethan. Somehow that curl hinted at the fiery, emotional man she knew lay beneath the custom-made suits and the multi-million-dollar deals.

"I certainly never learned how to paint or draw," Ethan said, with a convincingly proud smile of approval at his fiancée's handiwork.

While they chatted about the painting Fernando moseyed over to Ethan's desk. Out of the corner of her eye, Holly saw him snooping at the papers on top of it.

Fernando was making himself a bit too much at home. Funny that Holly felt territorial after only two days. She knew that Fernando used this apartment frequently. But he didn't keep any of his personal possessions here because other employees and associates of Benton Worldwide also used it when they were in New York.

Still, she didn't think Fernando had the right to be looking at anything Ethan might have put down on the desk. But it wasn't her place to say anything.

"Louise, would you like to sit down at the table?" Holly suggested.

She took Louise's elbow and guided her toward the dining area. Ethan and Fernando followed suit behind them.

Holly overheard Fernando hiss to Ethan, "I know what you're up to. You've found a wife so that Louise will retire and you can take over. If you think I'm going to spend the rest of her life getting sunburned on a boring island, you've got another think coming."

CHAPTER SEVEN

"SO FAR SO GOOD," Holly said as she placed four plates on the kitchen counter so that she and Ethan could begin to serve dinner.

"Except that I had forgotten how much I detest that little Fernando," he retorted.

Holly was only playing the role of soon-to-be member of this unusual family. She shouldn't be privy to the disagreements and resentments that might lie beneath the surface. So it wouldn't be proper for her to ask Ethan what Fernando had meant about not wanting to move to Barbados when Louise retired. Obviously the comment had made Ethan mad.

She removed the lid of the slow cooker. "Where did they meet?"

Speaking in a hushed voice, because Aunt Louise and her man-toy weren't far away at the dining table, Ethan explained. "Our office manager at Headquarters hired him. His title is 'Client Relations Coordinator,' or some such nonsense. He does scarcely more than order fancy coffees for meetings and come here to New York or go to Europe to spend the company's money. Of course I cannot fire him." Ethan gritted his teeth. "As much as I would like to."

With serving utensils, Holly lifted hearty chunks of the pot roast onto each plate. Ethan reached in with a fork to assist her. They worked seamlessly as a team, anticipating each other's moves. Now pros at navigating the square footage of the small kitchen.

"What does she see in him?"

"Companionship. I suppose he makes her feel younger. She was devastated after Uncle Mel died."

"She must miss Mel horribly."

"They were a partnership in more ways than I can count. Not being able to have children brought them even closer. Taking me in was another thing they did together."

With Ethan having witnessed such a solid marriage between his aunt and uncle, Holly wondered why he was so adamant that he himself would never marry for love. What had happened to close him off to the possibility?

Ethan ladled mashed potatoes while Holly spooned gravy on top. "So Fernando has been able to fill the hole left by your uncle's death?"

"Hardly. He could *never* step into my uncle's shoes. But I will grant that he provides a diversion. Within a year of Uncle Mel's death Aunt Louise began having symptoms of this hereditary neuropathy that she remembers her mother suffering from."

"Losing your husband and developing an illness, one after the other. That's awful."

"She could have sunk into a depression. Fernando at least gives her something to do. He keeps her busy with Boston society dinners and parties on Cape Cod. He will do the same in Barbados. I will remind him that *I* am the boss as often as I need to. We know a lot of people there. He can develop a social calendar for her."

"Give her things to look forward to?"

"Yes. Without children, there are no grandchildren on the horizon. Although I suppose she assumes you and I will have…" He trailed off.

Children. With Ethan.

The mere thought halted Holly in place. A home of her own. Filled with noise and food and laughter and love. Beautiful toddlers running around with reddish-brown tufts of hair falling onto their foreheads. Tall Ethan reaching down to hold little hands.

Did he ever think about having children?

He'd frozen too, holding a spoon in his hand, also lost in contemplation. Was he picturing the same thing?

He'd be a good father. The way he put so much care and thought into his aunt and what was best for her was like the devotion and concern she had for Vince, having practically raised her brother single-handedly because her mother had proved incapable. She had more of that kind of love to give.

Someday.

It wasn't going to be now.

That was much further far down the line. If ever.

No, this current arrangement was ideal. A new life for herself in New York. Not being pulled down by other people. Putting herself first. Free at last.

Everything was upfront with Ethan. There was zero chance of her being hurt. Zero love. Zero disappointment. So he was intelligent and intense? And gorgeous? That was ultimately irrelevant to the duties at hand. They were two professionals, doing their jobs.

Holly used tongs to crown each dinner plate with roasted carrots. Forging ahead. Although she wished her fingernails weren't spotted with paint.

"We did it. Dinner is served."

As she carried two plates to the dining table, she saw Fernando's hand atop of Louise's. The older woman's face did seem to have a livelier blush with his attention on her. Even if Fernando's intentions were less than honorable, Holly could understand the purpose he filled. Life was all about compromises.

Ethan brought the other two plates. While he poured water she ducked back into the kitchen for rolls and butter before sitting to eat.

"Holly, this is delicious," Louise proclaimed.

"I'm glad you like it. You sound surprised?"

"Indeed. I don't know that Ethan has ever dated a woman before who would know how to make an old-fashioned pot roast."

Ethan leaned to pat Holly's arm. She smiled at the unspoken compliment, as a fiancée should. "Aunt Louise, I have never dated a woman who has likely ever eaten pot roast, let alone prepared it."

"Where did you learn to cook like this?"

"I took a course in cooking classic American comfort food," Holly fibbed, without missing a beat. Louise didn't need to know that if she hadn't taught herself to cook she and Vince wouldn't have eaten. "I'll have to make cheeseburgers for you next time."

"Now, Ethan, dear," Louise said, "you have been keeping your delightful lady a secret. You must tell us everything about where and how you met," she insisted.

Fernando buttered a roll and gobbled it down.

Holly and Ethan, the happy couple, gazed lovingly at each other as if to signal that they were off and running. They'd been rehearsing. Now they'd be put to the test.

"Aunt Louise, I wanted to be absolutely sure of myself before I said anything to you," Ethan began. "Holly's brother is Vince Motta. He works for us in the Miami office."

Aunt Louise listened attentively as she continued eating. Fernando chomped on chunks of meat that he yanked off his fork with his lower teeth.

"It was at the groundbreaking ceremony for the Coconut Grove project," Holly continued. For accuracy, Ethan had filled her in on the details of that luncheon. "We were both reaching for the same shrimp on the buffet table. Our hands touched."

"And it was magic."

Ethan fluttered his eyelashes, which made Holly giggle.

She'd visualized this fairy tale over and over—to the point that now she would have sworn it had actually happened. The elegant outdoor celebration… Her in a pink dress, talking to her brother, Vince, and a couple of his coworkers… After excusing herself she left them to explore the lavish seafood table. And just as she reached for the plumpest, juiciest-looking shrimp on the tray a hand from the opposite direction nabbed the same one.

She tugged on her end of the shrimp, the other hand on the other end, until their fingers intertwined.

They turned to look at each other.

He surrendered the crustacean.

The skies parted.

The angels cascaded down from heaven playing trumpets.

"It was love at first shrimp…" They sighed in unison.

"How romantic." Louise was sufficiently charmed.

"We talked for hours that afternoon." Ethan laid it on thick. "But then I had to board a plane for Bangkok."

"We didn't see each other again for months."

Caught up in their "reminiscing," they moved their faces toward each other. Involuntarily. As if pulled together by a magnet.

Ethan bent in and brought his mouth to Holly's. Only it wasn't a feather-soft fake dinner kiss, meant to convince his aunt. No, his unexpected lips were bold. And hot. And they smashed against hers.

Their insistence didn't let her pull away. She swirled inside. Got lost in the moment. Let it go on several beats too many.

Until she could finally separate herself from him.

Holly feared that everyone at the table could hear her heart pounding outside her chest.

Ethan looked as shocked as she felt. But after a moment he picked up his fork and resumed eating. Following his lead, she did the same.

Fortunately neither Louise nor Fernando had noticed anything strange. Holly and Ethan were engaged, after all. Why *wouldn't* they spontaneously kiss?

But he wasn't helping her any with a kiss like that. Let that be a warning to her.

Louise inquired, "Are your people from Miami, dear?"

Holly barely had a moment to catch her breath—nowhere near enough time to recover from that inebriating kiss before there came the next flaming hoop she had to jump through. She didn't have "people." And the people she did have she needed to keep a secret. Her people were not Benton kind of people.

"No. Fort Pierce."

"Fort *Pierce*?" Fernando tossed back.

Certainly not the kind of stylish metropolis full of chic hotels, South Beach beauties and all-night parties that would interest him.

"We met again last year here in New York, when Holly was exhibiting paintings at a Soho gallery," Ethan fibbed to move their story forward.

"Then wasn't the next time when you came down and we visited Key West?"

He leaned over to brush the side of her cheek with the back of his hand. "It was then that I knew for sure."

His tender touch across Holly's face made it a struggle to keep her eyes open. Especially after that not so gentle kiss had rocked her to the bone.

Ethan sensed he had made her uncomfortable. "More water, anyone?" he said quickly, refilling glasses without waiting for an answer.

Thankfully giving her a moment to regroup.

After a couple of quiet sips Holly ventured, "I'm so happy we're finally together in New York. I haven't been here in five years."

Ethan, Louise and Fernando all looked at her.

Oh, no! Oh! No!

Fernando's eyes narrowed. "I thought you said you had a painting exhibition here last year?"

Gulp. Ethan's soft stroke to her face had thrown her off course. Let her talk before she thought.

Dead silence. Which was finally broken by the sound of a fax coming in on Ethan's desk.

"I meant that I haven't explored the city in years." Holly took a shot. "That was a work trip. I hardly left the gallery."

"Shall we have dessert?" Ethan did his best to defuse the moment.

"Let me help you, dear." Louise slowly rose and followed Ethan into the kitchen.

Fernando kept his glare on Holly one uncomfortable moment longer before he shot up to strut to the liquor cabinet.

Left at the table, Holly stood and began clearing the dishes. Not knowing how badly she had messed things up. Whether Ethan would be furious with her or sympathetic over her flub. Unsure if anyone had bought her quick cover-up.

Louise, even with her reduced ability, had offered to help Ethan with dessert in the kitchen. She must want to say something to him that she didn't want Holly to hear.

Careful not to interrupt Ethan and his aunt's private conversation, she stacked the dirty plates and brushed crumbs off the table. The dessert dishes and silverware were on a side shelf, so she set those out.

The evening had been going so nicely. Louise seemed

to like her. Hopefully Holly hadn't unraveled everything with one slip of the tongue.

With each passing minute Holly had come to like the idea of being Ethan's pretend fiancée more and more. She wanted to make this work. To have the art commission and a place to live. It was a peculiar arrangement, for sure, but a better starting point for a new life than she could ever have imagined. At almost thirty, it was time for her to re-wind and reboot. Put the bad choices—Ricky—and the bad luck—her mother—behind her.

When Ethan had sweetened the deal by agreeing to use his influence to help her brother, Vince, get a promotion, Holly had had to roll the dice and give it a try. Ethan had said he couldn't make any promises, but Holly knew Vince was a hard and devoted worker who could easily manage additional responsibilities. She'd never forgive herself if her mistake tonight had done anything to endanger his chances of success.

And, *wow*, she was going to have to lay down some ground rules about her physical interactions with Ethan. She was shocked at how she was drawn to him almost hypnotically, easily touching his arm and lightly laying a hand on the small of his back as if it was no big deal. Like a fiancée would.

But that kiss had shown her how quickly things could go too far. His mouth on hers had dizzied her, made her lose track of her thoughts, forget the company she was in. Ethan's lips were dangerous weapons. They could com-pletely daze her, leave her woozy and unable to do the job he had hired her for.

What she needed was to figure out a system whereby his touch had no effect on her. She'd work that out. This *was* playacting, after all.

The dessert and coffee dishes set, an odd sight greeted Holly when she turned around from the table. Fernando was again in front of Ethan's desk. This time he was peering at the fax they had just heard come through. His eyes widened and he snatched the piece of paper from the machine, folded it and slid it into his pocket. Not noticing that Holly was watching.

Because Fernando supposedly spent a lot of time in this apartment, the fax might be something he was expecting. But it irked her that he was again hovering around the paperwork and personal items that Ethan had spread out on the desk. However, she didn't know all the facts. He was Louise's husband. She couldn't question him even though she wanted to. She was a hired hand who didn't know what went on in this family.

She had already screwed up. Her job right now was to keep her nose down. And do her best to salvage the rest of the evening.

Ethan's arm around Holly's shoulder, they said goodbye to Louise and Fernando as the elevator door closed.

Back in the apartment, Ethan clenched his fist in victory. "Success!"

"Do you think everything went all right? I was so worried. And then I bungled up about not having spent time in New York."

"You recovered. Aunt Louise adored you instantly."

"She did?"

"In the kitchen she told me she could tell right away that you had good character and were not out for our money or the family name."

"If she only knew…"

Ethan mused on that truth.

Together they cleared the remains of the apple crisp and cinnamon-flavored coffee. The kitchen looked as if they had just fed a hundred people. Dirty pots and pans were strewn on every available surface. The sink was stacked with plates. Spills puddled on the countertops.

"I will pay the housekeeper triple to clean this tomorrow!" Ethan said.

"Do you want to go out?" Holly asked.

"Out? Right now?"

"Yes. It's not that late. And I'm full of nervous energy."

Ethan contemplated the idea. Aunt Louise had started to tire so easily the dinner had been over even earlier than expected. "Where would you like to go?"

"Show me some of the Benton buildings in New York."

He whipped out his phone.

Ten minutes later they were curbside as Leonard pulled up in the town car. It was a dry but very cold evening. Holly wore that favorite black leather jacket, and looked utterly lovable with a red beanie, scarf and gloves. Ethan didn't bring a hat, but dressed warmly with his own brown leather jacket and wool scarf.

Once they'd pulled away from the building Ethan recited to Leonard a quick list of addresses and the tour commenced. As usual, his driver maneuvered the car deftly through the always-present Manhattan traffic.

Holly had had the right idea. The crisp night was invigorating.

Or maybe *she* was the cause of the vigor he felt.

She had played her part to a tee at dinner, and he was sure Aunt Louise suspected nothing of his ruse. How fragile his dearly loved aunt had looked tonight. With those bruises on her face from the tumble she'd taken—in front of employees, no less—at Benton headquarters.

He plugged a reminder into his phone to hire an expert makeup artist for the gala.

But a nagging complication had plagued him throughout dinner. Nothing about the evening had felt fake. Everything had come naturally. From their comfortable banter to the way he and Holly had served the food together and the electrifying kiss they'd shared while telling the story of how they met.

Moment after moment had passed when he had almost forgotten this was a charade. Worse still, the feeling had filled him with a jarring elation and contentment.

This was new territory and it petrified him. He'd never given serious thought to a real-life real wife, and now was not the time to start. Concentrating on moving Aunt Louise into retirement and moving the company into a more charitable direction was plenty for the foreseeable future. Plus, he had vowed long ago never to be swayed into forgetting one critical fact.

Women were not to be trusted.

Aunt Louise was the only exception in his life. Didn't he know that well enough?

All—and that meant *all*—the women he had ever dated had betrayed him. Society girls, daughters of noblemen and businesswomen alike. They might have approached him as a colleague. Or cozied up to him as the wholesome girl-next-door. Others had come on stronger and seduced him with sexual wiles.

Not that he hadn't gone along with them.

He'd satisfied his urges. Indulged in temptations.

Several of them quite memorable.

Yes, maybe a few of them had made him imagine going past three dates or three weeks. But in the end they had always showed their true colors. They hadn't been who they'd said they were. Even some of their body parts hadn't been real. They had all been something other than what they had seemed. Out for something. A piece of *him*.

And his mother—his own mother—had been the worst offender of them all. That a woman could turn her back on her own son for personal gain was a hurt he'd do well to remember for the rest of his life. Apparently women were capable of the unthinkable.

So, even though his aunt sensed that Holly's intentions were good, he mustn't forget that they were performing in a play. All he could really know was that Holly was a competent actress. Instinct told him that this enchanting woman had a kind heart and honorable aims. But he'd only known her for a couple of days. She might prove herself to be just like the others. And there was plenty she could be hiding. Ethan hadn't received the background probe from his security chief yet.

"This is the Seventy-Fourth Street development we did about a decade ago." He pointed out the window when they reached their first destination. "Leonard, can you pull over to the curb?"

Lit from within, the gleaming glass tower shot upward into the night sky. Ethan leaned close to Holly, beside him in the backseat, to show off some details.

"We did the first story with a wider base, and then the remaining twenty-nine floors in a slender tower coming up in the middle. The larger platform of the first level allows for greenery to encircle building."

"Is the first-story garden accessible?" Holly asked, wide-eyed.

"Yes. It was designed so that employees in the offices can go outside into green space whenever they want."

Their next destination was Forty-First Street.

"This one is over twenty-five years old. It was the last project my father worked on before he died. Here they had the issue of erecting new construction in between two buildings from the nineteen-thirties," he explained.

"New York is amazing like that, isn't it?" Holly seemed to understand him.

"You can see that we did not build right up against the buildings on either side. We created those cement walkways and benches." He pointed. "We built our structure thinner than we might have, so that occupants in the buildings on either side could still see out of their windows."

Ethan was enjoying this tremendously. He was so proud of what his father, Uncle Mel and Aunt Louise had produced. He loved to visit the Benton properties that his father had helped construct. They were all he had left of his dad. Steel, glass and concrete. But they were monuments that would endure for years to come.

They rode downtown to look at a low-rise housing development near the East River. Holly asked a million questions about why a door was placed where it was and what materials had been used for what.

Next was a refurbishment in Greenwich Village from the eighteen-nineties. "We spent a fortune on those windows!"

"They look original." Holly nodded in appreciation.

"That was the idea."

Then Ethan had Leonard park curbside in front of the massive Chelsea construction zone. The steel skeleton columns were up for all five buildings. Architectural renderings of what the finished project would look like were hung on fences and announced it to be "Benton Chelsea Plaza."

"This is all one property?" Holly was surprised by the size of the site.

"Five buildings of living, working and retail space. And I have commissioned a talented and, I might add, beautiful painter to do the artwork for the public spaces."

"The Chelsea project! This is it!"

Despite the cold, she lowered the car window and jutted out half of her torso to get a better view. Ethan bent forward to get an arm in front of her and pointed out some features.

Although he'd make sure Aunt Louise received the accolades, this venture was really all his. He'd made the difficult decisions and agonized over the setbacks. He knew this endeavor would have made Uncle Mel and his father proud if they had been alive to see it. And it would allow Aunt Louise to go into retirement on a high note.

His chest pressed into Holly's back as he pointed through the window. Impulse ordered him to move her scarf aside, so that he could kiss the back of her neck. Sheer will kept him from doing so. But it was being sorely tested in this close proximity.

It wasn't difficult to envision losing power over himself in an instant and laying her down on the car seat, climbing on top of her and delving into her softness. A softness he might not ever be able to return from.

Which was not at all part of their deal.

In fact, that kiss at dinner had been much too much. He himself had been startled by the force of it. He could sense it had unbalanced Holly as well.

He'd only meant to enhance their charade with some harmless and sanctioned affection. Prior to that his "guard and defend" strategy had helped him withstand her casual pats on his arm and his back all evening. Yet his own lips had barely touched hers when they'd begun to demand more, and he hadn't restrained himself in time. That kiss had been out of the scope of what was necessary in both intensity and duration.

His actions had overpowered him—a phenomenon he wasn't accustomed to. Lesson learned.

He forced himself back to describing the project. "For Building One we have leases for three fine dining restaurants and a food court of six casual establishments."

"So all that open space will be outdoor seating?"

"Exactly. And we will have a retractable awning with heating units for the colder months."

"I can imagine it."

He continued telling her about the plaza's features. As

with everything Benton Worldwide built, Ethan hoped to live up to architecture's fundamental principle of providing a building with both form and function for its users.

"I just thought of one other building I would like to take you to see. It is not a Benton property, but I think you will agree it has merit."

"You've brought me to the Empire State Building?" As she and Ethan got out of the car Holly craned her neck up at the monolith.

"As long as we were looking at New York architecture," he said, nodding, "I thought we ought to give this grand dame her due."

Taking her hand, Ethan led her into the Art Deco lobby, with its twenty-four-karat gold ceiling murals and marble walls. "Whew!" she whistled.

"Do you want to go up to the top?" he asked.

"Heck, *yes*."

But as they rode the escalator up one floor to the ticketing level memory slapped Holly hard.

She didn't mention to Ethan that she had been here once before. With Ricky. They'd come to New York for a long summer weekend. Stayed in a cheap hotel room in New Jersey.

The Empire State Building had been one of the sights Holly had most wanted to see on their trip. The weather had been hot and humid and the ticket lines crowded with tourists. Unlike tonight—late on a winter Wednesday.

Ricky had got impatient. He'd wanted a beer. He'd tugged her back down to street level, found a bar and that had been the last Holly had seen of the Empire State Building.

"Are you nervous about the elevator ride up?" Ethan asked, reacting to what must be showing on her face.

"No! I was just…um…let's go!"

Rocketing into the sky, Holly felt excitement pump through her veins. She was happy to leave old memories as far behind as she was leaving the asphalt of Thirty-Fourth Street and Fifth Avenue.

When they reached the top Ethan guided her quickly through the indoor viewpoints and exhibits to the outside observation deck.

And there it was.

Three hundred and sixty degrees of New York in the dazzling clear night.

It was utterly freezing. Two sorts of chills ran through her—one from the cold and the other sheer awe.

"Oh. My. Gosh." That was all she could say.

The city was so glorious, with the grid of its streets, the grandeur of its buildings and the galaxies of its lights.

They passed a few other visitors as they circled the deck. Holly gawked at Times Square. At Central Park. The Chrysler Building. The Statue of Liberty. The Hudson River.

She begged for a second lap around. "Let's take selfies!" She grinned as she pulled out her phone.

"You look very beautiful," Ethan said in a husky voice. "Your cheeks are pink from the cold."

She sensed him watching her more than he was looking at the views. He'd seen the sight of Manhattan before. It was probably all ho-hum to a global traveler like him. He had seen all the wonders of the world. And was probably amused at Holly's enthusiasm.

But he gamely put his arm around her and they posed to get photos with the skyline behind them, the Brooklyn Bridge in the distance. Holly surrendered the phone to him, to lift it higher than she could. He clicked several shots.

As he handed the phone back to her he kissed her on the cheek.

"I am *so* sorry." He backed away. "I did not mean to do that. I have no idea why I did."

"Maybe because a million romantic movie scenes have taken place right here?"

"Yes, that must be it. My apologies. It will not happen again."

She braved it and said what she wanted to say. "Actually, I'm glad you did. At dinner in front of your aunt and Fernando I got so flustered when you kissed me. I think I'll need to practice physical contact with you until it feels more expected."

She wasn't sure if she had really said that out loud or merely thought it. Rehearse kissing Ethan? That was insane.

"You might be right."

He moved in front of her so they were face to face. With her back to the observation deck's railing. The glistening city behind her.

Her breath sputtered. "In order to be convincing…"

Ethan arched down and brushed his mouth ever so slightly against hers. A wisp of his breath warmed her lips when he asked, "So, for example, you need to practice doing that?"

"Uh-huh," she squeaked out.

Why did he have to be so attractive? This would be much easier if she had become the fake fiancée of an unappealing man who didn't ignite her inside.

Clearly practice was all that was needed. Practice would make perfect. Eventually she'd become numb to him. Kissing would be a choreographed action they'd perform like trained seals.

She was sure of it.

"What about this?" he taunted, and more strength applied a firmer kiss to her lips.

A jolt shot up her back. Her hips rocked forward uncontrollably.

"I… I…" She struggled to take in a complete breath. "I think I need to work on that one."

She tilted her head back for mercy.

Giving her none, he took both sides of her face in his two hands and drew her to him. He kissed her yet again. Harder. Longer.

"Do we need to rehearse this?"

Now he'd opened his mouth. And he didn't stop there. The tip of his tongue parted her lips. Forced her tongue to meet his. Drove her to take. Give. Insist on more.

A dark moan rumbled from low in his gut.

A group of tourists strode past, ignoring them and pointing out landmarks in spirited voices. Holly couldn't see them. Ethan was all she could see.

His hands slid from the sides of her face slowly down her arms to the tips of her fingers. His lips traced across her jaw and then he murmured into her neck, "Do you think an engaged couple might need to kiss like that on occasion?"

"I do," she whispered.

He took hold of her hips and crushed himself into her. Pinned her back against the railing. She stretched her arms up around his neck, going pliant and yielding against the steel of his body.

With New York as her witness, he kissed her again and again and again. Until they had only one heartbeat. Until there could be no doubt in anyone's mind that this was a couple who were deeply in love.

CHAPTER EIGHT

FLOATING ON A CLOUD. Ethan had heard that saying before but this was the first time he'd experienced what it meant. Yes, his physical body lay on the uncomfortable leather sofa that was too small to stretch out on. But his heart and soul wafted above him in a silken, curvy vision he never wanted to wake from.

Of course, real sleep eluded him. It seemed an utter waste of time when Holly Motta was in the world. Sleep would just be hours and minutes spent away from thinking about her. What if, during sleep, his subconscious drifted away from the cocoon of her embrace? No, sleep was not time well spent. Not when instead he could linger in this half-daze, filled with the memory of her velvety lips on his and her long arms wrapped around him.

Though reality nagged at him.

After that mind-bending interlude of kissing at the Empire State Building they both knew that something unintentional, inappropriate and very dangerous had passed between them. Something they were going to need to backtrack from. To run from. And to return themselves to the "strictly business" contract they had made.

During the car ride afterward they'd chit-chatted about the architecture of a couple of noteworthy buildings along the way. Once they'd got home Holly hadn't been able to get away from him fast enough. She'd emerged from the bathroom in a tee shirt and pajama shorts, poured herself a glass of water, voiced a quick good-night and then rapped the bedroom door closed with her foot.

Ethan hoped that she was in his bed, resting in peaceful sleep. At least one of them ought to be. If he was being honest, he also hoped that she was having sweet dreams about him. Just as he was drifting in his trance about her.

As the endless night wore on Ethan's elation turned to irritation. This was not what he'd signed up for. Lying awake thinking about a woman? *No deal!*

He couldn't afford to have that kind of preoccupation in his life. None of his plans included a woman.

Sure, he could enjoy the company of the exotic and enticing females that his travels put him in contact with. That was a game he could play indefinitely. He wanted something from them that they'd readily give in exchange for a taste of his affluence and the limelight. Then they would want more and he would move on. He knew the routine well.

For all his aunt's prodding, Ethan hadn't ever truly acknowledged the possibility of really devoting himself to someone and building an inner circle with them. A private life together. Not after what he'd seen of the world. Not after his mother.

Blasted Holly! She'd exploded into his life and detonated every stronghold he held.

Worse still, to all intents and purposes he had reached the point of no return with her. He'd already introduced her to Aunt Louise. The gala was in three days. It would be a huge setback to back out now.

There was no choice but to see this through. However, once his aunt had stepped down and was securely ensconced in the warm Barbados sand, Ethan might have to cut the Holly engagement short. He couldn't take much more of this.

Uncle Mel had taught him that admitting and analyzing his mistakes was the crucial first step toward moving forward. Ethan had made a grave error in misjudging his own ability to keep this a purely business transaction.

Or perhaps it was just Holly. He'd chosen the wrong person for the job.

Holly was testimony that his aunt and uncle might be right—that an authentic love might be out there in the world for him. A love that was worth bowing to and sacrificing for. That defined his future and ordered everything else to work around it.

Which was not at all where Ethan was headed.

Argh! The road not taken… If only he had stuck to his original plan to hire an actress. She'd have been a consummate professional who knew exactly how to separate reality from performance. Her expertise would have shown him the way.

Just for torture, he flicked on a lamp and snatched his tablet from the coffee table. He clicked onto the website of the talent agency where he had located his original choice. The—unfortunately for him—pregnant Penelope Perkins. The website featured headshot photos of the talent they represented. Tap on the photo and a short bio appeared.

Ethan leaned back on the couch and studied Sienna Freeman. A willowy redhead with a daisy in her hair. An inquiring click told him that she had performed at regional theatres throughout the country, portraying the ingénue in famous American musicals. She looked as if she could have easily been groomed to play the fiancée in Ethan's little domestic drama. A sweet-faced young woman.

Trouble was, she wasn't Holly.

Gabrielle Rivera was a temptress with dark hair and crimson lips. A substantial list of her appearances in television comedies and commercials proved she was capable of working in a wide range of situations. Gabrielle would probably handle herself beautifully at important occasions. A fine choice.

Her fatal flaw? She wasn't Holly.

Glamazon Zara Reed was picture-perfect for a socialite wife. With her blond tresses swept into an up-do, Zara looked born to hang on a wealthy man's arm. Add in her master's degree in psychology and small roles in quirky films, and you had one convincing package. A jaw-dropper.

But—poor Zara. She simply wasn't Holly.

Enough! Ethan put the tablet down, turned off the light and attempted his now customary bent position on the sofa. Every molecule in his body screamed Holly's name.

He tossed until dawn, exhausted and annoyed.

Ethan came into the kitchen after he'd showered. Holly was picking at the apple crisp from the baking dish they had managed to stick in the refrigerator last night after Aunt Louise and Fernando had left.

Before they'd gone out looking at buildings. And at each other.

He joined her in scavenging through the mess of the kitchen for breakfast. "Is there coffee?"

She nodded. Once again, the cramped space was making her uneasy. Holly winced at every accidental slide against Ethan's starched white shirt or suit pants as she prepared two cups of java.

There had been quite enough touching him last night. She needed a break.

With him carrying the coffee, she followed him to the table with the apple crisp. She licked bits off her fingers as she folded herself into a chair.

"We could use forks," he suggested, "like evolved humans."

"Sorry if I'm not civilized enough for you."

"I did not say that."

He imitated her by gnawing his own fingerful of the leftover desert. Trying to make her laugh. Unsuccessfully.

Not that he didn't look cute doing it.

"I think it's obvious," she sneered.

Truth was, she was more than a little ticked off at what had happened last night at the Empire State Building. Even though she had asked for it. But how *dare* he kiss her like that if it didn't mean anything to him? That went way beyond the call of duty in this assignment she'd consented to.

Of course she'd had her part in it. She certainly hadn't pushed him away. The opposite, in fact. His kisses had fed a vital nutrient into her body that she had been starved of for so long she hadn't even known she was ravenous for it.

Nonetheless, she was still furious at him for stoking that hunger.

"What I think is obvious…" he paused for a sip of coffee "…is that you are angry at me and I do not know why."

"Welcome to marriage."

"No surprise I have steered clear of it."

She undid and redid her ponytail, buying a moment to regroup. Deciding to be honest.

"We went too far last night."

"I agree completely," he replied quickly.

"You do?"

His kisses hadn't offered any apology. They had been the kisses of a man entitled to his desires, who confidently took them with no cause for second guesses.

"Clearly we need to define the parameters of our physical contact," he stated, as if he was discussing an architectural floor plan. "It is important that we keep any sentiment out of the framework."

Was he admitting that he had felt as much as she had in that transcendental swirl of urgent kisses and intimate embraces? Or was he scolding her for crossing boundaries?

"It's my fault," she said, strategizing. "I asked you for some practice kissing because I don't want us to appear awkward in front of other people."

He took a minute to measure her words, carefully contemplating them before he responded.

"We simply got carried away," he concluded. "We will not do it again."

Inexplicably, her heart crashed to the floor. Which made no sense—because not passionately kissing Ethan Benton again was exactly what *did* need to happen.

"Right…" she granted. Yet sadness ricocheted between her ears.

As a diffuser, she munched on another chunk of the apple dessert.

Clearly no longer interested in the leftovers, Ethan reached for his phone. He ignored her to swipe, read and type.

She looked at her painting of him on the wall. She had never painted Ricky, nor the other couple of men she had dated. None of them had gotten under her skin like Ethan had. Filling her not only with the inclination but with the outright necessity to bring her brush to his likeness.

Ethan was like the multi-faceted diamond she wore on her finger. Every way she turned she saw something new. Something more. Something unexpected. Something unfathomable. She could paint him a hundred times and still not be done.

Eventually he glanced up and observed her, as if maybe he had forgotten she was in the room.

"So. Shall we establish some ground rules?"

"O-okay," she stumbled, unsure where he was going with this.

"I believe we *will* need to kiss on occasion. We will certainly want a convincing display of affection at the shareholders' gala, when our engagement is announced."

Holly braced herself, suddenly unsure if she was really going to be able to go through with this charade. She felt ill-suited to the task. It was too much.

"I think it will be beneficial for us to define what type of kissing is necessary," he continued.

"Absolutely," she bluffed, shifting in her seat.

"For example, I see no need for our tongues to touch, as they did last night."

Well, that was for sure. Her head and heart couldn't afford any more kisses like last night's. The kind that made a girl forget that she was only an employee of the most compelling and sexy man she had ever met. A man who had made it clear that he had hired her to help him protect his aunt, the only woman he'd ever love.

A fact she'd be wise to keep in the forefront of her mind.

Which his kisses completely clouded.

"Got it—no tongues." She nodded once and reached her hand across the table to shake his in a gentlemen's agreement.

Ethan's mouth hooked up as he shook her hand. He was amused by her gesture of sportsmanship.

Except he didn't let go of her hand after the shake. In fact he fought to keep it like a possession he'd battle to the ground for. He turned it over and caressed the tops of her fingers with the pad of his thumb.

"I'd prefer it if you didn't press your body into mine." Holly yanked her hand free and continued. She sparked at the memory of last night's six feet and three inches of solid manpower searing into her.

"How far away shall I stand?" he asked, holding his thumb and forefinger apart as a measurement. "This far?"

"Further than that."

Widening the gap between his fingers, he tilted his head. "This far?"

"At least."

"And would that be all of my body? Or just certain parts?"

Oh, Lordy, he was mocking her.

"Probably all parts." She kept going. "Of course we should have friendly hugs, but nothing prolonged."

"Shall I program a timer?" He smirked.

She lifted her palms in surrender. "Look, it was your idea to lay down some guidelines."

"You are right. I did not realize how ludicrous it would sound stated aloud." He abruptly stood and gathered his phone, tablet, keys and wallet. "For the moment we need not be concerned about our proximity to each other. My schedule today is filled with appointments."

With that, he turned toward the front door. Holly shifted her eyes to spy him putting on his suit jacket followed by his overcoat. He picked up a roll of architectural blueprints that had been propped up beside the door, and out he went.

Holly wasn't exactly sure why a sharp tear stung her cheek.

The left side needed more of the muddy purple she had mixed. Holly dipped thin bristles into the unusual color and applied them to her canvas. When they'd been at the art supply store Ethan had insisted on buying her a full range of brushes—a luxury she wasn't used to. She flicked tiny lines with a brush that was ideal for the task of depicting the rain outside.

Music blared from her phone—a pop singer belting on about how it was time to move on from a man who had done her wrong.

A wild sprawl of buildings and weather... Holly couldn't

decide whether or not she liked this painting. It didn't matter, though. The important thing was the *doing*.

Painting had always been Holly's best friend. It had kept her alive during a tumultuous childhood with an unstable mother and a man she'd called her father whom she had seen so few times she could count them on her fingers. Painting had got her through a disaster of a marriage to a selfish man-child. And then through an ugly divorce.

Painting was her escape. Her entertainment. Her coping mechanism. Her voice. Her salvation.

Early on, her brother, Vince, had found sports. And she'd discovered canvas and color. It was unimaginable where they'd be without those outlets.

In the past few years she had been fortunate enough to have been able to make some money creating artwork for paying clients. But in times of trouble she still picked up her brush purely for emotional release. For safety. For comfort.

Which was what was required now. Because she was disturbed and confused. Art gave her a little bit of a sanctuary in an unpredictable world.

So she had re-created her little studio area after packing it up for Louise and Fernando's visit last night. And she'd got back to work.

As often happened when she was painting, her problems became evident.

She had developed strong feelings for Ethan. And if that wasn't bad enough, she sensed the same might be happening for him.

How he managed to be so volatile while remaining so formal she'd never understand. He was in control of himself, yet there was a barely masked vulnerability there. Manners and restraint mixed with something brutal and pounding.

Those kisses atop the Empire State Building had come

from somewhere organic inside him. Beyond rational intent. That kind of intensity couldn't have been plotted.

In spite of that he would never care for her as anything more than an employee. Plain and simple. Even if he did, he would clamp his emotions down and lock them away as soon as he acknowledged them. He was too strong and too true ever to be swayed once he'd made a decision.

A means to an end. That was all she was to him.

And he to her.

Her phone buzzed.

"Ethan, here."

"Hi."

"I wanted to apologize for making light of your concerns about what physical interaction between us would be appropriate."

"I just don't want to mess up at the gala. I'm worried I'm going to get flustered, like I did at dinner last night. I want everything to go right for you and your plan for Aunt Louise."

"I agree that we could use more training sessions where we are surrounded by other people. I have a charity event to attend tonight. You and I will go together. As colleagues."

That was a terrific idea. She wanted to fulfill her end of the contract and make this arrangement work with Ethan. He was offering her the door into a New York that she could never open on her own. How hard could it be? He'd contracted her for a job that she was capable of doing. She just needed to keep the right mindset, purpose and goals.

An evening as colleagues. *Perfect.*

A couple of hours later the building's doorman knocked and handed Holly a delivery. She thanked him and carried the large white box to the table. Untying the gold ribbon that gave the box the appearance of a gift, she lifted the lid. A notecard was tucked on top of the gold tissue paper concealing the contents.

Tiny dress. Warm coat.
See you at the dock.
Ethan.

She unfolded the tissue to discover a black sequined party dress. It was sinfully short, with thin straps and a scooped back. Holly sucked in an audible whoosh of air. She couldn't believe that Ethan had sent her this sexy slip of a dress. Was this what his *colleagues* wore?

Tingles exploded all over her body.

For all the clothes he had already purchased for her, he must have thought none of them were just right for the charity event he was taking her to tonight.

Anticipation rocketed through her.

The warm coat—cream-colored, in a heavy wool—he had already bought her. The reference to a dock must mean they were going to be on or near a boat. The mystery of it felt hopelessly romantic, even though with Ethan she knew it wasn't. Nonetheless, she could hardly wait until nightfall.

Leonard picked her up at the scheduled time and transported her to the Battery Park dock where Ethan was waiting to open the car door. He extended his hand to help her out of the car. It was chilly, but there was no rain, and she wore her coat open over the new dress. Admittedly to show it off.

"Thank you, Leonard," Ethan called to his driver and closed the passenger door. To Holly he said, after a leisurely once-over, "I knew you would look stunning in that."

Their eyes met. She smiled. The left side of his mouth curved up.

"Shall we?" He offered his bent arm and she slipped hers through. But then he glanced down and stopped with caution. "Oh. Right." He lightly touched her engagement ring. "I generally do not bring a date to events like this.

Because our arrangement—rather, our engagement—will not be announced until the gala, would you mind terribly...?" His voice trailed out.

"No, of course not," she responded, hoping he didn't see the rush of disappointment sweep across her.

She slithered the diamond off her finger. She also hoped that, in the moonlight, he hadn't noticed that she'd been unable to remove every fleck of paint from her cuticles. She'd scrubbed her hands raw, but this was the best she could do. With any luck the stylists he'd hired to spruce her up for the gala would have some magic tricks up their sleeves.

"Shall I keep it?" he asked, and he took the ring from her and secured it in his pocket before she'd had a chance to answer. "I will introduce you as a coworker. We can have the evening to practice being comfortable with each other's company in public and nothing more."

"Exactly."

He presented his bent arm to her again. "All aboard."

As they ascended the gangway, Ethan waved politely to a few people, this way and that.

"Who was that?" Holly asked. "Where are we going?"

"Tonight is a fund-raiser for a private organization I belong to that supports maintenance of the Statue of Liberty as state funding is not sufficient. We will cruise to Liberty Island. The vantage point is spectacular. I think you will enjoy it."

The yacht set off into the New York Harbor, away from lower Manhattan. Champagne was passed on trays. Ethan and Holly mingled with a few guests onboard, sharing mainly superficial banter.

He introduced her as part of his interior design team and she shook a few hands. When they were out of anyone's earshot he instructed, "You can discuss the Chelsea Plaza project. Tell people you are currently analyzing the requirements. That you are handling the art, and much will depend on what materials the furnishings are made of."

During their next chat, around a standing cocktail table, the project came up. Holly interjected with, "We are assessing how people will move through the public spaces."

Ethan subtly nodded his approval. Holly was grateful for the positive reinforcement. She had never interacted with these mega-rich type of people before. Many of them were older than her—men in dark suits and women in their finest jewels. Wall Street leaders, heads of corporations, prominent doctors and lawyers. All of whom, apparently, with their charity dollars, were helping to keep the Statue of Liberty standing proud.

There would probably be many more people like this at the shareholders' gala on Saturday. Ethan had been smart to bring Holly here, so she could get a taste of this world she knew nothing about.

As they ferried closer to Liberty, Ethan led Holly to the yacht's railing to gain the best view.

"She is amazing."

Holly could only gawk up at the massive copper statue, famously green with its patina of age. From the spikes of Liberty's crown—which Ethan had told her represented rays of light—to the broken chain at her feet symbolizing freedom, she was a towering monument to emancipation. And her torch was a beacon of enlightenment.

Lady Liberty seemed to speak directly to Holly tonight. Holly looked into her eyes and pleaded for her wisdom and guidance.

"'Give me your tired, your poor...' Isn't that poem about this statue?" she asked Ethan.

"*The New Colossus* by Emma Lazarus."

"'Your huddled masses yearning to breathe free.'" Holly

had been suffocating in Florida. All her ghosts were there. "Maybe in New York *I* can breathe."

"What has constricted you?"

Making up for her mother's failings, with no father in the picture. Protecting her brother. Appeasing her explosive ex-husband.

"Where I come from nobody thinks big. Everyone is just trying to survive one more day."

Ethan moved a bit closer to Holly. They stood side by side while the yacht circled Liberty, allowing them to observe her from every angle.

"Fate has such irony. I know so many people who have everything," he said, "and yet it means nothing to them."

"Gratitude is its own gift."

He smiled wryly and nodded.

"As I mentioned, after Aunt Louise retires I plan to move Benton Worldwide's new construction solely into housing ventures for disadvantaged people. I like giving houses rather than just money. Because I can supply the knowledge and the labor to build them properly."

Colored lights began to flash on the deck and a band started playing in the dining room. Guests progressed to make their way inside the boat.

Ethan didn't move, and Holly stayed beside him as the boat turned and the tall buildings of Manhattan returned to their view.

"I have seen so much poverty in the world," Ethan continued musingly. "People living in shacks. In tents. In cardboard boxes. If I can help some of them have a safe and permanent home I will have accomplished something."

"You can only imagine what a house might mean to someone who doesn't have one." Holly knew about that first-hand, having moved from place to place so many times as a child.

"In any case..." Ethan shrugged "...for all my supposed

wealth and success, giving is the only thing that is truly satisfying."

Once all the other guests had filed inside, Ethan gestured for Holly to follow him in. At the dining tables they sat with some older couples who were discussing a landscaping project for the grounds around the statue.

When the band began a tamer version of a funky song that Holly loved, she stood and reached her hand down for Ethan's. "May I have this dance, sir?"

Ethan's signature smile made its slow journey from the left to the right side of his mouth. He stood and followed her onto the dance floor, where they joined some other couples.

She faced him and began to swing her hips back and forth to the music. When her hips jutted left, her head tipped right. Then she flung her head left and he hips responded to the right. Like ocean waves, her body became one undulating flow. Back and forth. Back and forth.

The dress was slinky against her skin. She loved how it swung a little with every move she made. From what she could surmise in Ethan's watchful eyes, he liked the movement of the dress, too.

At first he just rotated one shoulder forward and then the other, in a tentative sashay. But after a bit any self-consciousness dissolved and he let his body gyrate freely to the beat of the music.

He had a natural rhythm—just as Holly had known he would. It was part of that primitive side of him—the part he kept hidden away. The part she wished she could access.

Their eyes locked and their movements synchronized until they were undeniably dancing together.

There was no doubt of their attraction to each other. But they were doing a very good job of keeping the evening friendly and nothing more, just as planned.

As a matter of fact, when he had been talking on the

deck earlier, about the good feeling of giving, it had been as if Holly was an old pal he could confide in. Pals were good.

Which was why when the band switched to a slow song Holly turned to leave the dance floor. Slow dances weren't for buddies.

But a strong arm circled her waist.

"This doesn't fit in with our no touching policy this evening." Holly shook her head in resistance.

Ethan pulled her toward him and into a firm clinch. He secured her against him with a wide palm on her back.

Her breath hiccupped. Tonight was supposed to be time off from physical contact with him. After their intimacy at the Empire State Building last night had gone far outside the realm of their contract. Tonight, the last thing Holly needed was to have her face pressed against his neck, with the smell of his skin and his laundered shirt intoxicating her into a dangerous swoon.

"We may as well have a run-through, future Mrs. Benton," he murmured into her ear. "We will be expected to dance together at the gala."

He lifted one of her arms and placed her hand on his broad shoulder. He clasped her other hand in his.

"I don't know if I can do it," Holly protested.

"Surely I am not *that* irresistible."

She laughed, although that was only half funny. "What I meant was, I don't know how to partner-dance."

"Well, young lady, you are in luck. I happen to be three-time champion of the Oxford Ballroom Dance Society."

"Really?"

"No. Of course not."

He began moving and she followed in line.

"But it is not that difficult. Can you feel my thigh leading yours…?"

* * *

When they got home, before they retreated to their separate sleeping quarters, Ethan retrieved the engagement ring from his jacket pocket.

As he replaced it on her finger, he asked, "Holly, would you marry me…again?"

CHAPTER NINE

"WHO ON EARTH would notice the difference between a napkin color called Eggshell and another called Champagne?" Ethan bellowed to Holly as she made her way across the vast hotel ballroom. "And good morning."

"There's actually a big distinction." Holly jumped right in and snatched the two samples from him. She held one up in each hand to catch some of the room's light. "See—the Champagne is iridescent. The Eggshell is matte. It's a very different effect."

"Thank you for being here."

About an hour ago Ethan had called Holly and asked her to meet him here to finalize the details for tomorrow's gala. Aunt Louise was not feeling well.

"I would call in my assistant, Nathan, but I have him on a dozen other tasks right now."

Ethan's brow furrowed as he remembered yet more specifications he needed to take care of.

"What's wrong with Louise?" Holly inquired.

"She said she felt a bit weak and lightheaded."

"Will she be okay by tomorrow?"

"I hope so. She will stay upstairs today, resting in one of the suites we booked for the week. Fernando is with her. Not that *he* is of any help."

"What do you think triggered it?"

"Rainy weather is especially difficult for her. And, even though she likes to be involved in planning these galas, I think the strain is too much."

He'd feel immense relief once his aunt had retired and no longer bore the weight of continuing as CEO of their billion-dollar company. With any luck she'd be flying in from Barbados for next year's gala, with no cares other than what dress she should wear.

"I'm here to help, Ethan. What can I do?"

Holly's concern softened his tension. He gestured to the table in front of him—the only one in the bare ballroom with a tablecloth on it. Several place settings were laid out for approval, each complete with different options for china, napkins, silver and stemware. There were modern styles, and those that were more ornate. Some in classic shapes, others unusual.

"Can you make these decorative decisions? You are the artist," he said, and added with a whisper, "and the fiancée."

There was no one directly in earshot, but hotel employees bustled about doing their work. With camera phones and social media these days, Ethan wanted to be sure details of his engagement weren't released to the world any earlier than he wanted them to be.

"Oh. Good grief."

"What?"

He pointed to her hand. "The ring again. I am so sorry."

She gamely glided it off her finger, handed it to him and filled her cheeks with air to make a funny face.

"It is ludicrous. I apologize again. Now, Aunt Louise had started to select a certain color palette. She picked out this tablecloth…"

Holly lifted a corner of the linen draping the table and found an identifying label underneath. "This color is called Stone. I like its earthiness. Instead of choosing a lighter napkin, how about a darker one? Can we see samples that might be called something like Pewter or Slate?"

"Sweetheart, you can see anything you want as long as you get this taken care of."

He immediately regretted the endearment. It had fallen from his mouth spontaneously. He supposed that was what he'd need to be doing once they were announced as an engaged couple, so he might as well get used to it. Still, he wasn't in the habit of referring to women by pet names. Holly's widened eyes told him she was surprised by it as well.

Thankfully, one of the hotel's event managers was passing by. Ethan flagged down Priya to come talk to Holly. And to get him out of the moment.

As the two women conferred he stepped away to return a couple of missed phone calls. Which was a bit difficult because the napkins weren't the only things that reflected light from the ballroom's massive chandeliers.

Holly's lustrous hair, flowing freely long past her shoulders, framed her face with a glowing halo. Her sincere smile came easily during her conversation. Sidetracking him from his call to the point when he had to ask his site supervisor on the Bronx project to repeat what he had just said. Which was both embarrassing and unacceptable.

How many reminders did Ethan need that a woman had no place in his life?

She bounded over to him after her consultation with the event manager.

"I hope you don't mind, but I've had a vision. I did go with a pewter napkin. And a minimalist kind of china and flatware..." She rattled off details at a mile a minute. "With a silver napkin ring to give it a sort of elemental look. Earth and metal, kind of thing."

He mashed his lips to suppress a smile, although he was charmed at her zeal.

"And, if it's okay," she persisted, "I thought we could do a sleek centerpiece with white flowers in clear glass vases, to bring in a water element as well. I think it'll all tie together with the lighting." She pointed up to the modern chandeliers with their narrow pieces of glass. "Do you think your aunt would like that?"

"She will appreciate your creativity," he said after Holly's debriefing. "Miss Motta, it sounds like you have a knack for this sort of thing."

She shrugged. "I guess it's just a painter's eye. And at my own wed—"

Ethan's phone rang. He lifted one finger to signal to Holly to hold that thought while he took the call. "Yes, Nathan?"

Holly's cheeks turned pink. She bit her lip.

Something he wouldn't mind doing.

Sweetheart. He'd accidentally called her *sweetheart.*

"Schedule me for a late lunch with him next Tuesday at that restaurant he likes on Jane Street. Thank you." He turned his attention back to Holly, "Sorry—what were you saying?"

"Oh. Um… Just that Priya says the tech crew are here if you're ready to go to the podium."

"Come with me."

He took her hand. After taking the few stairs from the ballroom floor up to the stage, Ethan and Holly turned to face the empty event space. Tomorrow night Benton Worldwide Properties would once again fête many of their shareholders with an evening of appreciation. Close to a thousand people—some from nearby, others who had traveled far—would fill this grand room for the annual event.

Holly whistled. "What a breathtaking location for a dinner." She pointed to the large gold wall sculptures that circled the back of the room. "Those give the idea of waves in an ocean, don't they?"

Ethan surveyed the familiar surroundings. "The burgundy carpeting is new this year. It used to be a lighter color. That is about the only change I have noticed."

"You hold the dinner here every year?"

"We have been using this room for as long as I can remember. These galas are as ingrained into my family as birthdays and Christmas are to others."

This year's event wouldn't be a run-of-the-mill evening, though, when his and Holly's engagement was to be announced.

Holly gestured with her head toward the podium on the stage. "Will you be giving a speech?"

"The baton will pass to me next year," he said. Uncle Mel had always given the speech and, after he died Aunt Louise had taken over the duty. "Only a few of us know that this is the last time Aunt Louise will deliver the CEO's report."

Louise's retirement wouldn't be revealed at the gala. Ethan and his aunt had decided that the first step in her exit strategy would be to introduce his fiancée. That would cause enough pandemonium for one evening.

Shareholders could be tricky. They didn't like too many changes all at once. Benton Worldwide had already made them a lot of money by sticking to the original principles Uncle Melvin and Ethan's father had established when they'd started the company with one small apartment building in roughneck South Boston.

So only the engagement announcement would come at the gala. In a month, they'd inform the shareholders in writing that Louise Benton was retiring after a distinguished career. A month after that they'd throw a splashy retirement party.

Tomorrow night would belong to him and Holly Motta. In addition to their proclamation to the shareholders, a press release would notify the world that Ethan Benton had finally chosen a bride. Photos of them would appear in the business sections of newspapers and websites across the planet.

Ethan peered at Holly by his side on the stage. Sudden terror gripped him. What if this masquerade was too risky? This pretty young woman appeared to be genuine and of good will. But what if she wasn't? What if she was like every other woman he'd ever met? Deceptive. Manipulative. Out for herself.

He'd only met her a few days ago, for heaven's sake. It wasn't long enough to put her intentions to the test. And he still didn't know much about her other than what she'd chosen to disclose. Hopefully his head of security, Chip Foley, would get back to him soon with any information he had found. If there was something he didn't want exposed he'd need to figure out how to bury it so that the press didn't have a field-day.

Doubt coursed through him. What if Holly simply wasn't as capable a performer as he'd hired her to be? Maybe she'd crack under the spotlight and the attention. Confess that this was all a set-up, causing Benton Worldwide embarrassment and loss of credibility.

His mind whirled. What had he been thinking? In his haste to plan Aunt Louise's departure from public life before her medical condition diminished her position of respect, Ethan had made an uncharacteristically rash decision. If it was the wrong one his family would pay dearly for it for the rest of their lives.

However, there was no choice now but to take a leap of faith.

"Are you ready for this?" He took Holly's hand, as he would tomorrow. Her fingers were supple and comforting, and immediately slowed his breath.

"I may faint afterward, but I promise to put on a show," she answered amiably, lacing her fingers in his.

"Imagine every table filled with people in tuxedos and evening gowns. Staring at you."

Her shoulders lifted in a chuckle. "Gee, no pressure there!"

Her humor reassured him that she could pull this off. She wouldn't have agreed to it if she didn't know in her heart that she could handle it. And she'd done fine on the yacht last night.

Aunt Louise wanted this one thing for Ethan before she stepped away and let him officially run the company. He was determined to give it to her.

An astute woman, his aunt knew that Ethan's constant travel was to avoid settling down. He didn't have any sustained commitments outside of work. Hardly had a base other than his rarely visited corporate flat near their headquarters in Boston. He dated women—and then he didn't. He spent months alone on a boat. Socialized, then disappeared into a foreign country. He was free. There was nothing to tie him down. He could do whatever he wanted, go wherever he pleased. And he did.

His aunt believed that a fulfilled life took place on terra firma. She wanted him to find a home. A home that would shelter him from the topsy-turvy world of highs and lows, change and disappointment.

Home wasn't a place.

Home was love.

An all-encompassing love that he could count on. That could count on him. That made life worth living day after day. Year after year.

Because of Holly, Ethan had now had a glimpse into what it might be like to coexist with someone. Like he had last night on the Liberty cruise, easily sharing his thoughts and plans and hopes.

But he would stay firm in his resolve to go it alone.

And that was that.

That was his fate.

That was his destiny.

So he'd give Holly to his aunt as a retirement gift. Deliver her on a silver platter. Let the one woman who had ever been good to him hold the belief she most wanted.

But Ethan would not forget the truth.

"Mr. Benton?" A voice boomed from a dark corner of the ballroom. "We'd like to do a sound-check from the podium, if you wouldn't mind."

"Of course," Ethan said to the unseen technician.

Still clutching Holly's hand, he led her to the side of the stage before they parted. His fingers were reluctant to let go. Yet he dutifully took his place at the lectern and adjusted the microphone. Substituting for Aunt Louise, who would be introduced tomorrow to deliver her speech.

"Thank you for joining us this evening at Benton Worldwide Properties' annual shareholders' gala. We are so delighted you are here… Test, test. Test. Testing…"

Ethan dummied through as the technician made adjustments to the sound system.

"Without our shareholders we would not have experienced the global development… Hello, hello. You give us the inspiration… Thank you, thank you. Testing one, two, three."

He turned to wink at Holly. She grinned in response.

"Thank you, Mr. Benton," the technician called out. "Now we'd like to run the video, if you'd like to watch and okay?"

"Will do."

Ethan escorted Holly back down the steps to one of the tables. They took their seats as a screen was lowered from above the stage.

"Hey, do we get to sample the food?" Holly asked. "Quality control?"

"No, that is one department Fernando *is* actually handling. He was here earlier, approving everything with the chefs, before he went to attend to Aunt Louise."

"Rats!" She snapped her fingers, cute as could be.

Which made him want to kiss her.

Which was more irrational thinking he'd need to get a handle on.

Kissing was only for show, when people were watching. No more recreational kissing. The Empire State Building kissing shouldn't have happened. Where he'd thought he might have been able to keep kissing Holly until the end of the world.

His body quirked even now, remembering.

He locked his attention on the screen as the presentation began with a graphic of the company logo and some sprightly music. A slick narrator's voice explained a montage of all the Benton Worldwide projects that had been started or completed during the past year.

In another montage employees were shown holding babies, celebrating their children's college graduations, tossing a football at company picnics.

A historical section flashed older photos—one of Uncle Mel and Ethan's father, Joseph, holding shovels at a groundbreaking ceremony.

"That is my dad." Ethan pointed. His heart pinged as the image quickly gave way to the next photo. Joseph had died when he was nine. Twenty-five years ago. "I do not remember much about him anymore," he admitted.

Holly put a hand on his shoulder. He prickled, but didn't pull away despite his automatic itch to do so.

"Tell me one thing you do remember about him."

"That photo shows him in a suit. I can only think of him in a casual work shirt. Uncle Mel was the businessman. My father was always at the construction sites."

One glimpse of memory Ethan did have of his father was of when he'd come home from work at night. He'd greet Ethan and then head straight to the shower to wash off his honest day's work.

His mother was not a part of that picture. She would sequester herself in her private bedroom before Ethan came home from school, and there she'd stay throughout the evening. It had been a nanny who'd tended to Ethan in the afternoon.

Another older photo had clients at a job site, with Joseph in a hard hat on one side of them and Uncle Mel and Aunt Louise on the other side.

"Do you have any pictures that include your mother?"

"Oh, she was in that shot. We had her edited out. We cut her out of every photo."

Holly tilted her head, not understanding. "Why?"

Now he shook Holly's hand off his shoulder. He couldn't take her touch.

"Because we did not want her in any way associated with Benton Worldwide."

"But *why*?"

"My father and Uncle Mel worked hard for every dollar they made. They earned it. They deserved it. And they were loyal to the people who were loyal to them. Values my mother cared nothing for."

Ethan's blood pressure rose, notifying him to end this conversation. When Holly started to ask another question, his glare shut her down.

Another photo documented him and Aunt Louise in front of a gleaming high-rise building. "Ah, the Peachwood Center in Atlanta. One of my favorites."

The last photo had Aunt Louise surrounded by ten or so Benton executives in front of their headquarters. Even though in reality Ethan had been running the company since Aunt Louise's health had begun to fail, he still made sure that she got all the credit and glory.

"Is everything correct on the video, Mr. Benton?" the technician called from the back of the ballroom.

"Yes—thank you."

"May I trouble you for one more thing, sir? Can I get an okay for sound and lighting on the dance floor?"

Ethan stood and made his way to the polished wooden floor in the center of the ballroom. Fully surrounded by the burgundy carpet and the tables defining the perimeter, the dance floor was its own little world, and it was lit as such with a yellow tint and spotlights beaming down from the ceiling.

"Mr. Benton, we'd like to check the lighting with some movement. Would you be able to find someone to do a quick waltz around the dance floor for me?"

Naturally Ethan gestured to Holly. Stretching out his arm, he beckoned. "So, we dance again."

Holly stood and navigated between the tables in the empty ballroom to reach Ethan on the dance floor. She envisioned what he had described—how tomorrow night the room would be filled with well-dressed shareholders gaping at her. Not giving in to panic, she reminded herself that she was here to do a job. To supply what she'd offered.

A love ballad suitable for ballroom dancing began from the sound system. Ethan started to dance and Holly's body fell in line with his.

He'd taught her well last night, and although she didn't think she could pull off any fancy ballroom dance moves she didn't trip all over his feet.

The lights were so bright on the dance floor that she could hardly see out to the tables. Which didn't matter that much because she really only wanted to close her eyes and enjoy the moment. The croon of the singer… Ethan's sure steps… His rock-sturdy chest…

Dancing with him, she thought they really were a couple—an entity that was larger than the sum of two individuals.

Ah... Her head fit so well underneath his chin as they danced. Being tall, she'd always had a sense of herself as being gawky around Ricky and the other men she had dated. She loved being encompassed by Ethan's height and width. As they glided across the dance floor, she felt graceful. A fairy princess. A prom queen. The object of attention.

All things she wasn't.

How would it be tomorrow, with a roomful of guests scrutinizing her? They wouldn't think she was beautiful enough for a man like Ethan! Everyone would know that she wasn't pedigreed and educated. They'd wonder why a Benton had settled for someone as ordinary as her.

Although she would be wearing the magnificent sky-blue gown covered in crystals. That gown alone would convince leaders and kings that she was one of them. Her hair and makeup would be professionally done. The smoke and mirrors tricks would be believable.

She'd hobnobbed with the New York elite last night and no one had guessed that she was not of their social standing. They hadn't known that she'd grown up in a trailer park with an unmarried mother who'd been too drunk to get out of bed half of the time.

Of course at the gala Ethan's fiancée would be under closer examination.

She tilted her head back to study her hand on Ethan's shoulder. Just as she had last night, she actually missed wearing the gargantuan diamond ring that labeled her Ethan's intended. She thought back to the paper ring he had used to propose to her. When he had bent down on one knee with a ring made from a beer bottle label.

And then she flashed back to the shopping spree on Fifth Avenue. To the blue topaz ring she had loved. But

Ethan was right, of course. The ring he'd chosen was one befitting the future Mrs. Benton.

Leaning back further, to look up into Ethan's handsome face, she asked him, "Being in the spotlight doesn't faze you in the least?"

"I suppose I have always been visible to the shareholders. They watched me grow up."

"You came to the galas as a child?"

His muscles twitched. "When I was younger I was kept upstairs in a suite with my mother, who hated these evenings. We would come down and make an appearance."

Holly had noticed that Ethan's voice became squeezed every time his mother came up in conversation. Hints of rage had come spitting out when he'd explained how they had edited her out of all the photos in the slideshow.

"Wasn't your mother obligated to attend?" Holly persisted.

"She would call the kitchen to find out exactly what time dinner was being served. A half-hour before she would trot me down here in a tuxedo. We would do our annual mother-and-son spin around this dance floor. Then she would tug me to the exit, offering excuses that it was my bedtime or that she had a migraine."

"What about your dad?"

"He was not much the tuxedo-and-martini type, but he would soldier through alone. My mother was not gracious, like Aunt Louise. She would not mingle and exchange pleasantries with the guests. Not even to support my father. He knew that she was not an asset to the company."

"Was it awful for you, being paraded around?"

"Not really. I understood at an early age that my mother was not good for business but that I was. Whether it had been a profitable year or a struggle, seeing that there was a next generation of leadership instilled confidence in the shareholders. I have always been proud to represent our company."

"Is your mother still alive?"

"I have no idea," he bit out. "Nor do I care in the least. I have always assumed the shareholders believe that she went into seclusion and retired from public life after my father died."

With that, he tightened his hold around Holly's waist, bolted her against him and guided her with an absolute command that started at the top of his head and ended at the tip of his toes.

Holly molded herself to him and allowed his confident lead. Knowing that talk of his mother had unleashed the beast that he had now locked back into the cage inside him.

As they circled the music got louder, then softer. The low bass tones became more pronounced and then were corrected. Lights were adjusted as well, becoming hotter, then diffused and milky.

"Just one minute more, Mr. Benton!" the technician announced.

The music changed to a swinging standard.

Ethan relaxed his grip and backed Holly away to arm's distance ready for a quickstep. He twirled her once under his arm. She stumbled and they chuckled into each other's eyes.

His head tilted to the side. They leaned in toward each other's smiles. Drawn to each other.

Out of the corner of her eye Holly saw Aunt Louise's husband, Fernando, enter the ballroom and scurry toward them.

When they had come to the apartment for dinner she had noticed the way Fernando walked with small, mincing steps. She hadn't liked how he had snooped at the things on Ethan's desk and taken a fax from the machine. And she had overheard him telling Ethan that he didn't want to spend his life in Barbados when Louise retired.

But at this moment it was important for them to unify for the sake of Louise. Since the older woman wasn't well today, Ethan and Fernando had taken charge of the final details for the gala. Ethan had to be grateful for whatever help Fernando was offering. Perhaps he had a report on the status of the menu...

"I've been trying to call you!" Fernando approached and yapped at Ethan.

Ethan glanced over to one of the empty tables, where he had left his phone while he was on stage at the podium and while he and Holly had danced. "Is everything in order?" he asked.

"No, it's not. Louise has taken a bad fall. I've called the paramedics."

CHAPTER TEN

ETHAN LED THE charge out of the ballroom and toward the hotel elevators, with Fernando and Holly racing behind him to keep up. When they reached the bronze elevator bank Ethan rapped the call button incessantly until one set of doors opened. Pressing for the twenty-sixth floor as soon as he'd stepped in, he backed against the gilded and mirrored wall of the elevator car.

His neck muscles pulsed. As the elevator ascended he kept his eyes peeled on the digital read-out of the floor numbers.

One, two, seven, twelve...

"What happened?" He forced the question out of a tight throat.

"Louise had been resting on the sofa in the suite's living room," Fernando reported. "She stood up and said she was going to make a phone call. Then, as she started to walk, she tripped on the coffee table and fell face-forward."

"Why did you not help her get up from the sofa in the first place?" Ethan seethed.

"She didn't tell me she was going to stand up. She just did it. I rushed to her, but it was too late."

Ethan's jaw ground as he fought to keep himself together. This incompetent idiot should have never been allowed to care for Aunt Louise. She was going to need full-time nurses. He'd arrange that immediately.

The read-out reached twenty-three, twenty-four...

On the twenty-sixth floor, Ethan pushed through the elevator doors before they had fully opened. Holly and Fernando followed. At the room's door, he snatched the key card from Fernando's hand.

Ethan rushed into the suite. "Aunt Louise?"

Louise sat on the floor with her back against the sofa. Angry scrapes had left red stripes across her right cheek and her knees. She massaged her wrist.

"I'm all right, dear," she assured him in a fairly steady voice. "Don't embarrass me any more than I've already embarrassed myself."

"There is no reason to be embarrassed," Ethan said, trying to soothe her. These incidences must be so humiliating for her. She'd always been such an able woman.

"Falls happen," Fernando chimed in. "We've been here before, Louise. You'll be fine."

Ethan fired a piercing glower at Fernando. He didn't need to try to make light of the situation.

"Oh, goodness. Holly!" Louise spotted Holly standing back from them. She managed a dry smile. "Somehow I've become an old woman."

"Thank goodness you weren't hurt worse." Holly nodded her respect.

"At this point we do not know if or how much she is injured," Ethan snapped, angry with everyone. "She needs to be examined."

Right on cue, there was a soft knock on the door. Ethan let in the hotel manager, who confirmed that they were expecting paramedics. Two emergency medical technicians filed in.

One checked Louise's vital signs, such as her blood pressure and heart-rate. He shone a small light into her eyes. Another technician asked questions about her medical history and what had happened.

While that was going on Ethan noticed Fernando pouring himself a cocktail. Holly had noticed too.

He and Holly raised eyebrows at each other. This was hardly a time for drinks.

Ethan clenched his fists and mashed his lips tightly. He stood silently.

Fernando had accused Ethan at dinner the other night of finding himself a wife just so that Louise would retire. Fernando had said he had no intention of spending his life on boring Barbados, as he characterized it, with Louise.

So, following that logic, Fernando should be doing everything he could to try to keep Louise as healthy as possible. Yet he obviously didn't bother with trivial matters, such as protecting her from falling. And now—with paramedics in the room, no less—he clearly thought it was cocktail hour.

"There don't appear to be any broken bones," one of the technicians informed them. "But, given her overall medical condition, we're going to transport her to the hospital for a more complete evaluation."

Ethan brought a hand over his mouth, overcome with worry. This woman had shown him so much love—had gone above and beyond the call of duty for him his entire life. Maybe his caring so much for his aunt was a sign. That he was capable of loyalty. Of devotion.

He refused his inclination to look over to Holly.

The technician issued instructions into his phone.

Fernando walked over to pat Louise gently on the shoulder in between sips of his drink.

"Can we take her down in a private elevator?" Ethan asked the manager, who waited quietly beside the door. "And out through a private garage? Many of our shareholders are staying here at the hotel, and we would like to keep this matter to ourselves."

"Of course, Mr. Benton."

Fernando settled himself closer to where Ethan was standing. "Clever…" he said under his breath. "Always thinking about image. I've got a little surprise for you with regards to that."

Ethan whipped his head to look into Fernando's eyes. "What on earth are you talking about at a time like this?" he demanded.

Two more paramedics came through the door with a stretcher.

Louise protested, "Oh, please, gentlemen—a wheelchair would do."

"It's for your protection, ma'am."

"I will ride in the ambulance with Louise," Ethan declared.

"No. *I* will," Fernando countered.

"Family only, please," one of the technicians said over his shoulder as he secured Louise onto the stretcher.

"I'm her husband."

"I am coming as well," Ethan insisted.

To the outside eye they must look like an odd sort of family. Elderly Aunt Louise. Nephew Ethan, who was probably being mistaken for her son, and Holly for his wife. Then Fernando, with his tanning salon skin and over-styled hair, who looked exactly the part of a cougar's husband.

The hotel manager headed the pack as the technicians began wheeling the stretcher out of the suite. Fernando and Ethan followed closely behind.

Ethan turned his head back to Holly. "You go home to the apartment."

"I'd like to come to the hospital, too."

Irritated at even having to discuss this further, Ethan

repeated his order. "There is no need for you to be at the hospital. Go back to the apartment."

The hotel manager led them to a private elevator and swiped her access card.

Ethan dashed a text into his phone.

"I could take a taxi and meet you there," Holly pleaded. "I want to be there for you and—"

He cut her off. "I have just instructed Leonard to pick you up in front of the hotel."

This was a private matter that Holly had no place in, despite appearances. While he had certainly become accustomed to having her around, she was still only an employee, and Louise's health was a personal thing. Ethan did not want Holly to overhear any discussions with doctors, or any information regarding a prognosis for his aunt. What Holly had just witnessed in the suite was beyond what his fiancée-for-hire should be privy to.

Ethan feared that he was starting to lose his better judgment around Holly. It was becoming so easy, so natural to let her into his life. If he allowed himself to, he might long for her support at the hospital. He knew it would be hours of waiting and worrying while Aunt Louise was examined.

He had nothing to say to Fernando. Wouldn't sitting with Holly in the waiting area, sharing a paper cup full of coffee, huddled together, be a comfort?

No! Once again, he reminded himself of Holly's place in this dynamic. Despite how they might appear, to the paramedics or anyone else, Holly was not part of this family.

Not. Family.

He pointed down the hall toward the public elevator they had ridden up to the suite. "Holly, please return to ground floor and retrieve my things from the ballroom. Thank you."

Louise was wheeled into the private elevator, and everyone but Holly got in.

Just as the doors were closing Ethan saw in Holly's eyes that he'd upset her by not allowing her to come along. But this was no time to focus on her. She should know and respect that.

"I will phone you as soon as I hear anything, all right?" He didn't wait for an answer.

So much for being part of the family.

Holly made it through the car ride home from the hotel, and it wasn't until she opened the door to the dark, empty apartment that tears spilled down her face.

Louise's condition was heartbreaking, and Holly hoped that she wasn't seriously injured after the tumble she'd taken. That she would be able to make it to the gala tomorrow night.

Ethan and Louise had such a finely tuned strategy to keep the extent of her illness hidden from the public. Holly admired their efforts. And thankfully the paramedics were only taking Louise to the hospital as a precaution.

She flipped on the lights. Slung her jacket on the coat rack. Kicked off her boots. And then she allowed in some self-pity. If she ever needed a reminder that this engagement was all a front, she had her proof. She was not, and nor would she ever be, a member of this clan.

Once they'd arrived at Louise's hotel suite Ethan had barely acknowledged her presence. Not that she would have expected him to pay lots of attention to her, but she had to admit she was surprised at how completely he had shut her out.

Holly had offered to go along to the hospital to be there for Louise *and* for Ethan—as a friend who rallied round when maybe a hand to hold would be welcome. But Ethan would have none of it, and hadn't been able to get her out of the picture swiftly enough.

Everything had moved so fast this week. How had she

got here? To feeling sorry for herself because she was left behind? How had she come to care so much for these people so quickly? She'd become so involved in Ethan's life she could hardly remember a time when she hadn't been. Had she forgotten who she was?

Holly Motta was an artist who had spent four long years married to the wrong man.

Ricky hadn't made it easy for her to leave. Even after she'd moved out of the last place they'd been living he'd shown up at her work and insisted on talking to her. Or he'd followed her car and confronted her at a supermarket or in a bank parking lot. It had got to the point that she'd had to change her phone number. Month after month he had refused to sign the legal documents divorcing them, leaving her hanging in limbo. Finally he'd given up and cut her loose.

It had taken her two years to feel truly unshackled from the demanding and possessive hold Ricky had on her. Now she was determined to move forward with her life. This prospect with Ethan had presented itself and she'd snatched it. The job, this apartment, the clothes…the promise of a glamorous escapade with an exciting man.

Nothing wrong with any of that. Life was throwing her a bone, for once. And she was taking it. Life on life's terms.

The problem was the illusion was so convincing that she was starting to buy it.

Twenty-nine years of hurt overtook her. She wasn't tough, like New York. She couldn't endure another defeat. Withstand another wound. Her heart functioned in broken pieces that were only taped together and could collapse at any minute. Maybe this masquerade was too dangerous. She didn't think she had it in her to bounce back from anguish yet again.

Restless, she went to the kitchen. Drank a full glass of water in one gulp. It had been hours since she'd eaten. A few slices of cheese and bread went down easily as she munched them standing up.

She hoped Ethan would get a bite to eat at the hospital. He'd be hungry, too. *Ugh!* She needed to stop caring about things like whether or not he had eaten. Had to break her habit of always looking after people.

She paced back to the living room. Judged the paintings she had been working on in the little studio area she had created by the window. They were a good start to the ideas she had in her head. A drawing pad perched on the easel. She mindlessly picked up a stick of charcoal and began to put it to paper.

After a few minutes she cranked up some funky music and swung her hips from left to right to the beat. A little sketching, a little boogie-woogie—that was always how she got through everything in her life.

Curved lines on the page. A man's jaw. Not square and chiseled like Ethan's. That buzz-cut hair. The thick swash of eyelashes.

A smile crossed her lips.

Small ears. The rounded shoulders. The only person she could count on. Her brother.

Yet she hadn't been honest with Vince about the events of the past few days. She had called him the first night she was here, when the mix-up with the apartment had started everything that had come since. She'd hinted that something had come her way. Vince had reminded her that it was *her* time now. That she should take hold of any prospect life threw at her.

They'd had so little in the way of support as kids. They'd always had to be each other's cheering section.

Straight up or fall down... Holly mouthed their childhood chant.

They had been texting every day, as they always did. She'd told him that New York was amazing. That it was mostly raining. But she hadn't told him about this weird arrangement she'd agreed to. Which had become a wild rollercoaster of feeling so right and then, in the next moment, feeling so wrong.

She hadn't even told Vince about meeting Ethan. And she hadn't told Ethan about her rat ex-husband, Ricky. It wasn't like her to keep secrets. But she didn't know where anything stood anymore. She didn't want to make things more complicated than they already were. Even if nothing were to work out for her here in New York, Holly needed to make sure that Ethan kept his word about helping Vince.

Her brother was a good man. She was so proud of him. Every day she hoped and prayed for a bright future for him. That separately, yet bound in spirit, they'd rise up like phoenixes from the ashes of their childhood.

She thumbed her phone.

"Holz?" Vince used his nickname for his sister.

"Vinz!" Holly sandwiched the phone between her ear and her shoulder as she finished drawing her brother's arm. Their builds were so different… It was only in the eyes of their mother where the resemblance was undeniable.

"How's New York treating you?"

"Oh… I kinda got involved in something I thought was one thing but now it seems like it's another."

As in tonight. Which had been reinforcement of the fact that Ethan would never regard her as anything more than a hired hand. That the feelings she'd started to have for him could only lead to misfortune.

"What are you talking about?"

"I don't know… I met a man."

"Well, sis, it's about time you met a man. You haven't dated anyone since you left the Rat."

"I know. But this might not be the right thing."

Somehow she couldn't bring herself to tell him that the man she was talking about was Ethan Benton. The bil-

lionaire vice president, soon to be CEO, of the company
Vince worked for.

"So you'll move on to something else. We've done that
enough times in our life, haven't we?"

"That we have, bro."

How often had their mother made promises? Then broken them.

"Straight up or fall down!" they recited in unison.

"Get some sleep, Holz. You sound tired."

Holly continued sketching after the call. Line after line,
listening to song after song. More glasses of water downed
in one go.

Finally she sprawled across the sofa and pondered the
painting of Ethan on the wall. His mouth… That urgent
mouth that had covered hers a few midnights ago atop the
Empire State Building. He had kissed her lips. Along her
throat. Behind her ear. Her eyelids.

They fluttered with the memory.

The phone woke her up.

"Hello?" Her voice was gravelly.

"Ethan, here."

"How's Louise?"

"Stable. She was not badly injured by the fall."

"Thank heavens."

Holly's eyes didn't want to open fully. The sound of his
voice caressed her, but didn't erase the sting of him ban-
ning her from the hospital yesterday. Despite wishing he'd
make mention of it, she knew he wouldn't.

She had to carry on forward. "What time is it?"

"Eight in the morning."

Tonight was the gala. Her end of the bargain was due.

"Are you still at the hospital?"

"No, I came back to one of the hotel suites to get some
sleep. I did not want to wake you by coming in during the
middle of the night."

Holly stroked the leather of the sofa where Ethan had been sleeping the past few nights. If he had come home he'd have found her conked out on it after she simply hadn't been able to stand at the easel any longer.

She'd done eight different renderings of Vince. Must have been some sort of homesickness, she mused to herself now, in the gray haze of the cloudy morning.

She stretched her neck. "What happens now?"

"Aunt Louise will be discharged in a couple of hours. Then I will send Leonard to pick you up. He will help you manage my tuxedo and your gown and whatever else you need. We can get dressed in this suite. I have ordered food. And a makeup artist and hairstylist are coming."

"Okay."

Ethan had everything so organized it made her head spin. How did he keep himself together? She needed a shower and coffee.

"Be prepared for a busy day and night," he continued. "I hope you are ready, my fiancée. Because it is showtime."

When the makeup and hair people departed the hotel suite, Holly and Ethan were finally alone for the first time all afternoon.

The last few hours had flown by. People from Benton Worldwide and from their public relations firm had come and gone from the lavish suite that had a bedroom, living room and dining table in addition to the spacious dressing area where they were now.

All of the suite's Zen-like furnishings and décor were made from precious woods and fine fabrics, while floor-to-ceiling windows provided panoramic views of the Manhattan skyline, where the gloomy and rain-drenched day had turned to dusk.

It had been a whirlwind of introductions as Ethan had presented Holly, although of course he hadn't yet revealed their engagement. Members of the shareholders' board of directors had been in to confer with Ethan. And Holly had finally met Ethan's trusted assistant, Nathan—a young man wielding four electronic devices in his two hands.

A sandwich buffet and barista bar had kept everyone fortified. Then the glam squad had arrived to give Ethan a haircut and work their magic on Holly, before filing out just now to do the same for Louise.

In the first quiet moment since she had arrived, Holly inspected herself in the mirror. She wore a white satin robe, but had already put on her jewelry and heels.

Shimmery eye makeup and soft pink lipstick gave her skin a luminous glow. The style wizards had managed to remove every speck of paint from her cuticles, so that a pearly pink manicure could complement the gown. Her hair was magically doubled in volume, thanks to the expert blow-dry she'd just received.

They had experimented with hairstyles, but gave Ethan veto power. Every time she'd asked his opinion of one of the looks they'd tried he had taken a long gander at her. He'd stopped to scratch his chin, or shot her a wink or half a smile. The way he'd studied every inch of her had been almost obscenely exciting.

And seemingly had had little to do with her hairstyle. Because each time he had decreed that he liked her hair better down.

Now she observed Ethan's reflection behind her in the mirror. He was perched on a stool in the dressing area, reading over some papers, already in tuxedo pants and dress shoes. His stiff white shirt was on, but had not yet been buttoned. She imagined her fingers tracing down the center of his bare, lean chest.

This was really happening. She was in this castle of a hotel, about to be crowned as princess and then ride off on a majestic horse with this regal prince.

Of course in real life at the end of the night they'd shake hands on a con well played. But what the heck? She might as well enjoy it.

"Louise was okay when you talked to her a little while ago?"

"Under the circumstances." Ethan didn't look up from his work.

"I have an idea for tonight that might make it easier on her," Holly said as she tightened one of her earrings in front of the mirror.

"Oh?"

"You were telling me that when it's time for her to give her CEO speech you'll escort her from the table up the stairs to the stage?"

"Yes."

"I was thinking it may be difficult for her to walk up the stairs after her fall. And it won't help to have a thousand people staring at her."

"What is the alternative?"

"I noticed that there is a side entrance to the stage from the waiters' station. While the video montage is playing, and it's dark in the ballroom, we could help Louise get away from the table and up to the stage that way. With no one watching her. Then, when she's introduced, all she has to do is come out from the side of the stage and go to the podium."

Holly followed Ethan's reflection in the mirror as he walked toward her. He came up behind her and circled his arms around her shoulders. He hugged her so authentically, so affectionately, she melted.

"Thank you for thinking of that," he said softly into her ear. "Thank you for thinking about it at all. My, my…. You have already gone far beyond what I expected of you. Please accept my gratitude."

She wanted to tell him how horribly it had hurt when

he hadn't let her go to the hospital yesterday. How much she'd wanted to be part of his family, and not just what her obligations required. How she longed to be there for him in good times and in bad.

She still had so much of her heart left to share. Nothing in her past had squelched that out of her.

But she'd never get to give that heart to him.

Even though she was now positive that he was the only man to whom she ever could.

Fearing she might cry, and tarnish her stellar makeup job, she flicked an internal switch and squirmed away from him.

"Can you help me into my gown? It weighs about ten pounds!"

Ethan went to back to the stool he had been sitting on and patted his tablet for music. A smooth male voice sang a romantic song.

Not taking his eyes off her, he drank a sip from his water bottle and then recapped it. "I would love to help you into your dress."

She raced over and punched into his tablet the upbeat music that she favored.

Ethan's grin swept across his lips.

Holly couldn't resist sashaying her hips to the rhythm as she turned and headed to the closet where her gown hung. She was sure she heard him gasp when she let her robe fall to the floor to reveal the skimpy undergarments underneath.

And so the pretend soon-to-be-married couple helped each other get dressed for the gala.

"Careful with the base of the zipper—it's delicate."

"Blast! Do this right cufflink for me. I am no good at all with my left hand."

"I hope this eye makeup doesn't look too dark in the photos."

"I do not know how women can dance in those heels. I am booking you a foot massage for tomorrow."

"Is my hair perfect?"

"Shoulders back."

"How do I look?"

"How do *I* look?"

The supposed future Mr. and Mrs. Ethan Benton exited the suite preened, perfumed and polished to perfection.

Just as they reached the entrance to the ballroom Ethan remembered he had the engagement ring in his pocket. He skimmed it onto Holly's finger.

Yet again.

They entered the gala to a cacophony of guests, cameras and lights befitting a royal wedding.

CHAPTER ELEVEN

THE BALLROOM VIBRATED with the din of a thousand people. Holly's heart thundered in her chest as Ethan maneuvered them from table to table for introductions. He charmed all the women and the men regarded him with great respect.

"Ethan, how has another year passed already?"

"Lovely to see you, Mrs. Thorpe. Good evening, Mr. Thorpe." Ethan pecked the older lady's cheek and shook the hand of her white-haired husband. "I would like to introduce you to Holly Motta."

Mrs. Thorpe's crinkly eyes lit up. "Well, now, Ethan, are we to believe that you have given up the single life at last?"

"Only because *you* are already spoken for," Ethan said, flattering her.

Holly was dumbstruck and could only squeak out, "Nice to meet you."

She felt horribly out of place. The giddy fun of getting dressed was gone now, and in this moment she felt like a young child in a Halloween princess costume. It was one thing to imagine being the fiancée of a respected and victorious billionaire. But it was another thing entirely actually to be presented as such.

"You look exquisite," Ethan whispered in her ear, as if he sensed her discomfort.

It offered no reassurance.

This wasn't going at all the way she'd thought it would. She hadn't felt this kind of pressure on the yacht the other evening, when Ethan had made small talk with casual acquaintances. The people here tonight knew him well, and she felt as if everyone—but *everyone*—was inspecting her. Panic pricked at her skin like needles, even while her brain told her she must not let Ethan down.

Taking short and fast breaths, she shook hands with a plastered-on smile.

"Henri!" Ethan clasped the shoulder of a mustached man. *"Cela fait longtemps."*

"Ça va?"

"Marie. *Magnifique, comme toujours.*" Ethan kissed the man's wife on both cheeks. *"Je vous présente Holly Motta."*

French. Naturally Ethan spoke perfect French. As men who take showers on private planes were likely to do.

As they walked away he told her, "Mr. and Mrs. Arnaud made a substantial personal donation to a low-income housing project we did outside of Paris."

"Merci!" Holly threw over her shoulder.

Ethan's eyes always took on a special shine when he mentioned those charity projects that were so important to him.

They approached a stone-faced man whose huge muscles were all but bursting out of a tuxedo that was a size too small. He stood ramrod-straight, with his arms folded across his chest. Holly saw that he wore a discreet earpiece with a barely noticeable wire.

"Holly Motta, this is Chip Foley, our head of security," Ethan introduced her.

Chip bent toward Ethan's ear. "I take it you received that fax with the information you requested, sir?"

Ethan looked confused. "No, I did not."

A Japanese couple were coming toward them.

"Ethan. *Ogenki desu ka?*"

The woman wore an elaborate kimono.

"Hai, genki desu," he answered back.

French wasn't intimidating enough. He had to speak Japanese, too.

The evening was starting off like a freezing cold shower.

Holly had imagined it was going to be easier. And more fun. What girl wouldn't want to be at the ball with the dashing prince she was madly in love with?

Madly. In. Love. With.

The four words echoed through her as if someone had yelled them into her ear. Especially the third word. Because there was no denying its truth.

She was in love with this sophisticated, handsome, brilliant man beside her.

Had it happened the very night she'd arrived in New York, when she'd opened the door to the apartment and found him reading his newspaper with that one curl of hair hanging in front of his eyes?

Had it been when he'd bought her all the painting supplies she'd been able to point to, because took her seriously as an artist in a way that no one else ever had?

Maybe it had been atop the Empire State Building, when those earth-shattering kisses had quaked through her like nothing she'd known before?

Or had it been on the yacht, under the tender shadow of the Statue of Liberty, when they'd danced together as one, late into the night?

It didn't matter.

Because she was in love with Ethan Benton.

And that was about the worst thing that had ever happened to her.

"We should make our way to the table now," Ethan said, after finishing his small talk in Japanese.

He took her hand and led them toward the head table, where Aunt Louise and Fernando were already sitting.

Awareness of his touch was a painful reminder that Holly would never have a bona fide seat at this family table. There would be no keeping the glass slippers. The Ethan Bentons of this world didn't marry the Holly Mottas. She was a commoner, hired to do a job—hardly any different from either a scullery maid or an office assistant in his corporation.

Ethan's world was a tightly coiled mechanism of wheels. She was but one small cog. Loving him was going to be *her* problem, not his.

She willed herself not to fall apart now. Overall, Ethan had been kind and generous to her. She had to hold her end up. That much she owed him. Despite the fact that she was crumbling inside.

Love was awful.

"Louise, you look wonderful tonight." Holly greeted the older woman with a kiss on the cheek.

The style magicians had worked wonders. None of the scrapes and bruises from her fall were visible. No one would guess she wore a wig that was thicker and more lustrous than her own thinning hair. Shiny baubles complemented her black gown.

Holly nodded hello to Fernando who, in return, lifted his nose and looked away.

Fernando sat on one side of Louise and Ethan the other. Holly sat next to Ethan. Rounding out their table were company VIPs whom she'd been introduced to earlier today but couldn't remember their names.

As the ballroom's lights were slightly dimmed a spotlight was aimed on Louise, and a waiter brought her a microphone. Louise stood, subtly using the table for leverage and balance. Holly saw a grimace pass quickly across her face.

"Good evening, Benton Worldwide extended family," Louise greeted the guests. "It's been another profitable and productive year for us, which you'll hear about in my report later. As you know my late husband, Melvin Benton, and his brother, Joseph Benton, began this company with the purchase of a one-bedroom apartment in South Boston. And look where we are today."

The ballroom filled with the sound of applause.

"Together we have made this happen. Melvin taught me many things. The most important of which is that money in our wallets means nothing without love in our hearts."

Louise smiled at Ethan and Holly.

"And so," she continued, "if you'll indulge an old woman before we get on to pie charts and growth projections, I'd like to share something personal with you."

A hush swept the room.

"Many of you have watched my nephew Ethan grow up over the decades. I hope you share in my pride at the man he's become. He's a leader who drives himself hard, a savvy negotiator who insists on fairness, and a shrewd businessman with a philanthropic spirit."

The guests applauded again.

Ethan bowed his head, clearly embarrassed by the accolades. Holly touched his arm. He turned his head slightly toward her.

"Yet there's been one thing missing. It has always been my greatest wish for Ethan that he would find a partner to share his life with. To rejoice with in triumph and to weep with in sorrow. To have a home. To have children. To know a love like Mel and I had. And it's with great joy tonight that I announce that Ethan has found that soul mate. And, although it's asking a lot of her to meet her extended family of one thousand all in one evening, I'd like to introduce you to Ethan's fiancée: Miss Holly Motta."

Ethan and Holly looked at each other, both knowing this was their moment. They rose from their chairs in unison and turned to face the crowd. Holly's chest crackled at the irony of the moment.

Applause and good wishes flooded the room.

"Bravo!"

"Bravo!"

"It's about time!"

"Holly!"

"Ethan!"

They smiled and waved on cue—as if they were a royal couple on a palace balcony. Guests began tapping their knives against their water glasses in a signal for a couple to kiss.

Without hesitation, Ethan leaned in to Holly's lips. Thankfully not with a passionate kiss that would have thrown her off balance. But it wasn't a quick peck either. Perhaps he was incapable of a kiss that didn't stir her up inside.

She felt herself blushing. When she giggled a little the guests cheered.

As planned, the chandeliers were dimmed further and the dance floor became bathed in a golden light. Ethan took Holly's hand and brought her to the center of the dance floor, this time as two thousand eyes fixed on them.

The love song from their practice session boomed out of the sound system.

Holly lifted one hand to Ethan's shoulder. One of his fastened around her waist. Their other hands met palm to palm.

They floated across the dance floor, bodies locked, legs in sync. The moment was so perfect Holly wanted to cry.

It was a moment she would never forget. Yet, in time she must learn to forget, if she was ever to love someone who could return her love.

With the gleam of lights beaming down on the dance floor and the rest of the ballroom darker, it was hard to see. Yet Holly's eyes landed on the table where they had been seated. Ethan turned her as they danced, but she kept craning her neck to focus on a strange sight.

Louise was chatting with a couple who had come over to the table. Meanwhile Fernando finished his drink and stood up. He reached into his tuxedo jacket's pocket and pulled out two pieces of paper. He placed one on the chair where Holly was sitting and the other on Ethan's seat. Then he smirked with a satisfied nod.

Holly was so spectacularly beautiful Ethan couldn't help glancing down at her as they danced. She was really just as fetching—if not more so—casual and barefoot in a tee shirt and jeans, having breakfast at the apartment. But to-night... The dance floor lights cast an incandescent glow on her face. The baby pink of her lipstick emphasized the sensual plumpness of her mouth.

It made him want to brand her with kiss after kiss, until he had to hold her up to keep her from falling to the ground. His body reacted—in fact overreacted—to the intimate feel of her breasts, belly and hips pressed to him as he held her close.

Every now and then the sobering fact that Holly wasn't really his fiancée would flit across his mind. There wasn't ever going to be the wedding, home and children that Aunt Louise had spoken of during her toast. He batted away the reality of those thoughts every time they came near. If only for tonight, he actually did want to believe the mas-querade was real.

He could risk that much.

Yet a voice in his gut pleaded with him to stop. Told him that he knew better. That his mission had been to guard and defend. That dangerous fantasies would confuse his intentions and lead to irrevocably bad decisions.

Opposing forces argued within him. So his rational

mind welcomed the distraction when he followed Holly's eyes to the table where they'd been sitting. He watched with curiosity as Fernando placed a piece of paper on his and Holly's chairs.

As soon as the dance was over Ethan nodded politely at the applauding guests to the left and to the right. When the next song began he gestured for others to join in the dancing. Couples stood and approached. Once the rhythm was underway, and the dance floor was well populated, he gestured to Holly to return to their table.

Ethan slipped the piece of paper on his chair into his jacket pocket and sat down, trying not to draw any attention to the action. When everyone was occupied with their first-course salads and dinner conversation, he'd discreetly look at it.

Holly held her piece of paper in her lap. She looked downward to read it.

Her face changed instantly. The rosy blush of her cheeks turned ashen white. The blue in her eyes darkened to a flat gray. She blinked back tears.

Trancelike, she slowly stood.

Her murmur was barely audible, and directed to no one in particular. "Excuse me…"

Fortunately, with the dance floor in full swing and one of the video presentations playing on several screens throughout the room, Holly's exit from the table didn't appear too dramatic.

Ethan watched her cross the ballroom as if she was headed to the ladies' lounge.

Instead she opened a sliver of one of the French doors that led to the ballroom's terrace. She slipped through and closed it behind her.

At the table, Ethan caught Fernando's eye. He grinned at Ethan like a Cheshire cat. Ethan's blood began to boil.

But he kept his cool as he rose. He moved slowly toward the terrace. And slid out through the same door Holly had.

The frigid and windy evening slapped across his face and straight under the fabric of his tuxedo. Holly stood across the large plaza of the terrace with her back to him. He figured she must be chilled to the bone.

What was it that had upset her so much that she'd had to leave the ballroom and retreat to this empty space that was not in use during the winter months?

With dread in his heart, Ethan pulled the paper from his pocket.

His temples pulsated louder with each word he read.

Fax to Ethan Benton from Chip Foley, Head of Security, Benton Worldwide Properties.

Regarding Holly Motta.

Per your request, I have gathered the following intelligence.

Holly Motta, age twenty-nine, last known residence Fort Pierce, Florida.

Internet and social media presence significant only as it relates to her occupation as an artist.

No criminal record.

Sometimes known as Holly Dowd.

Married until two years ago to a Ricky Dowd, age twenty-eight, also of Fort Pierce.

Married and divorced.

"Holly!" he spat.

Her shoulders arched at the sound of his voice.

She spun around and they marched toward each other. Meeting in the middle of the grand stone terrace.

"You had me *investigated*?" she accused, rather than questioned.

"You were *married*?" he fired back.

"Without telling me?"

"Without telling me?"

"That must simply be business as usual for you, Mr. Benton. Background checks on the hired help and all that."

"As a matter of fact, it is. My family has spent two generations building our empire. We had better damn well protect it with every tool we have."

"You might have let me know."

The hammering at Ethan's temples threatened to crack open his skull as he read the fax aloud.

"'Ricky Dowd, also known as Rick Dowd and Riff Dowd, indicted for armed robbery at age nineteen. Served twenty-two months in prison, released early due to penitentiary overcrowding. Indicted six months ago, again for armed robbery. Currently serving a sentence at Hansen Correctional Facility in central Florida.'"

Ethan broke away from the page to glare at Holly.

"Twice indicted for armed robbery?"

He felt heat rise through his body in a fury that, for once, he might not be able to contain.

Holly's face was lifeless. Her eyes downcast. She didn't even seem to be breathing.

Finally she muttered softly, "I didn't know Ricky was in prison again."

"But you knew who you married." Ethan's jaw locked.

"The first robbery was before we were married. This new incident happened after our divorce. I haven't seen or talked to him in two years."

"Yet you married a convicted criminal? And deliberately withheld that from me? How will that look to my shareholders? Do you not understand the importance of an impeccable reputation?"

Ethan was approaching cruelty. Rubbing salt into her wounds. But he couldn't stop himself.

Women were never who they seemed! Once again a female had betrayed him. Had not been honest. The same as every other woman he had known. The same as his mother.

This was exactly what he'd been warning himself of, despite his growing attachment to Holly. Why would she turn out to be any different from the others? How dense was he still not to have learned his lesson?

They'd spent so much time together this week. Yet all along she'd withheld the information that not only had she been married, but to someone convicted of serious crimes. She obviously didn't understand how, if that information was to be revealed publicly, it would become an integral part of people's perception of her. Of them.

What else was she hiding? Omission was its own form of lying. And he'd always known that if this engagement façade was to work, they'd have to be straightforward with each other. He'd told her about his future plans for Benton Worldwide. She knew about his aunt's health problems. He'd even let her witness Louise being wheeled out on a stretcher by the paramedics. Without measuring the risks of his actions, he had, in fact, trusted Holly.

Trust. Every year, at every shareholders' gala at this hotel, Ethan got a reminder that *trust* was a dirty word. One that he should never factor into an equation. After all, a boy whose father had just died should have been able to trust that his mother had his best interests at heart.

To read this background information about Holly, to confirm that he didn't know her at all, was an unbearable confusion. Just like the one he'd suffered as a boy, never really knowing his mother, or what could make a woman betray her only child.

A familiar fist pummeled his gut more viciously than ever. He wanted to scream. For the nine-year-old boy who'd lost both his parents within a few months of each other. One in a horrifying car accident.

To complicate matters even more, he was also seething

with jealousy that Holly had given her hand in marriage to another man. *Any* other man! Irrationally, he wanted her only for himself.

Ethan clenched his teeth and read on while Holly clutched her own copy of the fax.

> *Brother Vincent Motta, age twenty-six.*
> *Well-regarded employee at Benton Miami office.*
> *Mother Sally Motta, age forty-eight.*
> *Dozens of jobs, ranging from waitress to telemarketer to factory employee. No position held longer than six months. Never married. Motta appears to be maiden name.*
> *Father of Holly Motta—unknown.*
> *Father of Vincent Motta—unknown.*
> *Unknown whether Holly and Vincent have the same father.*

It was hard to say whose story was sadder—his or Holly's.

Her lower lip trembled uncontrollably until a sob erupted from her throat. "So now you know everything, Mr. Benton!" she cried. "Do you want to share my humiliating past with everyone in the ballroom?"

As tears rolled down her face she shivered in the cold and used both hands to rub at her bare arms.

"I do not know *what* I want to do!" Ethan shouted—uncharacteristically.

He yanked off his tuxedo jacket and wrapped it around her shoulders. "If you had given me all this information at the outset I could have discussed it with my team."

"Discussed it with your team?" She pulled the jacket closer around her. "What would you have done? Created a new identity for me? Erased the past? You masters of the world think of everything, don't you?"

"That is exactly what we have been doing, is it not? We have dressed you up and presented you as a suitable bride for me. Which is what we agreed upon in the beginning."

"Yes. Playing dress-up. Pretending someone like me could be *suitable* for someone like you. My mistake, Ethan. I thought we had become more than our contract. I thought we had…" She eyed the ground again. "I thought we had become friends."

He blamed himself for this predicament. It had been insanity to hire someone he'd only just met for this charade. In fact the whole ruse had been preposterous. Paying someone to pose as his fiancée in order to get Aunt Louise to retire. His heart had been in the right place, but he'd had a temporary lapse in judgment.

In fact he'd been deceitful to Aunt Louise. The one and only woman in his life who had always been truthful with him. Although he knew that no matter how big a mess he'd made of everything his aunt would still love him. That he could depend on.

For one of the only times in his life Ethan didn't know what to do. Didn't know how to reckon with all the events of the past few days. Just as he didn't know where to put the decades of shame that had mixed with the years of phenomenal successes.

And he surely didn't know how to make sense of his feelings for Holly. For once he was out of his league.

After a stare-down with her that had them both turning blue with cold, logic set in.

He wondered aloud, "How did Fernando get this fax from Chip Foley?"

Holly explained how she had seen Fernando take a fax from the machine when they'd had him and Louise over for dinner. Because Fernando used the apartment during his trips to New York, she hadn't thought it unusual that he'd receive a fax there.

"That weasel…" Ethan scowled with disgust.

All along Fernando had been conjuring up ways to ruin Ethan's engagement because he didn't want to move to Barbados with Aunt Louise. He no doubt planned to use Holly's history as a way to prove her an unbefitting bride.

"I will deal with him later. We will sort *all* this out later. For now, we will go back inside and finish the evening as planned."

"Okay," Holly whispered, but it wasn't convincing. She looked utterly shell-shocked with his jacket grasped tightly around her. The rims of her eyes were red and her makeup had smeared.

"I will slip back into the ballroom. You will go up to the suite and pull yourself together. I will meet you back at the table."

"Yes," she consented.

Ethan only hoped she'd be able to get through the rest of the night.

Once inside, Holly handed him his jacket and ducked toward the exit. Ethan soon got roped into a conversation with a Swedish architect. He returned to the table just as the wait staff cleared the salad plates. His and Holly's were untouched.

Ethan made small talk with his tablemates as the main course was served. Over and over again the information in the fax repeated itself in his brain. And he kept glancing in the direction Holly should be returning from. It seemed to be taking her an inordinate amount of time.

Guests were enjoying their surf-and-turf entrées of lobster and filet mignon. A pleasant buzz filled the ballroom.

Still no Holly.

Maybe she'd fallen and hurt herself.

Maybe she'd been taken ill.

Maybe she'd been so upset by the fax that she was crying her eyes out.

Ethan had to go find her. But just as he was about to get up the president of the board of shareholders, Denny Wheton, stood from his seat at the next table. A spotlight landed on him. A waiter gave him a microphone.

"Ladies and gentlemen..." Denny began.

Ethan scanned the whole ballroom for Holly, his insides filling with fear that Denny was going to make a toast to them.

"On behalf of the shareholders' board," Denny continued, confirming Ethan's worry, "I want to express our delight at the news of Ethan's engagement. As Louise said earlier, we've watched Ethan become the driving force of Benton Worldwide. His father and uncle would be proud. As to his bride...we haven't had a chance to get to know her yet, but we're sure Ethan has chosen her with the same diligence and discernment he puts into all his endeavors. To Holly and Ethan! Congratulations!"

Guests at the other tables lifted their glasses.

"Congratulations!"

Voices came from every corner of the room.

Ethan froze as a second spotlight beamed onto him. Hadn't Denny stopped to notice that Holly was not in her seat? He'd probably had too much to drink.

"Holly?" Denny called into his microphone.

The congratulations ceased. The room became silent.

"Holly?"

A microphone was handed to Ethan.

Who had to think fast.

"Thank you for your good wishes," Ethan stated robotically.

He'd kill himself if something bad had happened to her.

"I apologize that Holly is not present for this toast. She is feeling a bit under the weather."

"Under the weather?" Denny boomed into his microphone. "*Under the weather?* Will Benton Worldwide be introducing the next generation's CEO nine months from now?"

The ballroom exploded with applause and cheers.

CHAPTER TWELVE

HOLLY HAD NEVER been so relieved to be home in her entire life. She toed the apartment door closed and leaned back against it. With a deep sigh she dropped the couple of bags she had retrieved from the hotel suite before catching a taxi.

She closed her eyes for a few breaths, hoping to shut out all that had happened.

When she opened them again everything was still the same.

Only she had made matters worse by running away from Ethan and the gala.

En route to the bedroom, she heard her crystal gown swish audibly in the quiet of the apartment. A sound that hadn't been heard under all the activity at the gala. The sky-high heels were killing her, so they were quickly nudged off.

It was a struggle to reach the zipper of her dress. Much nicer earlier tonight, when Ethan had zipped her in. Eventually she was carefully able to wriggle out of the dress. Her impulse was to leave it pooled on the floor, but the adult in her at least managed to put it on the bed.

This gown wasn't her life.

Her jeans and tee shirt were familiar friends.

This wasn't her home.

It was time to go.

Time to cut her losses.

Holly had too much experience with that. Her marriage. Her mother. False hopes and grand promises that hadn't panned out. This was simply another.

With her tail between her legs, it was time to take two steps backward and keep striving for that next step ahead.

Sure, memories of New York would sting. Memories of Ethan would slice deeper than any wounds she'd ever endured before. But she was no stranger to pain.

Besides, she was supposed to be working on herself. Not getting mixed up in someone else's priorities. Not falling in love. This was the wrong road. Time to change direction.

Packing her clothes took less time than she'd thought it would. It was still the middle of the night. With plans to leave in the morning, she paced the apartment.

In the living room, the paper ring Ethan had made from his beer bottle label still sat on the coffee table. The one he'd used to propose to her with. When he had asked her to embark on a business venture that was *not* to become a matter of the heart. For the moment she still wore the enormous diamond that had been on and off her finger all week.

Holly rolled the ring round and round on her finger. She thought about the symbolism of rings—how the circle could never be broken. It had no beginning and it had no end. Continuous. Lasting. Eternal.

Undying love was *not* her and Ethan's story.

Their tale was of two people who had crossed paths in a New York City apartment. Now they both needed to continue on their separate journeys. Ethan built skyscrapers, but was determined not to build love. Holly had a past she could never escape.

His investigation into her hadn't even uncovered all her dirty laundry. He hadn't found out that she wasn't sure if the man who'd shown up every few years while she was growing up was really her father. Despite her mother's insistence that he was.

Wayne had been nice enough to her and Vince when he'd pass through town. He'd take them to get some cheap clothes that he'd pay for with a short fold of twenty-dollar bills he'd pull from his front pants pocket. Then they'd be shuffled off to a neighbor's house so that he could spend time alone with their mother.

Neither Holly nor Vince looked like him. But nor did they look like each other. It wasn't something they talked about much. They couldn't be any closer than they already were. What difference did it make? They could have DNA testing, but it wouldn't matter.

So she had never known whether she and her brother were half or full siblings. Or who their father—or fathers—were. They shared the same eyes as their mother. That was all Holly could be sure of.

Sally's blue eyes had been cloudy and bloodshot the last time Holly had seen her, five years ago.

Vince! Sorrow rained down on her. Her actions—lashing out at Ethan about the investigation and then abruptly leaving the gala without a word to him or to Louise—would cast an unprofessional shadow on Vince.

Her knees buckled and she sank down to the edge of a chair, vowing never to forgive herself if she had ruined her brother's chances at the promotion he'd worked so hard for.

Head in hands, she began to cry for all she and Vince had lacked when they were children. Not just material things, but adults to provide the care that every child needed. As much as they had looked out for each other, they'd always have holes in their hearts.

She wept for this week—for this failed chance to catapult her career to a potential high. For this lost opportunity to turn her goals into reality.

And she sobbed because she'd unexpectedly found a love in Ethan truer than any she could have imagined.

A love that the crux of her knew she would never have again. But she wasn't able to claim it.

Numbly, she picked up her phone. "Vinz…?"

"What's wrong?"

Only her brother would know after one syllable that she was shattered.

With the back of her hand she wiped the tears from her face. "I guess New York is not how I thought it would be."

"You wouldn't be the first person to say that."

"The thing is, I sort of think I've let you down."

Holly stopped herself there. She didn't have to explain everything right now. Maybe Ethan wouldn't hold all this against Vince. At this point she didn't have any control over the situation. All she had was regrets.

"Why would you have let me down? Because you took a shot and it didn't pan out? At least you did it."

"I'm just licking my wounds. I want to come home."

Where was home? She'd given up her dingy apartment in Fort Pierce to pin everything on her future. Neither she nor Vince had any current information on their mother's whereabouts.

"Fly here to Miami. My garage is yours to paint in. And my sofa bed has your name on it. I'll pick you up at the airport."

After the call, Holly took inventory of the mini art studio she'd set up by the window. Methodically she cleaned brushes. Tucked sketches into portfolios. She organized neatly, remembering the open tube of paint that had started this magical ride in New York. Cobalt Two Eleven all over her face.

Her gaze darted to the blue-painted sketch of Ethan on the wall. She was so proud of that piece—felt that she had

caught his spirit in each line. Power and gravity and sensuality, with demons fighting behind his eyes.

As a matter of fact she would take the painting with
her. It would either be a testament to the legacy Ethan
would hold in her heart forever. Or it would be a torment
that would haunt her for the rest of her days. Either way,
it was hers and she wanted it.

With a small knife she found in the kitchen she carefully removed the staples attaching the canvas to its frame.
She'd roll up the painting and buy a tube to transport it in
before she left town.

There was nothing more to do.

She wasn't interested in sleeping. Didn't want to give
up even one last minute of this magical city and its hex
that made people believe dreams could come true. These
moments were all she had, and she'd treasure them for a
lifetime.

She stared out the window. A million stories were un-
folding in the city. Hers would end here.

Inching off the diamond engagement ring, she placed
it next to the paper ring on the coffee table. Beside each
other they were as odd a couple as she and Ethan.

As usual, not knowing what else to do with her feelings,
Holly said goodbye to her fancy manicure and reached for
her charcoals.

Ethan closed the door on the hotel room where he'd managed a few hours of tortured sleep in a chair. He walked
down the hall to Aunt Louise's suite. Still in his tuxedo
pants, although his tie was off and the first two buttons of
his shirt were undone, he scratched his beard stubble. He'd
been unable to face a shower just yet, and had promised his
aunt they'd reconvene their discussion during breakfast.

"Come in, Ethan," Louise called out as soon as she
heard the keycard click to unlock the door.

"I have not had coffee!" Ethan managed a trace of a smile for his beloved aunt.

"I'll pour you a cup." Louise wore a dressing gown and slippers. She sat at the dining table in her luxury suite, heavy drapes open to the city.

Ethan took the seat across from her.

"Does anything look different to you in the light of morning?" She tipped her eyebrow to him in a familiar way.

When he was a teenager, living with her and Uncle Mel, if he'd been grappling with a dilemma or regretting a bad choice, Aunt Louise would always tell him to sleep on it and see if a new day brought any fresh insight.

The insistence in her arched brow today told him that she had decided what realization he should have come to. His intuition told him what her conclusion was. He peered into his coffee cup to try to shut the thought down.

Something like a tribal drum pounded inside him, urging him to lift his eyes and embrace the truth.

"Where is Fernando?" Ethan tried to change the subject—at least for a moment.

But on and on the internal drum sounded.

"Gone. Good riddance," Louise clipped. "Before dawn this morning I called Bob Parcell to draw up a non-disclosure agreement."

Ethan snorted. "Lawyers work around the clock."

"Ours do. I signed a generous check, contingent on the fact that Fernando never speaks a word about our family, our company or anything to do with us. If he does, our people will make sure the rest of his life is spent behind bars."

"Well done."

Louise took a sip of her coffee, then smacked the cup loudly back onto the saucer. "And *that*, my dear nephew, is the end of my foray into having a younger companion."

After Holly had disappeared last night he and Louise

had held their heads high until the last guest had left the gala. Then they'd sat up together until the wee hours. He'd confessed about the engagement ploy and his motivation behind it. Begged for her forgiveness. Told her about the fax and Fernando's part in it.

Now Ethan lifted his aunt's hand and gently kissed the back of it. "I am so sorry you fell prey to him"

"Don't you think I knew what he was doing?" she retorted. "His trips down here to New York while I stayed in Boston. The restaurant bills that were surely more expensive than dinner for one. Charges to women's clothing shops although I never received any gifts. Fernando was clearly taking advantage of me from the beginning."

"You never told me."

"The vanity of a rich old woman… Perhaps I thought I could simply buy myself something to replace the emptiness left by your Uncle Mel's death. But even with all the money in the world you can't purchase or declare love. You can't arrange it. It's love that rearranges *you*."

Ethan knew what she was telling him. The drum beat louder in his ears. Yet he couldn't. Mustn't. Wouldn't.

"I know that you're torn inside…" Louise continued.

For all her health problems, when Louise Benton was clearheaded she was a shrewd and intelligent woman.

"It's what I feared for you. That after so much loss you wouldn't be able to love. When your mother went—"

"You were the only mother I ever had," Ethan interrupted, taking her hand again. "Everything I have achieved is because of you."

Louise's eyes welled. "I must have done something right. You're a rare man to go through all this trouble to get me to retire. When I said I wanted you to be married and settled before you took over, I never imagined you'd concoct such an elaborate scheme just because I've been too hardheaded to see that my time has come. And I had no idea I'd raised such a skilled imposter!"

She snickered, forcing a crack through Ethan's tight lips.

"We Bentons do what we have to, do we not?" he joked in a hushed voice.

"My guess is that your playacting became real and you've fallen in love with Holly. Am I right, Ethan?"

He wanted to cover his ears, like a young child who didn't want to hear what was being said. *Love* her? Those drumbeats inside him sped up like a jungle warrior charging toward his most threatening battle.

Yes, he loved Holly. He loved her completely—like nothing he'd ever loved before. He wanted to give her everything she'd never had. Wanted to have children with her. Wanted to spend every minute of his life with her. Wanted to hold her forever as both his wife and his best friend.

That invisible opponent marched toward him and pushed him back behind the battle lines.

He lashed out without thinking. "Holly deceived me about her past. She lied to me. Look at what she came from."

"Oh, hogwash!" Louise dismissed. "How about what *you* came from? What *I* came from? Your father and Uncle Mel were brought up on the tough streets of South Boston without a dime or a university degree between them. I was a poor Southie girl whose father skinned fish for a living. It's not shame about Holly's past that you're concerned with. The time has come for you to let go of shame about your own."

Of course he wore shame—like a suit of armor. Who wouldn't be ashamed that his own mother didn't want him?

He studied his aunt's face. Hard-earned wrinkles told the story of a life embraced. Could he let go of his pain and open up to the fullness the world had to offer?

Could he gamble again on trust?

Gamble on Holly?

On himself?

In an instant he knew that if he didn't now, he never would.

He sprang to his feet. Leaned down to Louise and kissed both her cheeks. Moved to the office desk in the well-appointed suite. Wrote a quick note and then sent it through the fax machine.

"Wish me luck," he said as he flew out the door, too impatient to wait for a response.

In his hotel room, he shaved and showered. Called Leonard to bring the car around. He placed a second call to George Alvarez, manager of the Miami office.

"What are your thoughts about the site supervisor position?" Ethan asked him.

Liz Washington, the previous supervisor, had transferred to the Houston office.

"I've had a young guy apprenticing with Liz for a couple of years now. Done a terrific job," George pitched. "He's ready for the step up. Name of Vince Motta."

"Yes, Vince Motta," Ethan approved with relief.

He valued George, and wouldn't want to go against his expertise. But he knew that if he was able to help Vince it would mean a lot to Holly. That was the kind of sister she was. The kind of woman she was.

The kind of woman he was going to make his.

He raced down the hotel corridor to the elevators, and then out through the front entrance of the hotel. Because once Ethan Benton had made up his mind about something, it couldn't happen fast enough.

"To the apartment," he instructed Leonard as he got into the car.

After Holly had vanished from the gala last night Ethan had checked the hotel suites. She had been nowhere to be found. Even though there had been no answer on her cell phone, or at the apartment, that was where he figured she'd gone. A midnight phone call to the building's door-man had confirmed that Holly had indeed arrived by taxi.

Yes, he had called the doorman to investigate her where-abouts! How could she blame him for an action like that? He oversaw a corporation with thousands of employees all over the world. He couldn't possibly command that without being on top of all available knowledge. Information was power. Artistic Holly Motta might not understand that, but he relied on it. She'd have to get used to the way he thought.

Just as he'd have to get used to her freewheeling ways. How she slammed doors closed with one foot. Ordered pizza with everything but the kitchen sink on it. Said what-ever came into her mind. Needed to devote hours of scrub-bing to getting her hands clean of paint. Ethan thought he wouldn't mind spending a lifetime looking at and hold-ing those graceful fingers that brought art and beauty into the world. Seeing the ring on her finger that proclaimed her lo—

"Leonard! I need to make a stop first. Take me to Fifth and Fifty-Seventh."

Holly winced when she heard the key in the door. If only she'd stuck to her original plan and left at the crack of dawn after her sleepless night. She'd known that Ethan would make his way back here to the apartment. It would have been easier to slink away than to say goodbye in person. What was it that had kept her from going?

Her heart dropped in freefall to the floor as he strode through the door. She wanted to run to him. To put her arms around him. To kiss him until all the problems of the world faded away and there was just the two of them.

"Why did you leave last night?"

His eyes looked weary. His cheeks were flushed.

That one perfect curl of hair that always fell forward on his forehead was dotted with snowflakes. So was his coat.

Holly shifted her gaze out the window to see that it had started to snow. The whole week she'd been in New York it had rained and been cold and dreary. But it hadn't snowed.

She'd fantasized about walking the city streets during a snowfall. Seeing the soft powder billowing down as she crossed busy intersections and marveled at architectural landmarks that stood proudly dusted with white.

Instead she'd be returning to the sunny Florida winter. Snow—*ha!* That was what fantasy was. By definition not real.

"Answer my question," he insisted.

Holly's voice came out hoarse. "I'm truly embarrassed by my behavior. I know it was completely unprofessional."

She cut her eyes toward the floor.

"Look at me. How about the fact that I was worried about you?"

"What do *you* care? Let's be honest."

He stepped in and took her chin in his hand, lifting her face to meet his. "Certainly you leaving the gala without a word was not good business…" he began.

"I'm so sorry."

"But this is not business anymore, and if you want to be honest you know that."

"Know what?"

He moved his hand to caress her cheek tenderly, sending warmth across her skin.

"I love you, Holly. I *love* you. And I suspect you love me, too."

Tears pooled somewhere far behind her eyes. She fought them before saying what she needed to. "Now that you know the truth about me from your investigation, you've found out that I'm not who you want. I'm not a match for you. I'm damaged goods."

"You think you are the only one?"

"What do you mean?"

He let the hand that was touching her face fall to his side. His mouth set in a straight line.

"After my father died..." he started, but then let the words dangle in the air for a minute.

Holly anxiously awaited what he was so hesitant to say.

"Within a few months of my father dying, my mother—who was not much of a mother to begin with—met a man. And together they came up with an idea."

Bare pain burned in Ethan's eyes. Holly knew he was going to tell her something he had to dig out from the rock bottom of his core, where he kept it submerged.

"My mother told Uncle Mel and Aunt Louise that she and this man were going to take me away. That they would never see or hear from me again unless..."

He swallowed hard, his breath rasping and broken.

He regained his voice, "Unless *they* wanted to keep me instead. Which she would allow them to do in exchange for five hundred thousand dollars. In cash. She specified cash."

Agony poured from every cell in Holly's body. Grief for the little boy Ethan. And for herself. For her brother, Vince. For all the children unlucky enough to be born to parents who didn't give them the devotion they deserved.

"So, you see, my mother sold me to my aunt and uncle. I believe that means that you are not the only package of damaged goods around here."

The spoken words swirled around the room.

Again Holly wanted to hug the man she loved.

And again she didn't.

It was time for her to go.

He thought he loved her. He'd fallen for the drama they were starring in.

She'd have to have the cooler head. If she let him believe he loved her, one day he'd wake up and realize that he didn't want something this raw. That instead he could stuff his hurt right back down and act in a different play, with another kind of woman. With someone who'd never have to know about the betrayed and discarded child. About the gashes that still bled, the sores that would never heal. In his next pantomime he could be with a woman who knew only the functional and successful adult he'd managed to become.

She averted her eyes to the diamond ring on the table. To the beer wrapper ring beside it. She bent down for them and handed both to Ethan.

"I am glad you've returned these rings," he said. "They do not belong on your finger."

His words confirmed what she already knew. That it was time to leave.

He reached in his pocket and pulled out a small turquoise box. Holly's breath quickened.

He knelt down on one knee and held it out to her in the palm of his hand.

"Because an ordinary diamond ring does not fit the uniqueness of you. Like this, you are one of a kind."

He opened the box. Inside was the blue topaz ring she had admired from the private gemstone collection they'd seen that day they had gone shopping.

Uncontainable tears rolled down Holly's cheeks.

"I love you, Holly. I have loved you since you bounced through the door with that ridiculous blue paint on your face. I have never met anyone like you. Pretending to be engaged to you has shown me something I never thought I could see."

"What?" Holly asked, her spirits soaring.

"That our pain does not have to define us. That a past and a future can coexist. That there is beauty to be had every day. I want to share those miracles with you. To walk through life together. Please. *Please.* Will you marry me? This time the ring will never leave your finger."

She had to take the chance if he was willing to. To trust their authentic selves—scars and all. Together.

"I will." She nodded as he fitted the ring onto her finger.

Ethan stood. Holly reached her arms up around his neck and drew him into a kiss that couldn't wait a second longer.

Many minutes later he whispered, "Did you check the fax machine?"

"No." She'd heard the sounds and beeps of the machine before he arrived, but she hadn't looked to see what had come. She'd had quite enough of faxes already.

"Go," he prodded.

The piece of paper contained a two-word question.

Will you?

Had she read it earlier, she'd have known he was coming to propose.

She flirted with her fiancé. "Will I…?"

The smile kicked at the corner of his mouth. "Will you teach me how to draw?"

"It's a deal." Her grin joined his.

They pressed their lips to each other's in an ironclad merger, valid for eternity.

* * * * *

FALLING AT THE SURGEON'S FEET

LUCY RYDER

This book is dedicated to Kathryn Cheshire, whose encouragement and understanding got me through an incredibly difficult year. I simply could not have done this book without your support and guidance. You're awesome.

Also to my bestie, Marleine Dicks. Thanks for all the reading you had to do of my earlier—and really bad—manuscripts. I eventually got it right, but I appreciate all the loving support and encouragement. Thanks too for all the laughter you bring into my life. I just wish we could spend more time laughing.

CHAPTER ONE

"HEY, LADY! WATCH IT."

Dr. Holly Buchanan grimaced and threw a breathless "Sorry!" over her shoulder at the guy she'd nearly trampled as she dashed through the automatic doors into the huge marble lobby of West Manhattan Saints.

She was late. Late, late, *late*, damn it. And it was the second time this month. She should have suspected the morning would go to hell when she'd slept through her alarm and then broken the heel of her favorite designer pumps—hopping on one foot while trying to find the other shoe.

But nothing could have prepared her for the absolute chaos that greeted her when she'd opened her front door and found furniture and boxes piled up against her door, littering the stairs and sidewalk.

It had taken a few shocked moments to work out that the avalanche was meant for the neighboring brownstone and not hers. *Thank God.* Unfortunately, it had taken a lot longer to convince the mover—a scary tattooed guy who'd towered over her by at least a foot and a half—that the address he was looking for was right next door. *Not hers.*

He'd folded his huge tattooed arms across an even huger chest and stared at her with a level don't-even-think-of-messing-with-me-lady look that had made her quail in her strappy heels. And because he'd startled her, she'd blurted out the first thing that had come into her head: "Did you know that prison inmates in Russia use melted boot heels mixed with blood and urine to make tattoo ink?"

His answer, when it had come, had been accompanied by raised eyebrows and a wry twist of his lips. "Marine corps," he'd drawled in a voice that had seemed to come from his large booted feet. "One tattoo for every skirmish survived." And Holly had sucked in a mortified breath.

"Oh, my g-gosh, I'm s-sorry," she'd stammered, wanting the earth to open up and swallow her. "Th-thank you for your service."

He'd quirked an eyebrow and replied with a dry "You're welcome. Now, where should I put all this stuff?"

It had taken her time she hadn't had to convince him to call the moving company, which he did while guarding her door like a bouncer at a shady nightclub. After what had seemed like an age—during which Holly had bounced from foot to foot in extreme impatience—he'd finally apologized for the mistake. Then he'd reached over a box almost as tall as she was and gallantly lifted her as easily as if she were a child. To her shock he'd carried her down the box-littered steps and gently deposited her on the sidewalk with a cheerful "Wouldn't want you to twist an ankle in those shoes."

She'd mumbled a breathless "Thank you" and had risked more than a twisted ankle running for the subway.

Setting off across the huge lobby toward the bank of elevators, Holly dodged people heading in the same direction and tried to tell herself that elevators were mostly safe and that the hospital had a rigorous maintenance schedule.

She growled and skirted a crowd of nurses gathered around a large board the hospital used to announce upcoming events, lectures by visiting experts, and new staff appointments. She usually took an interest in any new announcements as she hoped her name would soon be featured when the plastic and reconstruction surgical fellowship was announced.

This morning, however, she barely gave it, or the oohing

and aahing women, a cursory glance as she streaked past, heels clicking on the slick marble floor. She hated being late for meetings with the chief of surgery. He wasn't exactly the kind of man you wanted to annoy—especially if you were a surgical resident hoping for that fellowship.

The doors of one lone elevator slid open with a ding and she sent up a quick prayer and dashed into the car just as a group of noisy teens emerged. As they shoved past, one sneakered foot caught Holly's ankle and sent her flying. She valiantly tried to halt her forward momentum by grabbing for the aluminum frame and forgot that she was carrying her briefcase. It went flying one way and she went the other, landing awkwardly on her hands and knees. She heard a muffled grunt and the next thing she knew the contents of her handbag and briefcase were exploding all over the floor.

The doors swished closed and there was a moment of stunned silence during which Holly thought, *You have got to be freaking kidding me!*

She sucked in air and snarled a few choice words that would turn her mother's hair gray. But, jeez, it had brought back memories she didn't like to think about. Memories of a wildly tilting elevator and frightened screams as it plummeted and then exploded on impact.

For a couple of beats she struggled with control before remembering having heard a grunt. She lifted her head, hoping Monday madness was giving her auditory hallucinations on top of everything else. The last thing she needed was someone having witnessed her graceless flight.

Please, let me be alone. Please, let me be alone.

Holly blew a few escaped strands of hair out of her eyes and froze when her vision cleared. Bare inches from her nose was a pair of large scuffed sneakers attached to the bottom of faded, soft-as-butter jeans. She blinked and followed the long length of denim up endless muscular legs to something that made her eyes widen and her mouth drop open. And before she could register that she was checking out some guy's impressive package, the man dropped to his haunches and Holly found herself staring into a pair of concerned blue-green eyes surrounded by a heavy fringe of sun-tipped lashes—on her hands and knees.

Sucking in a shocked breath, she wondered if she was more embarrassed by her position or the direction she'd been looking then promptly forgot everything when she felt the sensation of falling. Right into a swirl of gold-flecked blue and green. It was only when he opened his mouth and "You okay?" emerged in a voice as deep and dark as sin that she realized she'd been staring into his eyes as though she was submerged in the waters of the Caribbean and had forgotten how to breathe.

Her skin prickled and heated in premonition—of what, she wasn't entirely sure. But it felt like something monumental had just happened. Then, realizing what she was thinking, Holly gave a silent snort. *Yeah, right.* More like *monumentally* embarrassing.

His light eyes were startling in a tanned face that was both brain-ambushingly handsome and rugged. Like one of those naturally hot guys they used for advertising extreme sportswear. The kind of man who got his tan in the great outdoors—like standing on the prow of a pirate ship—and not from a tanning salon.

"Just peachy," she squeaked, swallowing her mortification at having sprawled at the feet of the hottest guy in Manhattan—maybe even America—and being caught eyeing his package then staring into his eyes like she'd been hypnotized.

Her belly quivered and for a second she wondered if the disrespectful little twerps had done her a favor. At least she now wouldn't have to suffer the additional indignity of swooning at his feet.

"You sure?"

"I'm f-fine," Holly croaked, her eyes dropping momentarily to his mouth, where the sight of well-sculpted lips tipped up in an almost-smile had her tongue swelling in her mouth like she was fifteen and crushing on a hot lifeguard. Her face flamed and she pushed back to sit on her heels. "Just incredibly embarrassed," she mumbled, brushing her hands together. "So, *please*…just ignore me and let me die with my dignity intact."

Crinkles appeared beside his amazing eyes and the corner of his mouth curled up even more, revealing—horror of horrors—a dimple. She caught herself staring at the shallow dent in his tanned cheek and gulped. *Darn*. He just had to have a dimple, didn't he? It was the one thing that could turn her into an awkward ninth-grader.

"I…er…" He cleared his throat and Holly looked up sharply, catching his attempts to suppress amusement. "I think it's a bit late for that."

She squeezed her eyes closed and gave a low moan of embarrassment. "G-great. Now I'm…." She sucked in a shaky breath and waved her hand in a quick dismissive gesture. "You know what, never mind."

Abruptly turning away, she looked around for her purse and briefcase. And there—in freaking plain sight for *everyone* to see—was her emergency stash of tampons, littering the floor like white bullets. And for just an instant she wished they were so she could just lock, load and pull the trigger to end her misery.

They reached for the closest tampon at the exact same moment and Holly squeaked, "I'll get that," quickly snatching it up and stuffing it into the bottom of her purse. She then pounced on the remaining cartridges, hoping he hadn't seen—but when she sent him a quick glance out of the corner of her eye and saw his teeth flash, she realized he had.

Oh, boy.

Pushing out her bottom lip, she huffed out a breath and lifted a wrist to shove aside tendrils of hair obscuring her vision. *Could her day get any worse?* Then a hand reached for hers and she forgot all about her crappy day when a snap of electricity bolted up her arm the instant their skins touched.

He too must have felt that audible little zap because he grunted softly and his eyes narrowed speculatively before he gingerly turned her hand over to inspect her scraped palm. She barely heard him rasp, "You're hurt," over the blood rushing through her ears.

The hand engulfing hers was large and tanned with long, surprisingly elegant fingers that drew her fascinated gaze even as they sent tingles rolling over her skin. Then his thumb was brushing gently over her scraped palm and the tingles became a raging firestorm of sensation that shot directly to her breasts and…well…further south.

Her eyes widened. *Oh…oh, wow.* What the heck was that? "It's n-nothing," she managed to croak, both to herself and him, before sliding her hand from his when she realized her mouth had dropped open and she was on the verge of babbling. She scooted back a little and sucked in a shaky breath, averting her face in the hope that he couldn't read her turmoil. Because, well…*darn.* The last time she'd been this flustered had been in the seventh grade when Jimmy Richards had caught her drawing hearts and flowers around his name.

Absently rubbing her tingling palm against her thigh, she stared at the jumble of her belongings and wondered what the heck she was supposed to be doing. It was only when she saw a half-eaten candy bar that she snapped to attention and began stuffing everything she could lay her hands on into her purse.

Holy cow. Where had all this stuff come from? She couldn't even remember having seen half of it before. Certainly not the gold pen or the roll of mints. And how many hairbrushes did one person need, anyway?

She left him to gather up her textbooks, study notes and stethoscope, thinking there was nothing in her briefcase that could embarrass her—until she remembered the old before-and-after photographs of herself that she kept as a reminder of why she was doing P&R.

Whipping around, Holly was relieved to see that the photos were nowhere in sight, but the guy was holding aloft a small foil square she hadn't even known she had. And if it *was* hers, it had to be at least two years old. Maybe even older.

Holly tried to look innocent, but it seemed the guy had an evil streak because he lifted a brow over gleaming blue-green eyes and drawled, "Medium?"

Oh, God, really? He was going to comment on the size?

"Keep it," she croaked. "Most condoms have a shelf life of four years, anyway. As long as you keep them in a cool, dry place." And nothing could be cooler or drier than the bottom of her briefcase, especially the past couple of years when she'd been focusing on the P&R fellowship and not relationships.

His grin turned wicked, deepening that dimple in his cheek. "Way too small," he said innocently, as though they were discussing a pair of shoes and not a freaking condom. He tilted his head and squinted at the printing on the back. "Besides, I think this one's already a year and a half past that four-year shelf-life date you were talking about."

Her face heated and she mentally rolled her eyes. *Way to let a hot guy know your sex life is non-existent, Holly.* She groaned silently and reached out with a growled "Just give it here," before tossing the package in the wall-mounted trash bin. For a couple of beats he stared at the stainless-steel receptacle then turned to her with a level look.

"You know someone is going to find that and use it, don't you?" He shook his head at her. "How do you think you'll feel knowing you had a hand—even unwittingly—in an unplanned pregnancy?"

"Ohmigod," Holly burst out, wondering if the torture of this day would ever end and what she'd done to deserve it. *"Fine!"* She opened the lid and fished it out, shudder-

ing when her fingers encountered something sticky. She shoved the errant condom into her pocket and glared at him challengingly. The unspoken words *Are you happy now?* vibrated in the air between them.

Eyes crinkling at the corners, he rose to his feet and offered her a hand but Holly ignored it and scrambled up—all embarrassing items finally hidden, thank God—before accepting her briefcase from him with a strangled mutter of thanks.

She was careful not to let their hands touch. Her body was buzzing with enough electricity to light up Manhattan for a day—and she hadn't even had her coffee yet.

Fortunately, the elevator dinged its arrival at her floor and when the doors opened she escaped, hoping she never saw him again. Just before the doors slid closed he called out a friendly "Don't forget to replace that condom, it's the responsible thing to do."

A few people heard and sent her curious looks but Holly ignored them, stomping down the passageway and muttering about *not* being responsible for her actions when it came to hot smartasses. It was only when she passed a startled nurse pushing a bassinet that she realized she was on the twentieth floor and not the twenty-second.

Muttering to herself, she changed direction and headed for the stairs, resigned to the fact that she was nearly fifteen minutes late for her meeting.

The moment she slipped into the boardroom she felt the eyes of every person in the room turn to watch her entrance, including the laser-blue stare of the chief of surgical residents, Professor Gareth Langley. Flushing, she ducked her head and murmured an apology, and slipped into the only open chair around the huge oval table.

Fortunately, with the day she was having, she wasn't scheduled for any surgery. She'd probably slice and dice her fingers—or worse.

Without looking up, she drew the nearest folder closer

and opened it, knowing she would find the new surgical schedule. There were other pages inside but Holly ignored them and quickly scanned the list, sighing her relief when she saw that she was scheduled for a number of procedures with Dr. Lin Syu and two with the head of plastic surgery, Dr. Geoff Hunt.

She lifted her lashes and caught Lin Syu's quick smile before she transferred her attention to the head of P&R, who was—*oh, joy*—looking right at her. She flushed beneath his questioning look and bit her lip but after a brief nod in her direction and a dry "Now that Dr. Buchanan has finally joined us..." Geoff Hunt turned away, shoving his hands into the pockets of his perfectly creased pants as he rocked back on his heels. "Perhaps we can get to the real reason Professor Langley is here this morning."

Now that the heat was off her, Holly let out a silent breath and relaxed into her chair, only half listening as Langley rose and began talking about the proposed expansion of the P&R department and the upcoming charity ball. It was a subject that he'd brought up before and one that Holly's mother—as CEO of Chrysalis Foundation—was involved in.

The Chrysalis Foundation worked solely for children and young people who needed plastic or reconstruction surgery but had no way of paying for the expensive procedures. It was also an organization her mother had started after Holly's own traumatic experiences.

Half listening, she let her gaze slide around the table but it came to an abrupt halt the instant she locked on a pair of amused blue-green eyes that were shockingly familiar. For the second time that morning—and it wasn't even nine a.m.—Holly felt the breath leave her lungs.

Her head went light, her stomach cramped and she thanked God she was sitting down because there in the chair next to Langley's was none other than...elevator guy.

Oh, God.

Her tongue emerged to moisten suddenly dry lips, and she wished she could grab the nearby water jug and drown herself before anyone noticed.

One eyebrow rose up his forehead and all Holly could think was... *Who the heck is he?*

Realizing she was staring at him all wide-eyed and open-mouthed, Holly jerked her gaze away to stare unseeingly at the columns of numbers on the screen, her mind racing with a kaleidoscope of images from the last half-hour. And when she realized she was absently rubbing her tingling palm down the length of her thigh she clenched both hands in her lap and struggled to control her breathing.

Maybe she'd dreamed up the entire episode. Maybe she was still asleep and dreaming.

Or having a nightmare, she snorted silently, and sneaked a peek at him. He was still watching her, his expression a mix of amusement and confusion—as though he didn't quite know what to make of her.

He wasn't the only one.

Frowning, she returned her unseeing gaze to Langley, nearly missing the part about the generous donation the hospital had recently received to expand P&R and finance the expensive new procedures they would be developing over the next five years, courtesy of a prominent Beverly Hills plastic surgeon.

It was the "Beverly Hills plastic surgeon" that caught Holly's attention and her gaze jerked back to elevator guy as a bad feeling landed in the pit of her stomach.

She sucked in a sharp breath at the wicked gleam lighting his changeable eyes and barely heard Langley's words over the blood thundering in her head.

Oh, God, please let me be wrong.

"I'm sure you all saw the announcement in the foyer this morning," Langley was saying, and elevator guy must have caught her stunned look because he gave a tiny shrug as though to say, You should have seen that one coming. But she hadn't. Not even close.

How could she have thought—even if she hadn't blown through the foyer—that the guy in the battered sneakers and well-washed jeans molded to every inch of his muscular thighs and well...*everywhere* was some big Hollywood celebrity cosmetic surgeon?

It's not him, Holly. It can't be.

Besides, where was the thousand-dollar suit, the eight-hundred-dollar, hand-stitched loafers and hundred-dollar haircut? She sneaked another peek at him and ran her gaze over all that tanned skin, sun-streaked hair and languid grace and decided she could see him gracing the cover of an extreme sports magazine—or maybe *Surf's Up*—more readily than a fancy Beverly Hills fundraiser.

But then Langley said, "I'd like to formally introduce Dr. Gabriel Alexander and welcome him to the West Manhattan family," and Holly realized with an unpleasant shock that the hot guy who'd made her knees wobble and her breath hitch in her chest was the very same man who'd been linked to rumors of new procedures and extreme body-sculpting of many Hollywood A-listers and supermodels. Including her famous sister.

What the heck was he doing in Manhattan?

He even had a dimple, *darn it!*

CHAPTER TWO

DR. GABRIEL ALEXANDER sighed and wedged himself into the movie-house-style chair, scooching down so he could tip his head back and finally close his eyes. It seemed like months instead of days since he'd shared a very interesting elevator ride with a certain surgical resident and he was exhausted—no thanks to said resident.

Crossing one ankle over the other on a backrest a few chairs down probably made him look like a long-legged spider squashed into a matchbox, but Gabe just needed some quiet time out from his hectic schedule. Besides, as a resident he'd slept anywhere; his favorite being observation rooms where it was usually quiet—especially after eight at night.

Popping his earphones in his ears, he sighed as rock music washed over him. It had only been four days since he'd been welcomed to West Manhattan Saints by a stunning briefcase-wielding assailant, but he kind of liked the vibe of being back in a large medical facility. Seems selling his partnership to some entitled young punk hungry for the Hollywood lifestyle had been the right decision after all.

For the past six years he'd been attached to a small private clinic that was so exclusive very few people even knew of its existence—except if you were famous, ultra-wealthy or both. Now, just thinking about what he'd left behind made Gabe shudder with an odd mix of pride, distaste and shame.

And if that didn't make him a candidate for the psych ward, nothing would. Not even his screwed-up childhood.

He'd had a mansion in Beverly Hills, a house in Santa Monica, a yacht and several luxury vehicles in his multiple-car garage and he'd been the most sought-after plastic surgeon on the West Coast. For a kid who'd spent his childhood believing he wasn't good enough, it had been a dream come true.

Looking back, he realized it had been a symbolic gesture to his rich and powerful grandfather. A man who'd used his connections to forcibly end the marriage of his son to a fellow student. A girl he'd deemed unworthy to carry the Alexander name—or the Alexander heir.

Only it had been too late for that. Third-year journalism student Rachel Parker had already been pregnant. When the old man had found out, he'd paid her a visit and along with thinly veiled threats told her to stay away from his family. Or else.

Afraid for her unborn child, Rachel had agreed. She'd moved across the country to ensure they never bumped into each other and Caspar Alexander had made sure that his son had been too busy—with his new wife and family— to be bothered with looking up his college flame. It hadn't stopped Rachel from telling her son all about his father and it hadn't stopped Gabe from dreaming—until he'd turned twelve—that his father would one day come to claim him. It had never happened. Both his father and his grandfather had conveniently gone back to their entitled lives as though nothing had happened.

Until about two years ago when the old man had decided he needed someone to take over the family business. It seemed Caspar's son and legitimate grandchildren were a huge disappointment and couldn't be trusted not to squander everything he'd spent a lifetime building.

The old man had told him how proud he was of Gabe's

achievements and that it was clear he was a chip off the old block.

Gabe had not so politely told him what he could do with his offer.

For a long time he'd been angry—at his mother and father—but especially the ruthless Caspar Alexander. And when he'd been invited to join the clinic he'd seen it as his ticket to the big league. *Look,* Gabe was saying to the old man. *I didn't need you or your family's money to become someone. I did it all by myself.*

Then his mom had been diagnosed with an aggressive form of leukemia and none of his money, contacts, fame or his skill with a scalpel had made a difference. By the time she'd slipped away, he'd realized his mother was right. He'd become the one thing he hated above all else. He'd become just like his grandfather. Ruthless, cold in his personal relationships and interested in only two things—money and status. It had been a rude awakening. One that had spurred him on to make some drastic changes in his life.

Someone bumped against the row of seats, jolting Gabe from the disturbing memories of his childhood and his nonexistent relationship with a man who'd pretended most of Gabe's life that he didn't exist.

Grateful for the disruption, he cracked open one eye to see that a small crowd had gathered at the observation window overlooking operating room three.

A quick look at the overhead OR screen gave him a close-up of an open torso and disembodied gloved hands wielding stainless-steel instruments with skill and precision. And considering that WMS had some of the best trauma surgeons on the east coast, whoever was on the table was in good hands.

Tugging on one earphone, he tuned into the murmur of voices around him and discovered that someone called Dr. Chang was working on a young woman who had landed beneath a bus during rush hour traffic.

He replaced the earphone and watched the onscreen action for a few more minutes, admiring the dexterity of the leading surgeon's hands, before letting his eyes drift over the observers.

They were painfully young and even if they hadn't been dressed in light blue scrubs, he would have pegged them as residents. Their fresh, animated faces reminded him of his own resident days, which meant they were probably not discussing whatever was going on below. Most likely it was about a hot nurse, or complaints about their supervisors.

Hospitals were like small towns where everyone knew everyone else and no one's personal business remained private for long. People gathered during quiet times to gossip about patients; nurses liked to complain about doctors and doctors liked to complain about everyone, especially Administration.

And Administration? Well, they were the common enemy because they hoarded funds like Scrooge, cutting costs and fighting every requisition from floor wax to MRI maintenance.

And, Gabe thought with a dry laugh, he hadn't even realized until now just how much he'd missed it. Not so much the gossip but he'd missed the camaraderie of a large medical facility where the haves and have-nots were locked in a daily battle of survival. It wasn't just a place where the rich and bored came to buy the latest style of face or body— or have a steamy affair with their attending surgeon. This was real.

Sighing, Gabe slid his gaze over the rest of the observation-room occupants before letting his eyes drift shut. He knew he should get up and return to his temporary digs, where a ton of boxes waited to be unpacked, but he just needed to—

Abruptly something he'd seen registered and his eyes snapped open to zero in on a familiar figure standing off to one side.

Dr. Holly Buchanan.

Mouth curving in appreciation, Gabe watched her focus on the overhead screen, her small white teeth nibbling on lush pink lips. A little frown of concentration marred the smooth skin of her forehead. Every so often her slender hands and long, elegant fingers would move in what he recognized was a replica of whatever was happening below—as though she was practicing or maybe committing the action to memory.

He'd spent enough time among the wealthy to recognize that Dr. Buchanan came from money, and lots of it. She even had that cool elegance that seemed to come naturally to the very wealthy. A cool elegance that sometimes hid an ugly belief that people they perceived as inferior were to be exploited and that their money and social status gave them that right.

He didn't have far to look for examples either. His own gene pool, for one. An old ex, for another. A girl he'd honestly thought had loved him enough to overlook the fact that he had been a half-starving med student from a very modest background.

But instead of standing up to her powerful family, she'd laughed at his declarations of love and told him she'd been using him to get back at her father—and have one final hot fling before she married a man eminently more suitable to their social circle.

Okay, so he'd been a young, foolish hothead, out to prove himself worthy. Prove that his story, at least, would have a happy ending. It had just proved to him that people born into wealth weren't interested in anything more than a hot fling with someone from the wrong side of town—especially someone they perceived as illegitimate.

But even though he knew Holly Buchanan was from a world whose vanity he'd happily exploited, he couldn't help watching her. Her appearance was as coolly classy as it had been the last time he'd seen her, scowling across the boardroom table as though he was personally responsible for the national debt.

But that's where the similarities ended. There was nothing cool about those large heavily fringed blue eyes. And knocked to her hands and knees, she'd muttered curses like someone tugging impatiently at the constraints of her upbringing.

Then there were those paper-thin scars that had been expertly covered with a light brush of foundation. Someone had either done a hatchet job on the stunning young surgeon or…or some horrific injuries had been expertly repaired. He wondered which it had been then decided it didn't matter considering both would explain her interest in plastic surgery.

But it was her eyes—or rather the unguarded expression in them—that had caught his attention. Despite that outer sophistication, Holly Buchanan, it seemed, wasn't as poised as she would like the world to believe, and he wondered what her story was.

He slid a hand to the bruise on his thigh where her briefcase had whacked him and spared a moment to be thankful that it hadn't connected higher. Any higher and he would have been on the floor, having an up-close-and-personal view of her tampons.

He chuckled, recalling the way she'd snatched them up and shoved them to the bottom of her purse as though they had been contraband and she'd been afraid he was the secret police. But then he'd found the condom packet and despite the wild color blooming in her cheeks, the ruffled kitten had flexed her tiny claws by insinuating he used a medium.

Gabe closed his eyes to the sight of her nibbling on her thumbnail and frowning at the overhead screen while she ignored the little upstart twerp trying to chat her up. There was something about her that struck a chord of familiarity but he was sure he'd never met or seen her before.

He was just drifting off when something made him open

his eyes to see her edging up the stairs, giving him a wide berth as though he was a slumbering tiger she didn't want to disturb. Suddenly several pagers began beeping and she froze mid-tiptoe, her eyes snapping toward him, widening in alarm when she caught him watching her.

The residents crowded up the stairs, elbowing each other and muttering curses about slave-driver supervisors as they bolted for the door. In the ensuing scuffle, Dr. Buchanan was roughly jostled aside and Gabe had a brief glimpse of one sexy heel catching on the stair runner. Her arms wind-milled in a frantic attempt at regaining her balance...and the next moment she was toppling onto Gabe with a muf-fled shriek.

His hands shot out to catch her but she landed with a startled "Oomph" right in Gabe's lap—and hard enough to have him seeing stars. When his vision cleared he had an armful of curvy, fragrant female squirming around like she was giving him a lap dance to end all lap dances. And because he was a red-blooded guy who hadn't been any-where near a woman in way too long, his body instantly reacted, waking up to the fact that a beautiful, sexy woman was butt-planted over his groin. He gave a low groan and she whipped around to gape at him like he'd zapped her with his shock stick.

Hey, not his fault. *Innocently minding my own business here, lady.*

One look into her mortified blue eyes and he realized that she was trying to get away and not turn him on but, damn...sue him, it had been a long time since he'd had *sex*, let alone been close enough to a woman to catch the heady scent of her skin.

Their gazes connected and she froze; her eyes wide on his. As though realizing her mouth was barely an inch from his, she gave a distressed bleat and tried again to free her-self, shoving at him at the same time as she tried to get her feet on the floor.

But the angle was wrong and the more she struggled, the more his eyes crossed and the more mortified she looked until he finally took pity on them both and rose to his feet in one swift move. She gasped at the abrupt change of elevation and clutched at him as though she anticipated being dumped on her ass.

It was probably that unflattering assumption that prompted his next action.

Instead of releasing her and stepping away like a gentleman would have, he kept one arm wrapped tightly around her waist and let her slowly slide down the full length of his body until her feet touched the floor.

He knew by the flicker of her lashes and the wild flush in her cheeks that she could feel more than the hard planes of his chest and thighs. The instant she got her feet under her, she sucked in air and shoved away from him, stumbling back a couple of steps. She would have fallen into the row of seats across the aisle if he hadn't shot out a hand and yanked her back.

Their bodies collided hard enough to momentarily knock the breath from his lungs and he wrapped an arm around her to keep her from flying off down the stairs. Okay, and maybe because he liked having all those soft curves pressed up against him.

"Careful," he murmured. "You don't want any more bruises to add to the ones you already have."

She froze and stared into his eyes, alarmed to find herself in the exact position she'd tried to escape from a couple seconds earlier.

"Who…who told you I have bruises?" she demanded in a breathless rush that made him wonder about things that he had no business thinking about. Like how she'd sound in the throes of passion. And where else she had a bruise that he could kiss better.

It was an entirely inappropriate thought—not to mention stupid given that his body clearly liked the visuals that popped fully formed into his head—to have about a younger colleague working toward a fellowship in the same department.

Realizing they were still plastered together like glue on paper, she made a sound of distress and eased out of his arms, this time careful not to make any sudden moves that might result in him having to save her.

She cleared her throat. "I mean, how do you know about the bruises?"

Gabe arched a brow and folded his arms across his chest, letting his gaze roam over the delicate creaminess of her face and neck. "You winced when you sat down at Monday's meeting and I'm guessing that creamy skin bruises easily."

She continued staring at him warily for a moment longer before she said, "Oh," as though she'd suspected him of following her into the ladies bathroom and spying on her as she'd checked out her smarting bottom and knees.

Gabe felt his mouth curve. He'd never met a woman whose every thought flashed across her face louder than Dr. Buchanan's. That they were hardly complimentary was an added bonus to a man who'd spent the last eight years of his life being wooed by women all wanting something from him.

"I'm sorry I disturbed your sleep," she said in that low, husky voice that seemed to reach out and stroke his flesh in places that hadn't been stroked in way too long. And when he lifted a brow she hastened to add, "And for…well, nearly flattening you."

"You hardly flattened me," he drawled. "Besides, I wasn't asleep, just resting my eyes. You learn a lot about people when they think you're comatose. Take the guy trying to get your attention." He could see she knew exactly who he was talking about when she bit her lip and looked away. "I overheard him bragging about his performance and wondered if he was talking about the OR, ER or someplace more private." Heat bloomed beneath her skin. "He's the kind of guy that gives surgeons a bad name."

Her eyes snapped to his and her face settled into a remote coolness that surprised him but not as much as her words. "The only surgeons who give us a bad name," she observed coolly, "are those arrogant enough to think they know better than God how to improve beauty."

Gabe was smart enough to know she was referring to him. He opened his mouth to defend himself but the anger and accusation filling her huge blue eyes stunned him into silence.

What the hell?

He wasn't to blame for her scars. Was he? He would certainly have remembered if she'd been a patient and there was no way he would have forgotten if he'd ever dated her—even briefly. Firstly, she wasn't his type and, secondly…well, secondly, he didn't think any man would be able to forget those big blue eyes or that lush wide mouth. Not in ten lifetimes.

Then he thought about her accusation and his anger died. She was right. For a long time he'd aggressively participated in the Hollywood pursuit of perfection until he'd reveled in the challenge of improving on Mother Nature's handiwork. A nip here, a tuck there and maybe even a complete body-sculpt to anyone who could afford it.

Thinking about it brought back the shame and disgust at the knowledge that he'd been as culpable as any one of his patients in their futile pursuit of perfection. But that didn't mean he was going to let her get away with her accusation—or her attitude, which, now that he came to think about it, had changed right about the time Langley had introduced him.

He shoved his hands in his pockets and rocked back on his heels. "Want to know what I learned about you?"

"No," she said quickly, and took a step toward him, only to stop abruptly when he didn't move aside because for some idiotic reason he didn't want to let her go. "I'm sure your insights are simply fascinating," she continued, frowning at her watch as though she was very busy and couldn't spare the time. "But I'm not that interesting."

Gabe smiled, because in the few days—encounters— that he'd known her, Holly Buchanan had been anything but uninteresting. He lifted a hand to scratch his jaw and paused, his eyes narrowing thoughtfully when she sucked in a tiny breath as though the rasp of beard-roughened skin was somehow too intimate in the quiet room.

"You're intensely focused, keep to yourself and practice with your hands without realizing it. You bite your thumbnail when you're concentrating and hate being the center of attention. In fact, you mostly present only one side of your face to people you're talking to."

She bit her lip and looked away. Zeroing in on the move, he was suddenly tempted to lean forward and bite that plump lip too. But she was carrying her briefcase again and he didn't want to tempt her to use it as a weapon. This time her aim might just reach ground zero.

"How am I doing so far?"

He was rewarded when she rolled her eyes and pressed her lips together as though her silence would discourage him. He'd spent enough time strutting around California beaches during his adolescence to know when a woman was disinterested. He'd bet his entire surfboard collection that Holly Buchanan had been just as affected by their little skirmish as he had. Her dilated pupils, wild rosy flush and that soft gasp she'd given when she'd realized how close he was—and how hard—were as telling as the shiver that had gone through her.

She was attracted but determined to fight it. The question was why. What had he done to offend her?

"Okay," he mused, studying her through narrowed eyes. "My guess is you did all the girly-girl stuff, like ballet, piano and deportment. You probably feel like you have to excel at everything you do…maybe to make someone happy. Mother? Father? Boyfriend?" Her mouth dropped open and he grunted with displeasure at the notion. "Is it a boyfriend?"

"As if!" she practically squawked, and he smirked, strangely pleased by her reaction. Seeming embarrassed by her outburst, Holly pressed her lips together and tried to look bored.

He scratched his jaw again before sliding his gaze over her face, touching briefly on those silvery white scars. "I'd say your interest in plastic surgery stems from your own experiences or maybe some deep-seated need to fix other people's mistakes."

Her hand rose swiftly and then froze in mid-air, as though she was fighting an instinctive reaction to hide her face, and Gabe felt his gut clench as though he'd been carelessly insensitive.

Fighting the urge to wrap his arms around her and pull her into the safety of his arms—which was shocking enough—he let his gaze slide over her classically classy outfit, lingering overly long on her breasts, covered but not hidden by the expert fit of her jacket. He suddenly knew exactly how to put that spark of rebellion in her eyes and get the stubborn tilt back to that Irish chin.

"Or maybe I've got it completely wrong," he drawled smoothly, making no secret of the direction of his gaze. "Maybe I'm not the only one into cosmetic surgery?"

For a moment she stared at him like he'd uttered an obscenity before she huffed out a breath and crossed her arms beneath her breasts, making Gabe wonder if it was to hide from his gaze or keep from taking a swing at him.

"That's just insulting," she snapped, and Gabe grinned. He kind of liked the idea that she was struggling with some pretty intense feelings and he didn't mind the idea of getting into a tussle with her if she did take a swing at him.

In fact, he would enjoy it. Probably more than he should.

He expected a scathing response—or maybe a request

for him to get the hell out of her way. What he didn't expect was for her to open her mouth and say, "Did you know that women with breast implants are three times more likely to commit suicide or develop drug- and alcohol-related dependencies?"

Gabe tore his attention from her breasts with a "Huh?" and wondered if he'd heard correctly. She flushed and sucked in air before continuing and he struggled to connect the random facts with what they'd been discussing.

"Two-thirds are repeat clients."

"O-o-okay...." Well, he could certainly attest to that fact. But what the hell did that have to do with—?

"In fact," she continued peevishly, as though she held him personally responsible for women's dissatisfaction with their bodies, "more than five million Americans are addicted to plastic surgery, spending about thirteen billion dollars annually on a variety of procedures. That's enough to rival the national debt of a small country."

She stared at him as though waiting for his response but he wasn't sure what he would say if he did. Instead, he studied her silently for a couple of beats, his mouth slowly curling up at one corner. "Uh-huh. That's quite fascinating but doesn't really answer my question."

She rolled her eyes and muttered something that sounded like "Never mind," before taking a bold step toward him, no doubt hoping good manners would prompt him to move out of her way.

"I have mace," she announced when he remained blocking her escape.

"No, you don't," he disputed, his grin growing into a chuckle when she blew out a frustrated breath. Her eyes narrowed to dangerous slits and her hand tightened on her briefcase as though she contemplated whacking him with it. "I know exactly what you have in there, remember," he said, angling his shoulders just enough for her to slip past but not enough that she could avoid touching him.

But Holly Buchanan was obviously no pushover because just before she stomped from the room she sent him a level stare all women seemed to develop in the womb that said he was lower than slime for behaving like a jerk.

But, really, he didn't know of one guy who wouldn't have.

For a long moment he admired the straight spine, slender, curvy hips twitching with annoyance as she headed down the passage. The strappy heels that had caused at least one of her accidents this week tapped out an irritated beat on the tiled floor that for some odd reason he found damn sexy.

"By the way," he called out, "did you know that the world's largest condom is two hundred and sixty feet long with a base circumference of three hundred and sixty feet?" And when she paused in her stride and sent him a *what-the-heck?* look over her shoulder, he shrugged. "I'm just saying. Mediums are only good as water bombs."

CHAPTER THREE

HOLLY ROLLED HER eyes and set off down the passage at a fast clip, muttering to herself about men never growing up. While it was mostly true and not worth losing sleep over, it certainly beat thinking about her humiliating tumble into the lap of the one man she wanted to avoid. Or his physical reaction to her squirming around on his lap like a second-rate stripper hoping for a big tip.

Her face burned. *And, boy, had she been given the biggest tip of her life.* Before she could stop it, her skin prickled and heated and her heart set off like a vampire bat scenting warm blood. *Oh, God.* And to think that humiliating little incident had actually turned her on. Maybe this all-work-and-no-play plan of hers was making her a little crazy. Maybe all she needed was a few hours of hot, sweaty, heart-pumping exercise—at the gym, she added hastily—and she could get back to focusing on her plan to get the fellowship.

Besides, she was so close that she couldn't let herself get distracted. Not now and certainly not by a guy who either nipped and tucked women into physical perfection or made the backs of their knees sweat.

Groaning inwardly, Holly increased her pace, as though she could outrun the memory of hard thigh and belly muscles pressed firmly against her bottom and then from chest to knee—and *everything* between—as she'd slid down the front of his hard frame.

She got a full-body tingle just thinking about it. A gasp of horror burst out. Full-body tingle? *Oh, God.*

Absolutely no freaking way. And not with him.

Focus on the plan, Buchanan, and *not* on the way he makes your knees wobble or the fact that medium was too small. No. Not too small, she corrected a little hysterically. *Waa-aay* too small.

Oh, boy. And since she'd inadvertently stared at his package, she would probably agree. She got another full-body shiver and muttered a curse when it slid down her spine like a delicious thrill.

Stop that, Holly, she ordered sternly, *he's the guy that turned Paige's respectable B-cups into C pods.* And for what? So he could make a few thousand bucks? So her sister could flash a bigger cleavage to all her adoring "fans" when she appeared on the latest magazine cover? Or went topless on Bimini?

Big deal. Especially when there were people out there scarred by life-altering events who didn't have access to even basic medical care, let alone cutting-edge plastic surgery.

Weren't there enough butchers willing to slice and dice in the name of vanity that West Manhattan could focus on building the best P&R center in the world? Besides, everyone knew that most women would never be satisfied with their looks, no matter what.

She was trying so hard to convince herself that there were no redeeming qualities about Dr. Hotshot from Beverly Hills that she failed to realize the man himself had caught up with her until a flash of movement drew her attention.

Her stride wobbled for an instant but she sucked in a fortifying breath and marched on, determined to ignore him. Besides, she needed all her concentration to keep upright or she might end up breaking something the next time she took a tumble.

She grimaced. She'd seen him a total of three times and

managed to embarrass herself each time. Despite her klutzy childhood, it was probably a new record.

She clenched her jaw and sent him a narrow-eyed look out the corner of her eye but he appeared oblivious to her presence, loping along beside her with an easy, loose-limbed stride that was deceptively indolent, as though he was alone and liked it that way.

Holly rolled her eyes and ignored the pinch in her chest. *Yep, story of my life.* The hot guys always ignored her—especially when they discovered she wasn't perfect, like the rest of her family. That she wasn't as outgoing as her famous sister or as warm and beautiful as her mother.

Not that she *wanted* him to notice her, she amended quickly, especially if it meant she didn't have to make conversation.

"Are you following me?" she asked coolly, rolling her eyes at the faint huskiness in her voice.

So much for not wanting conversation.

He turned his head and their eyes met for a couple of beats until Holly felt the soles of her feet tingle. "I'm headed home," he said mildly. "Although…I could probably be talked into dinner somewhere dark and smoky."

She caught his harmlessly hopeful smile, which did absolutely nothing to reassure her—especially when his eyes gleamed all wickedly amused and challenging. But it was the smoldering heat in them that stole all her bones right along with her breath and common sense.

Gabriel Alexander was about as harmless as a tiger in a supermarket and had most likely perfected the art of seduction before he could walk.

"No? Coffee, then?" he suggested in that deep hypnotic voice that invited women to do things they wouldn't normally do. Things *she* wouldn't normally do, but was suddenly tempted to try. "Besides being starving, I thought I might be useful."

Useful? Holly licked her lips. Completely against her

wishes, her thoughts turned recklessly to just how useful he could be—to her exercise plan, of course—and then wondered if she was advertising her thoughts like a neon sign in the desert when his teeth flashed white in his handsome, tanned face. And because the notion flustered her, she blurted out, "Did you know that silicone is a better choice than rubber for medical purposes because it is more heat- and UV-resistant?"

Realizing what she'd said, she squeezed her eyes shut and prayed for death. *Ohmigod.* Wouldn't it be easier to just walk into the nearest wall? Or maybe step out into traffic? Because clearly the man just had to look at her and her mouth disconnected from her brain.

"It's also better at resisting chemical and fungal attacks, which makes it more durable," she finished miserably and when he made a noise that sounded suspiciously like a chuckle she glared at him, only to find him looking back at her with polite interest—as if blurting out random stuff was normal.

"Now, that I do know," he revealed, hitching a shoulder in a smooth, boneless move that she envied. "I spent most of the eighth grade water-bombing the girls' locker room. The fact that latex is so flexible means it's more prone to breaking when stretched beyond its limits." His teeth flashed. "But don't worry, you're safe. I've grown out of the urge to hear girls scream at the sight of latex."

Yeah, right, Holly thought a little hysterically. *Safe, my eye. He was probably* still *making women scream—before wreaking havoc with their hearts.*

And when she felt queasy at the thought of him making some faceless woman scream, she turned away from his appealing smile before she gave in to the urge to return it—or maybe smack him for making her forget her plan.

Just then the automatic doors opened to reveal a uniformed porter and Holly could have kissed the older man in sheer relief.

On seeing her, the porter's face broke into a wide, craggy smile. "Evening, Doc," he greeted her in his heavy Brooklyn accent. "No big date tonight?" Holly shook her head as she did every time he asked and he clicked his tongue, sending the man beside her a reproving look. "It's a sad day when a beautiful girl doesn't have someone to wine and dine her at one of those fancy downtown restaurants. What is the world coming to?"

Dr. Alexander sent her a silent look and shrugged as if to say, *I did offer*. Narrowing her eyes, Holly was seriously tempted to lie. Besides, she did have a date. Sort of. That it was probably takeout from the pizza place around the corner from the brownstone she shared with a couple of other surgical residents, along with a bottle of wine and a gallon of ice cream, was beside the point. A date was a date.

Conscious of blue-green eyes watching her, Holly flushed. "Dating isn't in my plan," she told the older man. "At least, not right now," she hastened to add when a soft snort reached her, and she wished she carried a stun gun in her purse because he now also knew that she didn't date. And found it amusing. *The jerk.*

"Plans change, Doc. Besides, you're not getting any younger," the porter advised, and Holly ground her back teeth together when Dr. Hollywood's snort turned into a cough. "Want me to call you a cab?"

"I'm fine, thank you."

She was tempted to add that she wasn't entirely opposed to dating. Just not right now, thank you very much. Besides, the last guy she'd been serious about had taken one look at her sister Paige and decided perfection was better for his image than scarred and brainy.

That Holly had thought to surprise Terrence Westfield one night and had found Paige already there—in his bed—was beside the point. The two of them had been discussing Holly like she was a freak and laughing about how naive she was to think a handsome guy like him could be interested in her. It had been even more devastating to discover that Terrence had only dated her to get her father's attention in the hope that he could get an internship at her father's law firm.

She could have told him that Harris Buchanan only had time for his son and couldn't care less whom she dated.

When—*if*—she found a man who was either blind or could look beyond the surface flaws to the woman deep inside, she might risk it, but she first wanted to prove to herself that she didn't need to be perfect or beautiful to succeed.

Sighing, she turned to see Dr. I-Can-Make-Women-Scream watching her silently.

"What?"

His mouth turned up at the corners but his gaze was unreadable.

"Wanna share a cab?"

Holly quickly shook her head. She was suddenly eager to get away from him before she made a bigger fool of herself—which would be difficult after…well, everything that had happened.

"No. Thank you."

He studied her silently for a couple of beats until headlights lit them up like they were on Broadway, signaling the cue for them to launch into a heart-rending duet. But this wasn't a Broadway musical and she couldn't carry a tune to save her life.

He casually lifted his arm like a born-and-bred New Yorker and like magic the empty cab slid to a stop. Holly ground her teeth together. She usually had to step into traffic and risk serious injury before a cabbie deigned to stop. And then it was mostly to yell abuse at her for being a "crazy chick with a death wish."

"You sure?"

She swallowed an odd sensation that felt very much like disappointment—but couldn't possibly be—at his imminent departure, and nodded before she changed her mind. "I'm sure."

After a moment he shrugged. "Suit yourself." And leaning forward, he opened the cab door. Half expecting him to move aside so she could get in, Holly was momentarily distracted when he propped his arm on the top of the door and looked back at her, eyes dark and unreadable.

"See ya, Doc," he said, and slid into the cab, leaving Holly to gape at the departing vehicle.

Chivalry, it seemed, even California celebrity style, was well and truly dead.

The following week Holly had nearly double the number of scheduled procedures and didn't have a lot of time to brood. Her life was right on track with the plan and her goal was within sight. There wasn't time—or the inclination, she reminded herself—to be thinking about wicked blue-green eyes, let alone getting the opportunity to scream.

But that was easier said than done, especially when she happened to look up during a breast reduction plasty to see a familiar figure in the observation room. Only this time he wasn't sprawled bonelessly across the seats, head tipped back and eyes closed as his headphones pumped music into his ears.

With his long legs planted wide and his folded arms testing the seams of his black T-shirt, he looked like a modern-day pirate on the deck of his ship as he challenged the sea. And although his expression and his eyes were in shadow, Holly knew he was looking right at her.

She could feel the weight of that cool, assessing gaze and froze in familiar panic. It was only for an instant and scarcely noticeable by the people around her, but it sent her pulse racing and made her thighs tingle.

"Dr. Buchanan?" The calm voice of Lin Syu made her blink and suck in a fortifying breath. She dropped her gaze briefly to the attending surgeon, who was waiting for Holly's next move with a raised dark brow.

Altering her grip on the miniature scalpel, Holly prepared to make the inverted T incision that would both lift and reduce the size of the breast once the excess tissue had been removed.

She carefully followed the guidelines already drawn onto the skin. The patient, a thirty-four triple-D, with back, neck and shoulder problems, couldn't join her sports-crazy fiancé in outdoor pursuits because her heavy breasts caused discomfort, chronic pain and embarrassment. Kerry Gilmore had admitted that she'd spent her entire high-school years hiding her body and being unable to do things other girls did. Normal things like horseriding, swimming or joining the cheerleading squad. But it was the chronic pain that had finally made the decision for her.

She wanted her life back and Holly was preparing to do just that.

Exchanging the scalpel for surgical scissors, Holly carefully began separating the sectioned dermis from the breast tissue. The aim was to maintain a healthy blood supply to the nipple or it would turn necrotic. The drawback to any reduction was that large amounts of tissue were fed by a lot of blood vessels. Each time she nicked one of them, she waited while the OR nurse cauterized it and mopped up the blood.

Once the dermis had been properly detached from the breast tissue, Holly transferred it into the waiting hands of the attending nurse and went to work on excising the glandular and adipose tissue as per Lin Syu's murmured instructions.

By the time they'd removed five hundred grams of tissue from each breast, Holly was ready for the next stage. She and Dr. Syu made several complicated knots around the areola before gently lifting the nipple into its new position and nudging the remaining parenchyma into place.

She then temporarily closed and stapled the skin flaps so

she could assess the size, shape and position of each breast. The specialized operating table lifted the patient into a sitting position while Holly used the sizer to check the positioning before gently removing the staples and peeling back the skin flaps.

She attached strips of acellular mesh to the upper breast substance to strengthen the weakened muscles then patiently reconnected the mass to the dermal layers using a resorbable intradermal suture. This would reduce the pull of gravity and wound tension, speeding up recovery. It would also help keep scarring to a minimum.

She sutured the areola to the surrounding flaps before reaching for the staple gun for the final stage of the dermal resectioning procedure. When it was over she stepped back to allow the nurse to swab the wound sites with iodine in preparation for the daisy strips that would be applied around the areola in widening circles. They would serve a double function of protecting the wound from infection as well as provide additional support while the patient healed.

Five hours after the patient went under; Lin Syu supervised the insertion of the twin drains while Holly stripped off her mask, gloves and headgear.

"Excellent work, Dr. Buchanan," the older woman said, finally lifting twinkling black eyes to Holly. "We'll have you doing all our cosmetic procedures before long."

Holly grimaced, as Dr. Syu had known she would, and moved away from the table—her part of the procedure currently over. She sent a quick look up to the observation-room window and wasn't surprised to find it empty. Breast reductions weren't that interesting unless you were considering specializing in plastic surgery. And since Dr. Hot Celebrity was rumored to have done hundreds if not thousands of boob jobs, he had probably only wanted to rattle her.

And succeeded. *Darn it.*

"As long as the patient is satisfied with her new size," she said, stretching out cramped back and shoulder muscles as she moved toward the doors. She knew that she would have to perform cosmetic procedures but in this case it helped knowing she could restore someone's self-confidence while alleviating their pain.

Dr. Syu followed, stripping off her gloves. "You just saved her from a lifetime of pain and discomfort, Holly. That she wants to wear a bikini on her honeymoon doesn't make cosmetic procedures wrong."

Holly stifled a yawn. "I know," she mumbled, feeling somewhat chastened. "Besides being the object of curiosity and ridicule, Kerry Gilmore said she was tired of men making lewd comments about her breasts."

"Well, that's just juvenile and typical," Lin said in disgust. "Anyway, as long as she follows medical advice and wears the support garment, she'll be wearing her string bikini on her honeymoon come summer."

She untied Holly's surgical gown and waited while Holly returned the favor before saying over her shoulder, "You don't have to like them but you also shouldn't forget that cosmetics procedures—especially the big-bucks ones—help fund the reconstructions."

Holly sighed. Dr. Syu was right. Besides, she had first-hand experience of the emotional trauma caused by others' perceptions to be reminded of why she'd chosen to specialize in plastic and reconstruction surgery.

She'd spent her entire childhood struggling against the stereotype of beauty-versus-brains and was tired of people judging her by her looks or her family's accomplishments.

As a child she'd often thought she'd been adopted, switched at birth or maybe dumped on their doorstep by a wicked witch. It was only much later that she had accepted she was dark like her father and brother. At the time, though, she'd felt like an alien—a thin, scrawny, ugly duckling that her father couldn't possibly love.

She'd been clumsy, awkward and—she'd be the first to admit—cripplingly shy, geeky and snotty as hell. She'd hated being compared to her incredibly beautiful, blonde outgoing mother and her famous photographic model sister. And because she couldn't compete with her brother or sister for their father's attention, she'd tried to be the smartest so he could be proud of her too. And just when she'd begun filling out and growing into her large eyes, big mouth and long legs, she'd fallen a couple of stories when the cable on a glass elevator had snapped.

She'd been forced to undergo countless surgeries to repair the damage caused by flying glass, once again becoming the object of ridicule and pity. Boys who hadn't known about her accident had even called her The Scar, like she was some kind of comic-book villain or something.

"So," Lin Syu said casually, jolting Holly out of disturbing memories of her past. "What do you think of the new guy?"

Holly froze. "The new guy?"

"Yep." Dr. Syu dropped her soiled surgical gown into the hamper. "Our new celebrity hunk. I hear the nurses are all fighting to get on the surgical roster with him."

Holly rolled her eyes as heat crept up her neck. "I really hadn't noticed." Lin eyed her levelly, expression wry as though she could see right through Holly's lie. "What?" Holly asked, trying to look innocent. "I've been busy."

"So the looks that day at the meeting were my imagination?"

"What looks?"

"Everyone paying attention saw the looks, Dr. Buchanan." She grinned and waggled her eyebrows. "I just wondered if you two already knew each other or if it was lust at first sight."

Holly's head shot up, eyes wide with shock. "*Wha-at?* I don't… *Ohmigod!*" she spluttered, feeling her face burn with mortification as she thought back to those oddly intimate moments in the elevator and then again when their eyes had met across the boardroom. She hadn't thought anyone had seen. Clearly she hadn't been as discreet as she'd thought.

Her body instantly reacted to the memory of that weird sensation of the earth wobbling off its axis and she shivered and huffed out a breath.

"That's…um…" She gulped and cast around for something intelligent to say but all that emerged from her mouth was a strangled gurgling sound that Dr. Syu seemed to find hilarious.

Struggling to get her emotions under control and stall for time, Holly busied herself by carefully folding her soiled surgical gown and placing it neatly in the hamper.

"It's n-not what you think," she finally murmured, huffing out a couple of breaths like she was about to give birth. "But we…um, did meet in the elevator on the way up."

The surgeon pulled off her mask and cap and waited patiently for Holly to elaborate. When she didn't, Lin's brows rose up her forehead. "That must have been some meeting," she drawled, snorting out a laugh when Holly uttered a sound of distress. "I think he likes you."

Holly averted her head and wished she could sink through the floor. "That's…that's ridiculous," she denied a little too hastily. "Guys like him aren't…well…interested in people like um…" She gestured vaguely to her face. "Like me."

"You're a beautiful—yes, Holly," Lin insisted when Holly opened her mouth to argue, "beautiful and graceful woman. Not to mention a skilled and talented surgeon. Why wouldn't he be interested? He's a man, isn't he?"

"I wasn't always graceful," Holly admitted dryly, recalling how elegant she must have looked on her hands and knees. "It took a lot of hard work on my mother's part. Even now when I'm flustered…I, um…" She broke off, flushing when she realized what she was about to reveal.

"You what?

Holly sighed. "My…inner klutz emerges," she mumbled,

then grimaced when Lin snorted. "It's like I'm fifteen again and have no control over my feet or my mouth."

"And he flusters you? Hmm." Lin's mouth curved and her eyes twinkled with wicked humor. "I sense a story there," she said, just as her pager went off. "Which will unfortunately have to wait. Damn. Just when I thought I could finally get to know my kids again. They probably think I'm just the woman that comes in at night to sleep with their father before disappearing again in the morning." She sighed and threw "Great job in there, by the way," over her shoulder as she hurried off.

Holly took a moment to savor the senior surgeon's praise and went off in the direction of the locker rooms to change before heading home. She knew she should go to her office and catch up on paperwork but she'd promised her housemates that she'd be home for dinner.

It had been kind of weird since Kimberlyn Davis had moved in after her cousin Caren had left and then Tessa Camara, another surgical resident at WMS, had moved out, leaving Holly in a house of strangers. Okay, Sam Napier wasn't exactly a stranger but, then, the hot brooding Scot wasn't all that easy to get to know.

He mostly kept to himself but in a house filled with women she couldn't really blame him. She'd kind of had a little crush on him when he'd first moved in but he was a bit intimidating and didn't share himself with others. Thanks to her scars and her incredibly geeky adolescence, she still felt shy and awkward around him.

Tessa, who'd basically moved in with her fiancé, Clay, since she'd dropped the baby bombshell a couple months ago, had promised to join them for dinner. After the week Holly had had she was ready to talk about babies and forget about big bad celebrity doctors who could make women scream.

CHAPTER FOUR

GABE SLID INTO the back of a cab and gave the cabbie his Brooklyn address as he sank back against the seat. He'd been invited to join a few colleagues at a nearby bar but he'd been on call for over two weeks straight and he was exhausted. Besides, he still hadn't finished unpacking his boxes and he was sick of living out of suitcases and eating out of cardboard cartons.

He wanted real food that he'd cooked himself and he hadn't even had time to unpack his kitchen stuff.

When he couldn't swim or surf, cooking relaxed him. He didn't know if it was growing up in California, where everyone was a health nut or alternative lifestyle guru, but he liked eating freshly prepared food.

What he hated was eating alone. But that was something that couldn't be helped, especially after the telephone conversation he'd had earlier that day with his grandfather. Talking—if the cold, stilted exchange could be termed talking—with the old man always left him restless and angry.

He wondered how the old man had found out he was in New York then decided he didn't want to know. The less he knew about Caspar Alexander's business, the better. Besides, the only thing he had in common with his grandfather—or with his father, for that matter—was their last name and a few bad genes. Everything else he'd got was from his mom. *Thank God.*

The cabbie turned a corner and hooted at some poor pedestrian who'd had the bad judgment to cross at a green light, jolting Gabe out of his disturbing thoughts. This was a new chapter in his life and he didn't intend to ruin it by thinking about the sharks in his paternal gene pool. That was about as productive as standing in an observation room, watching a woman do a breast reduction plasty when he had rounds and a ton of paperwork waiting.

He may have been watching the skilled movements of Holly Buchanan's hands but he'd been thinking about those long, slender fingers on his skin. And when he'd realized that he'd been getting turned on, he'd left before someone in the OR had looked up and noticed his jeans had been a tight fit.

The cabbie pulled up in front of a neatly refurbished brownstone and Gabe got out, bending to glare at the guy through the open passenger window when he called out an outrageous fare.

The cabbie shrugged. "I have a wife and three daughters," he explained, accepting the notes shoved at him.

"My condolences," Gabe drawled, slapping a hand on the yellow roof as the cab roared off. He swore he heard the guy laugh and call him a crazy dumbass before the taillights disappeared around the corner.

Turning to survey the building he was temporarily calling home, he wondered if he'd made the biggest mistake of his life to have replaced his Santa Monica home with its sunny view of the ocean for this.

Sighing wearily, he shoved a hand through his rumpled hair and headed across the sidewalk. All those boxes waiting to ambush him weren't going to unpack themselves and he was tired of dodging obstacles and stubbing his toes.

Even before he'd received the phone call from West Manhattan, inviting him to join the P&R department, he'd been questioning the direction his life had taken. And thinking about that direction made him think about his mother, and his heart squeezed.

"Apparently you raised a crazy dumbass, Mom," he muttered, rubbing the heel of his hand over the pinch of grief in his chest. And then in the next instant he gave a rueful smile as he imagined how she'd react. She'd level her green gaze at him and say that it was better to be a crazy dumbass than a capitalist warlord—which was what she'd called his grandfather. His father, on the other hand, had the dubious honor of being the warlord's sidekick.

His mouth twisted in a bitter-sweet smile. *Damn* but he missed her. He missed her oddball sense of humor and the absolute joy she'd found in simple things; like growing herbs and making her own dandelion wine or chamomile tea, or scavenging wild herbs for her colorful salads. As a kid he'd been embarrassed by the weird stuff she'd made him eat and recalled how the other kids had used to torment him for being too poor to afford real food.

They hadn't been that poor and she hadn't tolerated any rudeness—from him or his friends. Her narrow-eyed stare had often been used to make him question some of his decisions. Like getting caught on camera, tp'ing the principal's car or being forced to clean the girls' bathroom after bombing it with paint-filled balloons.

He wondered what she'd have said about Holly Buchanan, blurting out random facts one minute, falling at his feet or into his lap the next, only to have her duck through the closest doorway to avoid him the rest of the time.

She'd probably laugh, say it served him right for being so pretty and then she'd tell him to hold onto the girl because she was obviously smart and he needed someone who wouldn't be taken in by his I'm-up-to-no-good smile.

But Gabe didn't need to hold onto anyone, especially a woman like Holly Buchanan. He'd fallen hard for a girl from her world once and had learned the hard way that they didn't consider guys like him suitable for anything but a good time. He'd been happy to comply ever since, keeping his relationships superficial and short-lived.

He'd never told anyone about his father out of respect for his mother. She was gone now but he no longer had any interest in people knowing that the owner and CEO of the company holding the largest US government defense contract was his grandfather, a man who'd told Gabe's pregnant mother to "get rid of it" because "it" wasn't good enough for the Alexander name.

Holly Buchanan might look at him like he was a decadent dessert and she was looking to fall off the diet wagon, but she'd made it perfectly clear that he wasn't part of her plan. No doubt she also had some eligible socially acceptable fiancé tucked away somewhere until she could fit marriage into her plan.

Besides not wanting to go down that path again, Holly was a colleague and Gabe didn't date colleagues—especially the young vulnerable ones depending on his professionalism for their career advancement.

He was heading for the stairs to his front door when he heard the sound of an approaching vehicle and turned just as a bright yellow cab pulled up beneath the streetlight. Even before the vehicle came to a stop, the passenger door opened and a strappy black sandal emerged.

Curious, he angled his head to get a better view and caught sight of a pale slender foot attached to the strappy feminine contraption. And when the sight set his heart pounding and his grip tightening on his house keys, he froze, because...because it was suddenly the most erotic sight in the world.

What the—?

Where the hell had that thought come from? Especially as he'd never had a fetish for women's footwear before. It either meant he needed sleep or had lost what was left of his mind. Considering he'd sold a hugely lucrative practice back in LA to join the staff of a Manhattan teaching hospital, it was most likely the latter.

His fascinated gaze took in the endless length of perfectly creased trousers and the slender curvy form that followed. He let out a soundless whistle when he recognized it as one he'd had plenty of opportunity to study over the past couple of weeks—usually disappearing through the nearest doorway to avoid him.

Oblivious to his scrutiny, she tugged briefly at the neat little black jacket and bumped the door closed with her hip while rummaging around in her shoulder bag.

She bent at the waist—giving Gabe an eyeful of her long slender legs and perfectly rounded bottom—and thrust her arm through the open passenger window. She said something to the cabbie that had him gesticulating wildly and Gabe decided she was probably cursing the hefty fare.

She turned with a muttered "Darn highway robbery," and stumbled back a step when Gabe chuckled in sympathy. Her sharply indrawn breath was clearly audible on the quiet street.

"Hey, careful," he called out before he could help himself, and breathed a sigh of relief when she didn't go ass over head into the street.

"*Ohmigosh*, D-Dr. Alexander, you scared me," she squeaked, and cast a nervous glance at the departing cabbie as though she was considering running after it. "Um... are you...are you coming to dinner?"

She cast a surreptitious look between him and the neighboring front door as though she was considering making a mad dash for it and suddenly all Gabe's moodiness and grief vanished and he found himself smiling.

Propping his shoulder casually against a huge earthenware pot halfway up the stairs, he studied her in the pool of light cast by the old-fashioned streetlamp.

Was the lady surgeon a neighbor or visiting? he mused. Or living with her husband or I—?

For some reason the idea of her with a lover annoyed him and then he wondered why the hell he cared. He didn't. Besides, she was exactly the kind of woman he'd promised he would never get involved with—the kind that fitted perfectly into his grandfather's world. Rich, classy and uptight.

He arched a brow. "Are you inviting me to dinner, Dr. Buchanan?"

A hunted look came into her eyes. "What? No...I mean... I thought that's why you're here." She sucked in an audible breath. "Aren't you?"

Gabe watched the conflicting emotions flash across her mobile features. After a couple of beats he took pity on her and held up his keys.

"Relax, Doc," he drawled, wondering why the idea of her going to dinner with some faceless man made his teeth ache. "These are my new digs."

She looked stunned and more than a little disturbed by the news as she edged up the neighboring stairs. "Your new, um...digs?"

"Uh-huh." He looked at her sideways and tried not to laugh at the sight of her nibbling on her thumbnail. It was something he'd noticed she did when she was disturbed. "Why, did you think I was stalking you again?"

"Wha—? No!" She gave an embarrassed laugh that ended on a cough. "Why would I think that?"

"I don't know," he said mildly. "Maybe because you're usually using escape-and-evade tactics that would do a marine proud."

"That's...that's just ridiculous," she spluttered, and even in the ambient light Gabe saw the guilty flush rise up her neck into her face. "We work on the same floor and..." She shrugged helplessly. "It's been hectic."

"Uh-huh." He folded his arms across his chest. "Would it help if I told you that you're not really my type?" He knew he'd thought it before but he'd been wrong. *She was so his type.* He shook his head and laughed again. This time at himself. Because, really, despite the uptight attitude, she was *everyone's* type.

Especially with those big blue eyes and soft mouth that made him think of deep, wet kisses in the dark. Maybe with a big fat harvest moon hanging in a midnight sky and bathing the street in a romantic glow. He could easily picture her beautiful features bathed in moonlight as she turned up her face for a kiss. His kiss.

Snorting softly at his uncharacteristically fertile imagination, Gabe decided he'd been in California too long if he was creating romantic movie scenes in his head.

She looked annoyed and maybe a little insulted, which dispelled his imaginary romantic scene. "What is your type?" she asked curiously, then, as though realizing what she'd said, grimaced. "No, don't tell me." She stomped up the stairs to her front door. "Blonde, stacked and vapid, right? And most likely a surgically enhanced beach bunny. *Yeesh.* Big surprise." She turned and glared at him. "Did you know that in ancient Greece, blonde hair was associated with prostitution?"

"Is that a fact?" Gabe grinned and realized with a jolt of surprise that he kind of liked the way she scowled at him—like a ruffled kitten ready to spit and scratch at the slightest move from the neighborhood mongrel. It made him want to reach out and stroke her until she arched into his caress and purred.

And as he'd never had any similar urges before, he decided that he'd slipped over the edge for real and should probably have himself committed.

"I thought the saying was blondes have more fun," he taunted, and chuckled when she snorted her opinion of his questionable taste in women...and in hair color.

"You're such a...a man," she growled in that oddly husky voice that did strange things to his gut. Shoving the key into the lock, she pushed open the door before throwing "Incapable of looking past bleached hair, a pair of large breasts and long tanned legs" over her shoulder. Then, without another glance in his direction, she disappeared into the building and slammed the door behind her.

For a long moment Gabe stared at the empty spot, gradually becoming aware of the growing lightness that had replaced his previous black mood. And when he realized he was grinning like a loon, he shoved a hand through his rumpled hair. He was vaguely surprised by his new neighbor's ability to make him smile when he hadn't felt like smiling in what seemed like forever.

Yet despite her prickly, less-than-friendly attitude, he kind of couldn't wait to see her again so he could tease an irritated scowl—or an adorable blush—to her face. Or maybe he just wanted to find out what other weird and wonderful facts she had tucked away inside that dark head.

He had a feeling she had one for every occasion.

With a cheerful whistle, Gabe turned and shoved his key in the lock and pushed open the door. "G'night, blue eyes," he murmured, before slipping inside. "Sweet dreams."

His day—and maybe the future—had just got a whole lot more interesting.

Holly's breath whooshed out noisily as she sagged back against the door. *Oh, boy,* she thought, feeling strangely buzzed and exhausted. And then, because she didn't know what else to think, she rolled her eyes, and said it out loud. "Oh, boy."

The sound of someone clearing their throat made her jump and squeak for the second time in as many minutes. Her gaze flew to where her friend and sometime housemate Tessa stood in the open doorway to the sitting room, watching her curiously. "You're late," Tessa accused lightly. "And you didn't answer your cell."

Dr. Enzo DellaToro, fiancé to a new housemate, Kimberlyn Davis, popped his handsome Italian head round the door. "She was getting ready to call the police."

"The police?" Holly squeaked, still feeling a little tongue-tied in his presence. "What for?"

He shrugged. "Maybe it's hormones."

Tessa waved that aside and folded her arms beneath her breasts. "Who were you talking to? I know for a fact that it's too early for Mr. Steiner to walk his dog."

Holly ducked her head. There was no way she could tell them about…well, him. Tessa would ask a million questions and try to set her up again and Holly was honest enough with herself to know that Gabriel Alexander was *way* out of her league. She'd learned a long time ago that guys who wore that casual confidence like a pair of soft well-fitting jeans mostly didn't even notice she existed. She was too serious, too quiet, too nerdy and…and boring.

Not to mention scarred.

"I'm sorry," she said with an apologetic grimace, "but did you know that the actual statistics for people going missing is lower than the reports?"

Enzo and Tessa exchanged silent looks and Holly hid a wince because she knew what they were thinking. Hoping she could head them off before succumbing to the guilty need to explain herself, she pushed away from the door and walked toward them, avoiding their searching gazes by focusing on the three large buttons on her jacket.

Ignoring the questions she could see Tessa was dying to ask, Holly led the way into the living room, where dinner was clearly under way.

"What happened?" Kimberlyn asked in her sexy Southern drawl before Holly could apologize for being late.

She felt her cheeks go hot and bit back a curse. Damn it. What was this, focus-on-Holly night? She tried for a casual "I don't know what you mean" only it emerged sounding defensive instead.

"You're flustered," Tessa, who'd known her the longest, said. "And you always come up with random facts when you're nervous."

"Nothing happened," Holly hastened to reassure them. "Not really. I…er…I just got home and there was a guy on the street."

"Is he still there?" Sam asked, wandering into the sitting room from the kitchen.

"Why didn't you use your mace?" Tessa demanded, and Holly laughed.

"Relax," she said, feeling her cheeks heat. "I, um…I didn't need to. It was the new neighbor."

"Ooh," Tessa said, eyes alight with curiosity. "Is he hot?"

Sam tapped the neck of the beer bottle thoughtfully against his lip. "Next door, huh?" he drawled, distracting Holly from asking Tessa what an almost married pregnant woman was doing checking out hot guys. "Isn't he the new cosmetic surgeon? The Hollywood guy?"

Holly blushed and gaped at him a little because it was the most she'd ever heard him say. She turned to throw her shoulder bag onto the nearest surface and shrug out of her jacket, hoping they hadn't seen that annoying tell-tale reaction that had haunted her adolescence.

"Yes…and it's, um…he's from…um, Beverly Hills." She rolled her eyes at herself. She'd gone for casual and ended up sounding like she had something to hide.

"Ooh." Tessa grinned, her eyes alight with glee. "She thinks he's hot."

She totally did.

"I do not!" Holly said defensively as she kicked her sandals off a little viciously. Her mother would have a fit to see the elegantly appointed sitting room littered with apparel. "Besides, sixty-five percent of men prefer surgically enhanced blondes with fake…tans, not pale brunettes who um…never…get…any…sun."

"Hey," Enzo and Sam objected simultaneously, both looking a little affronted by the "surgically enhanced blondes" quip. Holly rolled her eyes and huffed out a breath. Damn it, she was embarrassed enough, without getting into a discussion about blondes being more fun. Especially with Tessa—who knew a little about Holly's family—looking empathetic.

Better just to pretend it was no big deal. Because it hadn't been. *Really.* No big deal at all.

"Sorry, Enzo." She shrugged and sent Sam a look beneath her lashes because she'd seen a surgically enhanced blonde chatting him up at the hospital festival a few months earlier. She blinked innocently and added, "I was going to say he's okay if you like the tanned beach type. Which I don't."

"Oh, honey," Kimberlyn snorted. "Everyone does."

"Let's invite him to dinner," Tessa teased.

"No!" she practically squeaked, and Tessa laughed and threw herself into the nearest chair. She picked up a glass filled with what looked like mojitos from the sweating jug on the coffee table. "So-o-o," she said, sucking down a mouthful and licking her lips. "What's he like?"

Holly shrugged. "Okay, I guess," she lied blithely, and dropped onto the sofa, quickly releasing her hair from its high ponytail so it fell around her shoulders in a dark silky mass…hopefully hiding her expression. "And why are you drinking?"

"Oh, I'm not. Sam made me a virgin." There was a short pause as everyone absorbed that statement before Holly snorted.

"Won't Clay have something to say about that?"

Tessa's mouth curled and her eyes got that dreamy look Holly associated with people in love. The sappy one that made other women sigh with envy. "Of course he would." She waved aside Holly's attempts to change the subject. "Don't change the subject, Dr. Buchanan. Is he the tall, dark and handsome guy with blue eyes and a wicked smile?"

"That's your fiancé, Tessa," Kimberlyn pointed out, and Tessa blinked in surprise. Surprise that slid into a secret little smile, making her resemble a sleek cat that had recently swallowed a fat, juicy pigeon. "Oh, yeah, so it is. Lucky me."

Enzo snorted but Holly just felt relieved that their attention had finally shifted away from her. She exhaled with a soundless whoosh and reached for what was obviously the non-virgin jug of mojitos. She was in the process of pouring herself a hefty drink when she realized everyone had gone silent and was staring at her like she'd announced she was an alien from a distant galaxy who liked to suck guys' hearts out with a kiss.

"What?" She carefully replaced the jug, her gaze warily bouncing from one face to the other. "What's wrong?"

Behind Tessa's curiosity was concern. "Are you sure you're okay?"

Holly's brows wrinkled and she looked down at herself, half expecting to see her buttons open, that she was wearing a black bra under a white shirt or that she'd spilled something unmentionable on her blouse. Seeing nothing unusual, she looked up in confusion. "What?"

They all looked pointedly at the glass in her hand. "You're drinking cocktails now?" Tessa demanded, and Holly flushed, cursing Tessa's eagle eye and the realization that the encounter with their new neighbor had rattled her.

It had been bad enough that she had to see him at work, now she was probably going to fall over him every time she left her house too.

Instead of admitting that she was rattled, she shrugged casually, like she drank cocktails all the time, and sank back against the cushions with a sigh of relief.

Look at her, all sophisticated and casual.

"Well, since I'm not pregnant, I thought I'd stop being so predictable. Maybe I need to loosen up a little. Or…something. Anyway," she added quickly, as heat rose in her face, "it's been an exhausting day."

"You're acting weird," Tessa said, with a little frown. "What aren't you telling us?"

"Nothing. Really." Holly shrugged casually then exhaled a little shakily when she realized she hadn't sounded convincing even to her own ears. Maybe if she stuck with a half-truth they'd be satisfied and drop the subject. "Okay, it wasn't nothing," she confessed a little guiltily, and took a sip of mojito, grimacing at the strong taste of alcohol. *Yeesh, someone here had a heavy hand.* "I heard the code blue and full house call for OR three and went in to watch for a while."

A "full house" was the med students' term for a full trauma team consisting of all the main disciplines. It only rarely happened that a case needed so many specialists on urgent standby.

Suddenly ravenous, Holly snagged a large slice of pizza and between mouthfuls of crispy base, gooey cheese and spicy pepperoni she told them about the guy who'd fallen from construction scaffolding, thinking how amazingly clever she'd been to distract them.

Besides, she thought with a quiet huff of relief, they'd knocked back a couple of mojitos before she'd arrived and were already buzzing along quite nicely. Even Tessa, despite drinking the non-alcoholic version.

Although Holly rarely drank anything more lethal than white wine, she slugged down her first drink like it was medicine and found she kind of liked the tangy minty lime flavor and the way it made her lips tingle.

By the time her lips turned numb, so had her brain—which was great because it meant she could stop obsessing about her humiliating behavior and forget about the new neighbor.

So-o-o-o forgetting about the hot new neighbor.

Especially, she mused, surreptitiously fanning her hot cheeks, those embarrassing facts about blondes. Besides, if she wasn't his type, *he* most definitely wasn't *hers*.

Not by a long shot.

She tended to go for the serious business type. *He* was

too…um…the word *laid-back* came to mind and…and carelessly put together with an indolent, unconscious grace that made her feel like that clumsy awkward kid again.

Another thing that really annoyed her was his natural self-assurance. She would like to call it arrogance but it wasn't…not really. It was like he'd popped out of his mother's womb knowing his place in the world and didn't care if anyone disagreed. She had a feeling that air of casual affability hid a razor-sharp intellect. She'd seen ample evidence of a wicked sense of humor too and, *jeez*, she wished she didn't find that so attractive. Especially as it had being aimed at her most of the time.

Her cheeks grew hot when she recalled falling into his lap, only to find him huge and hard beneath her bottom.

She wasn't interested in him, she assured herself. He wasn't part of her plan—especially someone used to physical perfection. She was just annoyed to discover that after all the hard work she still hadn't outgrown the nerdy, clumsy adolescent that blushed and stuttered in the presence of a hot guy.

But later, when she slid between crisp, clean sheets and snuggled down into her pillow, along with a gently spinning room, Holly had a sudden and vivid image of a naked surf god sprawled across a sea of white on the other side of her bedroom wall. For the first time in her life she experienced a full-body flush that she promptly blamed on all those darn mojitos!

CHAPTER FIVE

WHEN SHE WAS stressed Holly sometimes had nightmares about the accident that had changed her life. She didn't often think about it but the following week she assisted a senior surgeon in repairing the face and torso of a maintenance worker who'd been caught in a gas explosion.

It had brought back memories of waking to a world of eerie silence filled with dust; the realization that she'd been unable to move and blinding pain when she'd tried.

She'd later learned that her face and right arm had been lacerated by flying glass as she'd been flung twenty feet from the exploding elevator car. The worst had been when she'd turned her head and seen the lifeless stare of a kid about her own age lying nearby. The sight of that empty eye socket where his merry brown eye had once been still haunted her dreams. One minute he'd been laughing and chatting with his friends, the next he'd been an unrecognizable bloodied mess.

Other than laceration injuries, she'd broken both arms and a collar bone and the ragged edges of her tibia had torn through the flesh of her right leg.

What she remembered most about the incident was the moaning and screaming.

Spooked by memories she hadn't thought of in years, Holly left the hospital and headed for the gym not far from West Manhattan.

Where other people enjoyed sweating and grunting through their workouts, Holly preferred the cool solitude of the pool. Besides, there was plenty of scientific evidence proving that submersion in water lowered blood pressure as well as stress levels. Besides relaxation, Holly liked the full-body workout swimming gave her. After the accident, it had been one of the physical therapy sessions she'd looked forward to and she'd eventually become a good swimmer.

And, boy, after the day she'd just had, she needed relaxation as much as she needed some alone time. Although she wouldn't have minded a little screaming to go with it, that wasn't on the cards. And until she landed the fellowship, the plan took precedence. Over everything.

She needed to do research for a paper she was writing on micro-surgical techniques but she was too wired to concentrate on anything and knew sleep would remain elusive if she went home. And recalling that what little sleep she'd managed lately had been filled with dreams of sun-warmed beaches, cool seas and…and hot surfers, Holly rolled her eyes because she was thinking of a certain hot celebrity surgeon. Again.

She dodged a couple necking on the stairs and entered the gym. Smiling a greeting at the girl manning Reception, she headed for the women's change room.

Within minutes she'd changed out of her street clothes and into her swimsuit. Scooping up her towel, she headed for the pool, hoping she would be alone. Alone meant she could get into her zone faster without having to dodge other swimmers. Alone meant she could get her workout done in record time and head home to food and her bed.

Okay, so she was also a little self-conscious about her scars, which were a lot more noticeable when she wore a swimsuit. Granted, they'd mostly faded but *she* knew they were there and in her mind's eye they were still livid and ugly.

Her heart sank a little when she saw the pool was already

occupied but after a few indecisive moments the need for the soothing feel of water closing over her head drove her onto the pool deck.

After a quick glance around, she realized that since the lone occupant appeared oblivious that he was about to have company, she could slip unnoticed into the water and pretend she was alone.

Dropping her towel over a nearby rail, she turned to face the clear blue water and wrestle with her hair. She twisted the heavy mass into a tight bun at the top of her head and secured it with a couple of holders as she approached the edge of the pool, taking a moment to admire the man's efficient, deceptively lazy style. He moved with the kind of fluid effortless grace only found in professional swimmers.

Pausing to stretch her tight muscles, she watched his long, tanned body power easily through the water toward her. Nearing the wall, he executed a languid racing turn as though it was as natural to him as walking. Fascinated, Holly followed the path his body made underwater until he surfaced some ten meters away, turning his head just enough to take advantage of his body's streamlining to breathe.

Darn, she thought with admiration as water glistened off his wide tanned shoulders and long powerful arms, she wished she could look half as good breathing, let alone swimming laps.

She spent another minute practically hypnotized by the dip and rise of wide shoulders and the shifting of muscles in a long tanned back until he abruptly disappeared in yet another turn at the opposite wall. Realizing she was standing transfixed by the sight of some guy doing nothing more interesting than swim up and down, Holly blinked as heat rose into her face.

What the heck are you doing, Holly? You came here to de-stress and get some exercise, not get all hot and bothered by some hunk out for his evening swim.

Feeling guilty for her somewhat racy thoughts, Holly took a deep breath and dived. Her foot slipped at the exact instant she realized she'd forgotten her goggles and instead of her usual graceful dive, she belly-flopped with a strangled shriek and sank like a stone.

The water was colder than she'd expected, closing over her head and rushing in on the heels of her startled gasp. For a few ragged heartbeats she panicked and flailed around like she'd forgotten how to swim, confused about which way was up. Just when she thought she'd run out of air, large hands clamped around her arms and hauled her upward.

Instinctively fighting the firm grip, Holly nearly lost what was left of the breath in her lungs when she was yanked roughly against a big hard body. They broke the surface in a tangle of limbs, gasping breath and gushing water.

"Jeez, lady," a deep familiar voice growled near her ear, and Holly's belly clenched before sinking as gracelessly as she had. "Are you trying to drown yourself?"

Gabe held the woman and waited while she spluttered and coughed, wondering if she'd pretended to drown, hoping to attract his attention. He'd had women do that and more, trying to get him to notice them.

It was only when she lifted her head and blinked huge dark blue eyes that he realized he was holding Holly Buchanan and she was staring at him like she'd suddenly found herself in the jaws of...well, Jaws.

"You?" she gasped.

He felt his mouth curl up at one corner and made no effort to release her. In fact, he drew her closer. "Well, well," he drawled softly, enjoying the feel of her body, still warm and incredibly smooth and soft, against his. The skin across his belly tightened in reaction. "What a...surprise. Are you by any chance stalking me?"

"Me?" she squeaked, her mouth round with outrage. "I was about to ask you the same thing."

"I was here first. Unless…" His eyes narrowed on her in mock suspicion. "Unless that was you hiding behind the pillar when I arrived earlier," he drawled, referring to the way he'd caught her ducking around corners or through the closest doorway when she'd seen him coming at the hospital.

Heat rushed into her face but she ignored his comment, her lips parting on a stuttered "I—I… Th-that was you? In the water, I mean?"

A frown tugged at Gabe's mouth at her incredulous tone. He wasn't sure she'd meant it as a compliment, which also meant she hadn't followed hoping to run into him. He ignored the odd feeling in his gut that couldn't possibly be disappointment.

"You sound surprised."

For a couple of beats she blinked myopically at him. It was fascinating to watch the conflicting expressions race over her features as if she couldn't decide if she was annoyed, impressed or embarrassed. It made him wonder what the heck was going through her mind to make her frown and blush.

"Not at all. It's just…" She suddenly blew out a breath and rolled her eyes. The idea that she'd been watching him was oddly satisfying, considering how much time he'd spent either thinking about her lately or watching her run for cover every time she saw him coming. Especially today, when evaluating her technique hadn't been the sole purpose of his presence in observation room six.

She licked her lips and he instantly forgot what he was thinking. "I…um…I didn't know you swam… At this gym, I mean."

His gaze dropped to her mouth and his skin tightened as heat gathered low in his gut. "And a good thing too or you might have drowned yourself."

"Don't be silly," she wheezed, lifting a hand to wipe moisture off her face. "I slipped, that's all. I'm an excellent swimmer."

He felt a chuckle rise in his throat. "Yeah? Then what was that incredibly graceful dive called? Because I can tell you I've seen preschoolers with more style than that."

She rolled her eyes. "The tiles are slippery," she muttered, dropping her gaze to his mouth. She sucked in a shuddery breath that pressed her breasts against his chest and made his eyes cross. It also made her realize she was plastered up against him like wet silk—okay, and maybe she'd discovered what the feel of her smooth warm skin was doing to him. She squeaked and tried to shove away but they were both slick and her hands kept slipping until she finally growled something that sounded like "Damn it, this is a nightmare" and managed to knee him in the thigh. He wasn't so sure that was an accident.

He muttered, "Wet dream is more like it."

She gasped and gaped at him. Her furious "*Ohmigod, I can't believe you just said that*" ended on a hacking cough, and Gabe shook his head as he slid his hands from her waist to lift her arms above her head even as she tried to take a swing at him.

"Come on, who didn't see that one coming?"

She choked and spluttered a bit more and he got kicked in the shin this time. He chuckled. "Breathe, Doc, before you hack up another lung or maybe knee me in the nuts."

"You...you deserve it," she croaked, when she could talk without spluttering.

He pulled back and dipped his head to peer into her face. "Is that any way to talk to the guy who just saved your life? For the fourth time, I might add."

"What are you doing here, *Dr.* Alexander?" she demanded in a husky voice that heated him up on the inside and gave him a few indecent thoughts. Thoughts he shouldn't be having about someone he was going to be working with. Thoughts about pushing her up against the side of the pool and practicing mouth-to-mouth.

"You mean, other than saving your sexy ass?"

Wild color rose beneath her creamy skin and Gabe was seriously tempted to lean forward and lick her pink mouth—see if she tasted as delicious as she looked.

"I'm perfectly capable of saving myself," she snapped, and shoved at hands that had ended up very close to her breasts—which were full and firm and incredibly enticing in that skin-tight black sheath. Did she know their hard points were practically begging for attention that he was all too willing to give? "And let me go, damn it."

His blood heated in his veins at the thought of getting his hands on her bounty and his grin turned mocking, as much at himself than anything. He was mostly a leg and butt man, probably because of all the boob jobs he'd performed. But despite the number of breasts he had his hands on, none of them had made a fraction of an impact on him compared to Holly Buchanan's shrink-wrapped curves.

And he'd just this instant become a breast man too.

"Aww," he drawled, his voice a rough rasp filling the inch separating them. "Do I have to?"

"No… Yes…I mean… *Damn it.*" Confusion chased annoyance and desire across her face as Holly put a couple of inches between them. Despite the move making him chuckle, the distance gave him an even better view. She saw the direction of his gaze, looked down and with an outraged squeak slapped her arms across her chest, glaring at him like he was a pervert for enjoying the view. "They're… they're all me," she snapped. "In case you were wondering."

He chuckled. "Yeah, I can tell."

His gaze drifted up her throat, past her stubborn little chin to her mouth, where he got stuck for a few heart-stopping beats. He finally locked eyes with her…and got caught up in the incredible dark blue depths surrounded by a heavy fringe of dark spiky lashes. For an instant his world tilted and then his heart rate spiked like he'd been zapped with a cattle prod.

The hair on the back of his neck prickled and a shudder of pure panic stomped up his spine with size thirteen army boots. Blinking, he shoved shaking fingers through his hair. *What the hell?* Next thing he'd be spouting poetry or something equally cheesy—not to mention freaking embarrassing.

When just the thought of it made his nuts shrink, Gabe didn't know whether to be relieved or freaked out. *Jeez.* This was exactly what happened when a guy went without for more than six months, he told himself. He got caught up in sexy blue bedroom eyes and starved his brain of oxygen when his blood drained south of the border.

"Stop…stop looking at me," she rasped, turning away from his gaze. He blinked her face into focus, finally realizing his scrutiny was upsetting her and that she was a little hunched over as though to protect herself. From him? What the hell?

"What are you talking about?"

"I feel like a…a bug under a microscope."

"A very attractive *wet* bug," he interjected, and dropped his gaze in time to see her bite her lip. And because he hadn't eaten since noon, he was tempted to take a nibble too but she turned wounded eyes up to his and he froze. "What? What's wrong?"

"I'm d-damaged."

He laughed but when her expression turned fierce, like she wanted to slug him, he frowned, confused as hell because the woman was damn beautiful. The last thing he'd call her was damaged.

Stunning, sexy and hot? Yes. Snotty as hell? Definitely. Damaged? No way. Scars and all. There was too much elegant bone structure, stubborn chin and lush mouth for that.

Frustrated, he shoved a hand through his hair. "What the hell are you talking about?" He felt like one wrong move from him and she'd… Hell, he didn't know, just that he'd go crashing through the ice any second and be plunged into deep frigid waters. She glared at him and he felt like an insensitive jerk. He didn't have a clue why.

"I'm damaged, flawed, broken," she muttered fiercely. "Take your pick. I've heard it all before, and more. Including ugly."

"Ugly?" He made a sound of irritation. "Did someone tell you that?" he rapped out.

She lifted a hand to cover the pale thin scars and blinked at him warily. "I've got eyes. I know what I look like."

He reached out and wrapped his fingers around her wrist, gently pulling her hand away so he could study the thin silvery scars marring her creamy skin with professional interest and clinical detachment. He had a feeling anything else would offend her.

Through the delicate skin on the inside of her wrist her pulse beat a rapid tattoo. Even if he hadn't felt the racing heartbeat, he couldn't ignore the anxiety leaking from every pore.

She made a sound of distress in the back of her throat and tried to tug free but he held her easily, lifting his free hand to gently turn the scarred side toward him.

He wanted to lean forward and kiss each imperfection, run his tongue along the pale lines. "I don't think you do," he said mildly. "Have you heard of body dysmorphic disorder?"

She jerked her chin away and flashed him a scowl of outrage. "Of course I have. Are you suggesting I have BDD or that I'm vain?"

Gabe shook his head and sent her a faint smile. "Neither. I merely wondered if you knew about it. I'm not going to lie and say your scars are invisible, Holly, but I think they're more noticeable to you because you know they're there."

She rolled her eyes and tried to twist free but he ignored her, his large, warm hand holding her captive. "I know they're there," she said in a low, fierce voice, "because I had to live through the stares as well as the endless procedures to get rid of them."

"And…" he guessed, lightly tracing one thin line across the top of her cheekbone to where it disappeared into her hairline. She sucked in a breath and after a moment a tiny shudder went through her. Gabe had to steel himself against the urge to wrap his arms around her, offer his strength. "You remember what they were like when they were new," he pointed out gently. "But unless you deliberately did this to yourself, it's not your fault."

"Of course I didn't do it to myself,' she snapped, then sucked in a huge breath that was probably an attempt to calm her but which nearly gave Gabe a heart attack when the round globes of her breasts swelled above the neckline of her swimsuit. "It was…an accident."

He had to clear his throat twice and fight the overwhelming urge to drop his gaze to her plump curves and drool like a guy. "Well, from a cosmetic point of view, even *I* couldn't have done better."

She snorted. "Modest much, Dr. Alexander?"

He chuckled. "No. In Beverly Hills you have to be good or word gets around and the next thing you know you're in Tijuana, doing budget nip-and-tuck tourist deals. Switzerland or Germany?"

She tugged again on her wrist and because he was somewhat distracted he let her go. She immediately wrapped her arms around herself. He could have told her it was too late. *Waa-aay* too late. Now that he'd seen—and felt them pressed against his chest—he was sure the image was burned into his brain for all time. And why he found that sexier than if she'd been naked, he didn't know. Clearly he'd lost brain cells along with his testosterone leakage.

"Switzerland. How did you know?"

At the question his gaze rose from watching her mouth form words. He blinked in confusion and got lost in the smoky blue depths surrounding enlarged pupils.

"I, uh…" What the hell were they discussing? Oh, yeah,

he thought with a rush of relief—her scars. "I recognized the technique from a study I did in med school."

She looked back at him and her expression was as dazed as his had been a few seconds ago. Clearly she was also having difficulty keeping up with their verbal exchange when their bodies insisted on conversing on a whole different level. A level that left his skin tight, his blood pounding through his veins and his body in pleasurable pain like he was an addict suffering withdrawal.

Holly licked her lips and Gabe's blood went instantly hot. She must have recognized the look in his eyes because hers widened and she edged away, watching him warily.

"Stop that!"

"Huh? Stop what?"

"Stop looking and…and talking about my flaws."

"Everyone has flaws," he murmured distractedly, his body following hers like he was a divining rod and she was a hidden source of water. He caged her against the wall with his arms, his voice a rough, low sound between them that heightened the feeling of isolation and intimacy.

Slick, naked skin brushed, sending goose-bumps marching across his skin like an invading army, and the water separating them heated until he thought he saw steam but maybe that was just his brain smoking. "My one ear is higher than the other and I have big feet."

She gaped at him like he was a lunatic for equating big feet with trauma scars. "You're kidding, right?"

"No, I'm serious. I bet if you looked you'd probably find a lot more. Like I broke my nose when my surfboard smacked me in the face."

She grimaced sympathetically. "What happened?"

"I was sixteen and showing off," he sighed. "Instead of being impressed, the girl fainted when she saw blood and the rest of my summer was ruined."

Her eyes lightened, as Gabe had intended, and he wanted to close the distance between them and kiss her, tease a

smile to her lush mouth. He wanted to make her laugh—
really laugh. Not the polite little smile he'd seen her aim
at people she wanted to keep at a distance. Hell. He'd like
any kind of smile, considering all she ever did with him
was scowl.

"That's really tragic."

Yeah, about as tragic as a grown man behaving like a
sixteen-year-old.

He gave a wounded look. "It was a traumatic adolescent
experience that scarred me for life," he accused, when she
smothered a snicker. "Anyway, in addition to a broken nose,
my one eyebrow arches more than the other and an old girlfriend told me I look permanently mocking."

"The one who fainted?"

"No." *Smartass.* "That one was history before I could
impress her with my manliness. It was another…girl."

"Well, you are mocking," she pointed out, and when his
lips curved up at one corner, her eyes dropped to stare at his
mouth and he knew she was as affected by their proximity
as he was. After a moment her gaze slid away a little guiltily
and when her tongue emerged to flick over her lips he felt
it all the way to his big feet—and every inch along the way.

"Maybe a little," he rasped, struggling to follow the conversation. "What I'm trying to say is that people are not
perfect."

"You haven't met my family."

"Why?"

The movement of the water bobbed them together and
their bodies bumped, skin brushing skin, soft curves against
hard. Her breasts brushed his chest, sending sensation zing-
ing through him until his back teeth ached with the effort
not to yank her against him and taste her soft mouth.

"My mother was a beauty queen," she was saying in a
husky tone, as though the accidental touch had affected her
too. *Damn.* Maybe he should move away. Maybe he should
get out of the pool and take a really cold shower until he

could breathe without inhaling the scent of her, move without the memory of her soft skin brushing against his.

But instead of getting the hell out of Dodge, he pressed a thigh between hers and shifted closer, until the plump curves of her breasts were pillowed against his chest and her thighs quivered and clenched around his. She made a little sound in the back of her throat that emerged as a gasping squeak and he nearly came out of his skin. It was so hot he was surprised the water didn't evaporate. It was so hot he felt the back of his skull tighten and his skin buzz.

She gulped and pressed herself against the wall before continuing. "She was…um…runner-up for Miss America and w-won Miss World that same year." She sucked in a breath. "She's beautiful and perfect. Like my sister Paige. Like my father and my brother Bryant."

Something tugged at his memory but when her tongue peeked out between her pink lips it vanished and all he could think about was tasting the moist pink pillows of flesh just beneath his mouth.

Maybe it was the hour or the fact that her eyes were heavy and smoky with the kind of need thundering through his own veins. But with her lips just below his and the smooth skin of her inner thighs making his gut clench with an almost violent need, he was powerless to do anything but slide his hand to the back of her neck and lower his head.

She gasped. "What are you…doing?"

Just before their lips touched, he murmured, "Proving how perfect you are."

Bare skin and thin elastane pressed into his belly and thighs. It flooded him with a need so powerful that he felt momentarily dizzy.

Oh, yeah, she was perfect all right. Perfect for him… perfect for his hands. Perfect for his mouth and he'd bet his grandfather's entire fortune she'd be perfect for his body too.

He reined himself in with difficulty but her breath hitched audibly in her throat and shot all his intentions—

to keep it light and teasing—straight to the bottomless pits of hell.

With a growl he covered her mouth with his in a kiss that instantly turned greedy and hot. He was thirty-five. A man who loved women; loved their bodies and the way their bodies felt against his. He loved the way they tasted and smelled and he loved the feel of their soft, firm flesh beneath his hands. He loved everything about them and he especially loved taking his time. But everything he'd ever learned about women went right out of his head the instant her mouth opened beneath his.

It was like he'd been sucked into a vortex created by her soft, wet mouth and soft, warm body and he couldn't think beyond getting more. More of her mouth, more of her silky curves pressed to the front of his jammer swimming trunks. More of her.

He pressed closer and when she uttered a breathy moan Gabe instantly took advantage and slid his tongue into her hot mouth. Without realizing he was doing it, he groaned low and deep in his throat and adjusted the fit of his mouth over hers, creating a light suction that made her whimper and arch into him, her hands clutching at his shoulders.

Blood roared through his head and he felt himself go under—submerged in liquid heat and drowning pleasure where his only lifeline was the feel of her soft mouth beneath his. And if he heard the alarm warning in the back of his mind, he ignored it in favor of murmured sighs that filled his ears and the slick, warm feel of her mouth beneath his.

Holly was aware of only two things. The big, hard body pressed to hers…the tangle of their limbs and the way his hand cradled her head as he devoured her resistance along with her breath. Okay, and she was also aware of the hard thigh between hers and the evidence of his arousal pressed almost painfully against her belly.

Her mind spun even as her eyes drifted shut and her

body softened, cradling that huge, hard shaft. He groaned. It came from so deep in his chest—like it'd been dragged up from the depths of his soul—that the responding vibrations swept through her like a subwoofer turned on high. And before she could remember her plan or think that maybe this was a very bad idea, she surrendered to the taste of him, greedily eating at his mouth and the hot, hungry kisses he fed her. Kisses that were deep and drugging and told her he was ravenous and that she was his next meal.

She'd never known kisses could be so hot or...hungry. Or that a man's mouth was capable of making her head spin, her belly dip and her body feel like one move and she'd go off like a bottle rocket.

And then there were no more thoughts as need and greed sucked her under, stole her breath along with any thoughts she might have to resist.

But there was no resisting the unstoppable force that was Gabriel Alexander and if she was honest with herself she didn't want to. Didn't want to push him away or stop the onslaught on her senses. Didn't want to resist his hot hardness sliding up to press against the apex of her thighs where she was hot and damp and aching with emptiness.

It was also wildly exciting to discover that someone like him could want her...with such rough urgency.

Then it didn't matter because all her thoughts drained away along with her breath, sucked out by his greedy mouth. But she found she didn't need breath as much as she needed this. This wild out-of-control feeling that sucked her under and sent her mind into a tailspin. And if she'd been in any condition to do anything but groan, slide her hands up the heavy muscles of his arms to his shoulders and press her body closer, she might have freaked at the ease with which he'd unraveled her defenses.

He fed her more deep, wet, hungry kisses that made her gasp and return them, just as hungrily, as if they were alone instead of in a public swimming pool where anyone might see them.

She didn't care. All she wanted was the hot, wet slide of his body filling the deep, empty ache within her. An ache she'd only discovered this very minute. An ache that she'd never thought existed, let alone experienced—especially in a brightly lit pool in central Manhattan.

He broke off the kiss to croak *"Damn,"* against her mouth and drag air into his heaving chest like he'd just sprinted three lengths of the pool without breathing. For several long beats they shared air until Holly lifted heavy lashes to see if he'd been as affected by the kiss as she had.

He looked a little shell-shocked. Kind of like she'd kneed him in the groin and he didn't know whether to throw up or pass out. Heck, she felt a little like passing out herself, and if she'd been in any state to do more than gulp air and cling to him, she might have panicked. Because…because, *damn.* Who'd have thought that Holly Buchanan would end up making out with Dr. Beverly Hills in a public swimming pool like a couple of randy teens? And want more? A whole lot more?

But her shock was about as little as the heavy evidence of his arousal, clearly outlined by his jammer suit practically shrink-wrapped to his lower body and visible beneath the water.

Okay, so she'd looked. It was better than seeing the hot blue-green eyes staring into hers until her thighs went up in flames. Her vision grayed at the edges and she thought she was having a panic attack until she realized she was holding her breath. She had to exhale or pass out.

And then he'd be forced to save her by performing mouth-to-mouth. *Oh, yes. Please.*

She must have swayed because his hands shot out to steady her. "You okay?" he rasped, and Holly stared up into his eyes and wondered why she'd never noticed how stormy they could get. Like the waters of the Caribbean stirred by hurricane winds.

"I…um…" And when nothing else emerged, he gave her a quick, hard shake to snap her out of her trance. But Holly was well and truly speechless. Who wouldn't be after that… that feeding frenzy?

"You going to pass out?" emerged rough and hoarse, as though he had as little control over his vocal cords as he had over his breathing. She inhaled and exhaled a couple more times until the urge to lose consciousness eased.

"Wh-a-at?"

A ragged chuckle scraped up from the depths of his chest and after a couple beats he shoved shaking fingers through his hair. "Damn it. I have to go." He sounded frustrated and a little like he was about to lose it. And, *oh, boy*, she could identify. "Are you going to be all right?"

"Oh…um…yes." She sucked in a couple more breaths and blinked up at him in confusion until she finally recognized the beeping noise she'd thought was the little warning sound in her head.

He was being paged and she hadn't even heard it over the pounding in her ears. Her head cleared a little more and she blew out a ragged "Go."

CHAPTER SIX

HOLLY WASN'T ABOUT to tell him that she felt like someone had smacked her against the head and left her ears ringing. She wasn't about to admit that every muscle in her body trembled—either with unfulfilled need or shock at her own behavior.

She white-knuckled the side of the pool with one hand and lifted unsteady fingers to her tingling lips, watching with dazed eyes as he hauled himself onto the pool deck. She felt shaken to her core. Kind of like finding out that aliens existed and that the government was helping them experiment on humans in return for their technology. Only... more.

Holy cow. Who knew anyone could kiss like that? Kiss *her* like that? As though he'd wanted to swallow her whole.

Water gushed down his body as he rose to his full height and she finally got a good look at what he'd been hiding beneath his jeans and sweatshirts—everything his jammer suit was supposed to cover, but didn't. *Gulp.*

She didn't realize her mouth had dropped open until he turned and caught her ogling his tight butt. His brow—the one that was usually arched in subtle mockery—rose up his forehead and a little lopsided grin sent that dimple creasing the lean planes of his cheek.

Oh, God. He'd caught her in the act of ogling him like he was a delicious pastry.

"Are you going to be okay? I hate leaving you alone when you're not such a great swimmer."

Holly's blush turned to a grimace at the reminder of her graceless dive. She didn't know what was worse—being caught leering at the goodies or…or having him witness her clumsiness. Again.

"I'm fine, Dr. Alexander. I…uh, slipped, that's all." She rolled her eyes as he wound a huge towel around his waist, his arched brow probably questioning her sudden attack of professionalism. But it was either that or drown herself at the memory of the way she'd whimpered and clutched at him like she'd been starving and he'd been a chocolate fudge sundae. "Maybe I'm not in your league, but I can hold my own."

"Uh-huh," he said, like he didn't believe her, and shoved fingers through his wet hair. Droplets showered around his head and shoulders and Holly felt equal amounts of glee and astonishment when she noticed his hands were shaking.

"I'm a great swimmer."

"If you say so." His phone started ringing and he grunted, looking for a moment like he'd love to toss the thing in the pool. But surgeons on call didn't have that luxury. "Look, I've gotta go. Promise me you'll be okay."

She rolled her eyes again, secretly pleased by his obvious reluctance to leave—although that might have something to do with his inability to walk in his…uh, condition. She bit her lip and watched his eyes go dark.

"I promise I'll be okay," she said hastily, and he finally sighed and gathered up his stuff.

He paused to send her one last look from beneath heavy, aroused lids. "A rain-check on the…other thing."

Holly shivered and dropped lower into the water to hide her body's reaction and stop her suit from melting beneath that laser-bright gaze. "The…thing?" One corner of his mouth curved and her breath caught in her chest. "Oh."

She swallowed hard and clenched her thighs together. "You mean…the, um…kiss?"

His grin turned wicked and his eyes burned a molten blue-green as they slid over her exposed skin, setting fire to her hair and her thighs. Jeez. It was a good thing she was submerged in water or her swimsuit—along with her thighs—would be history. "Oh, yeah," he rasped, his voice a dark slide of sin against her sensitized nerve endings as he turned and headed for the exit. "The kiss."

And just before he disappeared through the door she heard him say, "Definitely going to be another kiss."

And because he sounded so sure of himself—so arrogantly sure of *her*—she called out, "Don't hold your breath, Dr. Alexander. That was simply a thank-you for saving me." His response was deep laughter that floated across the pool and went straight to all her happy places that were feeling decidedly unhappy…and frustrated, *darn it*.

"Keep telling yourself that, Dr. Buchanan," rang in her ears, and Holly stared at the door for a few moments more before shaking her head as though to dispel the images lodged there. Sucking in a shuddery breath, she looked down to check that she was still clothed and wasn't sporting singe marks on her skin.

She was surprised to find that her suit hadn't vaporized and that the water hadn't boiled her like a lobster. Puffing out her cheeks, she blew out air in the hope that she could dispel the bubbles lodged in her brain. Because it was the only reason that would explain her wanton behavior. Especially with a man like Gabriel Alexander. A man who'd dedicated himself to the pursuit of perfection. A man who wasn't blind enough to ignore just how imperfect she was.

After a few moments getting her breathing under control, Holly squared her shoulders and sank beneath the water, ignoring the muscles trembling in her limbs like she'd just stepped off a carnival ride.

It was time to douse the fire and get into her zone, she

told herself firmly. A zone that didn't include sexy Hollywood surgeons with hot eyes, hard bodies and big warm... hands.

She had barely found her rhythm and was approaching the wall to turn when movement caught her attention. Stopping abruptly, she reared out of the water, her gaze automatically taking in a pair of battered sneakers at the edge of the pool.

She followed the long line of jeans-clad legs, over the bulge of a button fly and up a wide expanse of black T-shirt-covered chest to a tanned neck and square jaw gleaming with gold-tinted stubble. Stubble, she recalled with a shudder; that had scraped against her skin with rough eroticism.

She was surprised to see him. Dropping her head back, she quickly submerged then rose, lifting both hands to smooth her hair off her face. When she opened her eyes she found he'd dropped to his haunches and was looking hot and cool all at once. Their eyes met and a wild flush raced over her flesh at the memory of what he could do with his mouth.

"I thought you left?"

He shook his head. "I need you," he said, and the flush became a shudder, along with tightening breasts and clenching belly. Momentarily stunned, she gaped up at him as though he'd suggested something hot and forbidden...and incredibly tempting.

"I... You... What?"

He must have correctly interpreted her confusion because his mouth curved and that darned dimple made an appearance in his tanned cheek. "That'll have to wait for another time, Dr. Buchanan." He laughed and held out a hand as though he expected her to take it. Holly looked at his big brown hand and got a little dizzy just thinking about how it made her feel.

"Wha-at?"

He chuckled. "Pay attention, Doctor. I need you to get

out of the pool and get dressed. The hospital can't reach Dr. Frankel and we urgently need another surgeon. You're it."

"I'm not a maxillofacial surgeon."

"Close enough," he said a little impatiently, and waggled his fingers.

Without questioning him further, Holly took his hand and the next instant she was standing beside the pool, swaying a little on wobbly legs as water gushed down her body. He wrapped her towel around her shoulders and nudged her toward the exit.

"You have five minutes to change while I call a cab."

Holly walked into the gym lobby with a minute to spare to find Gabriel propped casually against the wall, laughing and chatting up a couple of women dressed in gym wear that looked three sizes too small. Both women looked taut and toned enough to bounce a coin on their tight butts and abs. And because she would never be able to do that, Holly was grateful her designer trousers and jacket covered her from the neck down.

The instant he saw her Gabe pushed away from the wall and wrapped his fingers around her elbow. The smile he aimed her way was warmly intimate as he called a quick "Night" over his shoulder. It also left her a little confused.

"Thank you," he murmured, steering her toward the automatic doors.

"For what?"

"For saving me from the barracudas." Oh, well, that certainly explained that, she decided with a pang that wasn't really disappointment. That smile hadn't been for her at all. Curious, she looked back over her shoulder and decided they did kind of resemble a couple of barracudas trawling the reef for a quick snack.

And to a woman who hadn't eaten all day, Gabriel Alexander was kind of snack-worthy.

"You looked like you were having a great time."

"Seriously?" He scowled at her as the doors swished

closed behind them. "Did you see how ripped they were? I was worried the blonde would wrestle me to the floor and put me in a headlock." *Or a something lock*. Holly hid a smirk. "It's humiliating," he muttered. "Besides, I don't like women who are so obsessed with the way they look they can't relax and have a good time."

The look he sent her made her hair smolder and her belly dip and quiver. "Women are supposed to be…soft," he murmured wickedly, his hot gaze dropping to her breasts. "Not have muscles in places they shouldn't. It makes a guy feel inferior."

He opened the cab door and stepped aside for Holly to get in. She couldn't see him feeling intimidated by anyone, let alone a couple of hot, sculpted gym bunnies. He'd have to care what people thought about him and he didn't strike her as a guy who worried overly much about that.

He got in behind her and she sneaked a peek out the corner of her eye when his thigh pressed against hers and their shoulders bumped. It sent warm little tingles of awareness pricking her skin.

She shifted over a little.

God, he was big, his wide shoulders taking up space she wasn't used to sharing with anyone and dominating it with a kind of smoldering masculine aggression that made her feel small and fragile when she looked most men in the eye.

By the time they arrived at the hospital Holly was wondering if she'd made a mistake by agreeing to accompany him after that kiss. She needed at least a week—okay, maybe a month…or three—to recover her equilibrium and stop wanting to either run for cover or…or jump his bones. Jumping his bones would be bad. Bad for the plan and bad for her heart.

"Get suited up and meet me in room two," he said briskly, with none of the misgivings or embarrassment she was experiencing. But, then, he was a guy. Kissing women and then going on to remodel a few breasts and thighs was all in a day's work. For her...? She sucked in air and let it out slowly. Well, not so much.

That kiss had been—

"You okay?"

Startled, she looked up into Gabriel's handsome face. "Of course." But instead of sounding coolly professional, she just sounded stunned and unsure. He must have thought so too because his eyebrow arched toward his hairline. "I'm fine, Dr. Alexander," she said, this time managing cool and confident, although it cost her. "But you might want to order me a glass of fresh orange juice. I can't remember the last time I ate."

One corner of his mouth curled. "I'll see what I can do. I'd hate for you to fall at my feet."

Holly rolled her eyes and hurried into the women's locker room. Falling at his feet was a habit she was determined to break.

She grabbed a pair of light blue scrubs, wondering how soon she would be permitted to wear the dark blue scrubs worn by all senior surgeons. It would be the final sign that she had reached the goal she'd work for years to achieve.

But there wasn't time to think about that now.

She quickly changed and headed for OR two, where the team would already be assembled. A ripple of anticipation tripped up her spine when she wondered what was waiting for her because she was fairly certain it would not be anything remotely cosmetic. Plastic surgeons didn't get called out for boob jobs or tummy tucks. Not at eight o'clock at night.

Maybe this would be her chance to show her real skills.

Already scrubbed, Gabe stood patiently while an OR nurse tugged the surgical gown over his shoulders and fastened the rear ties. Holly drank from the bottle of orange juice he'd ordered for her and waited for her turn to scrub up. When she'd finished she dropped the empty bottle into the trash and moved toward the basins.

He slid his gaze from the top of her dark head over the curvy body hidden beneath her scrubs, down her long legs to her surgical booties. Despite the outfit, she looked elegant and composed.

His gaze returned to her face and he frowned at the sight of her swollen lips. Lips he'd practically eaten off her face in his eagerness to taste that wide, lush mouth. Heat crawled up the back of his neck at the memory of the way he'd kissed her—like a green untried adolescent with his first crush. *Jeez.* It was no wonder she'd been stunned speechless. He'd been about as smooth as the Sawtooth Mountains.

"Is something wrong, Dr. Alexander?"

Realizing the nurse was addressing him, Gabe said, "Huh?" and tore his gaze from Holly. *Damn it.* He was standing here staring at her like a lovesick teen stunned stupid by big blue eyes and kiss-swollen lips.

"Is something wrong?" the nurse repeated, and Gabe dropped his gaze to her brown eyes for a moment before shaking off his odd mood. *Yep. Something* is *wrong. I'm wondering if I've lost my mind.*

"Just mentally preparing myself," he told her crisply, sliding one last hooded look at Holly and backing up to the swing doors. "Ready, Dr. Buchanan?"

Holly turned toward him, her face composed and serene as though that searing kiss hadn't happened. Then he caught a quick glimpse of her eyes before her lashes swept down and he realized she was fighting embarrassment and maybe apprehension. Whether for the upcoming procedure or the fact that he'd recently had his tongue in her mouth... he wasn't certain. Only that she avoided any eye contact as she brushed passed him and stepped into the sterile environment.

"Where do you want me?"

* * *

Three hours later Gabe lifted his eyes from where Holly's deft hands skillfully carried out his brisk instructions and recalled her last words.

Where do you want me? He could have told her that he'd have her anywhere he could get her but everyone was listening with big ears and he didn't want to provide fodder for gossip. He had a feeling Holly would do anything to avoid attention.

Over the last couple of hours he'd watched her carefully and couldn't suppress his admiration for her surgical skills. Watching from the observation room hadn't quite given him a sense of her abilities despite the video footage of other procedures he'd watched. He preferred the up-close-and-personal approach...of observation, he hastily amended. Working side by side with surgical residents gave him a better idea of their knowledge, skill and their surgical temperament. Despite what people thought, Gabe believed the difference between a good surgeon and an excellent one lay in their ability to stay calm and motivate people without resorting to temper tantrums or abuse. And he was pleased to discover that Holly's surgical temperament complemented his.

She was also a quick study. Calm and steady in a crisis, she didn't hesitate to follow his murmured instructions. In fact, she instinctively seemed to know what he would do next and was poised waiting for his cue or quickly moving in to assist when he'd appreciate another pair of hands attached to his brain.

The patient had been through massive facial trauma and ended up in reconstruction to stabilize his facial bones before something shifted and ended up in his brain.

Gabe had used a new technique he'd been developing to keep shattered bones stable while the swelling subsided enough for further reconstruction.

By inserting an ultra-thin malleable mesh beneath the

bones and over a specially made saline bag that would mold the cheekbone, he'd re-sculpted the facial bones to approximate the uninjured side. He'd explained that he was attempting to reduce the need for unnecessary additional re-construction, especially in heart patients. He'd only used the procedure once before, on a teenager who'd fallen off his snowboard and shattered his nose and both cheekbones. He'd had to resort to pins and wires to reconstruct the lower jaw, but the cheekbones had healed nicely with the new procedure, which included experimental bone-generating injections.

Once he was satisfied with the position and shape of the mesh-encased bone, he and Holly began the complex task of reattaching and re-forming the tendons in the jaw. It was tedious, painstaking work, requiring each connective bundle to be stretched and sewn onto its counterpart.

When he finally ordered the area closed with acelluar mesh, he could see Holly was exhausted but wildly buzzed. She'd just assisted in a ground-breaking procedure that was a first at WMS and had done remarkably well with the un-familiar procedure. The patient would still need ear, nose and lip reconstruction but that was for some time in the fu-ture when he'd healed from his other injuries and they could harvest skin and adipose cells.

They were finally wrapping up when Gabe noticed a tiny tremor move through her hands. She'd been on her feet since early morning and this had been her third lengthy proce-dure for the day. His gaze snagged hers, recalling how she'd gulped down the orange juice. But that had been hours ago and even he was ravenous.

"You okay there, Dr. Buchanan?"

Startled by the personal question after hours of imper-sonal orders and directions, she blinked a few times before nodding and dropping her gaze to where she was complet-ing the wound closure.

"Any special instructions?" Her voice was low and con-

fident and Gabe relaxed, stepping back from the action.
Rolling the two sets of latex gloves off his hands, he smiled
behind his face mask.

"You're doing fine," he murmured, dropping the latex
into the medical waste bin. "I'll leave you to finish things
while I write up a report and send instructions to ICU." And
with a quick word of thanks and congratulations to each
member of the surgical team, he left the room, stripping off
his gown, mask and bandana.

Leaving her to supervise the final stages was an unspoken vote of confidence that everyone in the room understood. It was well deserved. She might be an adorable klutz
in her personal life but there was nothing clumsy about the
way she handled herself in surgery. She just needed to believe in herself—go with her gut instinct. She knew what
she was doing and she was good. He felt confident that with
practice, expert guidance and encouragement she would
become a highly skilled professional.

A half-hour later he spotted her heading across the hospital lobby toward the huge glass entrance. It was almost two
in the morning and he was tired but knew from experience
that he wouldn't sleep. He was still buzzing with adrenaline
and though he usually preferred to be alone after a challenging procedure, he suddenly yearned for company.

Holly Buchanan's.

The realization that he was actively seeking out the company of a woman who usually went out of her way to avoid
him was a little disturbing. He shook off the unwelcomed
thoughts. This was just a post-operative conversation between colleagues.

That's all.

He quietly came up behind her, ignoring the fact that he
didn't quite believe it himself. "Wanna share a cab?"

Startled, she jolted and flashed a look across her shoulder
that could only be interpreted as guilty—especially when

her gaze slid away from his and color seeped beneath her creamy skin.

Gabe wondered what she'd been thinking and if it had been about him. It wasn't ego that prompted the thought, he told himself, because he rarely obsessed about women or wondered if they obsessed about him. In Holly's case it was only fair considering the number of times he'd been distracted by the scent of her, teasing his senses over the antiseptic smells of the OR.

"I don't know. Are you going to leave me on the sidewalk if I say no?"

He chuckled and steered her through the automatic doors with a hand to the small of her back. "Not this time." Her sideways look was loaded with suspicion despite the shiver he felt go through her at his casual touch. "Promise. Scout's honor."

"I don't believe for a minute that you were a Scout."

"Hey, I'm a helpful kind of guy," he cut in, stepping off the curb and lifting his arm when he spotted a lighted cab half a block away. "Just ask my mom. And I'm always prepared."

"For what?" Holly asked beside him.

He shrugged. "For anything. Everything."

"Like what?"

He paused for a couple of beats like he was seriously considering her question then a wicked glance across his shoulder prompted a raised eyebrow. "Like paying close attention to expiration dates."

She huffed out a startled laugh as the cab pulled up, her look filled with censure for bringing up the condom incident. "With all your surgically enhanced beach bunnies, I would hope so," she said primly as he stepped forward to open the rear door. "They probably don't last long enough *to* expire."

"That's not entirely true," he drawled as she slid across the seat and gave the cabbie her address. He wondered what she would say to the news that his most recent stash had been dangerously close to expiration or that he hadn't thought about replacing them. Which was about as pathetic as his need for her company. Besides, he'd been in a relationship when his mother had been diagnosed. A relationship that had tanked faster than the *Titanic* the second the woman had found out he was thinking of giving up his lucrative practice to move east.

He'd been somewhat preoccupied and had completely missed the signs that she'd already transferred her affections to one of the other partners. When she'd thrown it in his face in a fit of pique, it had just reinforced the notion that he wasn't relationship material. And when all he'd felt had been relief, he'd known then it was time for him to move on. Besides, with his mother gone, there was nothing keeping him in California.

Holly's eyebrows rose up her smooth forehead. "Planning to live dangerously?"

Recalling that they were talking about his stash, Gabe chuckled and slid in behind her. "Hell, no. I have no intention of being caught in that particular web of lies and deceit."

Her eyebrows rose in surprise. "Lies and deceit?"

"Do you know the lengths some women are prepared to go to snag themselves a rich doctor husband?"

"As a matter of fact, I do. It's a common enough problem in med school, even though most med students have huge study loans to pay off and won't make any money for years."

"Yeah." He shuddered. "I had a brief moment of terror in my fourth year that turned out to be a false alarm but a couple of buddies weren't so lucky. One is already divorced and the other heading that way fast." He watched the purity of her profile in the lights off Broadway and wondered at her belief that she was imperfect. Everyone was imperfect. It was what made people interesting.

He recalled something she'd said about her family and

wondered if it had anything to do with her scars. But that was probably just speculation from his dysfunctional perspective.

"What about you?"

She turned toward him and his eyes slid over the elegant lines of her face gilded in warm gold from the streetlights. He'd like to say his examination was purely professional but he'd be lying.

"What about me?"

At this angle her scars were in shadow and he caught his breath at the stark beauty of her bone structure. He knew a lot of women who would kill to look like Holly Buchanan, scars or no scars. In fact, they just made her more interesting and…alluring, especially with emotion simmering in her eyes or when they darkened to a deep smoky blue when she was aroused.

He tried to stretch out his legs and ended up pressing his thigh firmly against hers. Heat gathered where they touched and the slight tremor he felt zip through her sent arrows of hunger and need into his belly until his jaw ached and his skin felt tight.

"Did you have to fight off party animals eager to marry a beautiful rich doctor and live a life of leisure?"

Her mouth dropped open and he could see he'd shocked her. Whether by the beautiful and rich statement or fighting off men, Gabe couldn't tell.

"You're kidding right?"

"Actually, no. I've lost count of the number of guys I've seen checking you out."

She laughed, her genuine amusement filling the interior with warmth.

The sound settled into his gut alongside the clawing lust and made him stare. *Damn.* She should laugh more. It transformed her from merely quietly beautiful to breathtaking, and filled her eyes with warmth and light. She seemed suddenly *alive*. As if she'd forgotten her plan, forgotten to be serious and was simply living in the moment.

He wondered if she'd always been so serious or if her "perfect" family had somehow squashed the life and joy out of her. And the sudden impulse to bring her joy made the hair rise on the back of his neck.

Whoa. A trickle of unease slid down his spine like a drop of icy water. Since when did he fall over himself to make women happy? Maybe he was just tired and hungry. Maybe he just needed a shower, food and about twelve hours of sleep.

She sent him a sideways look filled with mischief and he swallowed. Hard. *Holy crap.* The back of his neck tightened and his chest clenched. *This is bad. Very bad.*

"You're a funny man," she said, her eyes sparkling like deep sapphires.

His eyes dropped to her lips, curved in merriment, and he thought, *Oh, yeah. I'm hungry, all right.* But it wasn't for food. "Maybe you should do stand-up comedy." He opened his mouth, although he had no idea what he was going to say.

"Huh?" was about the sum total of his brainpower.

"People stare at scars, Dr. Alexander," she pointed out gently. "You, of all people, should know that. It's what keeps plastic surgeons in business."

What he did know was that when she spoke, all he could concentrate on was her mouth…and her eyes. The rest just faded away, retreated to the edges of his mind. Okay, maybe not faded because he was always aware of her soft, curvy body, but he didn't see scars. He was too busy fighting the urge to yank her into his lap and study the shape of her with his hands and mouth.

"And maybe you should be more observant."

"What's that supposed to mean? I'm very observant."

"Uh-huh." The cab turned and headed into Brooklyn. Gabe shifted in the seat to relieve the growing tightness behind his button fly but he knew he was fighting a losing battle. With every breath he took, her subtle feminine fragrance filled the cab and flooded his senses. It made him feel a little drunk.

Maybe it was just exhaustion.

He *hoped* it was just exhaustion.

The cab finally pulled up in front of her brownstone and he let out a relieved breath that he could escape before he did something he'd regret.

Like pull her into his lap and suck on that lip. Or run his hands under her snug little jacket to her soft, silky skin and lush curves.

"I'll get that," he said when Holly reached into her purse for the fare. He pushed open the door and slid from the cab. "Consider it payment for leaving you stranded the other night."

CHAPTER SEVEN

HOLLY SCRAMBLED FROM the cab, bumping the door closed
with her hip. Gabriel straightened and stepped back from
paying the cabbie and she had a flash of him as he'd looked
earlier in Theatre. Tall, steady and *hot*—despite the laid-
back charm he'd dispensed with equal measure to everyone on his team.

Although she'd deliberately avoided any opportunity to
observe him in action, she could readily understand why
the surgical nursing staff fought to be on his team. Other
than the obvious hotness factor, he was patient and quick
to break any tension with supportive praise or a few wise-
cracks. He controlled the proceedings and the people around
him with such skillful ease that everyone practically fell
over themselves to please him.

Even her, she admitted with a frown. She could scarcely
believe how they'd worked together—perfectly in sync—
like they'd been doing it together for years instead of just
a few hours.

It had been a little unnerving to discover that the man
she'd been ready to dislike simply on principle wasn't the
spoiled Hollywood celebrity she'd been expecting. And
he was good, damn it. Good at kissing and making the
breath catch in her throat. Good at making her forget the
plan, and really good at saving a man's shattered face. So
good that she couldn't help the little niggle of jealousy at

the way he made things look so easy when she had to work so darned hard.

Sighing, she watched the cab disappear around the corner. A chilly wind had kicked up a few fall leaves and she shivered, hunching into her thin jacket as she looked up into a clear night sky. The moon was large and fat and seemed closer to the earth than usual and the halo around it promised a cold winter ahead.

She usually hated winter but for some reason it made her think of half-empty bottles of wine, a roaring fire and the flash of naked limbs and satisfied sighs. Her pulse leapt and heat rose from deep in her belly until it surrounded her in a shimmering glow—like a banked fire smoldering in her core, just waiting to burst into flame.

Puffing out her cheeks, she rolled her eyes because… because the tangle of limbs in her vision belonged to her and…and…

Another shiver moved through Holly.

She was in trouble.

Big trouble.

Spooked by her realization as much as the wildly erotic visions in her head, she turned and caught him watching silently from a few feet away. And in that instant her perception of him underwent yet another metamorphosis.

With only one side of his face starkly lit by moonlight and the rest in deep shadow, he looked big and bad and a little dangerous. Like a fierce golden angel banished from the heavens for inspiring illicit thoughts and needs in mortal women.

Gone was the laid-back flirt as well as the brilliant innovative surgeon with a knack for getting the best out of everyone. In his place was a man seemingly shrouded in mystery and…and aching loneliness.

The image made her heart squeeze in her chest and she had to resist the urge to go to him, press close to his big body and chase away the shadows she sometimes saw in his eyes.

But Gabriel Alexander was big and bad and beautiful and he certainly didn't need her. He didn't need anyone—especially someone scarred and focused on reaching her goals.

Shrugging off the uncomfortable realization that he was more than the hot, sexy Hollywood celebrity that made her tingle in hidden places, Holly became aware of the intensity of his gaze. His utter stillness unnerved her. She opened her mouth and said, "Did you know that Neil Armstrong was a Boy Scout?" before she could stop herself. "In fact, seventy one percent of astronauts," she continued determinedly, "are believed to have been Scouts."

His mouth curved, dispelling the image of a remote celestial being, and for once Holly didn't care if she sounded like a crazy person. She'd hated seeing that remoteness surrounding him like a thick, impenetrable cloud.

She bit her lip at the memory of the way his mouth had felt closing over hers. Of the way it had created a light suction that had made her breath hitch and her bones melt. She shivered again and this time it had nothing to do with the chill wind blowing from the north, announcing that winter was on its way.

Exactly what her shiver *was* announcing, Holly couldn't tell. Only that it made her heart pound, her skin tingle and her knees wobble like she'd tossed back one too many mojitos on an empty stomach.

"How did we get from being stranded in New York City to Neil Armstrong?"

"The moon, Boy Scouts…" she said a little breathlessly. "It seemed…I don't know…logical." She was helplessly caught in his eyes and the web of heat and tension that surrounded them. A tension that grew thicker by the minute, stealing her oxygen and her bones.

Her stomach chose that instant to growl loudly and she pressed a hand against the rumble, hoping he hadn't heard. But then it dawned on her that her weird dizziness—and possibly the hallucinations of lonely celestial beings—was simply a matter of low blood sugar. Her breath rushed out in a noisy whoosh of relief. *Oh, thank God,* she thought dizzily. All she needed was a quick meal, about ten hours of sleep and she'd be back to normal.

Whew. She gave a husky laugh that sounded a little too hysterical for comfort and headed for the steps leading to her house. *What a relief.*

She opened her mouth to call out goodnight and gave a surprised yelp when Gabriel took her elbow and steered her away from her brownstone.

Toward his.

"What…what are you doing?"

"Hmm?"

"That's your house, Dr. Alexander, not mine."

"I know, and don't you think we're past the stage of calling each other doctor?"

She wasn't going to talk about the kiss and calling him Dr. Alexander helped remind her that he was a colleague. She tugged on her elbow and growled when he ignored her attempts and continued to steer her calmly across the sidewalk, up the stairs past the late-blooming flowers in pots to the heavy wooden door. "Gabriel…why are you taking me to your house?"

The overhead light illuminated his features, revealing a wicked grin and gleaming eyes. She gave a mental eye roll. *Yeesh, so much for the lonely celestial being image.* He looked more like a fallen angel hell-bent on mischief and mayhem.

"Well," he said, fishing his keys from his pocket one-handed and jiggling them till he found the one he wanted. "I'm going to cook." He shoved the key in the lock.

She couldn't have been more surprised. "But…it's after one in the morning."

He arched that mocking brow at her and pushed open the door, drawing her closer despite her obvious reluctance. "You have a meal waiting for you?"

Hovering uncertainly on the threshold, she tugged on her arm and sent him a look filled with feminine exasperation when he tugged her closer instead. "Well, no, but…"

He drew her all the way in and shut the door, instantly surrounding them in deep silence that only emphasized her unsteady breathing and fraying nerves. "You haven't lived till you've sampled my…er…omelets." His grin flashed in response to her squeak as though he knew her mind had descended into the gutter. "Relax. I'll feed you and send you home. Scout's honor."

"I thought we'd established that you were never a Scout."

"No." He chuckled. "You established that."

Holly chewed nervously on her bottom lip as she looked around at the boxes still littering the floor. Not knowing what to do with her hands, she smoothed them over her thighs to disguise their trembling. "Maybe I should—"

He lifted a long tanned finger and placed it gently on her lips. "Food first." His touch made them tingle and she had to fight an overwhelming urge to open her mouth and lick him. Or maybe nibble on that long tanned digit.

She sucked in a sharp breath. *Holy cow.* She'd never had that kind of impulse before, which either meant low blood sugar was making her hallucinate or…or she was headed down a one-way street to disaster. She knew exactly which one *she'd* put her money on but hoped like hell she was just hallucinating.

His eyes gleamed as though he knew what he was doing to her, and in addition to her growing sense of looming disaster was an impulse to bite.

Huh.

Maybe she was just hungry after all.

"It's the least I can do after hijacking you at the gym."

At the mention of the gym, her face went hot and a little voice in the back of her head told her to run and keep running until the memory of those few minutes faded.

But he was taking her shoulder bag and briefcase hostage and to cover her tripping pulse she turned her attention to the furniture dotting the space not taken up by boxes.

It looked like one-tattoo-for-every-skirmish guy had simply dumped everything in Gabriel's sitting room and left.

"Interesting décor," she murmured, thinking there weren't even drapes at the windows and he'd been living here, what…three weeks already? But she'd seen his schedule and he'd probably only had time to come home, shower and sleep before returning to the hospital.

A glance over her shoulder caught Gabriel's grimace as he dropped her bags onto the nearest box. He pulled his black hoodie over his head, briefly exposing his flat, tanned belly before dropping the garment over her briefcase. The stark white T-shirt tested the seams of his shoulders and stretched across his chest, emphasizing the depth of his tan and the width of his biceps. She dropped her gaze to where she'd seen that flash of taut, tanned flesh and wondered why the brief sight of his belly button had seemed so…intimate. More intimate somehow than his earlier kiss. The one that had sucked the breath from her lungs along with her mind and any thoughts about her future.

"I haven't had much time to unpack or find someone to do it for me," he was saying, and Holly had to tear her gaze away from where her eyes had dropped to his button fly before he caught her ogling his package again.

Crap. Maybe she was losing her mind. Maybe this…this feeling of impending disaster was just the first sign of her unraveling mind.

Sucking in breath in an effort to calm her skittering nerves, she said, "My mother has a concierge service that could probably help." *There*, she silently congratulated herself. *That didn't sound crazy, did it?*

"Yeah? That'd be great." He thrust a hand through his hair, tousling the overlong strands even further, and she had to curl her hands into fists to stop from reaching out and smoothing the thick sun-streaked locks. "I hate unpacking," he admitted sheepishly, seemingly oblivious to her chaotic thoughts. "Even if I'd had the time, I wouldn't know where to put all this stuff. I just want my couch and TV set up so I can watch the games."

It was such a guy thing to say that she hid a smile and tried not to imagine his big body sprawled on his huge leather sofa, watching a ball game.

His body radiated clean masculine heat and where his hand touched the small of her back, as he ushered her toward the back of the house, an insidious heat spread across her flesh. She wanted to sink back into him and maybe rub against all that heat and hardness. Just as she'd done earlier.

Get a grip, woman, she ordered herself silently. *Since when did you have urges to lean on a guy for support?*

"I'll…um…call my mother in the morning." Her voice emerged low and slightly husky and she ignored the little smile teasing the corner of his mouth that she was tempted to bite right off.

She rolled her eyes. Clearly she needed food fast or she'd start nibbling on the closest patch of masculine skin.

Looking around his sparkling, modern kitchen, Holly discovered a mild case of kitchen envy but then he started pulling things out of his refrigerator with quick efficiency and she discovered another kind of envy too. The kind where she could wield a corkscrew or maybe a spatula with the same skill she handled a scalpel.

Gabriel Alexander—*the jerk*—didn't seem to suffer from the same challenges. He drew a bottle of white wine out of the cooler and efficiently uncorked it while he directed her to an overhead cabinet for wine glasses.

"I usually prefer beer," he said. "But good food demands a good wine."

She handed him the glasses. "You're a foodie?"

His eyes crinkled at the corners at her disgruntled tone. "You sound surprised."

She sighed, propped her hip against the nearest cabinet

and folded her arms beneath her breasts. "Not so much surprised as envious," she admitted. "I'm a kitchen klutz." His lips twitched and she narrowed her eyes to dangerous slits because she knew what he was thinking. He was thinking the kitchen wasn't the only place she suffered from klutziness.

He clearly valued his life because he just chuckled and handed her a glass of chilled white wine. "You're a cute klutz, though." Then he stunned her speechless by tracing a line of fire across her lips with his finger before turning away to reach for a bowl and a carton of eggs.

It took her a few moments—okay, minutes—to recover her breath and gulp down a mouthful of crisp Riesling. It jolted her back to reality before warming up her belly and clearing her head.

She offered to chop something but he shook his head and said he was off duty. She didn't know whether to be relieved or offended since he'd probably meant that he'd seen enough blood for one day. *Smartass.*

So Holly sipped her wine and watched him work, which, God knew, wasn't a hardship. It was also kind of hot to see a man so at home in a kitchen.

When she was stressed she liked to bake but her efforts were mostly inedible, which sucked because she loved chocolate-fudge brownies and chocolate-chip cookies. Granted, she made an excellent salad but she was ashamed to say she often just nuked one of the casseroles her mother kept stocked in the freezer for her. It was easier than cleaning up after her disasters.

She licked a drop of wine off the back of her hand, impressed by his one-handed method of cracking eggs into a bowl without adding a ton of shells. S*how-off.* He then went on to chop and sprinkle with quick efficiency until delicious smells filled the kitchen and her stomach set up an almost continuous growl.

Over another glass of wine and light, fluffy harvest omelets that he'd teamed with herbed bruschetta, Gabriel entertained her with stories of his youthful exploits. Holly found herself laughing more than she had in years and soon a warm glow radiated out from the center of her chest. She was flushed and light-headed—like she'd drunk too much champagne or maybe sucked on a little too much helium—and she could scarcely believe that she was sitting in a kitchen with the Hollywood Hatchet Man, actually enjoying herself.

Before she could remind herself that he'd seen countless beautiful and famous women—including her sister—naked or that he'd worked in an industry that was mostly to blame for the low self-esteem of ordinary women like herself, Holly swirled the wine in her glass and looked up, only to become snared by the sleepy heat in his eyes. *Yikes*.

"So what about you?" he asked.

Her laughter died and a palpable tension replaced the friendly mood—a tension that had absolutely nothing to do with her opinions of his former career. She blinked.

It didn't take a genius to know what he was thinking. It was there in the glowing heat of his gaze that set her pulse skittering even as a heavy ache settled between her thighs.

It might have been the wine, knocked back on an empty stomach, but her tongue felt suddenly too thick to form words. And like the night she'd slugged back mojitos, her lips went numb.

For long moments she stared into his eyes, hypnotized, until the thickening tension made it difficult to breathe. She blinked. "I...uh..."

Her voice came to her through a long tunnel and the breathless huskiness of it might have shocked her if she'd been thinking clearly...okay, thinking, period. But for the same reason her mouth couldn't form words, her brain couldn't form thoughts.

In slow motion she licked her dry lips and his gaze dropped to catch the path of her tongue. His eyes darkened and he said her name. "Holly." Just her name, but his voice, rough and deep as sin, scraped her already ragged nerves and she had to gulp in air or pass out.

Her skin gave a warning prickle an instant before her brain melted along with the muscles in her thighs.

"Hmm?" She was in big trouble and for some reason she couldn't seem to drum up the energy to care.

His eyes dipped to half-mast and she could practically feel the enormous control he was exercising over himself. It was there in the tight lines of his face and the sudden stillness of his body, which practically vibrated with tension.

And there was absolutely no mistaking the sensuality in his gaze.

"If you're going to leave," he rasped in a voice she scarcely recognized, "I suggest you do it now."

Feeling dazed and strangely lethargic, Holly sucked in a shuddery breath. "Um…now?" Frankly, she didn't know how he expected her to move. She was frozen to the spot by the laser-bright gaze, the gold flecks swirling in the blue-green depths having stolen her ability to move.

"I'm giving you ten seconds." The warning came as a low deep growl that sent a dark excitement skittering through her blood until her body was practically humming with anticipation.

His gaze darkened—"Nine"—and her pulse gave an excited little blip. Instead of scrambling to her feet and escaping, she continued staring into his eyes, wondering at this odd dark need to ride the edge of danger.

A voice in her head ordered her to move, but her body refused to obey. "And then what?"

He leaned forward until there was barely an inch separating his lips from hers. Fascinated, she stared into the swirling depths of his eyes and was stunned by the intensity burning in their centers. He appeared seconds away from pouncing and a thrill of alarm zinged across her skin.

Dropping her gaze, she found his finely sculpted mouth

almost touching hers. *Oh, God.* He was so close she could already feel the searing imprint of his mouth. She eagerly awaited a kiss she knew was just a heartbeat away.

And when he didn't so much as lean in her direction she was the one to make the move that closed the gap between their mouths. Through the roaring in her head she thought she heard him say, "And then I'm going to drag you over the counter and there'll be no escaping until—"

She froze. "Until?"

She felt him smile against her lips and the sensation of it sent a firestorm of sparks exploding in her brain like fireworks. "Until your eyes roll back in your head and..." Her breath escaped in a shuddery whoosh. "And you forget your plan."

She wondered why he was still talking when all she wanted was for him to grab her and make her eyes roll back in her head. Oh, wait. They'd already rolled back in her head to check out the state of her brain and "My plan? What plan?" popped out of her mouth in a breathless rush. It took a few seconds for her words to finally register. And when they did, her head cleared.

"Oh." She abruptly shoved back from the counter, nearly toppling the stool in her haste. For a breathless moment she stood, swaying, and stared at him with wide, panicked eyes. "I...um, I have to go."

Gabriel made a growling sound deep in his chest that had the hair on her arms lifting like she'd got too close to an electrostatic generator. Spooked by the sensations and the thoughts racing through her head, Holly backed away, turned on her heel and walked blindly into the wall.

"Careful," he murmured, and even without looking she knew he was fighting a smile. She rolled her eyes and altered her course, heading down the passage to the front of the house, suddenly eager to escape. Before she did something she regretted.

Like turn and grab him. Like lose herself in his hungry

caresses or forget that she had a plan that had no room for hot, sexy surgeons.

"I have to go," she repeated, feeling a little dazed and more than a little freaked out. Her ears buzzed and her knees shook so badly it was a miracle they didn't buckle and dump her on her ass.

"I'll see you home." His voice came from right behind her and a wide-eyed look over her shoulder revealed him fighting amusement. *Oh, God, how embarrassing.* She increased her pace until the urgent tap-tap of her heels on the wooden floorboards nearly drowned out her panicked thoughts.

"There's no need," she babbled, as she finally reached the door and tried to tug it open, only to find it locked. "Besides, I'm right next...door and—" emerged on a breathless squeak when she swung around to find him only inches away.

Gabriel regarded her silently for an endless moment before he scooped up her shoulder bag and briefcase. She held out a shaking hand. "I'll see you home," he repeated in a gravelly voice, and reached around her to open the door.

She might have escaped unscathed if she hadn't made the mistake of lifting her gaze off his white T-shirt-covered chest, up past his tanned throat, the hard square jaw and sculpted mouth to his gaze.

She froze.

His pupils were huge and very black, his eyes hot and steamy in his tanned face. More blue than green, they blazed with an emotion that was unmistakable even to a social klutz like her.

For long charged moments their gazes locked until with a savage growl Gabriel kicked the door closed and hauled Holly up against him. And before she could squeak out a protest at the rough treatment, he'd backed her against the door and closed his mouth over hers in a kiss so hot it singed her skin and set her hair on fire.

Ohmigod.

Incredible heat poured off him in waves that engulfed

her, threatening to drag her under and drown her in a flood of heat and urgency. *Help,* she thought an instant before his tongue breached the barrier of her lips, surging into her mouth and stealing her breath. *I'm in trouble.*

His tongue slid against hers and the next instant the kiss turned greedy, his mouth eating hungrily at hers. She moaned and desperation rose along with the heat in his kisses. Any thought of escaping faded.

In fact, if this was trouble she welcomed it, along with the slick slide of his tongue against hers and the warm press of his big hard body.

Fever rose in her blood and her skin prickled with an almost embarrassing need to be touched, a need for his big warm hands to slide over her naked flesh.

He broke off the kiss to feather his lips across her jaw to the delicate skin beneath her ear, leaving Holly fighting for breath and the urge to beg him to hurry. Heat exploded along her nerve endings and she shuddered, her breasts tightening until they ached.

She flattened her palms against his belly; the bunching muscles making her hands itch with the need to explore every hard inch of him, including the long thick evidence of his arousal against her belly.

Unable to resist arching closer, Holly angled her head and "Gabriel...I...um..." emerged on a low moan. She wasn't sure what she'd meant to say, only that a voice, somewhere in the far reaches of her mind, was urging her to get the hell away before it was too late. "I have to...I need to I think I should..."

"Don't," he murmured against her throat, and she murmured in dazed agreement. "Don't think." Nipping at the slender column, he drew her skin into his mouth, soothing the small hurt when she uttered a tiny shocked gasp. "Feel, Holly. Just...feel."

Okay, so that was doable. Besides, thinking took too much effort, especially with his mouth, hot and wet as it dragged across her skin, making secret hidden flesh respond with tiny spasmodic clenches.

She stiffened. *Oh, God.* He'd yanked her right to the edge so fast she was fighting to keep from exploding right out of her skin.

Then he was taking her mouth again in a hungry kiss, thrusting a hard thigh between hers and pressing his erection into the notch at the top of her thighs. His big hands slid to her hips, his fingers sinking into her soft flesh as he ground against her, groaning like he was in pain. And before she could give voice to the fiery need clawing at her belly, his muscles bunched and she found herself lifted off her feet.

Instinctively wrapping her legs around his hips, Holly clutched at his shoulders. Muscles shifted beneath her hands, a solid anchor in a world suddenly whirling with chaotic hunger, ragged breathing and wild exhilaration.

Her hair, a dark silky nimbus, floated around their heads. Somehow he'd unraveled her hair with the same ease that he'd unraveled her defenses.

"Hold on," he said, pushing away from the door to stand swaying for a couple of beats, breath sawing from his heaving lungs like he'd crossed the Brooklyn Bridge at a dead run.

"Wha-at?" Holly's lashes fluttered up and she stared at him uncomprehendingly. Without replying, he turned toward the sitting room, cursing when his foot caught on something and he staggered. She squeaked and tightened her grip and his muttered curse of "Damn boxes" became a soothing growl. "Don't worry," he murmured against her mouth between kisses. "I won't let you fall."

CHAPTER EIGHT

HOLLY HAD A brief thought that it was too late for that. Way too late to prevent her heart from getting bruised by a man as handsome and flawless as his celestial namesake.

Then a couple feet beyond the door his knees connected with something solid and the next instant she found herself literally falling. She sucked in a startled breath, tightened her grip, and before she could squeak out a protest she was on her back with Gabe's big body sprawled over the top of hers.

"Oomph."

"Sorry," he breathed beside her ear. "You're heavier than I expected."

"Or maybe," she retorted, unable to prevent the pleased grin from forming when she turned her head to give his earlobe a punishing nip and a groan accompanied the shudder moving through him, "you're not as manly as you think."

His response was an explosive snort that questioned her sanity.

"Oh, yeah?" he breathed, his teeth flashing white in the near darkness as he levered himself onto his elbows. The move pressed his hips closer, setting off an explosion of starbursts behind her eyes. "I'll show you manly."

She groaned, as much at the typically macho statement as the feel of him, long and thick and incredibly hard as he pressed tightly against her crotch. Suspended in sensation and every nerve ending firing simultaneously, it was more than she could handle. More than she could ever remember feeling. And just as a glimmer of panic threatened to break free of the haze of need and greed clouding her brain, Gabriel smoothed a hand from her bottom down the long length of her femur to her knee and back again.

"God, you have no idea how much I want you," he murmured, leaning forward to run his tongue from the corner of her mouth to the sweet spot beneath her ear.

But Holly did, and in response her core melted and clenched in anticipation.

He rose up onto his knees with a low, thrilling growl and reached for the back of his T-shirt, yanking it over his head in one smooth move that left Holly speechless. And not just from the speed of his actions.

His torso was a marvel of masculine perfection that she couldn't help but reach out and touch. She wanted to see him. Wanted to explore his physical perfection with her hands and her mouth.

Unable to stop herself, she slid her hands over his skin, reveling in the tanned skin, taut and smooth across his hard, ridged flesh. His skin was slightly damp beneath her questing fingers as muscles bunched and rippled at her touch.

Light spilled from the foyer, surrounding his darkened form like a full-body halo, and the image of a golden angel, fallen to earth to tempt mortal women to sin, returned. And, *darn it*, she was more than ready to become one of the fallen right alongside.

He was a beautiful man and for a blinding moment of panic she wondered what he was doing with her—what he would say when he saw the rest of her scars, especially the ugly one marring the length of her thigh. But then he fumbled, his hands shaking in his haste to undress, and she realized that she'd made him tremble. Her touch had made him shake like a boy.

It was a little overwhelming.

Then he was unbuttoning his fly. Her eyes widened along with every inch that became exposed and suddenly overwhelming was nothing compared to the sight of him.

"Wha-what are you doing?"

He looked up, his teeth gleaming in the near darkness. He took in her wide-eyed expression and rasped out an incredulous laugh. "Well, Doc," he managed roughly. "This is what's called getting naked. It's what happens before a man pulls out—"

Holly squeaked and slapped her hands over her ears in a move that belied her professional status. Gabriel's eyebrows almost disappeared into his hairline and he leaned forward to pull one of her hands free. "I was going to say protection, Dr. Buchanan," he finished dryly.

She gulped and fought the blush heating her face. "But… but we're in the sitting room."

He sent an indifferent glance across his shoulder at the huge bay window before turning back to renew his button attack. "I can't wait," he growled, lifting her up so he could strip off her jacket.

Her breath hitched at the impatience in his voice, his every jerky movement, and felt her core quiver in anticipation of the big event. "But…the curtains."

"No one can see you." He shoved the jeans down his legs and kicked them aside, settling back to study the lacy shell molded to her curves. "Besides, it's dark."

Not that dark, Holly thought. *You'll see me.* And, oh, boy, she could see him too.

"That's the point," he murmured in a voice as rough and deep as sin, telling her she'd spoken her thoughts out loud. "I can't wait to get you all the way naked so I can see you."

That's exactly what she didn't want.

"All of you, Holly." He dropped his hands to the hem of her shell, his fingers brushing the bare flesh of her belly. It quivered. "And then," he promised in a wicked whisper,

"I'm going to take you upstairs and I'm going to start all… over…again."

Her splutter of surprise ended on a gasp when he whipped her shell over her head and dropped it on the floor beside the sofa. She tried to shield herself from his gaze but he grabbed her wrists to prevent her from hiding.

Finally his eyes lifted and locked on hers. Holly sucked in a sharp breath as heat rose up her neck into her face along with the heat heading for her core. "Gabriel," she whispered beseechingly, but he leaned forward to trace a shaking finger across the tops of her breasts, interrupting her with a growl of appreciation when her nipples peaked.

"Don't hide, Holly."

She turned her face away. "You're…um…staring."

His chuckle was a deep velvet slide across her senses that made her quiver. "God, yes," he drawled. "You're so damn beautiful." And then quietly, as though he was talking to himself, he murmured, "More beautiful than I remember."

Her mouth dropped open and for a moment she wondered if he was hallucinating or drunk. Her words rushed out on a rising squeak of outrage. "You saw me naked? Wh-when?"

His hands soothed a fiery path up her arms to her shoulders where he slid his fingers beneath the lacy straps of her bra. "That black swimsuit doesn't hide a damn thing." He grinned, tugging them down over her shoulders.

Her mouth open and closed a couple times and he shook his head, although Holly wasn't sure what it meant.

"My plan…" she began breathlessly, but he leaned down and gave her a hard kiss.

"Will still be there tomorrow."

"Well, okay, then…" she murmured against his mouth. "I guess just this once…won't…um…hurt. Will it?"

"No." His voice shook with laughter. "I promise it won't hurt." Then his hands slid back over her shoulders. His knuckles brushed her collarbone as he moved to the tops of her breasts. It was difficult to read his expression.

Heck. It was difficult to think.

Then she stopped caring because his sensual mouth slid to her throat and his hand slid beneath the layer of stretchy lace to cup her bare breast. Her shocked breath was loud in the heavy silence and shudders of pleasure leapt and grew at the feel of his warm calloused hand cupping and squeezing her gently, his thumb scraping a line of fire across her flesh.

Her nipples tightened into hard points and she couldn't prevent a moan from escaping at the exquisite pain. Her back arched, the move pushing her breast into his warm, rough palm. Her hands moved across his shoulders, up his neck to fist his warm silky hair, pulling him closer...closer to where his mouth could close over her nipple and soothe the terrible ache he'd created.

If she'd been thinking she might have been horrified by her wanton behavior, but she wasn't...couldn't...because within seconds Gabriel had stripped her naked and the sound he uttered, a mix of pain and strangled laughter that came from deep in his chest, made her ache. And thrill. *God, what a thrill!*

Before she could get self-conscious or beg him to press his naked body to hers, he leaned down and placed a soft kiss on each breast. She trembled at the tenderness of the gesture and when he drew one peak into his mouth, his tongue sliding across her nipple, hot and wet and relentless, a ragged moan tore loose from deep in her throat.

He lifted his head. "Your heart is pounding." She blinked up into his face but his expression was hidden in shadow and she couldn't tell what he was thinking.

"What?"

His eyes were dark and fathomless. "Tell me you want me."

Oh, God. "Wha-a-at?"

"Say it and I'll give you what you need."

Holly sucked in a breath. "I...I..." For some reason she couldn't get the words past the hot lump of need in her throat. He lowered his head and gave her nipple a tiny punishing nip and the words finally escaped on a rush of air. "Ohmigodiwantyou."

And then, tired of waiting, Holly reached up and with hands fisted in his soft hair brought his mouth down to hers so she could kiss him, reveling in the ragged groan wrenched from deep within his chest. She loved the way he kissed; like he was starving for the taste of her. She was starving for the taste of him too and the kiss became an avaricious frenzy of mouths and tongues and grasping hands. And when Gabe shifted and thrust into her, Holly arched her back and begged for more.

Holly begged for more and Gabriel gave her more. More kisses, more climaxes and more…everything. He'd given her more than he'd given any woman in a long time. Maybe ever. And when it was over and she lay in a boneless heap across his chest, Gabe wondered what the hell had happened.

What had started out as simply satisfying a physical need had taken on a life of its own until he'd felt a desperation to take her someplace she'd never been. The only thing was—he'd been taken there too. And he wasn't entirely comfortable with the discovery.

They were both damp with exertion and his thundering pulse almost drowned out the sound of her ragged breathing.

Or was that his ragged breathing?

He felt completely wrung out and too lethargic to move them somewhere more comfortable. Like his bed.

He had plans for Holly and his bed.

After a few minutes, he groaned and lifted a large hand to soothe a line from her shoulder, down her back to her bottom. She was soft and silky and so touchable he couldn't resist repeating the move until she murmured in the back of her throat and shifted against him, so slowly and sinuously that he went instantly hard.

"Someone stole my bones while we were busy," he murmured sleepily, smiling when she grunted softly against his skin.

"Are you sure? I think I feel at least one they left behind," she murmured, her breath tickling his chest and sending arrows of heat into his groin, hardening his erection and fueling his hunger. "If they hadn't also stolen mine I'd help you find it."

She sighed sleepily and nuzzled closer. He slid his arms around her and nudged her closer, burying his face in her wild hair and breathing in her unique scent. It was warm and fresh with a hint of something elusive. Kind of like the woman herself.

Realizing he was breathing in a woman like she was his air, Gabe stilled. He'd never been a nuzzler. Or a cuddler, for that matter. He was usually looking for his clothes by now, ready to make his escape. But he didn't want to escape. In fact, he wanted to find the source of that scent and was prepared to spend the rest of the night searching for it.

He'd thought once would be enough. He'd rock her world, walk her home and go back to getting his life on track. *Hell.* Hadn't she been the one to put a limit on this?

And he'd been okay with that. Surprisingly, only a few minutes had passed since he'd climaxed but was already gearing up for round two.

Clearly he wasn't done with her yet.

"Damn New York thieves."

Her mouth curved against his skin. "What makes you certain they were from New York? Maybe they followed you from California."

"Yeah, and maybe you need to move your knee before you cut off my blood supply."

She snickered and gently shifted her knee until he swore he saw stars. He grunted and grabbed her thigh to halt her movement. She said, "Oops, sorry," in a voice that didn't sound very sincere. "Guess I found that bone." Then she yawned and stretched all those silky curves against him and the stars became firebursts of renewed lust.

"I guess it's also time to go," she murmured sleepily. "Make me go, Gabriel."

He didn't like the idea of her leaving. "Not yet," he said, wrapping his arms around her and heaving up off the couch where he stood swaying for a few beats while he waited for blood to reach his brain. "Later."

Much later.

Holly didn't know how she'd ended up in Gabe's bed. He'd hauled her into the shower, soaped every inch of her and then ensured she'd been completely soap-free with his hands and mouth. And when she'd been a boneless lump he'd wrapped her up in a huge towel and lifted her in his arms.

"And now," he growled in a voice as deep and rough as if he'd just awakened from a night of sin, "I'm taking you to bed."

The thought of getting to explore his big body sent tingles of anticipation racing over Holly's flesh. They'd been too desperate earlier to do more than race for the finish and Holly wanted to explore his big, brawny body with more than her hands. She wanted to use her mouth and tongue and eyes to explore every last inch of him. Her mouth watered.

Oh, and she wanted to discover the rest of him too.

He tossed her roughly on the bed, following her down to nip her shoulder lightly, chuckling when goose-bumps raced over her damp skin. Instead of ravishing her, like she'd thought—okay, hoped—he stretched across her body to pull out an unopened box of condoms from the bedside table.

"I thought you said you didn't have any," she said a little breathlessly, and reached out to untie the towel hiding his goodies from her.

Gabriel snorted out a laugh. "I lied."

"Some Boy Scout you are."

"I lied about that too," he admitted, straddling her body

and unwrapping her like she was an unexpected gift he'd found on his pillow. "I was too busy impressing the girls with my awesome skills." He chuckled at her expression and leaned forward to plant a lightning fast kiss on her mouth. "I meant in surfing." He fumbled with the box. "Damn it," he snarled, "I can't open this thing."

By this time he was panting and swearing and when Holly tried to help, the box popped open and silver squares flew everywhere. Gabe simply snatched one, planted a big hand in the middle of her chest and shoved her backwards. Holly gave a breathless laugh and before she could tell him to hurry, he'd covered himself and was sliding between her legs.

"Now, Dr. Buchanan," he growled, "I'm going to rock your world. Again."

Holly's skeptical snort ended on a long, low moan as he thrust into her, her body stretching deliciously as it accommodated his size.

Oh, God, he totally had, was her last conscious thought. *He'd totally rocked her world.*

Holly jerked awake with no idea of the time or where she was. One thing she did know was that something heavy pinned her to the bed. Something heavy, slightly hairy and toasty warm.

She frowned sleepily and stretched, wondering at the slight ache in her muscles. Like she'd spent the night in... rigorous...exercise... *Oh...my...God*, she thought, sucking in a sharp breath as recollection returned in a rush of heat and embarrassment and...and... *What the heck have I done?*

For several long seconds she lay there, not breathing, until a firm voice in the back of her head told her to get her butt into gear.

Exhaling shakily, she took stock of the situation and tried not to panic. But despite the overwhelming urge to jump up and run screaming from Gabriel's house, she couldn't help noticing the large body surrounding her like a living blanket.

Fine. So one would think that she'd noticed enough of that big, muscular body in the hours they'd spent… Yes, well, she wasn't going to think about that now. If she did she might lose it or…or jump his bones…again.

Kind of like she'd done in the deep, dark hours of the night.

Her face flamed. And when something else flamed deep in her belly, it galvanized her into action.

Holding her breath, she carefully slid out from beneath his sprawling body and felt cool air brush her exposed skin. She shivered. It was touch and go there for a while when every strand of DNA urged her to slide back against the heated furnace while instinct told her to get the heck out of Dodge.

Besides, they'd agreed. One time only. So maybe it had stretched to two and then three…*gulp*…but it was still one night.

Right? Her breath escaped in long whoosh. Right.

She made the mistake of looking over her shoulder at him and got stuck on the stark beauty of his long swimmer's body, sprawled face-down across the huge bed and illuminated by the light spilling from the bathroom. His back was a marvel of masculine perfection, the wide, powerful shoulders tapering to narrow hips, a tight butt—with those sexy little scoops at the sides—and long muscular legs ending in large brawny feet.

For one yearning moment she fought against the desire to reach out and touch but then he grunted and shifted as though he missed her already—boy, she could identify—and the instinct to flee returned.

Stifling a little squeak of panic, Holly slid off the bed and headed for the door. Her clothes were still downstairs—scattered all over his sitting room. *Yikes.*

She paused at the bedroom door, wondering if she should

wake him, but the thought of facing him after everything they'd done was just too disturbing. And considering where he'd had his mouth not too long ago—okay, and where she'd had hers—the last thing she needed was looking into his blue-green gaze and seeing knowledge and…awareness.

She'd rather run through the streets naked. Something she might have to do if she couldn't find her damn clothes.

Turning, she hobbled down the stairs in the dark, wondering where the heck all these aching muscles had come from. She stubbed her toe on her way into the sitting room and hopped on one foot as she hunted around for her clothes, pulling on items as she found them.

After a fruitless search for her underwear, she huffed out an impatient breath and swiftly buttoned her jacket over her unbound breasts. *Damn it*. She felt like everyone would know it too but the longer she lingered, the more chance there was of Gabriel waking and— And that was the absolute last thing she wanted.

So she'd have to ditch her underwear. Darn. And it was new too.

She knew she'd have to face Gabriel sometime but as for right this minute? No way in hell was she sticking around to find her panties and bra. Besides, glossing over someone's scars while in the grip of a desperate hunger was one thing, looking into his eyes in the cold aftermath of a hot night was something else entirely.

No. Not gonna happen. She'd rather lose her underwear and hope they'd disappeared altogether. Poof. Into thin air.

Grabbing her strappy heels, she headed into the foyer, where he'd dropped her briefcase and shoulder bag what seemed like days ago rather than a few short hours. Then with a quick guilty glance over her shoulder she quietly let herself out of the house.

Her one night of screaming exercise was over.

Time to get back on track.

It took her less than a minute to hightail it to her own

front door, all the while looking around guiltily and wishing she didn't feel like an errant adolescent sneaking in
after curfew.

She let herself in and quietly thunked her forehead
against the door a couple times, her breath escaping in a
whoosh of relief and for some reason fighting the urge to
cry. Damn it, what the heck was wrong with—?

"Long night?"

Holly gave a startled squeak and whirled so fast she
nearly fell over. She backed against the door to give her
shaky knees much-needed support and stared wide-eyed at
Sam, slouched casually in the sitting-room doorway, watching her over the top of his mug.

He was dressed in a pair of unbuttoned jeans…and nothing else. Just a few months ago the sight of his sculpted chest
would have sent her heart racing and her tongue swelling in
her throat. But now all she wanted to do was run and hide
and maybe freak out, because she'd seen Gabriel Alexander's awesome body and no one else could compare.

Sam's dark eyes took in her rumpled appearance and
his expression turned wry. "Ah," he drawled, and lifted his
mug in a silent toast.

Holly didn't need any interpretation of the brief flash of
amusement but she opened her mouth and "What?" popped
out before she could stop it.

"Really?" he murmured, his eyes going unerringly to
her mouth then dropping to her neck before lifting to lock
gazes with her. Beneath the humor was understanding. "You
want to go there?"

Holly assumed an innocent expression. "I don't know
what you're talking about."

"You bailed, Buchanan."

Guilt flashed like a neon light behind her eyes.

"I…uh…pfft… No."

"It's okay, Holly," he interrupted quietly, his eyes going
oddly flat. "We've all done it." And then without another

word he turned and disappeared, leaving Holly battling curiosity, embarrassment and a desire to go pull the covers over her head and hope that when she woke she'd find it had all been a horrible dream.

An image flashed into her head of Gabriel's expression as he rose over her and she got a full-body flush and shiver all at once.

Okay. Maybe not so horrible.

CHAPTER NINE

LIGHT STREAMED IN through the cracks in the curtain and fell across Gabe's face. He groaned and tried to lift his head but he felt like someone had run over him with a compacting roller—the ones they used on golfing greens—leaving him flattened.

Almost immediately he realized what had woken him. Firstly, his pager and his cellphone were both buzzing angrily in his ear, and secondly…his bed was cool and empty.

The buzzing was an annoying reminder that he needed to get to the hospital, but the latter…hell, he didn't know what to think. Only that he wasn't happy that she'd left without waking him—especially with the smell of her still clinging to his pillow and sheets.

He turned and sniffed his shoulder.

And his skin, damn it.

Rolling over, he grabbed his phone and told himself it was a good thing because now he wouldn't have to deal with any morning-after expectations. He just hadn't pegged Holly for the hit-and-run type. But what did he really know about her other than she wore class and refinement like a shield, and that she hated being stared at?

She was just another woman, he reminded himself, and he'd learned a long time ago that he wasn't cut out for more than a good time. It was coded into his genes.

Besides, she'd been the one to say this was a one-time thing and one-time things were his specialty.

He growled, "Yeah?" into the phone and listened to the nurse on the other end then ended the call. Then he rolled off the bed and headed for the bathroom. His day promised to be a whirlwind of surgeries and meetings, and with the information the nurse had just given him, he might just have to alter his schedule.

He arrived in ICU just as Holly was leaving. Her stride faltered when she saw him but even though she greeted him, she avoided his gaze. If he hadn't seen the wild tide of color surging beneath her creamy skin he might have thought she'd forgotten his existence the instant she'd walked out his front door.

But it was the sight of her, once again coolly elegant, that made him want to push her up against the wall and mess her up a little. Starting with her hair, which was pulled into a neat French twist.

She hadn't seemed to mind so much last night, he told himself, recalling with perfect clarity the dark, silky curtain framing her face and brushing against his skin as she'd memorized every inch of his body with her mouth.

Just that fast he was hard—harder than he'd been last night. Harder than he'd ever been, because now he knew that beneath the prim little suits and cool, professional mask was an incredibly enthusiastic woman eager to give as much as she received.

"Holly—" he began.

But she interrupted him with a hasty "Excuse me, Dr. Alexander, but I'm needed in surgery," leaving him gaping at her straight spine and swaying hips as she disappeared down the passage with an urgent tap, tap, tap of those sexy slingbacks.

What the—?

"Dr. Alexander?"

Gabe turned to see the head of ICU pop her head out the door. "Yeah?"

"We need you."

Yeah, well. Looks like you're the only one.

He sighed and shoved a hand through his hair, wondering if he'd lost his mind. Here he was, standing staring after a woman who'd made it abundantly clear that he was a one-time deal and… *Hell.* He shoved a hand through his hair again and blew out a frustrated breath. What the heck did he think he was going to do when…*if*…he caught up with her? Grab her? Push her up against the wall and kiss her until she moaned and looked at him through dazed, smoky eyes?

Jeez.

"I'm all yours," he sighed.

And chuckled when the older woman pretended to swoon and muttered a heartfelt "If only," before disappearing back into ICU.

Yeah, he thought dryly. If only. If only his one-night stand hadn't managed to rock his world. Three times.

Realizing he was standing around, obsessing about a woman who wasn't interested in a repeat, Gabe scowled and shoved through the doors, wondering when the hell he'd turned into such a damn girl.

Holly practically ran from ICU as if the paparazzi were in pursuit after an anonymous tip-off. Her skin burned with the mortification of having to face him so soon after…well, so soon. Because, frankly? She'd like to forget last night had ever happened.

Good luck with that.

"Oh, be quiet," she snarled to the annoying snicker in her head, startling a couple of nurses passing her in the hallway. They gave her strange looks but Holly was accustomed to people staring so she ignored them and headed for the nearest bathroom.

Once she made sure she was alone, she headed for the

basins and flipped on the cold water. Breathing like she'd stepped out and found herself at five thousand feet, she splashed her face until her ears stopped ringing and she didn't feel like her head was about to pop off her shoulders.

She made the mistake of looking into the mirror and nearly gave herself a stroke when she encountered her smoky, heavy-lidded gaze. *Ohmigod, I look like I just got lucky.*

A low sound emerged from her throat that sounded too much like a whimper for Holly's peace of mind. Her gaze dropped unerringly to her bruised, swollen lips and she recalled with absolute clarity the way Gabriel kissed. He'd consumed her like she was a rare delicacy he was determined to savor...as if his very life depended on it. A shiver of remembered delight skated up her spine. As if that light suction was an invitation to surrender, her soul along with her body.

Realizing she was hyperventilating, Holly splashed herself again. She didn't think she could walk out of this bathroom and not have people look at her without them knowing exactly what she'd been up to.

Groaning, she grabbed a wad of paper towels from the dispenser just as the door opened. Hoping it wasn't anyone she knew, Holly began patting her face dry.

"Holly?"

She froze. Oh, God. It had to be Tess, didn't it? Tess would see at a glance that she was a total mess.

"Are you okay?"

Sucking in a steadying breath, Holly met her gaze in the mirror, casually patting her skin dry. "Sure," she croaked. "Why?"

Tess moved closer. "Kimberlyn said she saw you tear out of the house this morning as though your underwear was on fire. Did something happen?"

At the mention of her underwear, Holly gave a strangled gurgle that she tried to cover up by coughing. Had something happened? Where to start? Forget that her underwear had practically caught fire—which was why it was currently gracing Gabriel's sitting room. Somewhere.

"No." Not going there.

The next instant Tessa was whipping her around, her eyes concerned as she took in Holly's expression.

"Oh, honey, what's wrong?" she urged. "It is your mother? Father?" Her concern abruptly turned to a gasp when she caught sight of Holly's neck. *"Ohmigod."* Her eyes widened with shock. "You've got a...*hickey*?"

"No! Jeez." Holly slapped a hand over the offending mark she'd discovered this morning—along with at least three others in embarrassing places—when she'd stripped in the bathroom, intending to wash away every trace of the night.

"It is." Tessa looked absolutely delighted by the sight. "It so is a hickey." She grabbed Holly's hand. "Let me see."

Holly squeaked and slapped her free hand over the mark. "Damn it, Tess." She covered her flaming face with her free hand and groaned. "What are we, in high school?"

"Oh, come on." Tessa spluttered with laughter. "Let the pregnant woman have her way or she'll get all hormonal on your ass." Then seeing the embarrassed misery on Holly's face she froze, her eyes going soft and concerned again.

"Oh, honey, why the long face? It's supposed to relax you, not make you tense enough to shatter."

Holly ignored her statement because she felt as though one wrong move and she'd— "I didn't mean for it to happen," she wailed helplessly as she pulled at her collar and turned to study the mark on her neck. There was another high on the inside of her thigh, one in the crease separating her hip and thigh and one—fine, two—on her breasts.

She blushed.

"Did the bastard say something about your scars?" Tessa demanded. "I hope you punched his—"

"N-no-o." Holly spluttered out a strangled laugh. "He didn't. He really didn't," she repeated, recalling exactly what he done to every single one of the blemishes marring her skin. With his lips and tongue.

Tessa's gaze turned sympathetic. "Oh, God, it was awful. Is that it?"

"Will you just stop?" Holly spluttered out on a mortified laugh. "No, it wasn't awful, it was…um…fine." By this time she wanted to climb into the basin and drown herself. Instead, she opened the faucet again, this time burying her burning face in her water-filled cupped hands, hoping Tess would just go away.

So, okay, it had been more than fine. Try spectacular. Amazing. Incredible.

And it was over.

Tessa was still there to hand over a wad of paper towels. Holly muttered her thanks and sent her friend a narrow-eyed sideways glance when her mouth twitched. Tessa quickly lifted a hand to hide her smile.

"Okay, so it was…*fine*," her friend said agreeably, but her voice wobbled as though she was fighting laughter. "Then why are you so…um…upset?"

Holly sucked in a breath and—*thank God*—was saved from replying by a sudden beeping. Whipping out her pager, she glanced at the screen. "I've got to go," she said apologetically, hugely relieved because she had absolutely no idea why she was freaking out and even less idea of how to explain it.

She dropped the wadded paper towels into the trash and headed for the door, yanking it open so fast she nearly bopped herself on the nose.

"I want details, Dr. Buchanan," Tessa called out, and a horrified Holly sent her a you-have-got-to-be-kidding-me glance over her shoulder. She left Tessa standing in the doorway of the bathroom with a secret smile.

Holly managed to avoid Gabriel for a whole week. And it wasn't easy. First, by being so busy she barely had time to think, and, second, by peeping out the bay window to see if the coast was clear before bolting from the house.

The nights? Well, she hadn't been so lucky there. Now that she knew where Gabriel's bedroom was located she realized they shared a wall. A wall that gave her endless nightmares—okay, sleepless nights—and really, *really* hot dreams that made her blush when she thought about them.

It was like her mind had…well, a mind of its own, emerging at night to torment her with images she was able to control during the day. Fine. Mostly control.

Besides, she'd known him, what…six weeks? And for most of that time she'd gone out of her way to avoid him. For most of that time she'd considered him the Hollywood Hatchet Man.

"I won't let you fall," he'd said. But he'd lied. Because Holly was in danger of doing just that and there would be no one to catch her. Fortunately for her, now that she knew the danger she could protect herself by continuing to avoid him like a tax audit.

Good idea.

No problem.

No problem at all.

"How's that working out?"

Holly's head shot up. "What?" She blinked at Dr. Syu over the final stages of the tissue expansion procedure they were performing on a snakebite patient.

"You said 'No problem at all,' and attacked that scar tissue like it's a blight on the butt of humanity."

"Just thinking out loud," she lied, returning her attention to what her hands were doing. Good idea to focus on what your hands are doing, Holly, instead of thinking about "it"…*oh, God*…and him.

Holly finally completed the task of reattaching the expanded skin over the wound and was stripping off her surgical gown.

"Great job as usual, everyone," Lin Syu called as she hurried for the exit. "Holly, go home, get some rest and work out those issues you're having with yourself. The noises in your head are starting to show."

An hour later, she was heading out, exhausted and seriously considering sleeping for the next few days—which she had off.

Her mother had called that morning, inviting her home for the weekend, ostensibly to talk about the charity ball, but Holly knew Delia had other motives. Like casually introducing some unattached guy she just happened to invite—along with a bunch of other people—to her father's birthday dinner.

She planned on showing up for dinner but there was no way—no way in hell—she was getting sucked into her mother's machinations, no matter how well intentioned.

Scrolling through messages and emails that had backed up over the past few days, Holly strode through the automatic doors and barely escaped colliding with a brick wall. Her gasp turned into a muffled shriek when the wall spun around and she caught a glimpse of surprised green-blue eyes.

He must have anticipated another graceful Holly moment—which was ridiculous considering both her feet were once again firmly planted on the ground—because warm fingers wrapped around her wrist and he yanked her against him, hard enough to knock a startled "Omph" from her.

For long moments she stared at the small white button an inch from the tip of her nose and tried not to notice that she was pressed up against the very chest, belly and hard thighs—*oh, boy*—that she'd spent the past week trying not to think about.

And failing spectacularly.

After a couple of beats she lifted her gaze up his throat and square jaw, shadowed with a day's growth of stubble, to his sculpted lips, where she got caught. Her mouth watered. One corner curled with what she knew was amusement at her clumsiness and she had to seriously tear her gaze away or end up drooling like an idiot.

"Good evening, Dr. Buchanan. Fancy bumping into you," he drawled, his deep, intimate voice sending shards of longing arrowing into places that should have gone back into hibernation. Should have, darn it. But hadn't.

Lifting her gaze almost reluctantly, her breath caught at the heat burning in the blue-green depths. Heat, irony and... and an odd emotion she would have sworn was loneliness. It flashed for an instant and then was gone and she was left wondering if she'd imagined it.

Lonely? Dr. Celebrity? *Phfft!* Yeah, right. There were probably a hundred women waiting this very minute for him to turn that sexy, sleepy look their way.

Wrestling with the shocking notion, she managed a strangled "Oh" and stared up at him, wondering why it felt like her chest was being squeezed by a giant fist. Finally realizing she was holding her breath and fisting his pristine dress shirt like she was afraid she would fall at his feet if she let go, Holly unclenched her fingers one by one and slowly exhaled.

She dropped her gaze to where her hands were flattened against his chest and tried unsuccessfully to smooth the wrinkled cotton. The muscles beneath her hand hardened and the raw sound he made, low and deep in his chest, had her gaze flying upwards. His eyes turned black and he sucked in a sharp breath as if he was struggling to control some pretty powerful inclinations. Inclinations she was fighting as well.

Realizing she was stroking his chest, she gave a bleat of distress and used her flattened palms to shove away from him. Okay, so she tried to shove away, but Gabriel's arms tightened and every part of her pressed against him did a happy celebratory dance—especially the parts that could feel *his* very substantial parts...part.

She made a helpless sound that she wanted to bite back

the instant it emerged. He growled out a ragged "Holly" and her head went light and her belly clenched at the rough, raw sound.

It scraped against her jangled nerves, making her shiver. A full-body shiver he couldn't help but notice. He cleared his throat and slid a fiery visual path across her features. "You've been avoiding me." There was accusation in his tone if not in his eyes—which were soaking her up like a sponge.

Guilt sneaked up on her and she blurted out, "Wha—? No...I—" His permanently arched brow rose up his forehead, the very move chiding her blatant lie. "It's just that... I...um." She broke off on a ragged breath and cast around in panic for a believable excuse. But she'd never been particularly good at lying. "It was a one-time thing," she reminded him weakly. "I just thought it would be easier if we didn't...I mean... Oh, God...help me out here."

"Have dinner with me."

The quiet request—that seemed not so much a request as a command—startled her. She cautiously eased herself out of his arms and drew in a lungful of air that smelled only faintly of him. *Thank God.* Plastered up against him, all she'd been able to smell had been something dark and masculine. Something that had hit her brain like a blast of pheromones and had made her sway dizzily, and when he reached out to steady her, she backed up like a startled deer.

She lifted a hand to her spinning head. "Dinner?"

Looking somewhat baffled by her behavior, he shoved his hands into his trouser pockets and stared at her, his normally wicked gaze solemn and a little brooding.

After a couple of beats, his mouth twisted into a wry smile that reminded her of that momentary flash of loneliness she sometimes saw.

"Yeah. You know. Dinner. Where two people walk into a restaurant, sit down, order wine and a meal and then...."

He paused for a moment and just looked at her. Before

Holly could stop herself, an image of what would happen "then" popped into her head and she actually blushed. And because he wasn't blind or stupid, his eyes lit with amusement and those darn dimples made their appearance, stealing her bones and her breath.

"And then we talk."

A frisson of panic skittered up her spine. Oh, God, that was almost worse than what she'd been thinking. Almost but not quite. Because she had no intention of going "there" with him again. She was back to focusing on the fellowship and her future, neither of which had room for hunky surgeons with sexy dimples.

She nervously licked her lips and sent him a wary look. "About what?"

"About why you bailed without at least thanking me."

She blinked. "Wh-a-at?"

"And letting me thank you."

"Uh…thank you?"

He inclined his head and studied her through narrowed eyes that gleamed with a host of emotions she couldn't read. "Yep. And then we're going to talk about you."

"We are?"

"We're going to be working closely together," he pointed out quietly. "And the tension between us is bound to cause gossip I'm sure you'd rather avoid."

She sighed and swallowed the instinctive urge to say she had other plans. Which might have been the truth but if she told him she had a date with her bed, he might offer to join her there. Maybe. Or maybe he was happy with the whole "This is just a one-off thing" and just needed some friendly company.

"Fine," she said a little impatiently, but it was mostly at herself for feeling a bit insulted by his "Then we talk" comment.

Abruptly realizing that she'd dropped her cellphone, Holly sighed and turned. She really had to stop doing this.

Suspiciously quiet, Gabriel bent to retrieve it.

"What?" she demanded, when hooded eyes continued to watch as she shoved it into her purse. He shook his head, a small smile teasing the corners of his mouth as he lifted a hand and tucked a dark, errant strand of hair behind her ear.

The move, the feel of his fingertips brushing her skin, sent a shiver of longing through her. A longing so powerful that even as her nipples peaked and her breath hitched in her throat, she experienced a moment of panic. Damn it. This was precisely what she'd wanted to avoid. Being reminded of what she was missing by the "this-is-a-one-off-thing" promise she'd made.

"Any preferences?"

"For?"

An image popped into her head about preferences and she had to bite back the urge to tell him she'd liked…loved… everything he'd done. So much so that she couldn't stop thinking about him…it.

Realizing she was having hot, racy thoughts while he'd been talking about food, Holly ducked her head to hide the heat crawling up her neck into her face.

Gabriel's warm hand curled around her neck and his thumb slid beneath her chin. Very gently he lifted her face. His expression was filled with simmering heat and gentle humor. "Dinner, Holly. Just dinner. Tonight I need a friend."

After the day from hell, Gabriel had honestly planned for *just* dinner. But that had been before he'd sat across a candlelit table from her and watched her expressive face go through a host of emotions he got dizzy trying to identify. She gradually relaxed enough to smile and laugh at his stories while sharing a little of her childhood—of herself.

"Tell me about the accident," he said, when it was clear that she wasn't going to go there without some prompting from him.

Her laughter faded and he tried not to feel bad. He had

a feeling her plan to avoid everything but her career had something to do with whatever had happened to her.

She dropped her gaze to the tablecloth and fiddled with first the silverware and then her wineglass until he reached out and took her hand in his. Her fingers jerked and a fine tremor went through them.

For long moments she stared at their hands, hers delicate and pale against the tanned bulk of his. Finally she slid her hand away and reached for her wineglass again, downing the contents.

Face pale, she cleared her throat and, still not looking at him, she said, so quietly that he had to strain to hear her, "I was with a few friends at a mall and the company contracted to service the elevators had a reputation for cutting corners. Their maintenance schedule was forged and the elevators hadn't been checked in nearly a year."

She drew in a deep breath. "Well, apparently there was some malfunction that had been reported but ignored. Anyway, I…um, left my friends in the music store to go up a couple of levels to the book store and took the glass elevator because the escalators were out. On the way down I had the misfortune of picking an elevator that a noisy group of boys followed me into. The instant the doors closed they started jumping up and down, trying to frighten me."

Recalling her terror and claustrophobia, Holly paused to suck in a couple of breaths. She hated talking about it and only had nightmares when she was stressed.

"Little bastards," Gabriel muttered, and when Holly lifted her head she caught the hard light in his eyes. Strangely, that angry glitter on her behalf steadied her as sympathy could not.

"They were just kids," she excused, recalling that one of the boys had paid for that stupidity with his life. She lifted her hand in a vague gesture at her scars. "The wheel casing on the elevator car that held the cable wheel snapped and we plunged nearly three stories. There was a lot of glass and twisted steel and…and I was in the way."

After a long moment he said quietly, "It's not your fault."

Holly sighed. "I feel like I should have done something."

His eyebrow rose up his forehead. "Like?"

"Like stop them from jumping up and down."

Gabriel grimaced. "A bunch of teenage boys? Not likely."

Holly gave a small laugh of agreement and shook her head. There was nothing she could have done and she knew it.

"I guess that explains a lot."

"About?"

"Your nervousness in lifts."

Holly groaned. "That was just clumsiness on my part."

His expression was unfathomable as he slid his gaze over her face. "It could have been worse." Yes, it could. She could have died along with that other boy. "You want dessert or coffee?"

Holly let out a shuddery breath of relief. He was giving her the space she needed to get her emotions under control again without spouting off a lot of platitudes. "Coffee would be great, thank you."

Although Gabe hadn't had more than a couple glasses of wine with his meal, by the time they stood on the street outside her house he felt a little drunk. And staring into her upturned face, he discovered he couldn't keep his promise.

He couldn't let her go. Not tonight.

Yanking her against him, he closed his mouth over hers in a kiss filled with heat and a wild desperation that might have scared him if he hadn't finally had his mouth and hands on her after what felt like a lifetime of frustration.

After her initial surprise, she wrapped her arms around his neck and clung, returning his kisses with as much hunger and heat as he felt. *God.* He'd never experienced anything like it. Like she was as eager to get as close as she possibly could, maybe permanently imprint the feel, the taste and the smell of her on his senses.

Unable to resist, he drew her closer and then closer still, sliding his tongue against hers even as he molded her against him until there was nothing between them but a few too many layers of fabric.

And before he knew it they were in his house and he was pushing her roughly against his front door to ravage her mouth and slake his raging thirst.

With shaking hands they tore at each other's clothing until he could thrust a hair-roughened thigh between her silky-smooth ones and take her breast in his mouth.

Clutching at him, Holly arched her back and emitted a long low moan that grabbed his gut and gave it a vicious twist. He didn't know how they ended up on the floor in a tangle of limbs and discarded clothing. He was too busy whipping her up again and again until she was moaning and begging him to take her.

And then he did. With one hard thrust that drew a ragged moan from her throat even as she arched her back, her inner muscles clamping down on him so hard he saw stars.

He froze, eyes locked on her face.

"Did I hurt you?" he gasped, his sides heaving like he'd run the length of Manhattan Island in three minutes flat.

Looking flushed and dazed and so incredibly beautiful that Gabe had to keep a tight rein on his inclination to pound his way to completion, Holly blinked her eyes open. Damn, he thought, feeling a little dazed himself, she took his breath away.

Or maybe that was just because she was wrapped around him like a ball of twine, arching her long, curvy body and making those breathy little sounds that had the top of his head threatening to explode.

"Whydidyoustop?" she demanded in a breathless rush, sinking her nails into his back, sending shudders of pure heat streaking down his spine to his groin.

"You…" He swallowed the groan building in his chest and felt his eyes cross when she slid her inner thighs up his flanks and clenched her inner muscles around him. "Damn it… Holly…stop a minute, will you?"

Her response was to lift her head to give his lip a punishing nip. He shuddered and the last slender thread of his fraying control snapped. Grabbing her hands, he tethered them beside her head and pressed her writhing body into the floor. "Look at me," he commanded, waiting until her eyes fluttered open and locked with his.

"I want to see your eyes when you come," he growled fiercely. "I want to look at you and know I'm all you see… all you feel."

"Gabriel…"

"Just," he murmured, dropping a hard kiss on her mouth, "just as I see only you." And then with a groan that seemed to originate from somewhere near his knees Gabe withdrew only to slam back into her body as though to fuse them together for all time.

Light burst behind his eyes and Holly cried out, trying to wrench her hands free, but Gabe knew if she touched him he'd lose it big time. He was that close.

He wanted this to last. Needed it to last.

Slowly, savoring the incredible sensations of being inside her again, Gabriel withdrew and with his eyes locked on hers entered her more slowly. She gave a soft mewl and her eyes darkened to midnight. Dropping his lips to the soft spot at the base of her throat, he smiled at the feel of her pulse fluttering wildly beneath the delicate skin.

Her hands tightened into fists. "Gabriel," she pleaded softly, her breath catching when he softly kissed the outward sign of her rioting emotions. Hell, his emotions were all over the place too and when he lifted his head and stared down into her flushed face the world tilted wildly on its axis. Some inexplicably painful emotion gripped him then and before he knew what was happening he'd lost the last fragile grip on his control.

All too soon Holly was arching in his arms, her smoky gaze locked on his as he pounded into her like he couldn't get enough—would never get enough. Then her eyes went dark, blind, and with a low ragged sound she went hurling off the edge, leaving him helpless against the violent storm crashing through him.

CHAPTER TEN

HE DIDN'T KNOW how long they lay there in a tangle of limbs, damp skins clinging as their thundering hearts slowed and their ragged breathing eased.

Tiny aftershocks spasmed through her, keeping him hard until she finally drew in a shuddering breath. "Oh, God," she rasped. "Wha—?" He felt her swallow convulsively and draw in another wheezing breath. "What the hell was that?"

He grunted. Besides being the only response he could manage, he didn't have a clue either. He hadn't had nearly the number of relationships that people liked to believe but he was thirty-five years old, for God's sake. Granted, he was more experienced than he cared to admit but not even when he'd been a randy fifteen-year-old had he lost it so completely.

With a groan he got his elbows beneath him and levered the bulk of his weight off her. He was about to roll off her but he caught sight of her face and he froze. She looked dazed.

His chest squeezed and he lost his breath all over again. This time with dread. "What?" She stared at him for a couple of seconds then blinked as though coming out of a trance.

"Sorry, what?" she rasped.

He frowned, beginning to think something was seriously wrong. "Are you okay?"

Her cheeks reddened. "Define…um…okay."

"Oh, God, I hurt you, didn't I?"

"What?" Her eyes widened. "No! Why would you think that?"

"You're acting weird."

Her eyes slid away. "Oh. Well…I…um…" She paused and licked her lips, another blush working its way up her throat. Her pulse beat a rapid tattoo in her throat. "You're… heavy, is all."

"Uh-huh." He didn't buy it for a minute. Especially not now when he'd shifted most of his weight off her. "Try again."

Her gaze slide to him and then away. She licked her lips, looking adorably flustered.

"You're saying I didn't hurt you?" he pressed. She gave quick headshake and tried to wriggle away but he was still buried deep, tearing a distressed squeak from her throat when he hardened even more.

"Holly."

Her breath escaped in a loud whoosh along with an eye-roll. "You're…um…you're still hard."

A smile of pure deviltry curved his mouth. "Oh, yeah. And I'm going to take care of it. Right now."

"Now?" she asked a little breathlessly, her eyes going wide. "So soon after…well, that?"

"Oh, yeah," he repeated, his voice emerging on a low growl when her inner muscles fluttered around him. "As soon as I can move without my blood pressure shooting out the top of my head, I'm going to try and repeat that."

She giggled and smoothed her hands down over his abs to where they were locked together like two puzzle pieces. Drawing in a ragged breath, Gabe gritted his teeth and slipped out of her body. He froze when she made a tiny sound of protest then surged to his feet in one determined move.

"But I'm not doing it here," he said, reaching down to

wrap long fingers around her wrist. With a tug he hauled her to her feet, wrapping his arm around her waist when her knees threatened to buckle and dump her on her very delectable ass. She clutched at him. Okay, they clutched at each other, because if he was being perfectly honest here his knees were a little shaky too. Especially when her incredibly good parts bumped his.

"Bedroom," he croaked.

"Can't move," she managed sleepily, smoothing her hands over his flanks to his back. And in the wake of that languid caress, his skin tightened and he was suddenly impatient for her all over again.

"That's okay," he murmured against her temple. "I've got this." *I've got you.*

Unlike the last time when she'd awakened to find something heavy and deliciously warm pinning her to the bed, Holly knew exactly where she was and how she'd got there.

And like the last time Holly blamed the wine. Okay, maybe it was also because she couldn't resist dimples and wicked blue-green eyes.

She was weak.

And it was all his fault.

For two years she'd managed to concentrate on her surgical career without once forgetting her plan or losing sight of her goal. Okay, and maybe there'd been no one who had tempted her, but then Dr. Hot Stuff had flashed his package and his dimples her way.

Her breath hitched.

Darn dimples.

And darn the hard warm body currently pressed against her back—heavy arm pinning her to the bed and a large hand cupping her breast—tempting her to repeat her mistakes.

Holly didn't normally repeat mistakes but it seemed all

he had to do was ply her with food and wine and she was a goner. No more, she told herself, she was going to be strong.

Slowly, carefully, she lifted each finger and then the rest of his hand from where it cupped her breast. Just as she was about to inch out from underneath his arm he moved, pulling her back against his body. His very aroused body.

She slammed her eyes closed with a muffled little squeak, hoping he'd think she was just moving and making noises in her sleep.

"Where are you going?" His voice, a sleep-roughened rasp in her ear, had her body tingling in unmentionable places. Holly held her breath, conscious of her heart trying to punch its way through her ribcage. She wondered if he could feel it too since the panicked *boom, boom, boom* shook the bed like a five on the Richter Scale.

He moved a hair-roughened leg between hers, his huge sigh disturbing the long tangle of hair obscuring her vision. Her breath escaped in a silent hiss when she felt something hard poke into her bottom. She rolled her eyes and stifled a snicker. *Damn.* Who'd have thought the sexy surfer would be a snuggler? Or that he'd awaken with his surfboard between them.

She waited until he was breathing evenly again before easing out of his hold. Once she was clear she edged her way carefully across the huge bed and was just congratulating herself on having made a clean getaway when he said, "Do I have to tie you down?"

Slapping a hand over the shriek that emerged, Holly cast a wide-eyed look over her shoulder and caught sight of Gabriel lying sprawled across the bed in nothing but gloriously tanned skin, looking at once satiated and exasperated.

Looking better than he had any right to look after being up half the night.

Finally realizing he was studying her nudity with open interest, she gave a strangled squeak and grabbed for the sheets. Unfortunately, she had to stretch about a mile for them and because he was closer he simply snagged the soft cotton and yanked it out of reach.

Her mouth dropped open and she glared at him for a couple of beats until she realized she was caught out in the open in nothing but her Wildman from Borneo hair.

Slapping both hands over her naked breasts, Holly blew hair out of her face and narrowed her eyes as she considered her options. It was either sit there like an embarrassed virgin or get up and saunter from the room.

Buck naked, of course. Because her clothes were littered all over Gabriel's entrance floor. Again.

He must have read her mind because he simply arched his eyebrow and waited. She finally sucked in air and made a dive off the bed, but he moved like lightning and before she could clear the edge of the bed he caught her, fingers wrapped around her ankle, holding her as effectively as if she'd been shackled.

Holly gasped at discovering she was face down and hanging over the edge of the bed—*oh, boy*—her position giving Gabriel a view that made her blush.

She gave a squeak of distress because he tightened his grip and began to reel her in until she was all the way back on the bed. There was a moment of silence. She sucked in air and waited—anticipation buzzing through her blood like a swarm of excited bees.

His hand smoothed a path of fire up the back of her leg to her knee. There he paused and something brushed the soft skin. Fiery heat that she'd thought extinguished in the dark early hours of the morning arrowed right up the insides of her legs to ground zero and Holly had to bite back a whimper of need. A quick glance over her naked shoulder told her he'd kissed that tiny erogenous spot and was looking up the long length of her thigh. Right where his touch had sent an erotic message.

Squirming with embarrassment, she gasped out a horrified "What are you doing?" drawing his hooded gaze.

"You planning on bailing again?"

Darn it. She'd wondered when he'd bring that up again. "No," she squeaked, feeling her entire body blush. "I, um… I need the bathroom. Really, really badly."

Holding her gaze, he bent his head and nipped the curve of her butt. Her muscles quivered. "If you're not out in three minutes I'm coming to get you."

"What? But…but I've got to…um…go. I've got an… um, thing."

"You've got the day off," he pointed out. "Heck, you've got the next three days off and so do I." He let that news sink in before saying, "I want to you spend them with me," in a voice that washed a heady eroticism over her. But it was his expression that had Holly stilling. He was preparing for her to say no.

"You…do?"

His gaze locked with hers, his thumb brushing the curve where her bottom joined her thigh. "Yes," he said seriously. "I do."

Over the long line of her naked back Holly searched his expression then nodded. She had to swallow the huge lump lodged in her throat before she said breathlessly, "Okay, but I have to attend my father's birthday dinner tonight and I still haven't got him a gift."

"We'll go together."

Surprise had her blinking. "Shopping? Or dinner?"

"Both," he said, before abruptly stilling. After a few beats he lifted his gaze from where he'd been watching his hand rub her bottom, his expression carefully neutral. Her pulse fluttered. "Unless you don't want me to meet your family." His hand slid away and he sat up, looking all hot and naked and pissy. "Unless you already have a date."

"No!" She turned, wondering what that was all about. But she had other things to consider. Like how she would introduce him to her family. Her mother would be over the moon that Holly had a date and would start reading all sorts of things into it, but Paige…? Unless…

Her belly quivered and she racked her brains, trying to remember if her mother had said anything about Paige being off displaying her expensive body for the camera somewhere.

The last she'd heard, her sister was in Fiji with her current lover. Holly hoped she stayed there.

In fact, taking Gabe to dinner would solve a lot of problems, the most urgent one being her mother. Delia kept throwing men at Holly like confetti, hoping she would find one acceptable, marry and give her more grandkids to dote on.

"No," she said again, this time more calmly as she mulled the idea over in her head. Not only would it keep her mother off her back but she wouldn't feel like a permanent fifth wheel. Or that awkward nerdy kid dragged to every social engagement against her will.

A smile grew. "I think that's a great idea." She paused and frowned as she thought about what it would be like for him. "Are you sure you want to be bored…? I mean, it's just family."

Gabriel's expression darkened. "You don't think I'll fit in?"

She rolled her eyes and huffed out a laugh. "God, no." Then, seeing his face, she hurried to explain. "That's a good thing, believe me."

"It is?"

"Heck, most of the time I don't fit in. Especially if my sister's there and if mother's invited all their friends." She made a face. "Believe me, boredom is nothing to what you're likely to experience with a bunch of dry attorneys and judges discussing the law." She shuddered. "If it wasn't my father's birthday, I'd invent something serious and cry off."

After a long moment during which his blue-green eyes

searched hers Gabriel nodded, a small smile lifting one corner of his mouth. "Okay, then," he murmured softly, reaching out to snag her hand. He yanked her down and rolled
her beneath him, his eyes hot and heavy. "What should we
do in the meantime?"

If Gabe had forgotten exactly where Holly had come from,
her childhood home reminded him. Set in the town of Stony
Brook, Long Island, it screamed old money. Surrounded by
expansive lawns and trees heavy with autumn foliage it was
everything he would have had if not for Caspar Alexander.

Pulling the rental to stop in the sweeping drive, he shook
off his odd mood and ignored the fact that he might be nervous. He wasn't. He had nothing to be nervous about. He
might enjoy spending time with Holly Buchanan—in and
out of bed—but he knew from experience that he wasn't in
any danger of falling for her. At least, not the forever kind.
Beside him she drew in a deep breath before flashing him
a brave smile. "You ready?"

She's nervous, he thought, exiting the luxury vehicle and
rounding the hood to open the passenger door. She nibbled
on her bottom lip, looking uncertain, which prompted him
to ask, "The question is, are you?"

"Me?" She shrugged, looking stunning in a dark blue
silky sheath the color of her eyes. "They're my family."
She drew in a deep breath, expelling it in a long whoosh
when he grabbed her hand and drew her from the vehicle.
"They can just be a little overwhelming…and protective,"
she warned. "My mother especially. She'll probably hug
you and maybe flirt a little."

"That's okay, Holly." He smiled, giving her hand a reassuring squeeze. "I'm good with that, especially if she's as
beautiful as you."

"Oh, I'm nothing like my mother," she said with a laugh,
and turned to gather up her purse and her father's expertly
wrapped gift. "She's beautiful and loves people—really

loves having them around. She doesn't look a day over forty and people often mistake her for Paige's older sister. My mother loves it but Paige?" She gave a short laugh. "Well, Paige's another matter altogether."

Before they'd taken a dozen steps a tall, slender blonde burst out of the house and swept down the stairs to gather Holly into a fierce hug. "Oh, my darling, I'm so glad you're here."

With such evident emotion shining in her beautiful face, there was no doubt that Delia Buchanan loved her daughter. Gabe felt his chest tighten and lifted a hand to rub the ache that settled next to his heart. He hadn't realized until this moment just how much he missed his mother and wondered if Holly knew how lucky she was.

Delia moved back to plant a kiss on each of Holly's cheeks. "Your father's going to be thrilled. It's been an age since you were home," she said chidingly.

"Hi, Mom," Holly said, kissing her mother's cheek. "Missed you too."

"Oh, let me look at you," she murmured, drawing back to study Holly's face. Her eyes, so much like Holly's, widened. "Oh, darling, you're…glowing. And since you left word with Rosa that you're bringing someone I guess I owe him for that."

She turned toward Gabriel and he got his first good look at the ex-beauty queen. She was indeed stunning and so much like Holly that he could understand people mistaking the two of *them* for sisters, as they had very similar bone structure and the same eyes.

She squirmed. "We just spent the day on Staten Island and the ferry…and, well, stuff. Gabriel's a…a surgeon."

He arched his brow at her a little challengingly but she sent him a desperate look that begged him to back her up.

"Don't be silly, darling. If anyone can get you out of that hospital and into the glorious fall air then I'm over the moon with gratitude." Still clutching her daughter's hand, she smiled at Gabe. It lit her entire face from within, exactly the way Holly's did. "And he's so handsome too, darling. Where did you find him?"

Holly blushed and elbowed her mother. "Mom, jeez. He's standing right there."

"I know," Delia said, sounding thrilled. "Isn't it wonderful? Oh, don't mind me." She laughed, taking Gabe's face in her hands and reaching up to kiss his cheek. "It's simply been an age since Holly was home, let alone brought a date."

"It's a pleasure to meet you, Mrs. Buchanan. I hope I'm not intruding on your family occasion."

"It's Delia, and don't be silly." She tucked her hand into the crook of his elbow and led him up the stairs to the front door, leaving Holly to follow. "It's just family and a few close friends. Bryant and Richard are here so you won't feel like you're the only young man among all the stodgy old men."

"It's been a long time since a beautiful woman called me a young man," Gabe said, smiling over his shoulder at Holly, who rolled her eyes and bumped the front door closed with her hip. "I can see where Holly gets her sweet nature."

There was a short silence and then both Holly and her mother burst out laughing. Delia grinned at him, gave him a fierce hug. "Oh, you're sweet. I think we'll keep you." She turned to Holly. "Darling, why don't you two go on into the salon? I'm just seeing to some last-minute food emergencies and your father's sitting around like a king waiting for his adoring subjects. And if he's smoking those awful cigars, remind him about what the doctor said."

Once Delia disappeared, Gabe drew in a deep breath and turned to Holly with a look of confusion. "I did warn you."

"No, I'm confused by the laughter."

"Oh, that." She shrugged. "No one's ever called me sweet before. Believe me," she added, when he arched his brow, "I was a really difficult kid. I was skinny as a pole, wore glasses and braces and I was forever walking into things and tripping over my feet. I used to hide when it was time to attend social functions."

Gabe's mouth curled up at one side and he let his gaze slide over her, from the intricate twist she'd managed to coax her long dark hair into, over her face and breasts to the slender, curvy body and dark blue strappy heels that made her legs look incredibly long.

"Well...maybe you're still a little accident-prone but no one could call you a pole and..." he leaned forward to add into her ear "...I know exactly how sweet you are. *All* over. Especially that spot..."

"Now, this," a coolly amused voice came from somewhere over Holly's shoulder, "is the true meaning of sweet." Feeling Holly stiffen, he flicked a curious look over her shoulder. In the middle of the stairs leading to the upper floors—and illuminated as though she stood in a spotlight for maximum effect—was a woman Gabe couldn't help but recognize. He'd have to be living in Outer Mongolia not to recognize supermodel Paige. And suddenly those weird flashes of familiarity made sense. Not to mention he'd also done a host of cosmetic procedures on the woman a couple of years ago.

Conscious of the odd tension pulsing off Holly, he straightened, watching as Paige Buchanan swept down the stairs in something long and floaty, trailing her hand on the banister as she descended. "Ms. Buchanan."

"Oh, Gabriel," she sighed with a pout as she floated closer, reaching up to pat his cheek. "There's really no need for all the formality. Besides, you've seen me naked and had your hands on my breasts...and...well, everywhere else." She blushed prettily and fluttered her lashes, before looking up at him in a move he remembered as being a tad overdone. It was as if she was constantly playing to an invisible camera. Her hand touched his arm. "And now here you are, with...Holly? That is surprising." She finally turned to her sister and did the air-kiss thing as Holly stood looking suddenly remote and cool. "Oh, sis," Paige crooned. "I'd love to hear how you two met. I'll bet it's an…interesting story."

"Not so interesting," Holly said smoothly, sending Gabe a hooded glance that he found difficult to read when before she'd been an open book. He narrowed his eyes on her, wondering at the undercurrents suddenly swirling around him like a thick fog, as well as the white-knuckled grip she had on the gift she clutched. "Gabriel's taken the opening in Plastic and Reconstruction."

Paige's smile widened. "Well, now, that's an amazing coincidence as I'm thinking about having a few things done."

Out the corner of his eye Gabe caught Holly's eye-roll. "I don't do cosmetics anymore," he told the model. "Dr. Syu at West Manhattan is an excellent cosmetic surgeon. Besides, you're beautiful enough without resorting to surgery. I told you that before."

"I don't want Lin Syu," she said, gazing up at him imploringly. "I want the best." She sent Holly a quick look under her lashes. "I want you." And for some odd reason Gabe got the impression she was talking about something else entirely. "Besides, it's just a few minor tweaks. Anyway…" She suddenly tugged playfully at his arm and drew him toward the double wooden doors to Gabe's left. "Do you have a drink? I can't believe Holly hasn't offered you a drink yet."

"We only just arrived," he said coolly, casting a look over his shoulder in time to see Holly's expression go carefully blank as if all the vitality had been sucked out of her. "In fact, we were on our way to see your father."

"Oh, don't worry about that. Holly will handle it and you can meet Daddy later. Besides, I'm parched and I'll just bet you are too."

Gabe was startled by the barely concealed hostility. "No. I—"

"It's fine," Holly said without expression. "You go ahead.

I'll just…" She gestured to her right before turning and hurrying down a short passage.

Gabe resisted Paige's attempts to pull him through the doors. Carefully removing her hand from his arm, he turned and narrowed his eyes at her.

"What was that all about, Ms. Buchanan?"

She looked startled. "I…I don't know what you mean."

"That little show you put on for Holly."

A secret little smile tugged at her famous mouth and she snuggled close, pressing her equally famous breasts—that he'd provided—against his arm. "Oh, relax. It's just a little game we play. We bring dates home and the other tries to lure them away. She does it all the time."

Gabe sincerely doubted that. His skepticism must have shown because Paige laughed, looking incredibly beautiful but to his discerning eye there was something off with her. A hardness in her eyes, a brittleness to her laugh.

"Oh, come on," she wheedled. "Let's have a drink. I'm in a party mood. Besides, Holly will be presenting Daddy with her incredibly thoughtful gift and hoping for a little paternal attention." She rolled her eyes. "You don't want to see that, believe me. It's nauseating in its desperation. And," she drawled lightly, "I've resolved never to gag before dinner."

CHAPTER ELEVEN

HOLLY FOUND HER father in his den with a couple of his closest friends, puffing on cigars and talking shop. Her breath caught in her throat, just as it used to when she was little and couldn't believe that such a handsome man was her father. Just as it did whenever she approached his den, wondering if he would even remember her name.

He was laughing as he turned and caught sight of her hovering in the doorway. "Holly," he said, discarding the cigar and dropping a brief kiss on her cheek when she stepped into the room.

"Happy birthday, Dad," she murmured, handing him his gift.

"I bet old Bergen wishes he was half as beautiful as you," her father's oldest friend said when he hugged Holly. "It might sweeten his disposition." He turned to the room. "Isn't she just like her mother?"

"The spitting image."

Holly rolled her eyes. It was a ritual everyone in the room had played since she'd been a shy, withdrawn teenager.

"When can I make an appointment?" her father's senior partner said, rising to greet her. "My foot is bothering me again. I need a second opinion."

Laughing, she hugged the old man. "If you're thinking about a facial reconstruction, Uncle Franklin, I'm your girl. But if you want to improve your fasciitis, you'll have to stop drinking red wine and smoking those cigars. Oh, and you might want to cut back on the red meat."

"You're as bad as Dr. Bergen," Franklin said in disgust, but his eyes twinkled, making Holly laugh.

"The girl's right, Frank," another partner added cheerfully. "Maybe a facial reconstruction will help. God knows, Sophie would probably approve. She might even agree to that second honeymoon you've been talking about."

With laughter filling the room, Holly left them to shop-talk. She headed for the salon and found Gabriel with her brother, Bryant, while Holly's sister-in-law chatted to the other guests. He looked perfectly content with Paige cleaved to his side like a surgical skin graft. But, then, why wouldn't he? Paige drew men like flies to a cadaver. She was beautiful, fun and exciting. According to a top men's magazine she'd also been voted as one of the ten sexiest women in the world. What man would want to look at—be with—*her* when Paige was around?

He looked up and smiled when he saw her but Paige pulled on his arm to get his attention. With her eyes on Holly, she leaned into him and reached up to brush some non-existent lint from his lapel before smoothing her palm down his abdomen to the waistband of his pants.

It was a game her sister had played since they'd been teenagers and suddenly her head was pounding like she'd spent the day drinking mojitos. She knew exactly how hard and touchable Gabriel's abs were and hated…really, *really* hated seeing her sister slide her hands over him as if she had the right, all the while silently challenging Holly with her eyes.

"Go over there and get your man," Delia murmured, slipping her arm around Holly's waist.

"He's not my man, Mom," she said wearily, and lifted shaking fingers to rub at the pain blossoming behind her eyes. "We're just colleagues."

"Oh, honey, I saw the way he looked at you and—"

"Yeah," she interrupted, turning away from the concern in her mother's gaze. "He's wondering how to ditch me so he can have Paige."

"Oh, my sweet girl. No, don't you look at me like that, Holly Noël Buchanan," Delia snapped. "You are sweet. I know we joke about it but you are, even when you're being an idiot."

Holly sent her mother a half-smile. "You have to say that, Mom, you're my mother. But I can't compete with Paige. I never could, and you know it. No, Mom, don't," she said wearily, when her mother looked like she was about to object, vehemently. "Let's be honest here, not many women can compete with someone on the top ten sexiest women list."

"You're not just any woman, Holly," Delia snapped. "And being sexy is more than flashing your body and pouting for a camera."

"It made her famous."

"It also made her spoiled," Delia said firmly. "For which I blame myself."

"It's not your fault, Mom. Paige always craved attention. She got it."

"And you shunned it."

"I liked books more. Anyway," she sighed, waving her hand dismissively, "I was just wondering what happened to Darian. I thought she was over the moon in love and planning to become Mrs. Darian Something…and now here she is." *All over my date.*

"It was Andreas," Delia corrected quietly, and Holly could see her mother's concern for Paige in her worried expression. "Darian was the one before." She sighed. "And like Darian, Andreas apparently forgot to mention that he was already married."

Holly rolled her eyes and nearly yelped when her brain threatened to explode inside her skull. She didn't say what was obvious to them both: Paige liked taking other women's men. It made her feel powerful and…desirable. And now it looked like she wanted Holly's. Again.

If only to prove she could.

Not that Gabriel was hers, she amended quickly. Two incredible nights didn't make him hers any more than it made her his. He was free to do anything he wanted and she…well, she'd had her exercise and now it was back to her plan. A plan that didn't include getting worked up over a man who could make women scream one minute and cozy up to another the next.

Holly pretended, for her mother's sake, to have a wonderful time but she couldn't wait for the evening to end. Her sister had somehow switched the name settings so she could sit next to Gabriel, whom she proceeded to manipulate with soft touches, coy looks and, Holly was certain, feeling him up beneath the tablecloth. Heck, she'd seen it all before. A hundred times.

Holly sat between Franklin and Richard Westchester, the son of a family friend that Delia had invited before Holly had called to say she was bringing a date. And if she smiled a little too brightly at Rick and leaned toward him a little too closely, Holly told herself it was simply because she was being a gracious dinner companion. It certainly wasn't because Gabriel was being attentive to Paige or watching *her* with a brooding expression.

The instant dinner was over she shoved back from the table and quietly excused herself. Her head throbbed like an open head wound and she headed upstairs to her parents' bathroom.

After downing pain meds and splashing her face with cool water, she made for the French doors that led to the balcony. Maybe a little fresh air and alone time would help soothe her aching head before she put on her game face and returned downstairs.

She let herself out and shivered in the cool night air but it was dark and quiet. Wrapping her arms around herself to ward off the chill, she leaned her hot forehead against the old stone pillar, staring out across the lawn toward the water.

She'd been out there a minute only when she became aware of murmured voices. One deep and achingly familiar, the other…well, it wasn't a surprise to hear her sister's smoothly amused tones.

She didn't mean to eavesdrop and wasn't in the least bit interested in Paige's plans to have some imaginary defect fixed, but when she heard her name she couldn't help peering over the balustrade and holding her breath so she could listen.

Paige was draped artfully in a pose she often used to display her amazing body to maximum effect. She took a sip of champagne from the flute she'd brought from the dinner table and Holly had to wonder how many times it had been refilled. She wondered too if her mother had noticed that as dinner had progressed, Paige had become more and more flushed and animated.

Watching now, she saw Paige tip back her head, luxurious waves of silvery blonde hair cascading over her naked shoulders. For a moment she thought Paige looked right at her and although she was in deep shadow, Holly drew further into the darkness.

"I came with Holly," she heard Gabriel say. "What do you want, Paige?"

"I just needed some fresh air and as I'm not feeling well…" her breath hitched dramatically "…I thought having a doctor around would help."

"You don't need a doctor to tell you that laying off the champagne would help."

Paige gave a dramatic sigh and set her glass aside before pushing away from the balustrade. "You're right," she purred, sliding her hands over Gabriel's chest and linking her arms behind his neck to smile up into his face. "You've got me. I know you came with Holly, but it's clear she's otherwise occupied and…well, I just didn't want you to feel left out, that's all."

Holly wondered if she was the only one who'd noticed that Paige had been the one feeling left out, which was why she'd attached herself to the best-looking man in the group.

"I saw you change the seating arrangements," he observed, putting his hands on her waist, whether to push her away or an excuse to touch her Holly couldn't tell. "I wondered about your motive."

"Oh, Richard's such a bore. I can't understand why Mother insists on inviting him but, then, I suppose it's because Holly always had a thing for him. Besides…" she pouted charmingly "…I just wanted you to myself without her watching every move I make. She's incredibly…possessive for someone who claims you're just colleagues."

"She said that?"

She shrugged. "Anyway, I thought I might convince you to change your mind about doing me that teensy favor."

"I've already told you I don't do cosmetic surgery anymore, Paige. Besides, I'm booked solid for the next six months. Probably longer."

Annoyance flashed across her features and she spun away to say sulkily, "Fine, then maybe you can use your incredible sex appeal to persuade Holly to have a little work done."

"Work?"

Light spilling from the salon illuminated Paige's face, giving Holly a clear view of the flirtatious look she sent over her shoulder. She gave a little laugh and turned back to slide her palm over his heart. "Don't pretend they're invisible, Gabriel." She shuddered delicately. "Those scars are awful and people don't realize how hurtful pitying stares are. In fact, I used to feel so bad when boys called her Scarface that I wondered if you could persuade her to have them…fixed?"

Like hell she'd felt bad, Holly thought darkly. She'd

laughed, telling Holly she should have an infamous comic book badass named after her.

"Hmm…" Gabriel rocked back on his heels as though he was considering her words.

Holly sucked in a sharp breath, the betrayal like a blow to her heart. She couldn't believe that after kissing every one of those scars, moving his lips against her skin and murmuring that she was beautiful, he— She bit her lip. Clearly, after seeing Paige's flawless beauty, he was reconsidering.

She pressed the heel of her hand to the spot between her brows as pain lanced through her head. Oh, God, she needed to get out of here. Away from…them. Away somewhere where she could fall apart in private.

She was about to turn away when she heard him say, "So what else would you suggest she have…done?"

Feeling the backs of her eyes burn, she waited with a huge hot lump of devastation in her chest for her sister's reply. When it came, it sliced at the self-confidence she'd spent so many years trying to build. And even though she understood that Paige's opinions reflected her own insecurities and jealousy, it made Holly feel like the ugly adopted sister Paige had always called her.

"Well," Paige said demurely, "I was thinking a breast lift and maybe since her hips and thighs are getting chunky, a little lipo? And she could certainly do with a nose job. What do you think?"

And when Gabriel laughed and said, "Chunky? You really think so?" she couldn't listen anymore because Paige reached up and twined her fingers in his hair.

His hands came up to her shoulders and the sight of them plastered together like a seal-a-meal ripped at the tender new feelings that had been blossoming inside her chest. But she couldn't…*couldn't* bear to listen to every one of her flaws discussed like a grocery list. She'd survived it once before when Paige had slept with and then dumped Holly's last boyfriend and she would survive it again.

Right now she couldn't bear to stick around and watch it happening again.

The last twenty-four hours had been fun but it was over and time to return to the real world. Time to return to planning for her future and time she forgot about a hunky surfer from California. No matter how hot he was or how good he was with his hands. And his lips.

Oh, God.

Turning, she walked blindly into the safety of her parents' bedroom, her mind spinning as she wondered how she was going to make a clean getaway. There wasn't time to fall apart however, as Delia entered as she was closing the French doors.

"There you are, darling," she said, catching sight of her. "We're getting ready to serve coffee so your father can blow out his candles." Holly turned and her mother stopped abruptly, her eyes widening when she caught sight of her expression. "I'm going to slap that girl," Delia said fiercely. "She's not too old for it."

"Mom…it's fine. Really," she insisted, when her mother opened her mouth to object. "Besides, I'm not feeling well and I wondered if you'd please tell Dad I'm sorry and make my apologies to everyone else?"

She searched Holly's face and then sighed, her eyes filled with so much compassionate concern that Holly was tempted to walk into Delia's arms and bawl. But that would only upset her mother more.

"All right, darling," Delia agreed softly, "but I think you're making a terrible mistake. I like him and…well, I guess I shouldn't interfere." She rolled her eyes before turning with a muttered "I promised myself I wouldn't interfere." Then over her shoulder she asked gently, "Do you want me to ask Gabriel to take you home?"

"No!" she yelped, and when her mother's eyebrow rose, she said more quietly. "Please, Mom…don't. I just…I…" She

heaved out a heavy breath and tried to wrestle her spinning emotions into submission. "I'll call a cab. You can tell Gabriel the hospital called."

For a long moment her mother silently studied her until Holly thought she might break down beneath that blue gaze. Finally she stepped closer and gave Holly a warm hug. "All right," she murmured softly, "but you're not calling a cab. I'll ask Richard to drive you back to the city."

Holly's eyes abruptly filled but she drew in a deep breath and willed away the tears. "Thanks, Mom."

Gabe was furious—with Holly for leaving without a word and with Paige for her machinations. But mostly he was furious with himself for thinking Holly was different. He also felt very bad for Delia Buchanan, who'd seemed genuinely upset when she gave him Holly's message.

"I'm so sorry, Gabriel," she said, taking his hands in hers.

"You have nothing to be sorry about, Mrs. Buchanan," he said. "This is not on you."

"No," she agreed quietly. "It's on both my daughters and I'm very sorry you got caught in the middle. Paige…well, Paige was always incredibly jealous of Holly even as a child, and after a while it was just easier for Holly to withdraw and let Paige have her way."

"That's insane."

"Yes, well," she said with a sad smile. "Paige is beautiful but there's just something a little fragile in her make-up. Holly was always the strong one, even when she was so adorably skinny and clumsy. She was smart and funny but couldn't get the hang of all those coltish arms and legs. I tried to help with ballet lessons, deportment and acting classes but I fear I just made things worse."

"You did what any mother would do," Gabe said, recalling the sacrifices his own mother had made for him. "But she's made her feelings perfectly clear."

"Yes, she has," Delia said sympathetically, laying her hand on his tense arm. "And you've misinterpreted her actions."

"How can I misinterpret the way she acted with Westchester during dinner or that she left with him the minute it was over?" he demanded, feeling once again like that poor med student invited to the mansion and humiliated by Lauren's family's condescending attitude.

"You appeared engrossed with Paige," she reminded him gently. "And for Holly at least, it seemed like history repeating itself all over again. So she did what she's always done when it comes to Paige. She withdrew. But I know she cares for you, Gabriel. She wouldn't have invited you or gone off like that if she didn't."

Sighing, Gabe thrust a hand through his hair. He didn't know what to think.

"Don't give up on her," Delia begged softly. "Get her to talk to you, please. And for God's sake don't get sucked into Paige's dramas. She has a bad habit of wanting what Holly has and destroying everything good in her own life."

But Holly didn't have him, Gabe thought furiously as he drove back to the city. She'd made it perfectly clear that she preferred someone from her own social circle. Someone from old money and an ancestry that could probably be traced back to Ellis Island. Maybe the Buchanan sisters were letting their history repeat itself but there was no way he was going to make the same mistake.

Not again, he vowed fiercely as Holly's phone again went to voicemail. He ground his back teeth together until his jaw popped.

Great. Now he was grinding his teeth into powder.

Disconnecting with a short jab, he ignored the angry honking around him and whipped across three lanes to take the Brooklyn exit. He was done with women, and he was especially done with Holly Buchanan.

So why, when he got home and smelled her on his pillow, did he get a hollow feeling in his chest that felt very much like grief? It wasn't, he told himself, lurching off the bed to strip the sheets and pillowcases.

It was humiliation and disgust with himself that he never seemed to learn his lesson. He was still hankering after women from the world his grandfather had denied him. Well, he was done with it, with her, he told himself as he threw himself across the freshly made bed that he'd shared with her. Twice. Which didn't explain why it suddenly felt so damn cold and…empty. Or why he couldn't stop thinking about her with another man.

He really hated thinking about her with—

Damn it!

He grabbed his phone and after a couple of indecisive beats hit redial. She'd done him a favor, he told himself, growling with frustration when the call again went to voicemail. Done him a favor by reminding him that he couldn't rely on anyone but himself and the professional reputation he'd earned through his own hard work and skill.

It had landed him the job of his dreams and he wasn't going to screw it up, especially not over some woman with big blue eyes that exposed her every thought and emotion. A woman who was soft and sweet even when she thought she wasn't. A woman who had a habit of falling at his feet and quoting random facts when she was flustered. A woman who— He stopped breathing and stared into the darkened room as the truth finally dawned.

Oh, man, he thought when he realized his mouth was curved into a sappy grin, he was in trouble. The kind of trouble that started with *L*.

His breath expelled in a hard, dry laugh.

He might as well go out and shoot himself.

CHAPTER TWELVE

INSTEAD OF GOING back to Brooklyn, Holly had Richard drop her off at her grandmother's summer house in Bay Shore. He offered to keep her company but she declined. She needed to be alone to work on her shaky defenses before facing Gabriel on Monday.

But when Monday rolled around, all Holly had to show for her days off were dark circles under her eyes and a bone-deep certainty that there was no way she could accept a fellowship in the same hospital—*oh, God, the same department*—as Gabriel. And as much as she hated the idea, she needed to review her options. And fast.

She spent the next week researching P&R programs in other cities while avoiding everyone, including her mother. She just happened to quite successfully avoid Gabriel too. Not that he'd come looking for her, she admitted with a pang. But, then, she hadn't returned his calls, even when he'd left a dozen *"Call me"* messages. And if she'd listened to his voice over and over again as she'd lain in bed at night, it hadn't been because she'd been yearning for the sound of his voice or the smell and feel of his body against hers.

He finally stopped calling and when she caught herself scouring the papers for pictures of Paige, or holding her breath every time her phone rang, she realized she'd been secretly hoping he'd... Well, she didn't know exactly, only that she'd hoped he wouldn't quit.

But he had. So…that was that, then.

The week was frantically busy. She stood in for another cosmetic surgeon whose wife went into early labor and ended up with more than enough to keep her busy and too tired at the end of each day to stay awake and brood.

The week leading up to the Chrysalis Foundation's annual charity ball she wasn't so lucky. On Tuesday she was called to Theatre for two late-night procedures when Gabriel's scheduled assistant called in with stomach flu. And because everyone was way behind schedule, Dr. Hunt assigned Holly to pick up the slack.

Fortunately there wasn't time for him to do more than study her with a penetrating blue-green gaze that made her heart flop around in her chest like a landed catfish and make quiet suggestions or give orders that everyone—including Holly—snapped to obey.

During the last stages of the second procedure, on a guy who had gynecomastia and wanted his man boobs removed, he was called away, leaving Holly to finish up the routine procedure.

She didn't see him again until late Friday afternoon as she left the surgical ward.

Scrolling through the dozen messages Delia had left about her dress and shoes for the ball, as well as her tickets, Holly rolled her eyes at her mother's OCD and…walked into a wall of living muscle and bone.

Startled, she lurched backwards—okay, shrieked and jumped about a foot in the air—and bumped into a nearby medicine trolley that hadn't been wheel-locked. A hand shot out to grab her but she yanked her arm away, the abrupt move sending the trolley skidding out from under her. She fell hard against the sluice trolley and went down in a tangle of limbs, another shriek and—yay—a half-dozen bedpans that crashed around her like the sounding of the Apocalypse.

For a couple of beats she lay there stunned until she became aware of two things. One: her notes were fluttering to the floor like confetti and, two—*oh, God*—Gabriel was dropping to his haunches beside her. Through the roaring in her ears she thought she heard him ask repeatedly if she was all right.

Realizing he was feeling her up, she jolted like she'd been shot. "What…what the heck are you doing?" she gasped on a rising inflection, shoving at his hands.

But he brushed her aside and growled, "Damn it, Holly. Stay still until I'm satisfied you're—"

The door burst open and three nurses spilled out, coming to an abrupt halt when they saw Holly flat on her bottom, bedpans and folio paper scattered all over the floor—and Gabriel Alexander's hands high up on her inner thigh.

Their eyes bugged.

"Dr. Buchanan?"

"Dr. Alexander?"

"Omigosh, are you all right?"

Sucking in a breath, she did a lightning-quick assessment and decided that other than her bruised bottom and her battered pride she was fine. "I'm…fine," she said, shoving Gabriel away and scrambling to her feet to hide her hot face.

Gabriel shot out a hand to steady her when she swayed and though she stiffened she didn't pull away. She did a mental eye-roll. Not after what had just happened—all because she hadn't wanted him to touch her.

"What happened?" the head nurse demanded, popping her head out the door and frowning at the debris scattered across the floor.

"The brake was off the meds trolley," Gabriel said, his voice more steely than she'd ever heard it.

"No," Holly hastened to say. "It was my fault. I wasn't looking where I was going and Dr. Alexander had to save me from—"

"It's not all right," he interrupted tersely. "Dr. Buchanan could have been seriously injured because someone didn't follow safety procedures." He frowned at the head nurse as the others scurried to pick up the scattered bedpans.

"Dr. Alexander—"

"Leave the papers," he ordered tersely, ignoring Holly's attempts to smooth over the situation. "I'll help Dr. Buchanan collect them."

Once the bedpans had been returned to their place and the trolleys locked, he waited until the frosted door closed on the cowed nurses before releasing his grip on Holly.

Without speaking, she dropped to her haunches and silently began gathering up her notes. She was shaking inside and had to bite her lip against the pain radiating from her elbow. She tried to hurry, wanting to escape without making even more of a fool of herself.

Unfortunately it was *waa-aay* too late for that.

She was on her knees when they both reached for the last page. Holly froze. With her heart in her throat, she was compelled to lift her gaze to his—and felt herself fall all over again. This time into a pair of blue-green eyes. *Déjà vu.* Blue-green eyes that swept over her face as though they'd been starved of the sight of her.

"Holly," he said coolly, his face expressionless. But there was a wealth of emotion in his eyes—anger, frustration, accusation, even concern, and something so dark and hot it sent hurt slicing through her.

Swallowing the sob that rose into her throat, she shook her head, snatching at the pages in his hand before surging to her feet in one smooth move. She abruptly swung on her heel and surprised herself by not falling flat on her face. Before she could stomp off with her head held high, he grabbed her arm.

Instantly pain ricocheted from her elbow to her shoulder and she flinched, unable to prevent a gasp from escaping.

He immediately released her. "What? What's wrong?"

Tears—that had little to do with the pain in her elbow—blinded her and she shook her head again and turned her face away. "Nothing. It's nothing. I just bruised my elbow, that's all."

"Let me see."

"No." She sucked in a steadying breath and said it again, this time quietly. "No. It's nothing, really. I'll be fine." She wasn't talking about her elbow. At least, not just.

"Fine, but we need to talk."

She gulped and thought, *Go away, Gabriel, can't you see I'm having a mini-freak-out here?* "There's nothing to say, Dr. Alexander."

His eyebrows flattened across the bridge of his nose and his lips firmed. "What's that supposed to mean?"

"It means you've already said everything I need to hear."

"What?" He looked so confused Holly almost relented but then she recalled the sight of her sister clinging to Gabe and her resolve hardened.

Folding her arms beneath her breasts, she thrust out her chin in silent challenge. "To Paige."

He rubbed the lines of exhaustion between his eyes and Holly was tempted to reach out and smooth them away. "Paige?" he demanded testily. "What the hell does Paige have to do with anything?"

Holly's mouth dropped open. "You're kidding, right?" Her hands curled into tight fists to keep her from taking a swing at his thick head. Maybe jolt his memory? Knock him out?

"I honestly have no idea—" He abruptly shook his head as though to clear it. "What about Westchester?"

She tried to look innocent. "What about Richard?"

"Yeah, right. It's fine to find fault with me when you ran off with him, leaving me to face your mother. Do you have any idea how humiliating that was? For both of us?"

"No more humiliating," she snapped, "than you discussing me…my scars." *Not to mention devastating.* She sucked in a steadying breath when she realized she was starting to hyperventilate. "Not to mention my sagging breasts and my huge ass and thighs!" She lowered her voice to a fierce whisper when a couple of nurses passed, eyeing them with avid curiosity. "With my sister?" She jabbed a finger at him and hissed, "My sister!"

He had the grace to wince. "You heard that?"

Suddenly Holly was exhausted. She'd been functioning on pure adrenaline since that night and she wanted to curl up in a ball and sleep for a month.

"Of course I heard it," she said wearily. "Paige made certain I heard it. Like she made certain I saw how she touched you and plastered herself…" She sucked in a steadying breath. "And how you did nothing…*nothing*…to stop her."

Her phone rang and she checked the caller ID, viciously punching the disconnect button when she saw who it was.

"Now, just a minute," he said incredulously. "*That's* what this is all about?"

Holly glared at him.

"*Damn it!* I can't believe—!" He broke off with a muttered oath and shoved his hands through his hair, looking agitated and…and hot, damn him. "Did you…did you hear everything I said to Paige out on the terrace?"

"I…I heard enough," she snapped. "Enough to know you agreed with her. But that's okay since it's nothing I haven't heard before," she said coolly. "A million times. But I can't believe you agreed with her. Not after—"

Fortunately Gabriel's furious "I did nothing of the sort" interrupted what she was going to say. Then her phone rang again and she was just about to throw the thing against the wall when she realized it wasn't Paige this time but her mother. "You know what, never mind. I have to go."

"We need to talk."

"I hardly think—"

His hand closed over her shoulder and whipped her around. "We're going to have that talk," he said firmly, his eyes glittering with determination and something else that Holly couldn't identify. It made her stomach drop then bounce back up like she'd fallen from the top of the Empire State building.

"I have to go. My mother's sent a car to take me to the hotel. I'm helping with the last minute details of the charity auction for the ball tonight," she explained when he looked like he wanted to throttle her.

"Fine," he said shortly. "I'll see you there. Save all your dances for me."

"You have an invitation?" she asked, mouth dropping open. She shook her head. Of course he had an invitation. "I mean, I might not have time—"

"I'll see you there," he ground out an instant before he yanked her against him and slammed his mouth down on hers in a hard, punishing kiss. It stunned her with its heated ferocity and even after he'd shoved back and disappeared into the surgical ward she stood open-mouthed, wide-eyed and more than a little dazed.

He'd tasted of anger and frustration, she thought dizzily. And a wild, wild lust that had just a hint of what she thought was desperation. But that was ridiculous. Wasn't it?

It took a passing med student asking, "You gonna answer that, Dr. Buchanan?" to realize she was staring at her buzzing phone as though she'd never seen it before.

A look at caller ID galvanized her into action. Once Delia Buchanan was on a roll, it took a force of nature to stop her.

Gabriel paid the cab driver and turned to look up at the blazingly bright façade of Manhattan's finest hotel. It figured that the charity foundation, which he now knew was run by Delia Buchanan, would host it here. Its five-star rating, as well as the richly appointed furnishings, would draw New York's social and moneyed elite.

It was clear by the number of glittery ballgowns and designer tuxes that the elite had converged on Manhattan for the prestigious occasion. Gabriel entered the hotel and was immediately struck by the intricate laylight high over-

He checked the seating plan on the easel at the entrance and headed across the dance floor. The live orchestra, all students from the Manhattan Music College, filled the ballroom with lively music, proving that Delia Buchanan supported young talent as well as raised funds for the disfigured.

She was a remarkable woman, he thought. Just like her daughter.

He skirted a group of people sipping champagne and debating the safety of air travel when a familiar voice purred behind him, "You all alone tonight, Gabriel?"

He didn't have to turn around to know that Paige Buchanan was on the prowl.

"No, actually," he said, turning to find a stunningly made-up Paige clinging to the arm of the man she'd not two weeks ago said was a dead bore.

"Ms. Buchanan, Westchester." He greeted the other man blandly but he guessed his feelings were pretty clear because Richard Westchester's brown eyes twinkled as he thrust out his hand in greeting.

"Alexander." His handshake was firm. "If you're looking for Holly, I saw her talking to the senator and Mrs. James over at the auction table."

A senator? "Thank you." He was just about to head off when Rick tilted his head, studying Gabe with narrowed eyes.

"You know, you remind me of someone. I thought so the other night but I just couldn't think who it was. Seeing you again has reminded me. Are you by any chance related to the Long Island Alexanders? Mark Alexander's son, Steven, is about your age, maybe a little younger, and you look a lot like him."

Gabe had known this moment would eventually come. Had prepared for it. But it still gave him a jolt. "No," he said casually. "I'm from California."

"Oh, that's right," Rick mused. "Funny how life is. I

guess it's true what they say about having a twin somewhere in the world."

Gabe was saved from replying by Paige. Clearly tired of being ignored, she tugged impatiently on Rick's arm. "Come on, Ricky." She pouted. "I want to show you the dresses I donated to my mother's little pet project."

"The auction," Rick said, by way of explanation to Gabe, who couldn't have cared less unless they brought in a lot of money.

"I'm sure the foundation is grateful for your loss," Gabe said politely. Paige sent him a cat smile.

"And you, Gabriel?" she purred. "How grateful are you? Considering most of the funds will be going to pay for your salary?"

"God, Paige," Rick groaned. "Give it a rest, will you? You know very well that Chrysalis can't afford to pay Dr. Alexander's fees. Anything made here tonight only goes to the medical costs for the miracles he performs."

Furious with Rick for daring to contradict her in front of Gabriel, she rounded on him. "I'm only saying—"

"Yeah, yeah," Rick interrupted wearily. "We get it. The great Paige Buchanan threw a couple of her old rags at the foundation and now everyone must be overcome with gratitude. You're thirty-one years old, for God's sake. Don't you think it's time you stopped behaving like a spoiled brat?"

"I am not that old," she whispered furiously, two spots of color appearing high on her famous cheekbones.

Rick sighed. "We're the same age, Paige, and I'm thirty-one. Almost thirty-two, in fact, which means—"

"I know what it means, Rick. It means you're an insensitive jerk and I never should have agreed to come with you tonight."

"No one else would bring you," he said brutally, to which she replied by sending him a look that should have sliced him to shreds before spinning on her heel and flouncing off.

After a short silence Rick shoved a hand through his

hair. "Sorry about that. The thing is…" He let his breath out in a long hiss. "I've been in love with Paige since I was six." He gave a hard laugh. "And you can see just how that worked out for me."

Gabe was confused. "If you're in love with Paige," he asked, "then what the hell was that display with Holly the other night?"

A dull flush rose up Rick's neck. "My pathetic attempt to make Paige jealous." He gave an embarrassed laugh. "I thought you'd arrived with Paige and…and ended up embarrassing myself. Look, Holly's the best, but Paige? Well, it's always been Paige for me."

Gabe understood because he had a feeling it would always be Holly for him. "My condolences."

Rick's laugh burst out and he grimaced. "Thanks. And now I think I'll just go drown my sorrows. Coming?"

He shook his head. "I need to speak to Holly."

"Hope you have better luck," Rick muttered.

After he left, Gabe spotted Holly across the ballroom and sucked in a hard breath at the picture she made; slender and stunning in a long column of ice blue that complemented her dark hair…and deepened the blue of her eyes.

She looked both touchable and as distant as a star, and she literally took his breath away. The one-sleeved dress was a feat of engineering that hugged and draped her curves before falling to the floor in a luxurious cascade of soft folds from an artfully draped row of fabric blossoms at her hip. It was at once modest and incredibly revealing, and while it cleverly covered her scarred right arm it exposed her flawless shoulder and arm entirely.

He didn't realize he'd been standing there staring at her like a lovesick schoolboy until someone bumped into him, jolting him out of his trance. With his eyes on her, he murmured an apology and started forward.

She must have sensed his stare because she looked up and their gazes locked. It was like one of those sappy movie moments when two people locked eyes across a crowded room. Everything faded—the people, the noise, the opulence—until there was only the two of them.

After a few heated beats a tentative smile trembled on her lips and warmth filled him, rising in his chest like bubbles in a champagne glass. Her gaze dropped to the dimple in his cheek and he realized he was smiling too.

Oh, yeah, he thought, she couldn't resist his dimples. Or his kisses. He just hoped she listened to what he had to say.

"Oh, Gabriel," a low feminine voice came from behind him. "I'm so glad you made it."

CHAPTER THIRTEEN

GABRIEL TURNED TO find Delia Buchanan at his elbow and wasn't the least bit surprised when she cupped his face in her hands studied him for a few beats before reaching up to kiss his cheek.

"Good evening, Mrs. Buchanan. *Wow.* You look amazing." She wore a simple off-the-shoulder black jersey dress only a true blonde could pull off.

"Oh, darn." She laughed up at him. "I was hoping the best-looking man in the room would call me by my name and make all the other women jealous."

Gabe smiled and kissed her cheek. "You're the most beautiful woman here, Delia," he murmured, his gaze sliding to Holly, who was watching them with an odd expression on her face. A kind of hopeful yearning that grabbed him by the throat and tugged him toward her. "After your daughter, of course."

She squeezed his arm. "And you're incredibly sweet, Gabriel. I only hope she knows how lucky she is."

"I'm the lucky one," he said, watching as color blossomed beneath Holly's skin. "Or I will be when I finally corner her and—"

She gasped softly, looking stunned and desperately hopeful. "Oh…oh, my…you're in love with her."

Gabe felt the back of his neck grow hot and grimaced. "It's that obvious?"

A lovely smile transformed her features and he caught his breath at how very much alike Holly and her mother were. "Only to a mother who's been waiting for this moment for a long, long time," she said on a rush of emotion. "For someone to love her enough to overlook the scars."

"She's beautiful," he murmured, taking in Holly's creamy skin, heavily lashed eyes and the tendrils of dark hair framing her oval face. "Inside and out." He turned to Delia. "Like her mother."

Tears filled her eyes and her breath hitched audibly. "Oh, you." She pressed her hand into the center of her chest and blinked a few times. She gave a soft sniff. "Look what you've done now. You've made me all weepy."

Gabriel felt his skull tighten. The last thing he'd wanted was to upset Holly's mother. Not tonight. Not ever. He shoved unsteady fingers through his hair and looked around for an escape route but there wasn't one.

Maybe he should have taken Westchester up on that drink after all. "Oh, man, I'm…sorry. Can I get you anything? Water, champagne? *Anything?*"

Delia laughed tearfully as she nudged his shoulder and he realized he'd started to sound desperate there for a second. "Look at you, getting all panicky over a few tears," she hiccuped. "Besides, what's a little smudged mascara when someone loves my baby?"

Embarrassed, Gabe rubbed the back of his neck and shifted his feet, feeling fifteen again. "Yeah, well," he said, clearing his throat. "Maybe I should see if she'll forgive me for being a colossal ass first."

"Oh, before you do," Delia said, as though she'd suddenly remembered. "There's someone I want you to meet first. He's a huge contributor to both the hospital and the foundation." She slipped her hand into the crook of his elbow and urged him forward. "In fact, he's responsible for the planned expansion of the P&R wing. And if I'm not mistaken, he was also instrumental in getting you here."

Gabe reluctantly allowed her to pull him forward.

"Me?"

"Oh, yes," she said with a lovely smile. "We only wanted the best for the program. In fact, the endowment depended on you heading up the team."

Gabriel frowned and wondered at the sudden bad feeling in his stomach. "That's a bit harsh. I'm sure there are other surgeons who could have filled the position."

"They wanted the best and apparently that's you." She squeezed his arm and sent him a proud smile. "Here we are," she said brightly, reaching out to touch the shoulder of a much older man who had his back to them.

When he turned, Gabe's blood froze.

Through the dull roaring in his ears he heard Delia Buchanan say, "Mr. Alexander, I'd like to introduce you to the hospital's newest acquisition. He's already made a huge difference to some of our recipients." As though she'd felt the instant Gabe's muscles turn to stone, she flicked him a concerned look before including the other members of the group.

"This is Dr. Al...ex...an...der?" Her eyes widened as enlightenment slowly dawned. She gave a shocked gasp, her gaze whipping up to his—looking suddenly shaken and distressed. "Oh." She lifted a trembling hand to her chest. "Oh, Gabriel, I'm so sorry."

As though Gabe's worlds weren't suddenly colliding, Caspar Alexander took Delia's hand and pressed a kiss to her cheek. "You're looking more radiant than ever, my dear. And the ballroom's never looked better." Then he straightened and turned his cold blue eyes on Gabriel.

He didn't offer his hand—probably because Gabe looked ready to take a bite of anything that moved. "Gabriel," he said smoothly. "You're looking well."

Gabe's reply, "Sir," as frigid as the north wind, slid like an icy blade into the sudden silence. He ignored the shocked expressions around him as he zeroed in on Mark Alexander, looking as stunned as Delia Buchanan. She tightened her fingers on his arm and pressed closer to his side as though she instinctively knew what was happening and was offering her silent support.

And Gabriel, grateful for her warm maternal presence, fell in love for the second time that day. He covered the hand gripping his arm and gave it a reassuring squeeze.

"Hello, Dad," he said with a blade-sharp smile. "Long time no see." And had the satisfaction of seeing Mark Alexander turn white. As though Mark had seen a ghost—or maybe his past coming up to bite him in the ass. And though Gabe wanted to hate him, he realized Mark was as stunned as the rest of the Alexander clan. A quick glance at Caspar showed the old man looking pleased, as though he'd orchestrated the events for maximum shock value.

Clearly Caspar wasn't done controlling his family. But Gabriel wasn't family and he had no intention of being manipulated by anyone. Especially the old bastard.

Oh, wait, he thought savagely. *He* was the unwanted son. *He* was the long "lost" grandson Caspar wanted to pull into his web of lies, deceit and tight-fisted control. He hadn't managed to bribe Gabe with riches and power three years ago so he'd gone for the jugular. He'd bought Gabe the one thing he'd needed after his mother's death—to do something worthwhile. To help people who really needed it, not just because they could afford to pay for their vanity.

The expression on her mother's face sent Holly's pulse ratcheting up a couple of thousand notches. Something was wrong, she thought, murmuring an excuse to Senator James and his wife. Seriously wrong.

Gabriel, looking coldly furious, appeared to have been

turned to stone but it was the distress on her mother's face
and the way she clutched at his arm that had Holly moving
quickly toward them.

She recognized the old man facing her and if she wondered what Caspar Alexander had said to make Gabriel so
mad, she arrived just as he turned to his son with a coldly
satisfied smile.

"Mark," he said airily. "Meet your son. Steven, Jade
and Courtney, meet your brother. *Dr.* Gabriel Alexander."
Holly's gasp was drowned out by other shocked gasps
around them. Gleefully enjoying the drama, Caspar turned
to Gabriel and with a gesture of disgust he said, "Son, meet
your family."

Holly froze, her eyes locked on the frozen tableau before her. Gabriel had stiffened even more until the air vibrated with tension.

"You don't get to call me son," he said quietly, lethally.
"You don't get to call me anything. You gave up that right
the night you tried to force my mother to have an abortion."

Holly's horrified gasp covered her mother's soft moan
and she grabbed Delia's hand and squeezed. The ballroom
had gone ominously quiet and people were beginning to
stare.

And to Holly's shock, instead of denying the claim, Caspar just snorted derisively. "I did you a favor, boy," he said.
"Look at you. You're a self-made man. If I hadn't, you might
have ended up just like them." He waved a whiskey-filled
glass.

"Father?" Mark Alexander asked faintly, looking alarm-
ingly pale. "Is that true? You threatened Rachel? You told
me she'd lost the baby. You told me she'd moved west to
get over the loss. How could you do this? I did everything
you asked of me."

"Yes, you did." The old man nodded, casually lifting the
whiskey tumbler to his lips. "Maybe I would have respected

you more if you'd defied me. Maybe these blood-sucking offspring of yours would have grown up to be more like Gabriel. More like me."

"I'm nothing like you," Gabriel snarled.

"Oh, yes, you are," Caspar interrupted. "You wouldn't have dragged yourself up from the gutter if you weren't."

Gabriel looked like he was contemplating murder. "I did it for my mother, not for you."

"I was wrong," Caspar said, but Holly's gaze was locked on Mark's face and knew the instant he was in trouble. "Rachel Parker was a fine woman, and a good mother. Look how well you—"

"Gabriel, your father—" Holly began, stepping toward the older man, who was clutching his chest and starting to buckle. Gabriel, quickly assessing the situation, leapt forward, catching Mark before he fell.

"Mom," Holly murmured. "Call 911." She dropped to her knees beside the gray and gasping man. "Gabriel, I'll do it," she began, placing her hands on Mark's chest to begin CPR, but Gabriel brushed her aside.

He pulled his father into a sitting position and thumped him hard on the back. "Cough," he said sharply. "And hard, like you've got something in your throat."

Holly's gaze snapped up. "What—?" Of course. "He's right, Mr. Alexander, cough really hard." Mark looked at them like they were crazy. "Please," Holly said, her eyes filling with tears. "It'll get your heart beating properly again."

Her encouragement worked and with Gabriel's help Mark started coughing, a little feebly at first, then harder until his color gradually returned.

Holly sat back, her eyes locked on Gabriel's face. He'd had every right to turn and walk away—had had every opportunity—yet he hadn't. And here he was, saving the man who hadn't been there for his mother. Hadn't been there for him.

As though sensing her gaze, Gabriel suddenly looked up

and their eyes locked. The stark fear and desperate hope in them nearly crushed Holly and it was in that moment she realized the naked truth.

She was in love with him and she would do anything—anything—to help him through this.

"I'll get some brandy," she said, and rose to her feet.

CHAPTER FOURTEEN

HOLLY PAUSED OUTSIDE the hospital room, her gaze riveted on Gabriel's broad back and the rumpled sun-streaked hair that appeared even more rumpled than usual.

She wanted more than anything to go to him and smooth the unruly locks that tended to flop onto his forehead but her heart was hammering against her ribs and she was still struggling to catch her breath after dashing halfway across the island.

Okay, she'd only dashed a few blocks, but in four-inch glittery heels and a long snug evening gown it was a miracle she hadn't broken her neck.

Her heart now, well, that was another matter altogether, especially when it gave a sharp wrench at the picture he made, silhouetted against the darkened sky. Her breath caught in her throat.

Oh, God. He looked so lonely and solitary…as if the weight of the universe rested on his broad shoulders. And suddenly she wanted to go to him, rest her head against his broad back and give him what he needed.

With his back to the room, and hands buried deep in the pockets of his tux pants, he faced the darkened window overlooking the lights of Manhattan. At any other time the view might have distracted Holly, but her attention was riveted on his tense back and the I-want-to-be-alone aura he'd wrapped around himself like an invisible cloak.

She'd returned to find Mark recovering nicely but planning to return to their room. There'd been no sign of Gabriel but she'd known instinctively where to find him.

"You shouldn't be here, Holly," he said quietly.

"Why not?" she asked, just as quietly, her heart suddenly aching with the realization she'd made a short while ago. She'd suspected she was in love after her father's birthday but she'd hoped it was just a little crush. Hoped it would fade with time. It hadn't. Wouldn't…ever.

"You said we needed to talk."

He gave a ragged laugh. "Really? You want to talk now?"

She stepped into the room. "It's quiet, we're alone. What better time?"

"I made a mistake." His voice was so low and ragged in the quiet room that she strained to hear the words that seemed to be wrenched from a place of deep pain. The suppressed emotion in it drew her across the room.

"With what?" she asked, joining him at the window.

He sighed heavily. "Coming here. You."

Oh. Her breath caught at the unexpected shaft of pain his words sent lancing through her heart. And she knew in that instant how it would feel—as though her heart was being ripped from her chest and crushed. "You…" She gulped. "You can't mean that?"

"Yes," he asserted, sounding unbearably weary. "I do. I knew I should stay away from you but now…" He sent her a brief glance.

"Now…what?"

He shook his head. "I can't imagine that you would want to have anything to do with me. Not now."

Her eyes widened and she licked her lips. "What do you mean?"

"You heard me, Holly." He gave a short laugh. "Hell, the entire ballroom heard me."

Holly was confused. Yes, she'd heard him but couldn't remember him saying anything to be ashamed of. "You mean when you called your grandfather a ruthless war-lord who didn't deserve to breathe the same air as the rest of humanity?"

He snorted out a laugh. "Yeah, that would be it."

She was silent for a couple of beats. "Is that the truth? Did he pay your mother to have an abortion?"

"Yeah. Pretty much. Although it apparently went more along the lines of 'If you don't take care of it the next person I send will make sure that thing doesn't survive another week' kind of thing."

"Well, then, the shame's on him, isn't it?" She bumped his shoulder with hers. "I'm glad your mother didn't take his money." She sent him a warm smile. "It showed guts. She must be awesome. I can see where you get it from."

His somber expression lightened. "She was. A real fighter. She lost the fight to cancer a few months ago."

She faced him now. "Oh, Gabriel, I'm so sorry. Is that... when you decided to move east?"

He frowned and Holly could see the subject change upset him. A muscle in his jaw flexed. "I got a letter from West Manhattan offering me my own team of top surgeons, promises of unlimited funds and the most up-to-date technology in the best teaching hospital in the world." He barked out a hard laugh. "I was flattered. I couldn't believe they'd chosen me to—"

He broke off with a muttered oath and turned away, fisting both hands as though he was controlling himself with effort. But she'd seen the fury and humiliation burning in his blue-green gaze and her heart broke for him. She could understand what it would do to such a proud, determined man.

"Do you have any idea how humiliating it is to find out that I was forced onto Langley, onto Hunt?" he demanded.

"Oh, Gabriel. My mother's devastated that she said anything. She didn't know. She would never do anything like that knowingly."

"It's not Delia's fault I handled it so badly." He shifted

his shoulders as though to loosen some of the tension there. "I can't think what she must think of me."

"My mother said if she was twenty years younger, she'd divorce my father and marry you herself."

He laughed and Holly's heart lifted at the sound, even though it was ragged and a bit rusty. "Yeah." His dimple emerged, distracting her from his next words. "I think I love your mother." And when they finally penetrated the jumble of emotion swamping her, she blinked.

"You…do?"

"How could I not?" he demanded. "When she's so much like her daughter."

Her heart stuttered and the fragile hope that had been slowly blooming in her chest shriveled. "What…what are you saying? Paige?"

"No, Holly," he said gently, taking her by the shoulders and turning her so she faced him. "*Not* Paige. You."

Her world tilted and swam, forcing her to blink up at him or pass out from shock. "M-me?" she stuttered, breaking off to swallow the rusty squeak emerging from her tight throat.

A half-smile teased his lips but his eyes were intense, watchful. "Yeah," he said firmly. "You."

"But I'm…you're—"

"I'm what? You're what?" he asked, when she continued to splutter and stare at him as though he'd suggested she jump from the window.

"Look at me, Gabriel. I'm…and you're…" She stopped because she was beginning to stutter and hyperventilate like she used to as a child.

"You're not making sense, Holly. Take a deep breath and try again."

Holly breathed in and then out a few times till the urge to pass out faded, staring at him silently for a few moments before gesturing to the window.

"Tell me what you see," she said quietly, her pulse hammering in her throat.

He searched her expression before turning to stare at their reflection in the window. "I see a beautiful woman with a soft heart and a quick mind. A woman who isn't afraid to face the world, even with her scars." He turned to stare down into her face. "I see a woman who's a little clumsy at times but only when she's flustered. And I kind of like that I'm the only one who makes her nervous." He drew in a deep breath and turned away. His next words were low and hoarse. "I see a woman who's too good for a man like me."

She blinked. "Wha—?"

"I'm the dirty little secret, Holly. Isn't that what this mess is all about? Caspar Alexander's unwanted grandson causing a scandal on your mother's big night?"

"*No!* How can you say that?"

"It doesn't matter, because I've decided to go back to California."

"You…you have?"

He sighed. "Yeah. It's best."

"For whom?"

He looked startled. "For you, of course. I would never humiliate you or your mother. My staying does that."

"Don't be an ass," Holly snapped, suddenly so furious she wanted to punch Caspar Alexander for what he'd done to Gabriel. And she wanted to punch Gabriel too; for letting the old man control his life. "That's just your pride talking."

"What are you talking about? I have no pride left. I accepted the position at West Manhattan because I thought they wanted *me*…not the Alexander money."

Frustrated, Holly grabbed his shirt and yanked him close until they were nose to nose. "I've seen you work, Gabriel. I've heard people talk about what you've done. The amazing techniques you've pioneered and not with vain, shallow women looking for bigger boobs or thinner thighs. But there…" She gestured wildly to the small bed holding a sleeping child. "Where a little girl disfigured by a dog attack is telling everyone that you're going to make her beautiful again. Or…or a man looking to rebuild his shattered face and self-esteem."

She drew in a shuddery breath. "That," she said fervently, smoothing her hands over the creases she'd made in his shirt front. "That's why you're here. Not because of the Alexander money." She looked into his stunned face. "Don't you see? We need you here. They need you here."

After a long pause, Gabriel asked softly, "And you, Holly? What do you need?"

"I…" She felt a shaft of panic go through her when he continued to stare at her, waiting. She sucked in air and took the plunge. "I…" She gulped. "I need you too."

"Oh, boy," he said, looking stunned and relieved and terrified all at once. His reaction confused her and she stumbled back a step but he gave a ragged laugh and yanked her close, wrapping his arms around her so she couldn't escape.

"Say it," he ordered, the expression in his eyes making her knees weak. Her eyes dropped to his mouth.

"Wha-at?"

"Say it."

She licked her lips nervously. "You…first."

His mouth curled up at one corner and his eyes shimmered with tenderness. "God, is it any wonder I love you as much as I do?"

Holly gasped as shock and happiness burst inside her head like a meteor shower. "I…uh, what did you say?"

He laughed and pressed a quick kiss to her mouth. "You heard me. I said—"

"I thought you were in love with my mother," she said breathlessly.

"No," he said with a chuckle. "I said I love your mother." He gazed at her for a long moment, his eyes touching on every inch of her face as though he was committing her face to memory. "It's you I'm in love with. Only you."

"Oh," Holly said, tears filling her eyes at the emotion blazing in his. "You're sure?"

He chuckled. "How could I not be?" He tucked her closer and bent to kiss her mouth tenderly. "You threw yourself at my feet; gave me a lap dance I'll never forget and tried to drown yourself to get my attention." He dropped a smiling kiss on her intricate hairdo when she gave an embarrassed groan and hid her face against his throat. After a few beats he cupped her neck and drew her back so he could look into her eyes.

"Every time you fell at my feet I was the one falling until there was no getting up from what you make me feel."

Her breath hitched. "I...I... *Oh!*"

"Say you love me, Holly. Say you'll stay in Manhattan and build a future with me."

She grimaced at the reminder that she'd discussed her plans to apply for a fellowship in another city. "You heard that?"

"Yes, and it sent me into a panic." He gave her a quick shake. "Now. Your turn."

For long moments she studied the face of the hottest man in Manhattan and decided that she'd never curse her clumsiness again. It had, after all, landed her at Gabriel's feet and she knew without asking that he'd always be there to catch her.

She lifted her hands to cup his cheeks. "I love you," she said, rising onto her toes and sealing the words with a kiss. "Always."

* * * * *

LET'S TALK
Romance

For exclusive extracts, competitions
and special offers, find us online:

f facebook.com/millsandboon

🐦 @MillsandBoon

📷 @MillsandBoonUK

Get in touch on 01413 063232

MILLS & BOON

THE HEART OF ROMANCE

A ROMANCE FOR EVERY READER

MODERN

Prepare to be swept off your feet by sophisticated, sexy and seductive heroes, in some of the world's most glamourous and romantic locations, where power and passion collide.

HISTORICAL

Escape with historical heroes from time gone by. Whether your passion is for wicked Regency Rakes, muscled Vikings or rugged Highlanders, awaken the romance of the past.

MEDICAL

Set your pulse racing with dedicated, delectable doctors in the high-pressure world of medicine, where emotions run high and passion, comfort and love are the best medicine.

True Love

Celebrate true love with tender stories of heartfelt romance, from the rush of falling in love to the joy a new baby can bring, and a focus on the emotional heart of a relationship.

Desire

Indulge in secrets and scandal, intense drama and plenty of sizzling hot action with powerful and passionate heroes who have it all: wealth, status, good looks…everything but the right woman.

HEROES

Experience all the excitement of a gripping thriller, with an intense romance at its heart. Resourceful, true-to-life women and strong, fearless men face danger and desire - a killer combination!

To see which titles are coming soon, please visit

millsandboon.co.uk/nextmonth